D0231476

Sorcerer to the Crown

Zen Cho

Sorcerer to the Crown

MACMILLAN

First published 2015 by Ace,
an imprint of Penguin Random House LLC,
a Penguin Random House Company, New York

First published in the UK 2015 by Macmillan
an imprint of Pan Macmillan
20 New Wharf Road, London N1 9RR
Associated companies throughout the world
www.panmacmillan.com

ISBN 978-1-4472-9945-5

1 3 5 7 9 8 6 4 2

A CIP catalogue record for this book is available from the British Library.

Printed and bound by CPI Group (UK) Ltd, Croydon, CR0 4YY

To Peter

Sorcerer to the Crown

PROLOGUE

THE MEETING OF the Royal Society of Unnatural Philosophers was well under way, and the entrance hall was almost empty. Only the occasional tardy magician passed through, scarcely sparing a glance for the child waiting there.

Boy children of his type were not an uncommon sight in the Society's rooms. The child was unusual less for his complexion than for his apparent idleness. Unlike the Society's splendidly liveried pages, he was soberly dressed, and he was young for a page boy, having just attained his sixth summer.

In fact, Zacharias held no particular employment, and he had never seen the Society before that morning, when he had been conducted there by the Sorcerer Royal himself. Sir Stephen had adjured him to wait, then vanished into the mysterious depths of the Great Hall.

Zacharias was awed by the stately building, with its sombre wood-panelled walls and imposing paintings, and he was a little frightened of the grave thaumaturges hurrying past in their midnight blue coats. Most of all he was rendered solemn by the seriousness of his task. He sat, swollen with purpose, gazing at the doors to the Great Hall, as though by an effort of will he might compel them to open and disgorge his guardian.

Finally, the moment came: the doors opened, and Sir Stephen beckoned to him.

Zacharias entered the Great Hall under the penetrating gaze of what seemed to be a thousand gentlemen, most of them old, and none friendly. Sir Stephen was the only person he knew, for one could not count Sir Stephen's familiar Leofric, who slept curled in reptilian coils at the back of the room, smoke rising from his snout.

The thickest-skinned child might have been cowed by such an assembly, and Zacharias was sensitive. But Sir Stephen put a reassuring hand on his back, and Zacharias remembered the morning, so long ago now—home, safety, warmth, and Lady Wythe's face bending over him:

"Never be afraid, Zacharias, but do your best. That will be quite enough, for you have been taught by the finest sorcerer in the realm. If the attention of so many gentlemen should make you nervous, simply pretend to yourself that they are so many heads of cabbages. That always assists me on such occasions."

Zacharias was pretending as hard as he could as he was propelled to the front of the room, but the cabbages did not seem to help. To be sure, Lady Wythe had never been called upon to prove the magical capacities of her race before the finest thaumaturgical minds in England. It was a grave responsibility, and one anyone would find daunting, thought Zacharias, even if he were a great boy of six.

"What do you wish to bring alive, Zacharias?" said Sir Stephen. He gestured at a small wooden box on a table. "In the course of his travels Mr. Midsomer acquired this box, carved with birds and fruit and outlandish animals. You may have your pick."

Zacharias had rehearsed the enchantment he was to perform many times under Sir Stephen's patient tutelage. The night before, he had fallen asleep reciting the formula to himself. Yet now, as he was surrounded by a crowd of strange faces, oppressed by the consciousness of being the focus of their attention, memory deserted him.

His terrified gaze swung from Sir Stephen's kind face, skipped over the audience, and roamed over the Great Hall, as if he might find the words of the spell waiting for him in some dusty corner. It was the oldest room in the Society, and boasted several interesting features, chief of which were the ancient carved bosses on the ceiling. These represented lambs, lions and unicorns; faces of long-dead sorcerers; and Green Men with sour expressions and vines sprouting from their nostrils. At any other time they would have captivated Zacharias, but right now they could give him no pleasure.

"I have forgotten the spell," he whispered.

"What is that?" said Sir Stephen. He had been speaking in clear ringing tones before, addressing his audience, but now he lowered his voice and leaned closer.

"No helping the boy, if you please," cried a voice. "That will prove nothing of what you promised."

The audience had been growing restless with Zacharias's stupefaction. Other voices followed the first, hectoring, displeased:

"Is the child an idiot?"

"A poll parrot would offer better amusement."

"Can you conceive anything more absurd?" said a thaumaturge to a friend, in a carrying whisper. "He might as well seek to persuade us that a pig can fly—or a woman do magic!"

The friend observed that so *could* pigs fly, if one could be troubled to make them.

"Oh certainly!" replied the first. "And one could teach a woman to do magic, I suppose, but what earthly good would a flying pig or a magical female be to anyone?"

"This is a great gift to the press," cried a gentleman with red whiskers and a supercilious expression. "What fine material we have furnished today for the caricaturists—a meeting of the first magicians of our age, summoned to watch a piccaninny stutter! Has English thaumaturgy indeed been so reduced by the waning of England's magic that Sir Stephen believes we have nothing better to do?"

Unease rippled through the crowd, as though what the gentleman had said sat ill with his peers. Zacharias said anxiously: "Perhaps there is not enough magic."

"Tush!" said Sir Stephen. To Zacharias's embarrassment, he spoke loud enough for the entire room to hear. "Pray do not let that worry you. It pleases Mr. Midsomer to enlarge upon the issue, but I believe England is still furnished with sufficient magic to quicken any tolerable magician's spells."

The red-whiskered gentleman shouted an indistinct riposte, but he was not allowed to finish, for three other thaumaturges spoke over him, disagreeing vociferously. Six more magicians took up Mr. Midsomer's defence, alternating insults to their peers with condemnation of Sir Stephen and mockery of his protégé. A poor sort of performing animal it was, they said, that would not perform!

"What an edifying sight for a child—a room full of men several times his size, calling him names," said one gentleman, who had the sorcerer's silver star pinned to his coat. He did not trouble to raise his voice, but his cool accents seemed to cut through the tumult. "It is all of a piece with the most ancient traditions of our honourable Society, I am sure, and evidence of how well we deserve our position in the world."

Mr. Midsomer flushed with anger.

"Mr. Damerell may say what he likes, but I see no reason why we should restrain our criticism of this absurd spectacle, child or no child," he snapped.

"I am sure *you* do not, Midsomer," said Damerell gently. "I have always admired your refusal, in the pursuit of your convictions, ever to be constrained by considerations of humanity—much less of ordinary good manners."

The room erupted into more argument than ever. The clamour mounted till it seemed it must wake the carvings on the box, and even the slumbering bosses on the ceiling, without Zacharias's needing to lift a finger.

Zacharias looked around, but everyone had ceased to pay attention to him. For the moment he was reprieved.

He let out a small sigh of relief. As if that tiny breath were the key to his locked memory, his mind opened, and the spell fell into it, fully formed. The words were so clear and obvious, their logic so immaculate, that Zacharias wondered that he had ever lost them.

He spoke the spell under his breath, still a little uncertain after the agonies he had endured. But magic came, ever his friend—magic answered his call. The birds carved upon the box blushed red, green, blue and yellow, and he knew that the spell had caught.

The birds peeled away from the box as they took on substance and being, their wings springing away from their bodies, feathers sprouting upon their flesh. They flew up to the ceiling, squawking. The breeze from their wings brushed Zacharias's face, and he laughed.

One by one the carved bosses sprang to life, and the dead sorcerers and the sour old Green Men and the lions and the lambs and the birds opened their mouths, all of them singing, singing lustily Zacharias's favourite song, drowning out the angry voices of the men below, and filling the room with glorious sound.

1

Eighteen years later

Lady Frances Burrow's guests had not noticed her butler particularly when he showed them into the house, but the self-important flourish with which he now flung open the door piqued curiosity. Those who broke off conversations, and raised their head from their ices, were duly rewarded by his announcement:

"Lady Maria Wythe and Mr. Zacharias Wythe!"

It had not been three months since Zacharias Wythe had taken up the staff of the Sorcerer Royal—not so long since his predecessor, Sir Stephen Wythe, had died. He was an object of general interest, and to the great increase of Lady Frances's complacency, more than one pair of eyes followed his progress around her drawing room.

Zacharias Wythe could not fail to draw attention wherever he went. The dark hue of his skin would mark him out among any assembly of his colleagues, but he was also remarkable for his height, and the handsomeness of his features, which was not impaired by his rather melancholy expression. Perhaps the last was not surprising in one who had entered into his office in such tragic circumstances, and at a time when the affairs of English thaumaturgy were approaching an unprecedented crisis.

Stranger than his colour, however, and more distressing than any other circumstance was the fact that Zacharias Wythe had no familiar, though he bore the Sorcerer Royal's ancient staff. Lady Frances's guests did not hesitate to tell each other what they thought of this curious absence, but they spoke in hushed voices—less in deference to the black crepe band around Zacharias's arm than out of respect for his companion.

It was Lady Wythe whom Lady Frances had invited, overbearing her protests with generous insistence:

"It is hardly a party! Only one's most intimate friends! You must take it in the light of a prescription, dear Maria. It cannot be good for you to mope about at home. Mr. Wythe, too, ought not to be left too much to himself, I am sure."

In Zacharias, Lady Frances had hit upon the chief remaining object of Lady Wythe's anxiety and affection. Lady Wythe's bereavement was great, and she had never been fond of society even before Sir Stephen's death. But for Zacharias she would do a great deal, and for his sake she essayed forth in her black bombazine, to do battle in a world turned incalculably colder and drearier by her husband's departure.

"I wonder what Lord Burrow is about?" she said to Zacharias. "It cannot do any harm to ask him about your spells to arrest the decline in our magic. Sir Stephen said Lord Burrow had as good an understanding of the science of thaumaturgy as any man he knew."

It had formed no small part of Lady Wythe's desire to attend the party that Lord Burrow chaired the Presiding Committee that governed the Royal Society of Unnatural Philosophers. Lord Burrow had been a friend to Sir Stephen, but he had regarded Sir Stephen's scheme to educate a negro boy in magic as an unfortunate freak—an eccentricity only tolerable in a man of his great parts. The turn that had bestowed the staff of the Sorcerer Royal on that negro boy was not, in Lord Burrow's view, one to be welcomed. He was learned enough not to ascribe Britain's imminent crisis of magical resource either to Zacharias's complexion or to his inexperience, but that did not mean he looked upon Zacharias himself with any warmth.

His support would do a great deal to bolster Zacharias's position, however, if it could be got. It was with this thought in mind that Lady Wythe had chivvied Zacharias along, for Zacharias was as disinclined for society as Lady Wythe could be. Though he had, at four and twenty, all the ease and assurance that could be imparted by a capital education and a lifetime's intercourse with the good and great of the magical world, by nature he was rather retiring than sociable, and his manners were impaired by reserve.

He had agreed to accompany Lady Wythe because he believed society might enliven her spirits, but he balked at her directive to make up to Lord Burrow:

"Like as not he will think it an absurd impertinence in me to presume to have identified a solution for our difficulties, when so many better magicians than I have failed. Besides, my researches had hardly advanced in any degree before they were suspended."

Before Sir Stephen's death and Zacharias's subsequent elevation, Zacharias had devoted the bulk of his time to the pursuit of thaumaturgical inquiries. He had surveyed the household magics clandestinely transacted by females of the labouring classes, to which the Society turned a blind eye; he had studied the magics of other nations, producing a monograph on the common structures of African and Asiatic enchantments; but in the period preceding Sir Stephen's death, he had been chiefly engaged in the devising of spells to reverse the ongoing decline of England's magic.

It was a project of considerable practical interest, but Zacharias had not so much as looked at it in several months. For Zacharias, as for Lady Wythe, Sir Stephen's death was the point at which the ordinary course of time had been halted. What ensued after that date had been life of quite a different kind, scarcely connected with what had gone before.

"I should not like to show my spells to anyone, in their current state," said Zacharias now.

Lady Wythe was too wise to press the point. "Well then, perhaps we ought to see to your being introduced to some of the young ladies here. Lady Frances said they might get up a dance after dinner. There cannot be any objection to your joining in, and it would be a pity if any young lady were compelled to sit out a dance for want of a partner."

Zacharias's look of consternation was comical. "I scarcely think they will be pleased to be offered such a partner. You forget in your partiality what a very alarming object I am."

"Nonsense!" cried Lady Wythe. "You are precisely the kind of creature girls like best to swoon over. Dark, mysterious, quiet—for a young man who talks a great deal always seems a coxcomb. The very image of romance! Think of Othello."

"His romance came to no good end," said Zacharias.

It seemed he was in the right of it, for it soon became evident that Zacharias was having a curious effect upon the other guests. Whispered discussions were hushed suddenly as he passed. Thaumaturges who might be expected to greet the head of their profession nodded to Lady Wythe, but averted their eyes from Zacharias.

Zacharias was not unaccustomed to such treatment; if it troubled him, he had no intention of letting Lady Wythe know it. Lady Wythe was not so hardened, however. Though the other guests' withdrawal was scarcely overt, her powers of observation were sharpened by affection, and what she saw wounded her.

"Can I credit my eyes?" she said in a low voice. "Did I see Josiah Cullip cut you?"

Zacharias said, in a dishonourable fit of cowardice, "Perhaps he did not see me."

"Zacharias, my dear, I do not believe I am misled by partiality when I say you are impossible to miss in this room," said Lady Wythe. "To think of that linen draper's son presuming to cut you, when you recommended him to Sir Stephen to be Secretary of the Committee! What can he be thinking?"

"I am not popular, you know," said Zacharias. He had already suffered and swallowed his bitterness regarding Cullip's defection. To show he minded it would only increase Lady Wythe's distress. "I suppose he thinks to curry favour with the Society by disowning his connection with me."

"But what complaint can the Society have with your conduct? I am sure you have done nothing but what redounds to the credit of your office. If anyone has a right to repine, it is your friends, for the Society has taken up all your time since you became Sorcerer Royal."

"There is the decline in our magic," said Zacharias. "It is not surprising that my colleagues have linked our difficulties to my investiture. It affords the possibility of a simple cure: remove me, and all will be well again."

"It is never surprising for thaumaturges to latch on to a silly notion, but that does not excuse their stupidity," said Lady Wythe. "This lack of magic plagued Sir Stephen for years, yet no one ever thought to fault him for it. It is those wicked fairies that will not let us have familiars, and that is nothing to do with you. Mr. Cullip ought to know that."

"He cannot help feeling the prejudice against him," said Zacharias. "A large part of the Committee dislikes the notion of any but a gentleman being counted among their number, and Cullip has a wife and children to support. Without his post he should have been compelled to give up thaumaturgy."

"Now that is the trouble with you, Zacharias," said Lady Wythe.

"You will go out of your way to help the most undeserving creature, but never have any regard to yourself. I wish you would not run yourself ragged for these ne'er-do-wells. You are quite grey! If I did not know better, I would suspect you of having contracted some illness and concealing it from me."

Discomfited, Zacharias rolled his shoulders, as though to shrug off Lady Wythe's searching gaze.

"Come," he said, with an attempt at lightness, "are not we at a party? We are hardly making a fit return to Lady Frances for her kindness. Should you like some punch? Or I believe there are ices—I am sure you would like an ice."

Lady Wythe looked wistfully at Zacharias, but she knew that despite his mildness, he had all the traditional stubbornness of a sorcerer. She should like an ice of all things, she said.

Zacharias was as anxious that Lady Wythe should be easy as she was concerned that he should be well—and well liked. It was not within his power to reassure her on either point, and there was more she did not know, that he knew would only distress her further. In his preoccupation he did not hear John Edgeworth say his name, though he spoke it twice.

"I say, Wythe!"

"I beg your pardon, Edgeworth," said Zacharias, starting. "I did not think to see you here."

John Edgeworth was the scion of an old thaumaturgical family, but though he had inherited his ancestors' intelligence and enterprise, he had, alas, none of their magical ability. He had made the best of an awkward situation, and was much esteemed in the Foreign Office, where he was valued for his understanding of Britain's wayward thaumaturges and their relations with France's *sorcieres*. These days Edgeworth was more likely to be found at the dinner parties of political hostesses than among the Fellows of the Society.

"I don't propose to remain for any time, for I've another engagement and cannot be late," said Edgeworth, glancing around as though he was anxious not to be overheard. "Great men, you know, will not be kept waiting! But I had thought there might be a chance of catching you here. Indeed, Lady Frances gave me her word I should. The fact is the Government is in a quandary, a *magical* quandary, and I have been tasked with bespeaking your assistance. Will you come and see me tomorrow?"

Zacharias hesitated. They both knew this was not truly a request. In theory the Sorcerer Royal was independent of the Government, and even of the Society. His only allegiance was to the nation, and it could not be allowed that anybody but a sorcerer was capable of judging how magic might best be employed for the good of the nation—certainly not any mere politician or civil servant.

In practise, however, a Sorcerer Royal whose profession was facing such a scarcity of magical resource must endeavour to keep his Government in good humour. The Government knew the Society's influence had waned of late, even if it did not know of the extent of its difficulties, and it would be on the alert for any sign of weakness or incompliance. Yet it sat ill with Zacharias to overturn his plans at such a peremptory order.

"I have a meeting of the Committee of Thaumaturgical Standards tomorrow, which cannot easily be postponed," he said, but John Edgeworth cut him off:

"Then you must come on Wednesday. But stay, you are in the Sorcerer Royal's quarters now, are not you—those vastly alchemical rooms? They would be just the thing. We will attend upon you on Wednesday. Whether we come in the morning or afternoon will be no great odds to you, I am sure."

Before Zacharias could protest, or ask who was encompassed within Edgeworth's "we," his interlocutor had swept off, leaving Zacharias in a state of suppressed indignation, and with a rapidly melting ice. The latter prevented his lingering too long upon the former, and he hurried back to where he had left Lady Wythe.

England's scarcity of magic was a matter of common knowledge among the magical. Edgeworth could not have escaped knowing something of it. But magicians were a secretive lot, and no one but a practising thaumaturge could know how very ill matters stood. If the Society were to retain its position and privileges, its dearth of resource must be concealed—most of all from the Government, which had little fondness for England's magicians.

Was the significance of Edgeworth's air of mingled mystery and importance that thaumaturgy's secret had been discovered? Zacharias would not know till Wednesday. It was a pity his research had been interrupted! If only he had been able to complete his spells to increase England's magic, it might have been within his power to take the sting out of these anxieties. If he had time to travel to the border of Fairyland, he might yet be tempted to try them.

Lady Wythe was absorbed in conversation with their hostess when Zacharias approached. Lady Frances Burrow affected a penetrating theatrical whisper when imparting confidences, which had the effect of drawing far more attention than her accustomed tones. She was saying to Lady Wythe, very audibly:

"My dear, you could have knocked me down with a feather when Mrs. Quincey told me! I did not credit a word of it, of course, but I hope you will forgive me if I did not quarrel with her over it."

Zacharias did not hear Lady Wythe's response, but Lady Frances seemed disconcerted. She protested, in a whisper more piercing than ever:

"But you know, Maria, that Mr. Wythe should have been the last creature to see Sir Stephen alive is rather strange. And then to emerge from Sir Stephen's study the master of the staff, and Leofric nowhere to be seen—you cannot deny it all looks very odd! You could not fault Mrs. Quincey for wondering."

This time it was impossible to miss Lady Wythe's reply.

"I find myself perfectly capable of faulting Mrs. Quincey for wondering whether Zacharias might have murdered my husband and his familiar," she said. "If she believes Zacharias of all people would be capable of lifting his hand to anyone, much less he who was a father to him, she is even more foolish than she seems. And I am surprised that you should repeat her ill-natured fancies to me, Frances!"

"Why, Maria," cried Lady Frances, injured. "I only wished to help! As for its being merely Mrs. Quincey's fancies, you should know that it is not only Mrs. Quincey I heard it from. It is being talked of everywhere one goes, and it will look very bad for Mr. Wythe if he does not put a stop to it. If you must know—"

But Lady Wythe would never hear what she must know, for Lady Frances caught sight of Zacharias, and blushed scarlet. Lady Wythe's eyes were damp, and her nose reddish, for to her own vexation she always wept when she was angry.

"Zacharias, I was just saying to Lady Frances that I think we had better go home," said Lady Wythe, composing herself. "Your Committee meets early tomorrow, does not it? And I find I am too tired to remain. But Lady Frances will forgive me, I am sure. She is too good-natured to hold a grudge."

Though she had been chiding Lady Frances but a moment ago, Lady Wythe pressed her hand now. To Lady Frances's credit, she responded splendidly:

"I should, only there is nothing to forgive! It was kind of you to come. I only hope," she added in a lower voice, "I only hope I have not added to your troubles, Maria, my dear."

Though her friendship with Lady Frances was salvaged, Lady Wythe's evening was beyond repair. Once Zacharias had handed her into the carriage, she burst out:

"Wretched creatures! How can they say such appalling things! They would never have dared to be so odious in Sir Stephen's day. How I wish—!"

She took a handkerchief out of her reticule with shaking hands, and pretended to blow her nose. Zacharias knew exactly what she would have said, however, if she had permitted herself to conclude her sentence, and she could not have wished for Sir Stephen to be restored to his life and office more urgently than he.

"How I wish I could help you," she said instead.

"I beg you will not let such talk distress you," said Zacharias. "My office confers on me immunity from any charge, you know, so it is only an unpleasant rumour, and cannot have any real consequence. I do not let it concern me." This was not wholly true, but he spoke evenly enough, he hoped, that Lady Wythe would believe him untroubled.

Lady Wythe lowered her handkerchief and fixed anxious blue eyes upon Zacharias. "You had heard this rumour before?"

Zacharias nodded. "I hope—" But he could not say what he hoped. It would make it too clear what he feared. He averted his face, so Lady Wythe could not see his expression, and said, with difficulty, "He was—dead, you know—when I arrived."

"Oh, Zacharias," said Lady Wythe, distressed. "Is there any need to explain yourself to *me*? Sir Stephen told me of his complaint even before he confided in his physician. We knew his heart would be the death of him. I only wish we had prepared you for it. Sir Stephen knew he ought to tell you, but he could never bring himself to the point: he could not bear to think he must leave you so soon. He would be so proud if he could see how well you have done—and so sorry to have caused you such trouble."

Zacharias shook his head, twisting his hands together—a nervous habit Sir Stephen had sought to rid him of, but to which he reverted in times of intense emotion. He opened his mouth to speak, scarcely knowing what he was about to confess, but the ghost spoke first.

"If you tell Maria about me, I shall never forgive you," said Sir Stephen.

Zacharias did not choose to address his guardian's spectre, but sat in furious silence throughout the remainder of the journey, to poor Lady Wythe's confusion. It was only when she had been restored to her home, and Zacharias was safely ensconced in his study, that he exclaimed:

"I wish you would not jump into my conversations! It is extraordinarily difficult not to betray you by my response. Did not you say we should do everything within our power to prevent Lady Wythe's becoming aware of you, since she has such a horror of ghosts?"

Zacharias would never have spoken so abruptly to Sir Stephen in life. Though they had by no means always been of one mind, Zacharias had not often ventured to make Sir Stephen aware of the fact. Perhaps there had lurked in him the old childhood worry, that if he did not make every effort to please—if he showed any sign of being less than his benefactor desired—he might find he was no longer wanted.

But death, in its backhanded kindness, had torn that ancient fear from him, even as it had robbed Lady Wythe of her chief support, and Zacharias of the man he had esteemed most in the world. There was now no reason to put off any quarrel, and Zacharias could not doubt Sir Stephen's disinterested attachment when his ghost continued to haunt him with such unwelcome persistence.

"Had I remained silent, you would have forgotten your bond," said Sir Stephen, with an aggravating lack of remorse. "You promised me, you know, that you would not tell her of what happened that night."

Zacharias shook his head.

"Lady Wythe ought to be told," he said. "Of all people in this world or the next, she has the best right to know what happened the night you died."

"If it were only the manner of my death that would be revealed, I should not disagree," said Sir Stephen. "But to confide in Maria would be to entrust the details of the Exchange to a member of the laity—a female, no less! You are unpopular enough, Zacharias, not to draw your colleagues' opprobium upon you by divulging sorcery's greatest secret."

"There can be no question of Lady Wythe's breaking a confidence," argued Zacharias. "The comfort it will give her to know that you are well will be incalculable, and . . . even she must wonder." His voice dropped, so that only someone possessed of the preternatural hearing of the dead could have heard his next words: "Even she must doubt."

Sir Stephen was a tall, bluff man, still vigorous despite the grey in his hair. His broad frame recalled that of a general more than a scholar and sorcerer, but the frank countenance and clear blue eyes concealed an unsuspected shrewdness. It had been said by his thaumaturgical enemies, half in disapprobation and half in envy, that Sir Stephen ought to have set himself up as a politician: he would not have ended as anything less than Prime Minister.

"Maria, doubt whether *you* might be a murderer?" cried Sir Stephen with an air of incredulity. "Never believe it, Zacharias! Because she knew Nurse's authority must not be questioned, she would pretend to credit the stories of your wickedness, but when punishment had been dealt and you were borne off bawling to the nursery, what dark suspicions Maria raised then! What aspersions cast upon poor Nurse Haddon's probity! 'She was not certain Nurse understood Zacharias. He never meant to be naughty. Such a nature as his needed only patience and affection to govern it.' It would take more than the whisperings of a parcel of ill-bred magicians to shake her faith in you."

But nursery reminiscences would not do. Zacharias's countenance wore a stubborn look with which Sir Stephen was intimately familiar. So had Zacharias frowned when he was four, and did not wish to eat his porridge. So he looked now, twenty years later, when prevented from doing what he believed to be right.

"I might be persuaded to release you from your promise, if you agreed to tell Maria of your complaint," said Sir Stephen. "She might be able to help relieve your distress."

"My complaint is not such as any mortal can remedy," said Zacharias, but he said no more. His battle was lost, as Sir Stephen knew it would be the moment he referred to Zacharias's illness. That was an aspect of the secret of Sir Stephen's death that Zacharias would not willingly speak of, however highly he valued honesty.

Zacharias proceeded to busy himself with preparations for the next day's work, as though he had not already begun to feel unwell—a pretence that would not have deceived Sir Stephen even before he possessed the intuition of the dead.

"Does it hurt you much?" said Sir Stephen.

"Not much," said Zacharias. This line of inquiry made him uneasy, and when he spoke again it was to divert the conversation:

"Do you have any notion what Edgeworth desires of me on Wednesday?"

It was not necessary to explain to Sir Stephen anything that had happened, now that he hovered between the mortal and celestial realms. He seemed to know every detail of Zacharias's days as well as Zacharias did himself.

"I expect he will want a spell," said Sir Stephen. "It will be some outrageous overturning of nature that he wants—a tripling of the Navy's ships, or the undoing of some military reversal. The Government can never ask for a simple chantment—an illumination, say, or a glamour to enable Members of Parliament to doze unnoticed in the Commons."

"I shall have to decline to assist, then," said Zacharias. He paused, glancing sideways at Sir Stephen. "What ought I to say to him? The

Government has habitually overestimated our powers, but it cannot be wished that it should be disabused of its notions of our abilities."

"No, indeed!" said Sir Stephen. "No monarch has ever liked a sorcerer, and it is only wariness of how we might revenge ourselves for any incivility that has kept our Government in line. It is a delicate point, and will require finesse."

But he cast a knowing look at Zacharias, who had assumed an ingenuous air of attention.

"Very well!" said Sir Stephen. "You know I like nothing so well as to be asked my opinion. But mark, Zacharias, your reprieve is but temporary. I shall not forget our quarrel!"

2

THERE IS NOTHING so prolix as a committee of magicians. It was six o'clock when Zacharias's colleagues had done opining on thaumaturgical standards, long past the time he would ordinarily have sat down to his dinner.

He was engaged to dine with a colleague, but fortunately his friend kept polite hours, and would not deem even half past six too late for his meal, so that Zacharias mounted the broad white steps of the Theurgist's Club with nothing but his own appetite to quicken his pace.

The Royal Society of Unnatural Philosophers regulated the affairs of English thaumaturgy, but it was within the less stately and more modish corridors of the Theurgist's Club that thaumaturgy took its ease. In the Theurgist's handsome rooms congregated augurers, alchemists, diviners, warlocks, soothsayers, invocators, tempestarians, mages and even the occasional sorcerer. The only conditions of membership were that the candidate possess some *soupçon* of magical ability, and that he pass for a gentleman.

In recent years the requirement of birth had assumed rather more importance than that of magic, as England's magical resource began to dwindle and thaumaturgy lost some of its lustre as a profession. In truth magic had always had a slightly un-English character, being unpredictable, heedless of tradition and profligate with its gifts to high and low. Save in the grand old thaumaturgical families—the Burrows, the Edgeworths, the Midsomers and their ilk—magic-making was now really only deemed a desirable profession for younger sons.

In consequence the dining rooms of the Theurgist's were swelled with gentlemen who cared more for whist than wizardry. Serious-minded unnatural philosophers fled for the refuge of the Society's august halls and hushed libraries.

It might have been expected that Zacharias would join them, but in fact he found the Theurgist's young bucks and dandies more congenial company. He had not been admitted as a Fellow of the Society, despite fulfilling all the requirements of learning and ability, until he had taken up his staff, and even then the Society's acceptance of its new Sorcerer Royal had been grudging at best.

Boisterous as the Theurgist's dining rooms were, within them, at least, Zacharias could trust that his colour was no bar. There he was merely Zacharias Wythe: "Gentlemanly fellow, Wythe, even if he does talk like a book." Zacharias always experienced a sense of relief upon stepping over its threshold, a relaxation of his guard he could enjoy nowhere else in public.

A group of thaumaturges was busy spell-making in the grand front sitting room of the club as Zacharias passed through. They were reflected in tall looking glasses, so that it seemed as though the room were full of dozens of lounging magicians.

Josiah Cullip stood among them, wobbling on his feet, and declaring, in the deliberate, portentuous manner of the foxed:

"All this talk of Puffett's impenetrability is humbug! Any middling thaumaturge could cast it. All that is needed is a modicum of ability—and a candle, of course."

"Well, we have an abundance of candles here," said an associate. "Perhaps you would condescend to demonstrate Puffett's for us, since it is so straightforward."

The exchange was nothing remarkable. The execution of trifling illusions and glamours was the accustomed dinner entertainment at the Theurgist's, so commonplace that Zacharias would be deemed very eccentric for raising any objection to it. He might nonetheless have remonstrated with his colleagues for their extravagance—Puffett's fireworks in miniature was in fact rather a ticklish spell, requiring a significant expenditure of magical resource—but that speaking would entail reproving Cullip. In the common way of men, Cullip's guilt led him to resent Zacharias for having been kinder to him than he deserved, and Zacharias had no wish to increase the ill feeling between them.

The footman who greeted Zacharias knew whom he was there to see:

"Mr. Damerell asked to be put in the Blue Room, sir, being quieter than the main hall. Will you be having the lobster as well?"

"A boiled fowl will suffice for me, thank you, Tom," Zacharias was saying, when there was the most extraordinary noise behind him. It sounded like nothing so much as a thousand deep resonant voices saying at once, *"Blurp."*

Zacharias turned to see Cullip brandishing a silver candlestick above his head, like a sword. It held no candles, but Cullip now wore a top hat, made not of beaver or silk plush, but of pure white wax. Small orange flames blazed on wicks sprouting from his ears, illumining his baffled countenance.

Tom tutted. "I knew he would come a cropper! I never saw a man that could carry off Puffett's when he was in his cups. I doubt whether even Sir Stephen could have done it!"

The thaumaturge who had egged Cullip on said drily:

"I doubt that is quite what Puffett intended! But I am sure you are right, Cullip, and I vastly overrated the difficulty of the spell. I should think it is a problem with the candles." Noticing Zacharias, he cried:

"Why, we have the Sorcerer Royal among us! He will shed some light on this. Do not you think, sir, that it is a false economy to have candles that will not permit of Puffett's success? For the skill of the magician cannot be doubted."

Cullip went crimson, snatching off his wax top hat and hurling it to the ground. He exclaimed:

"Are we to defer to the Sorcerer Royal's judgment? If the office were held by one deserving the title, English thaumaturges might not be reduced to scrabbling for magic for every inconsequential spell!"

Zacharias stiffened, but he had received snubs worse than this before, and swallowed his resentment.

"There is only so much even my wealth and influence can do to counteract the prejudice against you," Sir Stephen had told him once, long ago. "In time you will prove yourself, Zacharias, and your accomplishments will leave no one in any doubt of your worth. Till then your only defence against impertinence must be patience and courtesy. By such means you may win your enemies over—but it is certain you cannot afford the alternative."

The nearest Zacharias could approach the requisite patience and courtesy now was to ignore Cullip. He said to Tom:

"In the Blue Room, did you say?"

But Cullip was too angry and incautious to let the matter lie.

"At least he knows his place well enough not to seek to defend himself," he said to his acquaintance. "It is only a pity he has not the wisdom to surrender his office to a true English thaumaturge!"

Zacharias was no paragon, despite his long training in enduring insults. The sneering tone of Cullip's voice could not be borne. He turned and snapped:

"You need only one candle for Puffett's—tallow, not wax—and if you had recited the correct formula, you might have carried it off. As for the rest, sir, I shall not dignify it with an answer—save that if English thaumaturges spent less of their magic in foolish diversions, perhaps they might have more to serve their country with!"

Cullip was already so purple from claret and temper that he could not turn redder, but he flung down the candlestick and drew himself up, swelling like a bantam.

"Well, sir, I believe you know where I am to be found—" he began, but he was interrupted.

"You are shockingly late, Zacharias. What can you be about?"

No one could recall ever having seen Paget Damerell perform an enchantment, though he had somehow contrived to attain the much-coveted status of sorcerer. He pursued a life of the completest inutility, flirting with interesting women, eating handsome meals, paying scrupulous attention to his clothes and making it the sole business of his life to know every scrap of news floating about the thaumaturgical world. For this, as much as the silver sorcerer's star pinned to his coat, he was respected and even feared at the Theurgist's, and his appearance threw Cullip off his stride.

As he hesitated, Damerell lifted a quizzing-glass to his eye, saying in a tone of mild surprise:

"Those flames in your ears are a clever trick, Cullip, but dangerous, do not you think? I daresay I am an old fogey, and flaming ears are all the rage. I do not like to take Mr. Wythe from such delightful society, but there is the matter of my lobster, you know." Damerell's manner was apologetic, but that of a man who is serene in his conviction of doing what is right. "A gentleman cannot keep a lobster waiting. You will understand, I am sure."

By the time Cullip had formulated a response to his own satisfaction, Damerell had hustled Zacharias to the refuge of one of the small private dining rooms.

"I am loath to discourage you from calling out Cullip, for if any man deserved a drubbing it is he," said Damerell. "But a Sorcerer Royal *cannot* duel his brother-thaumaturges. It is not at all the thing."

His ears burning, Zacharias said:

"I had no intention of calling him out, and must thank you for interrupting us before he could commit us. I ought not to have addressed him in such intemperate terms. Cullip's thaumaturgy was always better than his judgment, but I have not that excuse."

"Your estimation of his parts is kinder than he merits, if that is his notion of Puffett's," Damerell observed. "At any other time I should congratulate you on your intemperance—*I* would call it candour. But this is not the time for it, Zacharias. Do not you know what they are saying of you?"

"That I am a murderer?" said Zacharias, after a moment. No other man would have ventured to speak so openly of the dark rumours that circled Zacharias, but Damerell's was a nature that thrived on picking up rocks and making amusing comments on the manners of the creatures scurrying underneath.

Damerell shook his head. "Not only that."

He slid a pamphlet across the table. Upon the frontispiece was a caricature of a leering old man in thaumaturgical blue, making his leg to a dark-skinned gentleman with a leopard skin slung over his shoulders and bones entwined in his hair. Emblazoned above the curious pair was the title: *ENGLISH MAGIC UNDER SIEGE.*

"This was on the floor of my entrance hall this morning," said Damerell. "You have not seen it?"

Zacharias had not, though he had seen many depictions like it. Unkind portraits of him had begun appearing in the press since Sir Stephen had announced his adoption. These had fallen off as the Society grew accustomed to his existence, but his appointment as Sorcerer Royal had lent fresh inspiration to the pens of the caricaturists.

The tension in Damerell's manner suggested that this was no

ordinary joke, however, and Zacharias bent his head to examine it with a sense of dread. The pamphlet proclaimed:

> *Its most faithful supporters cannot deny that English magic is now at its lowest ebb. We count fewer sorcerers among us than ever before, and in the past twenty years only a single magician has dared venture into Fairyland, where before there was a continual traffic across the border. As for familiars, those most valuable vessels of magic, England has received not a one since the ascension of our King.*
>
> *Is it any surprise, however, that English thaumaturgy should find itself in such a state of degradation, when it willingly bends its knee to a woolly Afric? One who, so far from overcoming his native savagery, has repaid his benefactor in the coin of villainy, and been rewarded with the staff of the Sorcerer Royal?*
>
> *England's magicians, throw off your shackles and wrest the ancient staff that is your birthright from the hand of the interloper! Were we to cease this foolish forbearance and exact justice, Zacharias Wythe could not withstand us—and we would do our nation a service that would not soon be forgotten.*

Zacharias dropped the pamphlet as if it burnt his fingers.

"This is a call to action, Zacharias," said Damerell. "It would be unwise to ignore it."

"Do you have any notion who the author is?" said Zacharias, striving to keep his voice even.

"You rejoice in such a number of enemies it would be difficult to trace this delightful confection to any one of them," said Damerell. "That it refers to Geoffrey Midsomer suggests he might have something to do with it, perhaps."

Geoffrey Midsomer had recently returned from a year's sojourn at the Fairy Court, against all expectations, for visits by seemly young gentlemen to the Fairy Queen were rarely curtailed by anything short of their demise.

"But I should be surprised," Damerell continued. "Vaulting ambition he always had, in common with all that family, but Geoffrey never struck me as possessing sufficient enterprise to o'erleap himself. But it is clear there is a general feeling against you, Zacharias. It is not promising that Cullip was so ready to snub you, and this"—he shook the pamphlet—"worries me more than his incivility—there is an ugly tone in it I have not seen before. It would be just as well if you were to make yourself scarce for a time. I wish you would leave London."

"Leave London?" exclaimed Zacharias. "At such a time as this?"

Damerell was prepared for Zacharias's obstinacy. He lowered his chin, and said:

"I should be worried for your safety if you stayed. I know you do not like to abandon your duties, but you are to consider, Zacharias, that it will not do one jot of good how many meetings you attend, or what scores of letters you write, so long as we want for magic. Did not you design spells to increase the influx of magic from the Fairy border? I cannot think of a better time to make a trial of them. Why do not you go to Fobdown Purlieu?"

Zacharias shook his head. "Any attempt to extract magic from Fairy must be a delicate operation, and I should wish to perfect those spells before I ventured to cast them so near Fairyland. I need not tell you what perils attend any instability at *that* border."

"Well then," said Damerell, without much hope, "perhaps a holiday . . ."

But then a voice rang across the room, full of joyful relief:

"Why, there you are, Poggs! I had begun to despair of finding you."

As he bounded into the room, Rollo (christened Robert Henry Algernon) brought irresistibly to mind a golden-haired cocker spaniel. He was a typical specimen of the younger son in avid pursuit of mediocrity with which the Theurgist's teemed: the cut of his coat was faultless and his neckcloths were fearful in their construction, but he had never managed to inspire in anyone a serious suspicion that he was capable of magic. He seemed to have been admitted to the Theurgist's largely on the ground that he was a particular friend of Damerell's.

"What fellows you are to be dining in this poky room, when you could be in the main hall watching the fun," he said. "You would enjoy it, Zacharias. They are making their reflections recite poetry. It is vastly philosophical."

"We wished for peace," said Damerell lugubriously, whisking the pamphlet out of sight. No one could doubt Rollo's good will, but his discretion was less to be relied upon. "It was a foolish fancy—but how pretty, while it survived! Did not you promise me that you were dining with your aunt?"

"Didn't I dine with my aunt!" said Rollo, with feeling. "Would you believe Aunt Georgiana has a friend that runs a school for young ladies?"

"I cannot say that intelligence provokes either surprise or interest," said Damerell. "Rollo's aunt Georgiana," he added as an aside to Zacharias, "is one of those eccentric relations that goes travelling about by themselves, and picks up all manner of unsuitable acquaintance in out of the way places—silk weavers at Macclesfield, and baronetesses at Tunbridge Wells. What does it signify if she has a friend with a school for young ladies?"

"It signifies when my aunt has a mind to offer me up as a sacrifice to the wretched creature," said Rollo. "It seems it is a school for gentlewitches, of all things, and nothing would do the friend but that I should come and give a speech to her girls on 'Magic, the Purposes and Dangers Thereof.' Can you conceive of my giving a speech to a gaggle of gentlewitches? What do I know of the Purposes and Dangers of Magic?"

"Why, very little, to be sure," said Damerell. "You might have to read a book about it if you are to give this speech. Have you any books? Zacharias might let you borrow one, if you do not."

"But I can't give any blasted speech," said Rollo. "It is positively against nature that I talk as much as I do. My pater never opened his mouth without there was dinner waiting at the other end."

"Then you must tell your aunt you will not do it."

"One might have thought you had never met my aunt Georgiana," said Rollo, with the steeliness of despair. "She is the one with the false curls and glowing eyes and smoke rising from her jaws. Do not you recollect her?"

"She did strike me as possessing unusual force of character," admitted Damerell.

"Whereas I haven't any character to speak of," said Rollo. "If I were to say anything to Aunt Georgiana that she did not like, she would devour me in two bites. I doubt she would even wait to reach for the fish knife."

"Well then, Rollo," said Damerell, "it seems you are in for it."

"I should have thought two intellectual fellows like you would be able to think of some means of rescuing a friend in a pickle," said Rollo bitterly. "Here's me, who can't tell one end of a word from t'other, being made to give a speech, when one of you is the Sorcerer Royal, and the other is always wittering on so a fellow hardly knows where he's at . . . !"

He broke off. Light dawned upon his face. "Here, Poggs, why do not *you* go and—"

"I have it!" said Damerell quickly. "Zacharias will give the speech in your stead."

Zacharias had been making swift progress on his boiled fowl as his friends argued. At this he sat bolt upright. "Hold up!"

"I was about to suggest that you might do it, but that is an even better notion," said Rollo to Damerell. "Landing the Sorcerer Royal would be a coup for that headmistress. Aunt Georgiana could have no reason to object."

He looked relieved. Damerell could be a froward customer when he chose, but you could rely upon Zacharias. Sort of fellow who would lend you a guinea and never ask to see it again. He would certainly help a friend in need.

But Zacharias had no compunction in disenchanting Rollo.

"It is out of the question," he said. "There is this business of the Committee of Thaumaturgical Standards to settle, and I have a meeting with John Edgeworth tomorrow."

"I am not meant to go down for a fortnight yet," said Rollo hopefully.

"No one could reproach you for your absence from London, with such excellent reason to be gone," added Damerell. "Your visit would be as good as a tonic for the young ladies' constitutions. The inmates of every good girls' school are perpetually on the brink of expiring from boredom, and you would stir them up nicely. Women find you so frightening, and so romantic."

"Indeed, Zacharias, I have no notion what I will do if you do not help me," pleaded Rollo. "A speech is nothing to a fellow like you, but imagine me standing up before a pack of ravening schoolgirls! I expect I shall go into a decline before I ever reach the school."

Zacharias glared at them. "Much as you are to be pitied, Rollo, I have a great many things to attend to, and I have no intention of delaying them to make a cake of myself before a parcel of schoolgirls."

"But—"

"Let us have an end to this, if you please," said Zacharias. "I have heard enough. You must simply give this speech yourself, for I will not do it, and that is my final word on the matter."

3

EDGEWORTH HAD NOT troubled to confirm the time of day when Zacharias might expect him, but he did not leave Zacharias in suspense for very long. Zacharias had not been in his study for an hour when his manservant knocked on the door, begging pardon for interrupting. Mr. Edgeworth had arrived with his guests.

"Foreign gentlemen, sir, two of them," said Simpson. He hesitated. "And a lady—I believe the wife of one of the gentlemen."

Zacharias saw the reason for his hesitation soon enough. The two gentlemen Edgeworth ushered into the room were impressively attired in rich foreign dress, but it was the fourth member of the party who made Zacharias stare.

"Your Highness, may I present to you Mr. Wythe, our Sorcerer Royal?" said Edgeworth, addressing the more gorgeous of the two gentlemen.

"Sultan Ahmad governs the island of Janda Baik in the Malaccan Strait," he added, turning to Zacharias. "His companion is Mr. Othman, and this is his royal wife. I hope you do not object to Her Highness's joining us. The sultan cannot be comfortable leaving her alone in a foreign land, as I am sure you will understand."

Edgeworth's pointed look recalled Zacharias to his manners, and he averted his eyes from the sultana, his cheeks warm. She was a pretty creature, very young, but it was her incongruously large belly that had drawn his gaze. It seemed extraordinary that she should have undertaken the rigours of travel in her condition.

"Yes, of course," he said. "Pray take a seat, Your Highness. I beg you will not be concerned by the skull at the window—it is only a harmless relic. In life it belonged to Felix Longmire, who was exceedingly mild-tempered as Sorcerers Royal go."

This did not seem to assuage his visitors' nervousness. Zacharias's study bore the marks of his predecessors, whose taste had run decidedly stoicheiotical. They had had a fondness for skulls with burning lights in their eye sockets, crystal balls in which mysterious shapes came and went, and dark velvet window curtains traced with obscure runes.

Though Zacharias had asserted himself so far as to cover the walls in a light sprigged paper, which did wonders for the room, the study was still wont to induce unease in the unmagical. His guests sat at the edge of their seats, drawing their feet away from the mystic sigils inscribed upon the floor.

Zacharias was scarcely more comfortable than they. At least it did not seem likely that Edgeworth would confront Zacharias with the dwindling of English magic, since he had brought a foreign potentate with him. But if Edgeworth had not discovered their crisis of magical resource, then his visit must be for the usual reason the Government sought out the Sorcerer Royal—in reliance upon that magic, and in expectation that it should be used for whatever purpose the Government deemed best.

"Janda Baik, alas, is beset with magical difficulties," began

Edgeworth unpromisingly. "When Sultan Ahmad approached us for assistance—for His Highness knows what an interest we take in everything concerning his nation—I told him I knew just the fellow to help him. Mr. Wythe would settle these wretched females in a trice!"

"Wretched females?" said Zacharias, glancing at the globe by his desk. Janda Baik was a minute speck in the Malay archipelago, so small it seemed hardly to merit a name—but to the east lay the riches of China; to the west, the vast waters of the Indian Ocean, to which Bonaparte had such convenient access from the Isle de France. The reasons for the Government's tender concern for Janda Baik were obvious.

"I daresay the trouble is best explained by the sultan himself," said Edgeworth.

The sultan was a slender, handsome man, not much older than his wife. Though he had looked askance at Zacharias upon their introduction—a black man could not have been his idea of Britain's first magician—his manner was courteous when he spoke. Mr. Othman interpreted.

"Our kingdom is afflicted by a group of old women who profess to practise magic," Sultan Ahmad began. "Aunts and grandmothers, whom we have tolerated out of respect for their great age, and because we believed they did no harm with their chantments."

"Witches, in short!" interjected Edgeworth, who was enough of a thaumaturge to grimace at the notion. Nothing disgusted a thaumaturge so much as a witch. Shameless, impudent, meddling females, who presumed to set at naught the Society's prohibition on women's magic, and duped the common people with their potions and cantrips!

"At first they contented themselves with rain-making and wave-settling, to which we made no objection, since it pleased the people," continued the sultan. "But now we have reason to regret our magnanimity. Of late our witches have entered into commerce with evil spirits, even taking these creatures into their own homes. We find ourselves overrun by monsters! The lamiae swarm our isle, so that decent people cannot sleep peacefully for fear they will be devoured in the night. It is to succour our people that we travelled here to seek assistance."

The young sultana leant over to whisper in the interpreter's ear. Mr. Othman cleared his throat and said:

"The French approached us with an offer of support, but we declined. We hate that tyrant Bonaparte, and our loyalty to our friends could not permit of our accepting aid from their enemies. We knew that the British would not fail to help us!"

"His Highness knows Britain is a friend to Janda Baik," said Edgeworth. "Our man Raffles made the introduction, and I assured the sultan we should do everything in our power to help."

"Certainly," said Zacharias, after a pause. Addressing the sultan, he said:

"I hope you will forgive my ignorance, sir, but Oriental lamiae are a species of magical creature of which I have had no experience. I have read Du Plessis's monograph, and understand them to be a type of ghoul—the vengeful spirits of mortal women wronged in life—but though his is the best exposition we have of the subject, Du Plessis says nothing of how they may be dealt with. If you would be so good as to explain, what form of assistance is it that you seek?"

His sentence had scarcely been conveyed to the royals when the sultana sat up and let out an urgent stream of words. This was translated succinctly.

"Guns!" said Mr. Othman.

"That is out of the question, of course," Edgeworth said hastily. "As your Highness knows, mere artillery would be nothing to witches and vampiresses. We discussed that yesterday, if you recall."

Zacharias wondered, not without a touch of irony, whether they had also discussed the fact that the Government was nearly as overstretched as the Society. The long war had drained the nation's resources. Britain was pressed so hard that it was very unlikely it could spare either troops or ships for a squabble over a remote island, however commanding its position.

"Mr. Edgeworth is in the right of it," he said. "Lamiae being already dead, guns would not frighten them." Before he could wonder aloud whether cannon might nonetheless be efficacious in blowing the lamiae apart, Edgeworth cried:

"We are of one mind! I have already told His Highness that you will be only too happy to oblige with some thundering piece of magic—some fearsome hex, vastly better than any number of guns, which will put these vampires in their places. Sultan Ahmad was delighted. His Highness understands that the Sorcerer Royal is an enchanter of considerable powers."

Zacharias was so taken aback that he scarcely knew what to say, or how to look. This, then, was the reason Edgeworth had given him no forewarning of what would be asked of him. Edgeworth knew how little likely Zacharias was to agree to any involvement in a foreign dispute. The Society's policy of non-interference in affairs of state was of long standing, and the history of the vexed relations of England's thaumaturgy to its sovereigns had proved its necessity.

But Edgeworth meant to back Zacharias into a corner. He knew Zacharias could not easily object in the sultan's presence, or express his indignation at Edgeworth's high-handedness. No one would have dared play such a trick on Sir Stephen, but Zacharias was untried. Perhaps Edgeworth thought the new Sorcerer Royal might be more docile than an Englishman—or ought to be.

Zacharias went to the window, turning his back to his guests. He was in such a state of cold anger that he could not trust himself to speak. It was tempting to leave both Britain and Janda Baik to resolve their own difficulties.

But Zacharias's was a changed world. Unlike the sorcerers before him, he could not retire to a tower and spin curses in splendid isolation.

Like England herself, Zacharias ignored the world beyond at his own peril.

He turned, swallowing his indignation, and began, "I should counsel against rushing into any sort of violent action—" when Felix Longmire toppled off the windowsill.

A faint persistent magic lingered in everything to do with a sorcerer, and the skull fortuitously avoided collision with anything that might cause it injury. It dropped onto a cushion that had fallen off an armchair, where it was forgotten by the living—for their attention was engrossed by the crystal ball vibrating upon the sill.

Zacharias made occasional use of the shewstone for scrying, and to commune with fellow magicians in distant lands. When it was not in use he covered it with a black velvet cloth, partly to shield it from dust, but also to preserve the sensibility of any unmagical guests. Shewstones collected traces of atmospheric magic, resulting in the appearance of disturbing images upon their surface: horrid impish faces, mystic letters, tiny desperate figures running from some lurking doom.

Seizing his staff, Zacharias snatched the cloth away, and caught the crystal ball when it juddered off the windowsill. Within the glass loomed two giant dark orbs, and a harsh, ancient voice bellowed:

"Raja Ahmad!"

The sultan sat up, his eyes starting from his head. The sultana clasped his hand, her face pale.

"What—*what* is that?" cried the interpreter.

All at once the shewstone became as hot as a poker taken off the fire, scalding Zacharias's fingers. He dropped it with a cry, and the crystal ball rolled across the room, catching up at Sultan Ahmad's feet.

The dark orbs within the crystal resolved into ordinary eyes, set in the face of an elderly female. She was a foreigner, like the sultan and his companions, with skin several shades lighter than Zacharias's own. Her grey hair was partly concealed by a scarf, her face wrinkled and sere. Despite her scowl there was little in her appearance to inspire fear, but Sultan Ahmad jumped out of his seat as though he had seen a snake.

"Who is that woman? What is she saying?" hissed Edgeworth, grasping Zacharias's arm. Zacharias drew a quick symbol in the air, murmuring a formula. The woman's speech sprang into clarity.

"You thought you would escape without anyone's discovering your purpose, but you ought to have known you could not evade Mak Genggang so easily!" she said. "I know what you have been about! Pleading with the British King for cannons and blunderbusses, the better to attack your own people with. Is this the reason the Achinese restored you to us, Raja Ahmad? Better that you had never come home, if so!"

The sultan was crimson with fury and embarrassment. He swept Zacharias and Edgeworth with a raging look, crying:

"I am betrayed! Damn you all for traitors and villains!"

He stormed out of the room, followed by the sultana. The interpreter only paused at the door to snap in a trembling voice:

"That is a poor attempt at a translation spell, for you ought to know that he called you a *black-faced villain*, and I quite agree!"

"Is that you, Othman?" cried the old woman in the glass. "See what cowards these men are! They are bold enough to bow and scrape to foreigners, but they would rather flee than look poor old Mak Genggang in the eye. You may tell your master from me that he has ground his face in the earth for nothing, Othman. All the broadsides in the world will not affright the witches of Janda Baik!"

THIS is a pretty pickle!" exclaimed Edgeworth.

Zacharias picked up the shewstone. The woman's face had vanished, and the glass was cloudy again, showing only the fleeting images produced by atmospheric magic. But traces of Mak Genggang's spell still lingered, stinging his fingers.

It had been potent magic that had allowed the witch to enter the shewstone though she had not been summoned, all the more as she was working her spells in Janda Baik. It was possible in theory to cast any enchantment from afar, but it required considerable skill—more than Zacharias would have expected from the type of village witch Sultan Ahmad had described to them. But it was clear neither the sultan nor Edgeworth had told him the whole story.

"What can have possessed you to spring that hag upon the sultan?" Edgeworth continued. "With a little effort we might have made a valuable friend for England, but now you have sent him off in high dudgeon, and the work to cultivate him is all to do again!"

Vexed as Zacharias was, he was almost tempted to laugh. He had not expected an apology, but still it seemed extraordinary that Edgeworth should be reproaching *him* for springing unwelcome surprises upon his guests.

"I did not summon the witch," said Zacharias. "She inserted herself into the proceedings."

"Oh, indeed!" said Edgeworth. "I was always told that the Sorcerer Royal's quarters and possessions were hedged about with wards, but I am a mere layperson and cannot claim to know anything about the matter."

"The shewstone is warded," said Zacharias, holding it up to the light. "But the dimensions within it belong to anyone who can master the spaces between the worlds. A shewstone must be open to any influence that is capable of entering it, or it could not perform its ordinary functions. It says much of this witch that she was capable of penetrating it, however. Sultan Ahmad has good reason to be anxious."

"Nor is he the only one," said Edgeworth. He seemed to have a great deal more to say, but he cut himself off and exhaled, striving to govern his irritation. After a moment he said, with a tolerable appearance of complaisance:

"Come, Wythe, cannot we arrive at a suitable agreement? The

Government longs to consolidate our power in the Indian Ocean, for if we do not, like as not Boney will pip us to the post. We cannot afford to offer Janda Baik either men or ships, but if there were some means of placing the sultan in our debt—some knockdown spell, say, which would put paid to these harridans—the Government would be very much obliged, and I am sure it would show its gratitude in a fitting fashion."

Zacharias said he should be sorry to disoblige the Government, but he was sure it would not depend upon him for any knockdown spell. "It would, you know, be rather like making war against these witches. The Government will recognise how impossible it is for thaumaturgy to involve itself in anything of that sort. The Government will not have forgotten our treaty with the French *sorcieres*."

It was Sir Stephen who had negotiated the entente between France's *sorcieres* and English thaumaturgy at the beginning of the war. Both sides appreciated the profound devastation that would be wreaked by a magical war, and neither wished to provoke it. Fairy commonly scorned to take notice of mortal skirmishes, but a fairy never lived who could resist adding its hexes to a magical scrimmage, and *that* was a result no one could desire.

Thaumaturgy benefited from the treaty, for it enabled English magicians to avoid testing their declining powers against the French, who had given no sign of suffering from any lack of magic. But it also suited the French *sorcieres*: they were as froward and jealous of their independence as any illusion of magicians, and they had no desire to be ordered about by their government as though they were no better than the military. They had agreed with the Society that no magician would advance the political aims of either nation by magic, so long as the war continued.

"Any use of military magics to assist the sultan risks breaching our agreement, and provoking France's *sorcieres*," continued Zacharias. "I need not tell you, sir, that we are already sufficiently embattled, not to court the addition of magic to Bonaparte's arsenal."

He and Edgeworth had both been pretending that neither of them was as annoyed with the other as they really were—Zacharias with rather more success, for his life had been such as to cultivate his ability to feign complaisance even when he was angriest. For all the privileges Sir Stephen's patronage had lent him, Zacharias could not often afford the liberty of honest emotion.

Neither his colour nor his birth was such as to render such habits of self-control necessary for Edgeworth, however, and his composure began to fray at the edges.

"And I suppose we have no magic to frighten Boney with!" he snapped. "We are a laughingstock—a nation of hundreds of enchanters, and nothing to enchant with!"

Zacharias's face went stiff. This was what he had feared all along, that the Society's weakness should be revealed to the Government. In a moment he had recovered his equanimity, but not quickly enough. Edgeworth had seen his look of alarm, and said:

"Oh yes, I know of our want of resource, and what is worse, I am not the only man in Government who suspects it. I need not tell you what that is likely to mean for the Society. You know the Government has never liked magicians above half: they are expensive creatures to keep, and they hardly pay for the keeping. Your arrogance may have served in the old days, when thaumaturgy had the power to justify its independence. Now, however—!"

He paused and took a turn around the room, his forehead creased with worry.

"I ought not to tell you—it is as much as my position is worth—but I am a friend to magic, little though magic may believe it," said Edgeworth. He seemed to arrive at a decision, and continued, with more assurance:

"To own the truth, I brought the sultan to you in hope that you might put it in my power to do the Society a favour. The Government has grown doubtful of the utility of continuing to support the Society—the Society benefits, as you know, from various emoluments, and has not paid a penny in rent in hundreds of years. You cannot conceive what anxious attention the Government gives every farthing in these difficult times, and the Treasury has been pushing for a removal of the Society's privileges for an age.

"Now, I do not know how the laity got wind of the Society's difficulties—*I* never breathed a word of them—but there are those within the Government who have a notion that it may no longer be such a risk to offend Britain's magicians. It is proposed that we require a Fellow of the Society to demonstrate the measurement of atmospheric magic levels at the Spring Ball, when everyone who is anyone will be in attendance, and the results could not be concealed. If what the Government suspects is proved—if English magic is shown to be no more than a bogey to frighten children with—why, then, it will feel at liberty to do what it can to make savings.

"And you may trust that that will be done," concluded Edgeworth. "So long as thaumaturgy clings to its famous independence, and refuses to lift a finger for King and country. I ought not to have told you even so much, but I wished you to understand why it is vital that the Society oblige the Government for once, even if it never did before."

He looked at Zacharias with unfeigned earnestness—but it was, thought Zacharias, no great surprise that Edgeworth should be earnest, since in his view the Society's good was bound up with his own advantage.

Zacharias could not agree. It was the Sorcerer Royal's duty above all to serve his country, and that overrode any other obligation, including any he owed to the Society. Even if it might help the Society's position for Zacharias to attack Janda Baik's witches on the

Government's behalf, it could not be thought of, when weighed against the risk of provoking the French.

If Zacharias agreed to one harebrained scheme proposed by the Government, founded on what was very like blackmail, it would be only the first of many. And his compliance would not address the root of English thaumaturgy's difficulties: its want of magic.

It was clear what he must do. His dismay fell away. He said:

"I am afraid we must disappoint you. Though I am loath to disoblige the Government, I would rather risk its offence than offer France's *sorcieres* an invitation to join the war. I am obliged for your confidence in me, however, and you may trust it has not been misplaced."

Edgeworth took his umbrella from the stand in icy silence.

"Then I do not see that there is any need for me to detain you," he said. "I will see you at the Spring Ball, I suppose."

"If I return in time," said Zacharias. At Edgeworth's look of surprise, he added, "I am leaving town tomorrow, though I shall try my best to attend the Ball, of course."

"I should have thought you were so taken up with your duties that you could not spare any time for rusticating," said Edgeworth, all freezing astonishment.

"It is my duties that call me out of London," said Zacharias, but Edgeworth's suspicious expression spurred him on to add, "I am going to address a school of gentlewitches, in fact. The headmistress is a great friend of the Threlfall family."

"It is no great odds," said Edgeworth, losing interest at such a tediously unexceptionable reason for a trip. "You will hear what occurs at the Ball whether you are there or not. I expect there will be a great deal of talk of it this year."

"There always is," said Zacharias tranquilly.

But England's crisis of magical resource would not be one of the subjects talked of if Zacharias had anything to say to it. He would travel to Fobdown Purlieu, to the border that separated Britain from

Fairyland. As Fairy was the source of Britain's magic, so it must be the source of its difficulties—and where he might find a solution.

He had hoped to have more time to perfect his spells for extracting magic from the border, but the experiment could not wait. By the time the Society opened its doors for its annual Spring Ball, it would have sufficient magic with which to dazzle all its guests, even the most fastidious, most disbelieving representatives of Government. Zacharias would see to that.

4

TWO DAYS BEFORE the Sorcerer Royal was due to arrive at Mrs. Daubeney's School for Gentlewitches, Prunella Gentleman was shaken awake at four in the morning. Mrs. Daubeney stood over her, holding a taper aloft and looking like Lady Macbeth in a lace cap.

"Prunella, the worst has come to pass!" she said in a tragical whisper. *"He is come!"*

A zephyr had knocked upon Mrs. Daubeney's window to inform her that the Sorcerer Royal's journey had proceeded more swiftly than expected. He would be upon them, not in two days, but—that very morning!

"I do not see that it makes any great odds," said Prunella, in no very complaisant spirit. She was no lark in any event, and Mrs. Daubeney had woken her at an unpropitious time. The night before the schoolgirls had fallen to talking of the parties and balls they had been to, or glimpsed through the banisters, at home. As a result Prunella had been dreaming of improbable glories: herself, dressed enchantingly, wafting around a glittering ballroom upon the arm of a faceless gallant.

Waking brought with it the reminder that she had been up till midnight the night before, not dancing, but polishing the silver at Mrs. Daubeney's insistence. The cold dark of early morning scored into Prunella's bones how unlikely it was that she would ever see a ballroom or go to a dance, save in her dreams.

Only her affection for Mrs. Daubeney enabled her to suppress her impatience and moderate her impulse to snap. She said mildly, "I am sure the school has never been so clean, and all the girls have been told what they must say and how they must look, and Clara has practised her curtsey a thousand times, and told she must not lisp when she gives Mr. Wythe his posey. There is scarcely anything more to be done, and Cook will be sure to have something to set on the table—she has been deep in preparations for weeks."

"But Prunella, think of the state of the attics!" said Mrs. Daubeney. "You know I said we should be sorry if we did not make haste to clear out the attics, and now here we are, with the Sorcerer Royal nearly upon us, and the attics uncleared!"

It was a curious contradiction that even as the rest of England languished for want of magic, the school was afflicted with more than it knew what to do with. Being a school for gentlewitches, it did not, of course, instruct its students in practical thaumaturgy. Mrs. Daubeney knew just what parents desired her to inculcate in their inconveniently magical daughters: pretty manners, a moderate measure of education and, above all, a habit of restraint.

But despite the mistresses' vigilance, they could not prevent forty high-spirited girls from breaking out in spells on occasion, and the garrets, tucked away beneath the roof and rarely visited, were an ideal location for mischief. A scent of leftover chantments lingered always about the attics, making the more susceptible servants sneeze as they passed.

"I am sure no one has looked in the attics for years, and there is bound to be some dreadful spell or talisman hidden there by one of the girls," Mrs. Daubeney continued. "That is just what I should do if I were a careless girl, with no notion of the trouble I was likely to cause."

"But I do not see why it should cause any trouble, even if it were true," Prunella objected. "The Sorcerer Royal is only here for half a day, and he will hardly wish to see our attics."

"Prunella, I am surprised at you!" cried Mrs. Daubeney. "Do not you realise the Sorcerer Royal's visit may be the making of this establishment? He is acquainted with every thaumaturge in England, and need only say a word to persuade them that they should send their daughters to this school. Only consider what Mr. Wythe would think of us if he smelt magic from the attics! Like as not he would insist on going up to see them, and stumble upon some magical hoard left by an old girl! Then he will accuse us of harbouring witches, and the girls' parents will take them away, and we shall have to sell the building and send away the servants, and we will end our days in the poorhouse!"

Prunella flung off her sheet. "If that is to be the consequence, I suppose I had better clean the attics!"

"Blessed girl!" said Mrs. Daubeney, brightening. "I don't know what I would do without you. You will know just what to do to rid us of these emanations. I need not worry about you, I know, where magic is concerned."

Prunella was accustomed to Mrs. Daubeney's swiftly changing moods. Still, it is provoking to be told you must clean an attic within half a day, to which you had intended to devote a week. When Henrietta Stapleton found her in the attic, Prunella was too hot and vexed to receive with patience the news that Miss Liddiard had retreated to bed, felled by an illness. Miss Liddiard taught the eldest class, and it was inconsiderate of her to be poorly on this of all days.

"A plague on all Miss Liddiards, and all Sorcerers Royal!" said Prunella.

"I am sure Miss Liddiard would rather not be ill, Prunella," said Henrietta in a tone of mild reproof. "She has a horror of giving trouble." At seventeen Henrietta was as good as out, and really too old for the school, but she had been sent back for another term by her mamma, who fretted about her continuing tendency to levitate in her sleep.

"But that is just what she is doing," said Prunella. She had stubbed her toe twice already, and been alarmed by the appearance of the largest rat she had ever seen. *She* would not mind a return to bed—not that anyone would offer her the opportunity! "A female may be poor or delicate or a spinster, but it does seem ill-advised of Miss Liddiard to combine all three."

This was an indelicate way for a young female to talk, but Henrietta was accustomed to the wild things Prunella said. It seemed to the schoolgirls that Prunella had been with the school forever: darting from Mrs. Daubeney's boudoir to the kitchen, chivvying the little ones through their baths, and substituting for the mistresses at times.

They were puzzled to describe her position whenever their parents took notice of the pretty, well-spoken girl who was Mrs. Daubeney's shadow. Prunella was not quite a servant, though she was as likely to be sent out to buy a black pudding for Mrs. Daubeney's dinner as to take a cup of tea with the headmistress. Nor did she seem to be any relation of Mrs. Daubeney's, for though they were both dark, Mrs. Daubeney's was a thoroughly English darkness, while Prunella's clear brown skin spoke of foreign antecedents.

When questioned Mrs. Daubeney only said, "Oh, her father was a friend of the family. Poor Gentleman, he died when she was still a babe, and entrusted her to my care." But she would not be drawn any further, and Prunella was as ignorant of her own origins as any of the girls.

That there was a special connection between the headmistress and Prunella everyone knew, however, and Henrietta looked at her hopefully. "Could not you speak to Mrs. Daubeney? She is so busy with the

Sorcerer Royal I do not like to trouble her, but I know she intends to show us to him, and it will look so bad for us to lack an instructress."

"Show you to him? What does she mean to show?"

"We are to demonstrate the Seven Shackles," explained Henrietta. "Mrs. Daubeney thinks the exercise will make a remarkable impression upon the Sorcerer Royal. She says no other school makes its girls perform it." Henrietta made a face. "I wish we did not have to! It makes one feel so cotton-woollish and good for nothing."

Prunella shook her head.

"I am under strict orders to keep out of the Sorcerer Royal's way," she said. "I could not speak to Mrs. D without attracting Mr. Wythe's attention—that is, I suppose I could make myself invisible, but likely he would see through that, and Mrs. Daubeney wishes me to stay away precisely because I am too magical! The class will simply have to amuse itself, Henny, and demonstrate its Shackles without Miss Liddiard's guidance. The girls are all old enough to know how to behave themselves."

"I would not be so sure," said Henrietta darkly, but she rose to leave. "I hope Mrs. Daubeney may not scold Miss Liddiard. She was dreadfully cut up, and kept insisting she would stay, but she was so pale we were all afraid she would do herself an injury."

"If good nature were all that were needed, no one could object to Miss Liddiard," said Prunella. "But a female making her own way in the world requires more than that to get on!"

This exchange with Henrietta left Prunella rather solemn. Despite her cross words she liked Miss Liddiard, and her position struck Prunella as pitiable in the extreme. Miss Liddiard was not strong, and the solitary life of a schoolmistress, with its tedious routine and its innumerable little snubs, did not suit her. But her father had bequeathed her nothing but his own uncertain constitution upon his death; it was necessary for her to earn her own bread.

If she were a man she might be a thaumaturge, and employ her magical abilities to good purpose. Since she was a female of gentle birth, however, she could not, in propriety, employ her magical talent to *any* purpose. If she could not marry, her best hope of establishing herself lay in teaching other females afflicted with magical ability how best to avoid using it.

From Miss Liddiard's position it was a natural progression for Prunella to consider her own, for this subject occupied an ever greater part of her thoughts as she grew older. She had always been set apart from the schoolgirls, even as she had passed her life among them. The fact that she remained at the school only at Mrs. Daubeney's sufferance would have ensured this in any event, but the distance was increased by the colour of Prunella's skin, the cast of her features, and the likelihood both suggested that her mother had been a native.

Mrs. Daubeney had not separated Prunella from the others by any deliberate measure. As a child Prunella had attended lessons, played and dined with the schoolgirls, and she had scarcely noticed the difference between their position and her own.

At nineteen, however, Prunella was no longer quite a girl. The older girls' tales of their families and dreams for their futures brought her own prospects into stark relief. No chance of a glittering Season in London or a grand marriage for Prunella. For as long as she wished she might stay with Mrs. Daubeney, and do everything desired of her for no wages, but that was as much as she might look forward to in the coming years.

Of course, if she were patient and tractable, there was a chance she might inherit Mrs. Daubeney's worldly possessions, but: *I am the most impatient, intractable creature I know!* thought Prunella.

In her reverie she might easily have missed the valise, for she was bundling things into chests without stopping to examine them. But as Prunella gathered another armful of objects she felt leather under her fingertips, and a curious sensation came over her.

She thought she stood, not in the familiar dusty attic, but in a different room altogether. A room in an alien land, for though it was dark and cool she knew somehow that it was a blazing-hot day outdoors. She felt the grit of dust between her teeth. The very air smelt different, perfumed with foreign scents—warm air, sluggish water, and earth baking under the sun.

"There you are!" said a soft voice. Though Prunella longed to see who it was, she could not raise her eyes, struggle as she might. The things in her arms clattered to the floor. She wrenched her gaze up, and saw—

Nothing. She was alone in the attic, stupefied with magic.

"Oh!" said Prunella. She put her hands over her eyes. She felt as if she had lost something terribly important, though she could not say what it was. For a moment she feared, absurdly, that she might cry. Then she remembered the touch of leather beneath her fingers.

On the floor, jumbled with split embroidery hoops and a stuffed owl, was a valise. It was made of brown leather, scuffed and worn as though it had been much used, though Prunella could not recall ever having seen it in Mrs. Daubeney's possession. There were initials engraved upon it: *HRG*.

"Was not my father's name Hilary?" said Prunella, and started at the sound of her voice echoing in the empty room.

"Prunella!" said Henrietta behind her.

Prunella jumped. Acting on an unexamined impulse, she hid the valise under a dusty old piece of tarpaulin. She was inclined to snap when she turned to greet Henrietta, but she forgot her irritation when she saw the girl's anxious face.

"Why, what's amiss?" she said.

"Emily Villiers and Clarissa Midsomer are quarrelling," said Henrietta. "I hate to play the informer, but you know what Clarissa is like, and she is so cross I believe she would not stop at murder. She has *bit* Emmy!"

"Wretched creatures! I hope they may bite each other's heads off!" Prunella exclaimed, but she divested herself of her apron. "If the

Sorcerer Royal arrives while I am there, you will simply have to distract him, Henny. I declare there are times I do not know if I am in a school or a travelling circus!"

When Prunella entered the classroom, Clarissa Midsomer was trying to bang Emily Villiers's head against a desk. Emily was resisting this, screeching in a manner fit to bring the ceiling down.

"That is quite enough of that!" said Prunella, pushing between the combatants.

She was no taller or sturdier than Clarissa or Emily, and they were neither of them inclined to attend. Yet after a moment's confusion they found their struggle suddenly at an end, and themselves on opposite sides of the desk.

"What can you be thinking, to be brawling on the very day of the Sorcerer Royal's visit?" demanded Prunella.

Clarissa looked away haughtily. She was one of the few girls who would not condescend to address Prunella as an equal, and she clearly believed it beneath her dignity to respond. Prunella was used to such snubs, however, and she looked at Emily.

"Clarissa was being an utter brute, and I told her she ought not to talk so about Lord Duchemin, for he *is* my cousin, and even if George is not very clever, he has the kindest of hearts, and it is a beastly lie to say that Millicent is only marrying him for his money!" said Emily all in one breath.

"I did not say that at all," interjected Clarissa. "I am sure the prospect of being a countess is as much an attraction as his fortune, to the daughter of a grocer! But I do not like a mésalliance. I suppose"—she glanced at Prunella—"*some people* would see nothing wrong in it. Some people would make themselves ridiculous if they thought they had half a chance at rank and fortune."

"I know I should certainly take any opportunity of uniting myself to a viscount," said Prunella cheerfully. "But I think you will find that society frowns on trying to break the heads of one's schoolfellows even more than it does on marrying outside one's station. What would the Sorcerer Royal think of finding a parcel of fishwives where he was told to expect a charm of gentlewitches? He does so much for the nation, I am sure we ought to spare him the disappointment."

Clarissa gave a hateful titter, by way of showing she, for one, would not be squashed by an upstart. "Indeed, he does a great deal!"

To Prunella's surprise, Henrietta leapt into the fray.

"Has any Sorcerer Royal done as much?" she said. "Mr. Wythe is known for his generosity. Think of all he did for that ingrate Mr. Cullip, who writes such shocking things of him in the *Thaumaturgical Gazette*!"

"I do not blame Mr. Cullip for doubting whether Mr. Wythe merits his office," said Clarissa. "Zacharias Wythe is not even a proper sorcerer."

"No one can say he is not a sorcerer," said Henrietta hotly. "The Committee confirmed his claim to the staff. But perhaps you think the staff of the Sorcerer Royal may be used by anyone who is so disposed?"

It was not a serious question. The girls were given a serviceable education in thaumaturgical history, which contained so many instructive examples of the unfortunate consequences of women's practising magic: Queen Mary's horrific blood magics among them, and the outbreak of untrammelled witchery that had caused such chaos in the Middle Ages.

So, too, they had all been taught about the staff of the Sorcerer Royal, which only the true Sorcerer Royal could wield. The fraud Edmund de Bourgh had been blinded when he tried it. Richard of Kinnersley was slain by the very spell he cast to murder his rival. Jeremiah Larke had been sliced neatly in half, both ends of his divided person cauterised by the spell. These were preserved in one of the schools of magic, where he could still be seen, a pitiful look of surprise frozen on his face.

There was no denying that nothing so unpleasant had occurred to Mr. Zacharias Wythe, but Clarissa tossed her head. "All I can say is, I have never known a sorcerer that did not have a familiar!"

She looked around in triumph, as one who had produced a trump. All the girls had grown up in the thaumaturgical world, and understood its hierarchies. Any man could be a magician; any gentleman a thaumaturge; any scholar an unnatural philosopher. But only a magician that commanded the loyalty of a familiar could claim the title of sorcerer.

Without the assistance of a familiar, a spirit from the Other Realm bound in service to a magician for the duration of his mortal life, a magician had no access to the expanded world of wonder that was a sorcerer's rightful demesne. He must rely upon his own imperfect perception and mortal frame in his spellcasting. But a sorcerer had the senses of his familiar to draw upon: his mind was intimately connected to that of a being of pure magic, and he had in his familiar a living channel to the power of Fairy.

"Does not Mr. Wythe have a familiar?" said Prunella, intrigued. Passing her days within the school grounds, she had little opportunity to hear the news of the outside world, which the girls imbibed upon their visits home. "Of course there have not been any new familiars for a great while, but I should have thought Mr. Wythe would have inherited the old Sorcerer Royal's familiar. Did not Sir Stephen Wythe have a familiar?"

"Leofric," said Clarissa, forgetting any intention to remain aloof in the pleasure of showing off. "My father knew him well. They used to lend each other books on insects—Leofric was a great entomologist. He had been familiar to the Sorcerer Royal for so many hundreds of years that he was nearly civilised, but Papa always said he was too ready to trust those he ought not. Poor creature! Now look what has happened to him!"

"When *I* spoke to Mr. Wythe at Papa's party," said Henrietta, blushing, "he assured me that Leofric is in good health, and much as he ever was, though he has retired from public life. I expect he has returned to Fairyland, and I do not see that there is anything to pity in that."

"Oh, if you pretend to credit that, there is nothing to say!" said Clarissa contemptuously. "But everyone knows what truly happened, and if you were not so in love with him you would too. Everyone knows your precious Mr. Wythe is a murderer!"

The roses in Henrietta's cheeks deepened to a flush.

"Henny!" cried Prunella in a tone of warning, but she had left it too late to avert disaster. Henrietta could never govern her abilities at times of strong emotion. She did not mean to cast spells when she was happy or sad or angry, she said, but the spells seemed to cast themselves.

The air in the classroom grew thick with magic. A strange light shone upon the girls, so that Henrietta's curls appeared to writhe like serpents, and glowing sparks clung to Clarissa's dress.

Henrietta stamped her foot, her grey eyes drowned in green light.

"I will teach you a lesson for that!" she cried. "How *dare* you call him my precious Mr. Wythe! How dare you say I am in l-love!"

5

"I CANNOT BEGIN to describe our gratification at your condescension, Mr. Wythe," declared Mrs. Daubeney. "No Sorcerer Royal has ever showed any interest in the magical education of females. The girls feel the honour of your visit extremely, I assure you."

Mrs. Daubeney was not at all what Zacharias had expected. Knowing what he did of feminine magic, he had envisioned a grey-haired, discreet sort of woman, wise in the ways of girls—horsey, perhaps—but certainly not magical.

Instead Mrs. Daubeney possessed all the glamour that the ignorant layman might have ascribed to her. She was tall and handsome, with silver-streaked black hair and a nose tending towards the beaky. She dressed in a picturesque style, with a great deal of purple and velvet. If spells could be cast by pure drama of gesture, she would have been a veritable sorceress. She was perfectly fitted for running a school for gentlewitches, however, for she did not in fact appear to have any magical ability whatsoever. What she did possess was a brain as keenly alert to the main chance as any politician's.

"Of course, dear Sir Stephen—what a loss to the nation!" Mrs. Daubeney's voice dropped, and she looked solemn. "And yet, you know, he visited the thaumaturgical schools at Seaton and Yarrow, but never seemed to think of our magical girls. I am glad *you* recognise their importance, Mr. Wythe, for if we continue to neglect our girls, the nation will suffer for it!"

Zacharias had been brooding on the challenge awaiting him at the border, and the troubles he had left behind him in town, but this embarrassed him out of his abstraction. He muttered some civil platitude: he believed the magical education of females deserved more attention—commended Mrs. Daubeney for her sterling work.

"It is a shamefully neglected subject, and I fear we will repent of our inattention," said Mrs. Daubeney. "What sad tales have I not heard of females driven mad by their magic! Of the sorrow they have caused their unfortunate family and friends! Yet what do we do to prevent these tragedies? We scold our girls if we catch them in spell-casting; we forbid them from reading grimoires—but we do no more, and are shocked when we find they have learnt night-spells from Nurse, and cantrips from Cook.

"If a girl-child makes her dolls dance, her parents admire her cleverness, and say it is of no account, for little Susan will soon outgrow such amusements. If, when she is turned fifteen, she is discovered in charms to curl her hair or brighten her eyes, she is reproved for her vanity, and told she must stop, lest she is thought fast. But no effort is made to make her understand the seriousness of her breach, and she comes to womanhood believing there is no harm in indulging in minor magics, provided she does it discreetly. And what is the result?"

Zacharias was at a loss for a reply. He knew, of course, what the Society would have him say. Magic was too strong a force for women's frail bodies—too potent a brew for their weak minds—and so, especially at a time when everyone must be anxious to preserve what magical resource England still possessed, magic must be forbidden to women.

Yet Zacharias had seen too many hags in kitchens and nurseries, too many herbwomen and hedgewitches in villages around the country, not to know that women were perfectly capable of magic—at least, women of the labouring classes. Among their betters it was genteel to turn a blind eye to such illicit activities. One would not like one's own wife or daughter to indulge in witchcraft, but it did not serve to be overscrupulous when feminine magic could prove so convenient in one's servants.

Fortunately Mrs. Daubeney was ready with her own answer.

"In consequence of our criminal lenience, our girls are committing acts of magic every day!" she said impressively. "You may think I exaggerate, sir, but we see it in all our new arrivals. They are so accustomed to easing their way with little charms and devices, they cannot easily leave off. It is no small matter, changing a girl's fixed habits, but we have learnt a great deal about how the change may be effected."

"Indeed?" said Zacharias. "How—"

"I had hoped you would ask!" exclaimed Mrs. Daubeney, delighted. "But stay—why should I bore you with explanations, when I can show you? We have a class in session at this very moment, a class of our eldest girls, to whom we have imparted such a sense of their duty of restraint, as I believe you will not find in any other crop of magical females in this country."

She leapt to her feet as though the idea had just occurred to her, though in fact she had been resolved upon it from the moment she heard of the Sorcerer Royal's visit. For Mrs. Daubeney had grand plans for her school.

Miranda Daubeney had begun life as rather a silly woman, and she might have continued as such if not for the lucky turn, twenty years ago, of her husband's dying and leaving an encumbered estate. She had been compelled to advertise for paying lodgers, and it was this necessity, painful as it had been at the time, that transformed the entire course of her life.

Mr. Hilary Gentleman had seemed a dubious proposition when he first applied for lodgings—haggard and tanned from his roving life in India, with a child tucked under his arm and a wicked-looking old leather valise he would never put down for a moment. But he had offered such a substantial sum that Mrs. Daubeney could not turn him away, and when she came to know him better, she did not regret her decision.

In time she had begun to nurture a secret hope that she might become something more than a friend to dear Gentleman. She had even grown fond of his child, despite the dusky tint to its skin, and its unfortunate predilections. Even then Prunella had begun to show troubling signs of being magical—signs which she needed the help of a mother to curb. Mrs. Daubeney would not have objected to being called upon to discharge that responsibility, but alas! It was not to be.

Mrs. Daubeney would never know what had driven Gentleman to drown himself, for the brief note he left, confiding Prunella to her care, explained nothing. She could not bring herself to send the child away: it would have to go into the poorhouse, or be boarded with some poor widow and like as not die of neglect, for Mrs. Daubeney could not find out that Gentleman had possessed a relation in the world.

But Prunella could not have an ordinary nurse, who would be frightened by her making little people out of soot, and drawing birds upon the wall that flapped and squawked as though they were alive. Mrs. Daubeney was puzzled to know what to do with her, when by chance she made the acquaintance of a village woman who had formerly been employed in a lord's nursery.

Prunella's eccentric ways disconcerted Mrs. Tomlinson not at all: "She's an uncanny creature, but then so was my lord's second girl, Annabel, and I never had any trouble with her. You need only be firm with them, ma'am, and show you won't stand for their wickedness, and they will settle down soon enough. Annabel is a great lady now; she married a lord herself, and you may trust she never thinks of doing any magic now she is grown."

Mrs. Tomlinson had proved so capable in caring for Prunella that when the squire's wife confided in Mrs. Daubeney that her cousin Stapleton was sadly troubled by her daughter's propensities—"she acts strangely at times, and they fear it may be *magic*"—Mrs. Daubeney had no hesitation in suggesting that this cousin should send her daughter to Mrs. Daubeney, who would see to it that the child's propensities were checked. For Cousin Stapleton had married a man with twenty thousand a year.

It soon became evident that Mrs. Daubeney could not rely on Mrs. Tomlinson alone to educate the Misses Stapleton of the world. She found herself mistresses from the ranks of impoverished gentlewomen who knew from bitter experience how to suppress and conceal their talents from a world that wanted none of them.

To Mrs. Daubeney's own surprise, it seemed she had a remarkable facility for management, and eventually she found herself in possession of a small but thriving girls' school. Five years after she had taken in Prunella, she refused an offer of marriage from a widowed thaumaturge with three daughters, and only regretted that her decision was likely to deprive her of three potential students.

She was no longer content with being mistress of a small school, however. Mrs. Daubeney dreamt of an establishment for the education of magical females on an unprecedented scale, and she had every intention of making the Sorcerer Royal's visit count to that purpose.

"Miss Liddiard is teaching our oldest girls the Seven Shackles today," she announced when they arrived at the classroom door. "If practised regularly, the exercise will extinguish seven of the most common types of magic of which the mortal frame is capable. It is an admirable device, and I beg you will not be misled by its appearance. We shall find the girls droning on together, looking half-asleep, but you must not think our girls are usually so dull!"

She flung the door open with a flourish, revealing a scene of utter pandemonium.

A cluster of girls clutched at one another, shrieking in dismay. At the other end of the room, a young lady crouched behind a barricade of desks. She had one arm wrapped around a wriggling girl's neck, and a small hand clamped over the girl's mouth, stifling protest (which the captive nonetheless continued to issue with unabated vigour).

The young lady did not regard this. She was engrossed in blocking the hexes flung by another girl, who stood in the middle of the classroom screaming curses, her eyes blazing with red light, and all her red hair standing on end.

Mrs. Daubeney looked for a moment as if she considered fainting, but the situation was too dire for that. She gasped:

"Prunella! What is the meaning of this?"

"Oh, Mrs. Daubeney!" said the young lady. "Pray summon one of the mistresses! If someone could deflect Miss Midsomer's hexes, I would be able to deal with Henrietta in a manner less injurious to her dignity. There, Henny, I know it is provoking, but I cannot very well release you, for you know you will try to strike Miss Midsomer dumb, and that would not be at all *gentlemanly*!"

"Mr. Wythe, I do not know what to say," stammered Mrs. Daubeney. "What you must think of us!"

Zacharias stared. Prunella was light enough for exertion to lend her cheeks a brilliant colour, but that she was not of wholly European extraction was clear from the warm hue of her skin and the profusion of dark curls tumbling over the back of her drab brown dress. Her small, three-cornered face was screwed up in a look of intense concentration that did not injure its beauty.

But it was not this alone that fixed Zacharias's attention. Prunella was stopping Henrietta's mouth not only with her hand, but with a spell—a spell hastily cobbled together, but of such ingenious construction that he would not have expected to see it from anyone but a trained thaumaturge. That she was contriving to maintain the spell while blocking Miss Midsomer's hexes—which were also more advanced than Zacharias would have expected from a schoolgirl—was nothing short of extraordinary.

Prunella cried in vexation:

"Oh, don't *flap*! Is that the Sorcerer Royal you have got there? He might be so good as to put a stop to Miss Midsomer's antics, and grant me some respite!"

"To be sure!" said Zacharias, starting. "I beg your pardon."

It was simple enough for him to draw a barrier around Miss Midsomer to contain her endeavours, but in fact it was not needed, for both girls suddenly lost their appetite for battle at the words "Sorcerer Royal." Miss Midsomer stopped mid-screech and stood staring at Zacharias with a purple face, as though she had swallowed one of her own curses. Henrietta tore Prunella's hand from her mouth, shrieked, "Oh, it is *not*!" and swooned to the floor.

"Good gracious!" said Prunella. She added, in a tone of reproach:

"If you were going to strike anyone down it should have been Miss Midsomer, for she was most provoking, and she knows perfectly well Miss Stapleton cannot help doing magic when she feels strongly on any subject."

"Prunella!" said Mrs. Daubeney chidingly, but Zacharias was bending over Henrietta.

"This is Miss Stapleton?" he said. "Miss Henrietta Stapleton? But I know her father."

"I do not see how that helps matters. I expect he will be very cross to hear you have hexed his daughter," said Prunella severely.

She knelt and raised her fallen friend's head with all the gentleness her manner towards Zacharias had lacked: "Poor Henny! To think that you were defending the Sorcerer Royal, only to be so served out by the wicked creature!"

"I did not—" Zacharias began, but he had no opportunity to complete his defence, for Henrietta sat up and said:

"Prunella, if you do not stop upbraiding Mr. Wythe, I declare I really will faint, and I expect I will do myself an injury, and then you will be sorry for being so shrewish!"

Whereupon she burst into tears.

PRUNELLA was more relieved than not to be sent to her room in disgrace. She had not a high tolerance for sentiment, and within five minutes of Henrietta's dissolving into tears, half the class had followed her. Prunella had been rather enjoying herself till then, but when faced with a class of upset girls the fun of the affray had drained out of her, leaving her cold and uncertain. She had been in scrapes often enough, but she had never seen anything quite like the look on Mrs. Daubeney's face.

She was uneasy as she let herself into her little room, tucked in the draughty east wing of the school. On any ordinary day she would have taken advantage of the unexpected luxury of leisure to take a nap: sleep could not be overvalued by one who rose at five and often did not get to bed till eleven. But she was too restless. The look on Mrs. Daubeney's face would recur, though of course Mrs. Daubeney could not blame Prunella for her students' bad temper—could she?

"She ought to pick better-humoured girls to instruct, or at least teach them to avoid politics once she has them," Prunella said to herself. "Mrs. D is always saying that a female ought not to know what to think about anything, but ought to do that prettily. Not but what she is shockingly bad at that herself!"

As she paced her room she caught a glimpse of herself in the small, cracked green looking glass on the wall. Her dress bore grey patches of dust, which must have been acquired in the attics. Clothed in this, she had appeared before the Sorcerer Royal!

Not that she gave a fig what the Sorcerer Royal thought. Only it was provoking to have looked so bedraggled before such a very handsome young gentleman. (Prunella saw now what had lent Henrietta such fire in arguing her cause against Clarissa's. A single dinner party would quite suffice to make any susceptible young lady fall desperately in love with a gentleman as beautiful and melancholy as Mr. Wythe.)

"Bother those attics!" she said.

But in a moment Prunella had forgotten all about Mr. Wythe, for her own words reminded her of the attic she had been cleaning. In that large, cold, cluttered room sat a piece of old tarpaulin—and under it, a certain valise.

The valise could not conveniently be hidden under her arm or her dress, so Prunella ran all the way from the attics down to her room. Her pulse beat high in her throat, though no one was about.

"It is not *theft*," she thought. "Not truly theft, if it is really my father's." If it was not her father's valise she would return it to the attic, of course, but the only way she might find out was by looking into it.

In her bedroom she dragged a chair over to the door. Having secured herself as much privacy as was possible for her, she opened the valise, sneezing as the dust flew from its surface.

How odd she felt! But hexes always excited the stomach. She was not nervous about what she might find within the valise. Like as not it was not her father's at all, and had nothing of interest in it. Indeed, why should she care if it was her father's, since she had never known him?

Despite these brave prophylactics against disappointment, Prunella was inclined to be crestfallen when she drew out of the valise a sheaf of old papers—newspapers and torn receipts, of no account. But the next thing was a worn old journal, bearing the name *Hilary Reuel Gentleman*, proving she was no thief—and then a black velvet pouch, which promised to be of even greater interest.

Still, this was so little that when she had emptied the valise she overturned it and shook it out, to make sure she had missed nothing.

Something clinked on the floor, and would have rolled away into the darkness under the bed if Prunella had not caught it.

It was a small, heavy silver ball, engraved all over with intricate curlicues and dots. Among the swooping strokes and flourishes could be discerned the occasional exotic flower and animal, represented in miniature. Strange hues gleamed upon its surface: first it was silver, but then it was illuminated by a purple light, then green, then blue, the colours following each other in quick succession.

The weight of the ball in her palm seemed curiously disproportionate to its size. It felt as though it contained a great deal more than could be encompassed by anything so small.

"Perhaps it is a locket," said Prunella, and set about prying it open, but there was not a join or gap to be found upon it. After some fruitless striving she surrendered the attempt.

She looked at the journal, but decided to leave it to the side for the moment, though she would not admit even to herself why she avoided it. "Doubtless it would take a vast time to puzzle out"—(letters were not Prunella's strong point)—"most likely it is nothing worth reading—scribbles about his day, and what he ate, and what the weather was like."

The black velvet pouch seemed safer, and Prunella harboured a faint hope that it might contain jewels, or perhaps gold guineas. It was nothing of the sort, however. She poured out upon her palm seven blue stones.

"This is my treasure!" she exclaimed. "A trinket, seven stones, a bundle of old papers, and a journal! Mrs. Daubeney need hardly begrudge me such an inheritance."

There was nothing for it: she must look into the journal now, while she had leisure to examine her find. Prunella opened the book and smoothed its pages, with hands that did *not* shake—and even if they did, it did not signify, for no one saw her.

Though her lips moved as she read, and it was necessary for her to rely upon the aid of a finger to trace the lines, she was soon engrossed. The owner had only used about ten pages, filling them with scattered notes. But he had preserved letters within the leaves of the journal, and stray pieces of paper upon which he had copied out what seemed to be quotes from books—books on magic.

There was enough to keep Prunella occupied for several hours. When she finally looked up from the journal, it was almost time for the Sorcerer Royal's speech. She was stiff and cold.

Prunella took out the stones again, noting the trembling of her hands with a philosopher's detachment. She shivered partly from the cold, but partly, too, from what she had learnt. It seemed strange that she should still be the same Prunella, possessed of the same chapped hand.

The stones looked as obdurately dull as ever, save for their colour. They were a pure, pale blue like robins' eggs, but veined with gold.

"What Mrs. D will say when I tell her!" said Prunella. Her laughter rang out, bell-like, in the stillness of the room.

6

ZACHARIAS WOULD NEVER make a sensation as an orator, but luckily his speech for Mrs. Daubeney's gentlewitches did not require any great oratory from him. He congratulated the young ladies on their good fortune in being educated at such a school, under the auspices of such a Mrs. Daubeney. He elaborated upon the perils to the fairer sex of venturing into the rarefied realms of thaumaturgy, and praised the instructresses who laboured to prevent his audience's meeting that dreadful fate.

Even as he recited the conventional objections to women's magic, however, Zacharias was mulling over the arguments in favour of it. He had been struck by the scene in the classroom. The spells Miss Gentleman had cast had been crude enough, but they had appeared to be of her own devising, and spoke of skill startling in an untrained female. That she had contrived to juggle such a number of enchantments while under attack, and in such infelicitous conditions as obtained in that room of weeping girls, was impressive.

But could female ability be any argument for encouraging women to exercise it? Surely feminine magic must be curbed, magic being so peculiarly detrimental to women's delicate frames. Besides, magic was too hard to come by in these days for it to be frittered away in women's frivolities—ballgowns and christening gowns and gowns of other descriptions.

Yet the moment this thought passed through Zacharias's mind, his conscience presented the image of Lady Wythe as a counterpoint. Anyone less likely to waste magic in fripperies was impossible to imagine—unless it were the cooks, maids, charwomen, herbwives, and other females of the lower classes, who were permitted to practise their craft in peace, because they employed it for the benefit of their betters.

For that matter, what could be more wasteful than the manner in which the heedless young members of the Theurgist's amused themselves? Magical fireworks and talking reflections were the least of their extravagances.

At this juncture, Zacharias's speech and (somewhat more to his irritation) his thoughts were interrupted by a disturbance in the audience. A small crowd formed around a girl who had fainted.

When Zacharias approached he found Miss Gentleman kneeling by the girl, trying to revive her by the application of sal volatile. Mrs. Daubeney waved him away.

"Pray do not be concerned, Mr. Wythe!" she said. "Such a to-do over a trifle! The silly girl ought to have known she was permitted to suspend her exercises today."

"It was instead of lines," said a pale maiden. "Olivia said she would rather chant the Seven Shackles all day than look at another line. She had lines yesterday for impertinence, and then today she was late to breakfast."

"Is the young lady unwell?" said Zacharias. "If her indisposition is connected to magic, I beg you will permit me to examine her."

"It is nothing to do with magic—quite the contrary," said Mrs. Daubeney, who would have been most grateful if Zacharias had had the decency to remove himself from the scene. "A little faintness is a natural consequence of the Seven Shackles. The girls are told never to do it but on a full stomach. I suppose the silly creature missed her breakfast, but insisted on continuing with the exercise even during your speech, so that it would be finished sooner. Olivia never can take thought for the future."

"Oh, but she was," said Prunella. "She must have been thinking of plum pudding at dinner today—the Seven Shackles during dinner would quite ruin her appetite. And there is the excursion tomorrow, that Miss Mortimer promised her class. If Olivia had postponed the exercise, she should have been too ill to go."

"But what is this exercise?" said Zacharias, who was appalled by the unconscious girl's appearance. Her countenance was bloodless, her lips blue, and her chest barely moved with her breath.

"My dear Mr. Wythe, do not you know? The Seven Shackles are quite the finest innovation of our age!" cried Mrs. Daubeney. "I make sure to have our girls practise it regularly, and it has a most salutary effect."

"I have never heard of it in my life," said Zacharias. "And you will allow me to say, Mrs. Daubeney, that I hope never to hear of anything like it, if this is its effect!"

"Mr. Wythe likely knows it under another name," said Prunella, apparently addressing Mrs. Daubeney. "You know, ma'am, that it is based upon Pobjoy's taking."

"Pobjoy's taking?" If Zacharias had been alarmed before, now he was horrified. "But that is a killing curse! It has been prohibited by the Society for hundreds of years, for its effect of draining magic from its victims."

"But there can be nothing wrong in the girls' doing it to themselves, you know, for it is not as though they inflict it upon anyone else," said Mrs. Daubeney eagerly. "Besides, you must not mislead Mr. Wythe, Prunella. It is not quite Pobjoy's taking, but an adaptation by one of our mistresses. The Seven Shackles only cause a mild enervation, which need not lead to any lasting damage if proper precautions are taken.

When it has drained the girls' magic, it releases it into the air, counteracting the general decline. So you see it is a most ingenious device!"

"Most ingenious! A curse I would not put upon my worst enemy!" said Zacharias.

"But I do not know why there should be any objection," said Mrs. Daubeney, in tears. "It is only a little inconvenience—nothing to speak of—and in consequence the girls are preserved from magic, and magic preserved for thaumaturgy. Why, I wrote of the Seven Shackles to Lord Burrow, and he commended the practise. He said it is just what the country needs!"

"She is waking up!" exclaimed Prunella. "You ought to be ashamed of yourself, Olivia. You have frightened everyone out of their wits. Let us get you to bed, and never worry about the plum pudding, for you may be sure Cook will save you a piece."

Zacharias reined in his indignation. He had no wish to distract attention from the girl.

"You are quite right," he said, his voice as even as he could make it. "I beg your pardon, Mrs. Daubeney. It is an excellent innovation, I am sure. I was only a little taken aback. But if the Society approves it . . ." He allowed his voice to trail off.

He was still simmering at what struck him as a reprehensible breach in an institution with so many young lives in its care, but a lifetime's practise of self-control enabled him to conceal this. Mrs. Daubeney curtseyed, smiling graciously (if a trifle wetly). Zacharias would have had no doubt that he had brought it off—if not for the sardonic light in Miss Gentleman's eye.

After the extraordinary interruption to the Sorcerer Royal's speech Mrs. Daubeney retired to her boudoir. The mistresses were tasked with entertaining Mr. Wythe while she recovered her spirits—and told Prunella off.

Prunella was not overly exercised by the summons. Mrs. Daubeney would scold her for the morning's work, no doubt, but her trespasses must have been thrown in the shade by Olivia's display. Besides, though Mrs. Daubeney did not know it, Prunella now possessed a potent weapon—such intelligence as would make Mrs. Daubeney forget all her complaints.

Prunella might have concealed her discovery of her father's valise if there had been nothing in it but the journal and the trinket, for those could be of no value to anyone but herself. Now that she knew what she possessed, however, it was clear that the good fortune must be shared with Mrs. Daubeney.

Mrs. Daubeney was reclining upon an ottoman when Prunella entered the room, her eyes fixed on some dreadful invisible sight. She looked like the lead actress in a tragedy, but this accorded with Prunella's expectations. Mrs. Daubeney would enact her theatricals—alternate between tears and vapours, and rain down voluble reproaches upon Prunella's head—but she would feel all the better for it, and there would be an end to the matter. Mrs. Daubeney never held a grudge.

"This morning's scene in the eldest class, Prunella!" she exclaimed. "How could you have permitted the girls to run so wild? For the Sorcerer Royal to have witnessed such brazen indulgence in magic at my school, when magic is the one thing I have set my face against—oh, it is beyond anything!"

Prunella had resolved to wait out Mrs. Daubeney's complaints, but she was full of her news, and she could not resist the opportunity to introduce the subject.

"But you must not be too prejudiced against magic, you know, Mrs. Daubeney," said Prunella. "Why, only consider, if it were not for magic you would not have a school at all."

"I should be pleased to give up the school if it meant no girl in England was afflicted with magical ability," said Mrs. Daubeney mendaciously. "But pray, Prunella, do not seek to change the subject. I am not sure you have a proper consciousness of what you have done. You ought to have considered me, but no one ever does, and it puts me in an impossible position!"

Mrs. Daubeney dissolved into tears. This might have dismayed anyone who knew her less well, but not Prunella. She rose and searched in a pretty japanned cabinet, unearthing a handkerchief, and thrust this into Mrs. Daubeney's unresisting hand.

"I am sure I have done my best for you," wept Mrs. Daubeney. "Indeed, no one expected that I should do so much. When your dear father died, my friends advised me to send you away. Why should I burden myself with the care of an infant unconnected to me, they said? But I ignored their counsel."

Prunella was properly grateful, and said so, but she added, "My father did leave some money for my upbringing, ma'am. You know he left enough to feed and house me, till I turned eighteen."

"But you are now nineteen," pointed out Mrs. Daubeney between sobs. "Not that I begrudge the care I have given you, but money does not go as far as it did when dear Gentleman died, and all he left is spent."

Mrs. Daubeney had nonetheless suffered very little from permitting Prunella to continue at the school. Prunella had started teaching the littlest girls when she was fourteen, and she had run errands and helped with the work of the household even before then. She did not remind Mrs. Daubeney of this, but for the first time it occurred to Prunella to wonder whether it really was the best course to tell Mrs. Daubeney of her discovery.

"You know the one wish of my heart has been to help England's magical womanhood," said Mrs. Daubeney. "There are not so many magical schools for young ladies, and with a little effort we might easily become the first among them. The Sorcerer Royal's visit was the answer to all my prayers, and to have such an opportunity squandered is what I will not stand for."

"Was the Sorcerer Royal very cross?" Prunella ventured. "He did not seem excessively put out this morning."

Mr. Wythe had seemed far more vexed by the Seven Shackles, she thought. If Mrs. Daubeney had observed this herself, however, she did not mention it. In common with most of humanity, she possessed a convenient capacity for forgetting anything that might cause her discomfort.

"Why, what could he do but disapprove of an establishment that allows its girls such latitude?" said Mrs. Daubeney. "But he is not the only one whose opinion must be considered. Clarissa Midsomer has told her family of what passed. It seems her brother taught the wretched girl to pass messages by zephyr, which is the worst possible thing he could have done. Why the family sent her to us if they were only going to spoil our work by teaching her spells, I'm sure I don't know! The result is that Mr. and Mrs. Midsomer have said that I must send you away, or they will ruin me. And they are perfectly capable of it, Prunella! All they need do is tell their friends what happened today, and everyone is bound to take their daughters out of the school, for who would educate their girls at an institution where they were permitted to brawl like prizefighters?"

"Good gracious!" said Prunella in dismay. "What a shabby thing to have done!"

Even then it did not occur to her to be alarmed. She could not conceive that Mrs. Daubeney would really send her away for such a trifle as a spat between the girls. But Mrs. Daubeney said, in a voice trembling with passion:

"That is to understate the matter altogether! You have no notion of how very little stands between us and disaster. How could you, indeed? You have never known what it is to be at the mercy of a mortgage!" Mrs. Daubeney shuddered at the hideous word.

"I have laboured for years to establish this school, and if the Midsomers choose to set everyone against us, it will all be for nothing," she said. "Just when I have contrived to pay off poor Daubeney's debts, and am nearly able to put us out of the reach of want forever! If our credit with the world is not to be destroyed—if I am to preserve all I have worked for—I must be seen to take every possible step to prevent a recurrence of this morning's incident."

The bottom seemed to drop out of Prunella's insides, letting in a draught that chilled her to the heart. Mrs. Daubeney had never before spoken to her in this manner, with this combination of trepidation and self-righteous resentment.

"What will you do?" said Prunella. She was so determined she should not sound frightened that her voice was toneless, lending her words an insolence she did not intend.

Mrs. Daubeney bridled. Prunella was never ingratiating at the best of times, but it seemed outrageous to Mrs. Daubeney that she should be so unconciliating just now.

"Less than you deserve!" snapped Mrs. Daubeney. "I ought to send you away, but I could not bring myself to do it when I thought of your poor father. In truth, if you have ideas above your station, I must take some of the blame, for it was I who indulged you, and gave you a greater sense of consequence than your position can support. But that will certainly change, and I do not think Mr. and Mrs. Midsomer can object to my penalty. You ought to be grateful, Prunella. It is not such a great alteration, after all. You have done such work all along."

"What do you mean?" said Prunella. Her hands, folded in her lap, tightened their grasp until the knuckles were white, but her voice was steady.

Despite Mrs. Daubeney's anger, she was not so composed, and she fidgeted with her bracelets as she spoke:

"Henceforth I must ask you to conduct yourself in accordance with your station. You may not teach any more classes, not even the infants, and you must not take your dinner with the girls, or address them by their Christian names. It does not do to be so familiar with girls whose station in life is so far above yours. I have told the servants, and they will expect you in the kitchen this evening. I think it best to begin today as we mean to go on."

Prunella was stunned. It was one thing to clean out an attic or two, or to help with the dinners, to oblige Mrs. Daubeney. Mrs. Daubeney had been known herself to scrub a floor or make a bed, especially in the earlier days of the school.

But it was another thing altogether to be told she must have her meals in the kitchen, and call the girls "miss." Prunella was on cordial terms with the servants, but she had no wish to be counted among them.

Her silence discomfited Mrs. Daubeney. She was genuinely fond of Prunella, and felt she had been forbearing. Any other woman in her position would have conceded to the Midsomers' demands, rather than offering them a compromise with which they were only half-satisfied. No doubt Prunella was put out, but she was really very fortunate, and must be taught to take the correct view of the affair.

"I know it is not what you expected," said Mrs. Daubeney, more gently. "But there is nothing else to be done, Prunella. I had thought, before, that you might teach the girls when you were older, but it would not have answered. The parents expect our mistresses to be of a certain quality, you know, and poor Gentleman! Who knows what indiscretions he might have committed in his youth? No one knows anything of your mother. She might be anyone."

She did not add that it was clear, at least, what Prunella's mother could *not* have been—an Englishwoman. Prunella was as conscious of this as anyone could be, and though she flushed, she said nothing.

"What is more," said Mrs. Daubeney, "and indeed what is worse, you are *too magical*, which is what of all things an instructress of gentlewitches must not be. For you work spells before the girls, Prunella—you know you do."

At this Prunella's shame receded, anger taking its place. Mrs.

Daubeney did not reproach her for working magic when the results suited Mrs. Daubeney. Why scold Prunella when her magic made polishing the silver or scrubbing the stairs or hustling the little ones through their breakfasts easier and quicker? There was a great deal Prunella did for the school with the judicious application of magic, and both of them knew it.

"I should not have done it if I had known you disliked it," she said, in a cold fury.

"I am sure there is a great deal we would both change, if we could," said Mrs. Daubeney, dabbing at her eyes. "If your father were alive . . . ! He is not, however, and we must do the best we can. You will not mind it so much, Prunella, once you have grown accustomed to the change."

Prunella was not weeping as she flung herself into her room. She never indulged in tears, and she would have disdained to give way to them for such a trifle.

She dropped to her knees, drawing out the valise from underneath the narrow white bed. *Her* valise, containing *her* treasures. Mrs. Daubeney could lay no claim to them now. She had lost all right to them when she forfeited Prunella's confidence and affection.

Prunella laid out the seven blue stones, and opened her father's journal. She read again the hastily scribbled fragment of text that had transfixed her before.

> *Endure: it is only a brief suffering. With what great reward! I have won a king's ransom, and once I have learnt to unlock it, my fortune, my name and my place in history are assured. What will not the Society do for even the mere travelling magician, Hilary Gentleman, now that he possesses riches beyond its conception—now that he calls himself master of seven familiars' eggs?*

Prunella had been surrounded by the daughters of thaumaturges all her life, and she knew how highly even one egg was likely to be valued by the Society. Seven eggs were a king's ransom.

She had had no thought of hoarding such wealth to herself. She had hoped Mrs. Daubeney would speak to the Sorcerer Royal, and obtain his advice as to how they might best profit from her discovery. But nothing could be hoped from Mrs. Daubeney now, or ever again.

So much for her foolish belief that she might be named Mrs. Daubeney's heiress! Mrs. Daubeney would scarcely consider doing so much for a half-caste female whom she believed better placed in the servants' hall. Prunella would be fortunate to receive a servant's legacy if she stayed—and that only if she were patient; if she did what was required of her without complaint; if she suppressed all heart-burnings and swallowed her resentment and never showed a sign if it sat like a live coal within her.

It could not be borne. It would not be borne. Prunella had in her father's treasure the key to free herself. What would not society do for Prunella Gentleman, when she was able to supply such a reason for generosity?

She must leave the school, it was clear. As for where she would go, where better to learn about familiars' eggs than the seat of English thaumaturgy—the greatest city in the world—London?

Even amid her revulsion from Mrs. Daubeney and all she stood for, Prunella did not think of attempting to hatch the eggs and employing their power for her own ends. It was a matter of orthodoxy that a woman's weak frame could not support an excess of magic. Prunella would have supposed, if she had considered it, that the power supplied by a familiar would certainly exceed any female's limits.

Besides, she had witnessed how little magic counted for in a female. Her life at the school had been a thorough education in the snubs magical women received, and the mortifying shifts to which they were put to suppress their abilities. Prunella was aware of what little worth society ascribed a Miss Liddiard, and she had no intention that Miss Gentleman should share her fate. There was no place for a magical woman in the world, unless she learnt to conceal her magic. After all, what had Prunella's own magic done for her, save to persuade Mrs. Daubeney that she ought to be a servant?

A woman possessed of a key to magic, however—a woman who might at her pleasure grant or withhold men's access to power—that was a different matter! Such a woman need never worry about poverty or obscurity. With such leverage Prunella did not doubt she would gain all she desired—position, influence, security—provided she were canny and careful.

She closed her hands over the stones, her decision made. She could not go to the Society with her treasures till she understood them better, but once she did, ah, then! She would know how to employ them to gain all she desired, and all she desired lay in that bustling metropolis, of which the girls had told such dazzling stories.

Everything might be accomplished in London. After all, if Emmy Villiers's cousin was so foolish as to marry a grocer's daughter, who was to say there were not more susceptible lords in London, rich enough to please themselves, and willing to be pleased by such a one as Prunella Gentleman?

7

SILENCE PREVAILED WITHIN the carriage as it trundled back to the Blue Boar, where Zacharias would pass the night before travelling to Fobdown Purlieu the next day. Sir Stephen broke this finally with an encouraging:

"It must be a weight off your mind to have that done with, eh? I did not envy your dinner. If that joint ever came of a goat, the creature must have been as old as I upon its expiry."

"Is that so? I did not notice it," said Zacharias.

Sir Stephen believed Zacharias was low-spirited, not without reason. The day had not been a success, and the dinner that had wound it up had been painful. Mrs. Daubeney's eagerness to please could not conceal her private distress, and Zacharias's mind was clearly elsewhere. Receiving no better response to her brave sallies than "Indeed, yes. No. I beg your pardon," Mrs. Daubeney had finally retired from the field, and waited out the dinner in stony silence.

Sir Stephen cast about for a means of raising Zacharias's spirits.

Zacharias must feel he had done nothing right today, but then he had hardly been prepared by his previous life's work for the occasion.

"I think you did very well, all things considered. It is a difficult thing to know how to deal with females when one has no experience of the creatures," said Sir Stephen. "But practise would give your manners the polish they want. I tell you what it is, Zacharias, you do not mix enough in society. Maria wishes you to pay court to some young lady, does she not? You are perhaps young for marriage, but it might do you good to get up a harmless flirtation. Why should not you turn the Spring Ball to your advantage, and contrive to be introduced to a few agreeable females then?"

This suggestion jolted Zacharias out of his waking dream. He stared at Sir Stephen in astonishment.

"Get up a flirtation, at such a time as this?" he exclaimed. "It is not to be thought of. I shall be too busy to have any time for society. Such a wholesale reform will require a great deal of time and energy."

Now it was Sir Stephen's turn to stare. He said:

"Wholesale reform? What in heaven's name are you talking about?"

"The reform of the magical education of women, of course!" cried Zacharias. "I wonder that you need ask. Surely there can be no question that reform is needed. Pobjoy's taking! I have never heard the like! Of course, it targets the seven centres of magic within the body; I ought to have known it by the name they gave it. But I would never have conceived of its being put to such ends. They are fortunate they have killed none of their students yet!"

Zacharias did not often allow himself the indulgence of being out of temper, but he was a young man, as few other than Sir Stephen and Lady Wythe now remembered, and he was deeply affected by all he had seen at Mrs. Daubeney's school. The longer he pondered the day's events—and he had ample time for pondering over dinner, since he had not troubled to make conversation—the more convinced he was that he had been wrong on the subject of feminine magic. *Everyone* was wrong on the subject. But that would certainly change.

Zacharias had been engrossed in schemes of improvement all evening. In his fancy he had trampled over old articles of faith, won a reluctant Society to his cause, and built vast palaces of learning peopled with healthy, useful thaumaturgesses. This prepared him ill for Sir Stephen's response.

"Perhaps it is a little foolhardy of those women to employ Pobjoy, but it does not seem to have done the girls any harm. It is a clever thing they have done, to funnel the magic back into the ether. If we could persuade more of our women to practise the exercise we would be all the better for it. I declare I do not see what you are so alarmed about."

"No, indeed. Why should I be alarmed that we require women to suppress their powers and disregard their instincts?" said Zacharias. "Why should it distress me that we punish any deviation so cruelly?"

Sir Stephen was surprised, though he was intimately familiar with the zeal for reform that lurked, unsuspected, within Zacharias. He had done his best to curb these instincts, and when the young Zacharias had protested, "Why, sir, you are a reformer yourself!" he had replied placidly, "But you have not my advantages, you know. Besides, I know my limits, my dear fellow—I know my limits!"

But that was the trouble with children, Sir Stephen reflected. They were confoundedly liable to pattern themselves upon one's conduct, when one would rather they simply did what they were told. Of course Zacharias was no longer a child, but the years had not dampened his fervour. Zacharias had ever placed what he believed to be right above what was politic.

"You had always a soft heart, and I suppose you were distressed by that girl," said Sir Stephen. "But consider the privations a thaumaturge must suffer, Zacharias. You know better than anyone the cost of sorcery." His voice dropped. "Think of how you are placed yourself—think of Leofric, and all you have suffered on his account, and mine. Would you subject women to that?"

Zacharias hesitated for the first time.

"I do not propose that women seek to pass for sorcerers," he said slowly. "Indeed, I could wish the nation had no need of sorcerers at all. I have no anxiety regarding the effect of ordinary magic on women, however. You have met many a house- and hedgewitch yourself—they invariably live to a great old age."

"Oh, that sort of thing is all very well for charwomen and chambermaids," said Sir Stephen impatiently. "But their use of magic to lighten their burdens is no argument for imposing such evils upon females of the better classes."

"What needs to be stifled by daily recitations of a curse can hardly be described as an imposition," retorted Zacharias. "I am not sure I credit these tales of the peculiar dangers of magic for women. After all, did not the Society say much the same of me? That my body could not support, nor my mind comprehend, the subtleties of the craft? You championed my abilities in the teeth of their opposition. Can you truly say, sir, that I should not seek to do for women what you did for me?"

Zacharias had not always been grateful for the form Sir Stephen's defence of his abilities had taken in the past. Though he had never doubted his guardian's attachment, being Sir Stephen's protégé had at times felt like being a touring attraction—a dancing bear on its lead. But Zacharias knew he could say nothing so well calculated to silence Sir Stephen.

Sir Stephen looked as though he did not know whether to be pleased or dismayed. He assumed a cantankerous expression, and said, huffing and puffing:

"There were no pamphlets calling for *me* to be strung up for invented failures! But I suppose you will pursue these crotchets whatever I say. You are of age, and if you will not consider your own security, there is nothing I can do to prevent your risking yourself. But I wash my hands of the matter—I throw you off entirely, mind! When it all ends in disaster, remember I told you I would have nothing to do with it!"

"You should certainly include a chapter on goety," said Sir Stephen.

Since Zacharias could only start for Fobdown Purlieu in the morning, he had begun sketching out his plan to reform women's magical education, by way of putting his evening to good use. He lay down his pen, stealing a look at the clock.

It was a quarter past eleven, and he was the only living person in the coffee-room, the inn having given over the apartment to him. He longed to massage his forehead, but he had no wish to remind Sir Stephen of his malady—Sir Stephen was bound to insist that he go to bed.

Zacharias knew he would suffer an attack of his complaint that evening—it was presaged, as always, by light-headedness, and hallucinations of strange shapes, lights and noises. But it would only strike at midnight, and he was loath to stop his labours before then. If he left off now it was a matter of real doubt when he would return to them again.

Sir Stephen had hovered at Zacharias's shoulder, muttering imprecations, but he was soon absorbed in the work despite himself. The task of devising a suitable syllabus was too interesting for him to refrain from commenting, however doubtful he might feel of its utility.

"I cannot think necromancy a suitable subject for girls," said Zacharias.

"This is what comes of being acquainted only with missish London females," said Sir Stephen, who had, not an hour ago, been inveighing against teaching women any magic, for fear it should be too much for them. "Childbirth is no very delicate process, and it is women who lay out the dead, so pray include the study of necromancy, and let us have no more argument. If you insist on instructing females it must be a comprehensive education, and no magical education can be complete without imparting a proper understanding of the darker arts."

"I wonder whether necromancy ought not to be followed by the study of household magics," said Zacharias musingly. "That might serve as a capital counterbalance to spirit-speaking."

"I thought you wished to train serious practitioners," exclaimed Sir Stephen. "If your desire is to turn out a phalanx of magical cooks, there is no need for reform. Your magical females can apprentice themselves to any village witch or wise woman—there are scores of the creatures, however hard the Society may try to pretend they do not exist. But I cannot see that their lore has any earthly relevance to a thaumaturgical education."

"Why, as to that, the low magics may produce spells as intricate and exacting as anything by the name of thaumaturgy," said Zacharias. "One witch, a Mrs. Hudson, showed me a spell which ensured her cooking never burnt, the principle of which was as philosophical as any thaumaturge could wish. The spell bound together time and the ideal, compelling both to meet at the desired point. An ingenious receipt, one she learnt at her grandmother's knee. I took a copy of it."

He rose to look for the receipt among his journals, but it was not among the books he had spread out upon the table and floor. Zacharias reached for his luggage, which sat in a dark corner of the coffee-room, but as he did so he stumbled over an obstacle he had not perceived before.

"Pray do not step on my case," said a small, clear voice.

Zacharias realised three things:

Sir Stephen had vanished.

At his feet was a worn old valise, which was not his.

On the floor sat a young woman. She rose, moving stiffly, as if she had been sitting for a considerable time.

The room, lit by the dwindling fire in the grate, was full of soft dark shadows, and the lamp on Zacharias's desk threw only a small circle of light. But his visitor had not relied upon the dimness of the room to conceal her presence. She still wore the rags of an invisibility enchantment, that Zacharias had torn by treading upon it.

It was a cleverly worked spell, surprisingly original in design, but it would not have so practised upon Zacharias's senses if he had not been tired and taken up with his thoughts. He had not expected to see anything other than shadows in the corners of the room, and so he had seen no more.

Even so, he was horrified at his lapse. He gazed openmouthed at the young woman, and this was when Zacharias arrived at a fourth realisation: it was Miss Gentleman, whom he had seen that morning fending off hexes.

"Now you have seen me, please may I sleep on the chaise longue?" she said. She seemed perfectly collected, as though it were an everyday matter to her to intrude upon the most prominent magician of his generation. "It is late, and I should like to rest for the journey tomorrow."

Zacharias was so perplexed by the situation that he let this pass without comment. "How did you contrive to enter this room?"

"I turned left before the stairs, and opened the second door," said Prunella. "The maid's directions were clear enough, and there are not so many rooms that one is easily lost."

It briefly occurred to Zacharias to wonder whether the young woman was speaking a foreign language, and he had simply failed to notice it. He did not seem to be following her meaning at all.

"There must be some mistake," he said. "How did you persuade the landlord to let you in?"

"Oh, that was no trouble at all," said Prunella. "The Headeys have a new maid, who does not know the village. I told her I was a courtier from Fairyland disguised as a mortal female, and that I had an appointment to confer with the Sorcerer Royal. She is a superstitious creature and let me in directly, so I came up here to wait for you."

"How long were you sitting here in the dark?" said Zacharias. He undertook a hasty mental review of his conversation. How fortunate it was that he had been engaged in a discussion of educational reform. As explosive as the Society would find his plans, they were not nearly so great a secret as the Government's negotiations with Janda Baik, or the manoeuvrings of the Fairy Court.

"I came when everyone had sat down to dinner," said Prunella. "I slept a while, so I was not very bored. The floor was excessively uncomfortable, however. I should much prefer the chaise longue, if you have no objection."

Another man, surprised by a female so abandoned to all considerations of propriety as to saunter unasked into his room and demand the use of his chaise longue, might have so forgotten his manners as either to eject her without further ado, or to grow offensively familiar. Not so Zacharias. The latter course would never have occurred to him, and if the former presented any appeal, it was banished by the chatter of Prunella's teeth as she spoke, and the trembling of her hands.

The instinct of hospitality Lady Wythe had instilled in Zacharias came to the fore. The girl must be returned to the school, it was clear, but first she must be looked to.

"Pray sit," he said, handing her to a chair by the fire. "I will ring the landlord for tea. May I ask why I have been honoured with this visit?"

Prunella seated herself, holding the battered old valise on her knee. "Of course," she said. "I am coming with you to London."

8

PRUNELLA'S FIRST THOUGHT had been to board the stagecoach to London at the Blue Boar, but the difficulties inherent in this scheme soon made themselves obvious. Chief of these was expense: she had taken sufficient funds to supply her wants for a period, but the longer she could preserve that amount untouched, the better.

If only Mrs. Daubeney were going to London! Not that Mrs. Daubeney would take Prunella along, since she was in disgrace. But if only Mrs. Daubeney had a friend who was going there, who might permit Prunella to accompany him; if only she knew anyone travelling in that direction . . .

When Prunella recollected that the Sorcerer Royal was leaving the next day, she felt that the fates had contrived to give her such a chance as she ought not to throw away. No doubt the Sorcerer Royal was travelling in his own chaise, which would save the expense of a stagecoach, besides being a vast deal more comfortable. Had not Henrietta spoken of his good nature? It seemed to Prunella that she possessed such a piteous tale as would persuade anyone who had not a heart of stone to help her.

When she arrived at the inn Prunella had every intention of employing the time till Mr. Wythe's return in concocting a plan for inveigling him into taking her to London, but she betrayed herself. No sooner had she settled down on the floor of the coffee-room and drawn her invisibility enchantment around herself than she fell asleep, worn out by the misadventures of the day.

She started awake when Mr. Wythe entered the room, but before she could decide what to do, he began to talk. After a moment's confusion Prunella realised he was not speaking to her. Indeed, he did not seem to be addressing anybody that she could see.

This was pleasingly sorcerous of Mr. Wythe. Prunella refrained from announcing her presence in favour of following his monologue. There is nothing so revealing of a person's character as the manner in which he conducts himself with his nearest connections. His language, gestures and attitudes, what he does and does not say, all serve to give the completest illustration of who and what he is.

Prunella did not know that it was to this useful species of discourse that she listened. But it was soon evident to her that the Sorcerer Royal was, as she had hoped, precisely the sort of forbearing gentleman upon whom it might just be possible for an unscrupulous young woman to impose.

"I beg your pardon," said the Sorcerer Royal, when she had declared her intention. "I cannot have heard you aright."

"It sounds strange, I am sure," said Prunella, trying to look tragic. She ought to be very good at it, she reflected, with such a model as Mrs. D constantly before her. "It must seem inconceivable that a gently bred female should lower herself to such a shift. But my desperation must be my best defence, for— Oh, sir, you are my only hope!"

She descended into noisy weeping, but not being much of a hand at acting, Prunella was forced to have recourse to a large white handkerchief, appropriated from Mrs. Daubeney's boudoir, to conceal the absence of tears. Fortunately Mr. Wythe was so befuddled that he did not seem to observe the pretence.

"My dear young lady!" This manner of address would have seemed impertinent in any other gentleman of Mr. Wythe's youth and handsomeness. But his manner possessed such a splendid unconsciousness of these attributes—he spoke so much like a man who believed himself over the hill, and beyond all flirtations—that Prunella was overtaken by an irresistible fit of the giggles. She hastily contrived to bury them in counterfeit sobs.

"I beg you will be calm," said Zacharias. "I am sure it is not so bad as it seems, whatever the trouble is. Shall I ask the landlord to summon Mrs. Daubeney?"

"No, call no one else! You are the only creature in the world who can help me, if you would," declared Prunella behind the shelter of her handkerchief. "I knew when I saw you that you would understand. Some instinct told me that you would not support those who would oppress a female, and deny her her birthright of magic!"

Above the lace edge of the handkerchief, Prunella's sharp eyes saw Zacharias stiffen.

"I knew that you would understand the secret I have been forced to conceal for these many years," she continued, infusing her voice with a passionate intensity. "For you must know, sir, that I *long* to study thaumaturgy! All my life I have dreamt of nothing else. I had scarce means enough to attain my dream, but I learnt what little I could from our ill-stocked library and untrained mistresses. I was happy in picking up scraps and rag-ends of wisdom. But that is all at an end. Even what little opportunity I had of acquiring magical learning is beyond me now—unless you, sir, condescend to help me!"

Mr. Wythe's defence to his invisible interlocutor of the need to educate magical females had given Prunella some notion of how to craft her petition. It was, after all, only an exaggeration of the truth.

Prunella *had* picked up all her magic from books and indifferently taught lessons. She had learnt even more from the schoolgirls—both in getting up mischiefs with them as a child, and in restraining their inventive wickedness when she grew older—but she was not about to confess that to Mr. Wythe.

The only falsehood lay in the wish she expressed to study thaumaturgy. Prunella had no more interest in magical lore than a fish has in the philosophical properties of water. Magic as a substance, a living force, was the air she breathed and the ground beneath her feet: she would no sooner give it up than she would willingly surrender her sight or speech. Stuffy old thaumaturgy, however—by which Prunella meant magic in books, particularly the deadly tomes to which Mrs. Daubeney's schoolgirls had access—was another matter altogether.

But the Sorcerer Royal was a scholar, and she had formulated her little speech with that in mind. Even so, she was charmed by its effect. Mr. Wythe was all sympathetic attention, his eyes fixed upon her countenance with a glowing look of interest.

"But this is extraordinary," he exclaimed. "Fate must have directed you here. I shall certainly try to help you, to the extent that it is within my power."

This readiness to enter into her feelings surprised Prunella. But she had not accounted for the fact that a passionate yearning to steep oneself in the principles of unnatural philosophy must seem the most natural thing in the world to a young man bred to the office of Sorcerer Royal. Nothing needed less explanation to Zacharias than a professed love of magic and a desire to know more of it.

He was not to be so easily persuaded of the wisdom of abetting an unaccompanied maiden in her own abduction, however. Even as Prunella's spirits rose, and she began to think this business of running away very easy, he continued:

"It may take some time to convince Mrs. Daubeney of the utility of teaching women thaumaturgy, but you will be patient, I know, Miss

Gentleman. My office lends me some authority, and it is to be hoped that that authority will lend weight to my appeal. The change will feel slow to one of your laudable ambition, but it will certainly occur in time. Such a foolish, unjust system as now obtains cannot long survive determined resistance. And in the meantime, there are books!"

"Books?" said Prunella blankly.

"Yes, for even Mrs. Daubeney cannot object to my supplying her library with books," said Mr. Wythe. "Even if she disliked their contents, it is unlikely she would refuse such a mark of attention from the Sorcerer Royal. You see there is no reason to lose heart, Miss Gentleman! Much benefit may be gained by solitary application. A good tutor makes learning pleasanter and quicker, of course, but many of our best thaumaturges had no teacher but books."

"I am obliged to you, but books will be no earthly good to me," said Prunella firmly. "For I cannot stay at the school. That is why I must come with you to London. There is nothing here for me!"

Zacharias had already begun to devise a suitable reading list, but this returned him to earth with a thud that knocked all the titles out of his head.

"But what is the matter?" he said, looking at Prunella with concern. "Have you disagreed with Mrs. Daubeney? Is it possible that I might assist in resolving the conflict?"

Prunella had not expected this solicitude. To her astonishment she felt tears burn her eyes. She blinked furiously, looking away: Prunella might have no compunction in indulging in a show of weeping, but she had far too much pride to give way to real tears in the presence of a stranger.

She thought suddenly, *I could tell him about the treasures*. Mr. Wythe was kind; he seemed honest; and he would know, if anyone did, what to do about seven familiars' eggs locked by an enchantment. The mere revelation of her secret must guarantee what she most desired: an escort to London.

But the memory of Mrs. Daubeney's perfidy stopped her. If Prunella could not trust the one creature in the world she had known from her infancy—the one soul who remembered her father—what reason had she to trust a stranger?

"I have parted from Mrs. Daubeney forever!" said Prunella, and she did not trouble to suppress the tremor in her voice, since it served to reinforce the impression she wished to give. "She thinks me too magical, and has ordered me to give up all enchantery. I may not even devise illusions to amuse the children, or soothe them to sleep with charms! I could not endure such a life. Sir, you are a friend to magic. If you deny me, I do not know where I shall turn."

Mr. Wythe looked at her with pity. Speaking gently, but with an immovable resolution, he said:

"You are distressed, Miss Gentleman, and not without reason, but if you were to reflect upon your request in a calmer spirit, I am persuaded you should see it would not do. Besides, I am headed not for London but for Fobdown Purlieu on the morrow. I would advise you to return to the school. I can see that with your ability you must find it a sadly restrictive environment, but even such a system as Mrs. Daubeney's will give you more exposure to the theory of magic than if you were anywhere else."

"Not more than if I were in London!" said Prunella bitterly.

She had hoped to work upon Zacharias's sentiments by appearing as a weeping, clinging, trembling creature in need of aid. Mrs. Daubeney was always saying pointedly how little gentlemen liked *pushing* females, whose tongues were never still, and who had a stomach for anything.

But her lack of success made her reckless. Speaking with real candour, Prunella said:

"I beg you will put yourself in my position, sir. Someone owned you as a son. There were those who had a stake in your success. But if you were me—with no family, no one upon whose charity or affection you could depend—would not it seem to you that there was no place in the world for such a one as yourself?"

Zacharias looked at her in surprise. But he could not fail to understand her meaning. Prunella was not nearly so dark as he—perhaps Sultan Ahmad would not recognise her as anything but a European—but to Zacharias, and more importantly, to any Englishman or -woman, it was evident that she was not—could not be—altogether English.

"Someone owned me, indeed," he said slowly. It was not an inaccurate assertion, though it was long since he had been emancipated. Sir Stephen had got around to signing the necessary papers when Zacharias turned thirteen—a curious birthday present for a thirteen-year-old boy. "I should like to help you, Miss Gentleman, but consider, would you be any better in London? How would you live? The city is no kinder than the country to those who have no place in the world. Here, at least, you have food and shelter, even if you have fallen out with your mistress."

Prunella flushed, remembering her last encounter with Mrs. Daubeney. To be obliged to her any longer was intolerable!

"I think I may seek better than to be beholden to the likes of her for food and shelter!" she said. But the Sorcerer Royal was not listening.

He said nothing, but his countenance altered all at once. He put a hand to his forehead, reaching out with the other, as though he sought support. But in fact he was only fumbling for the clock on the mantelpiece.

"Mr. Wythe," said Prunella, "are you well?"

"So late!" said Zacharias in a harsh voice, so changed that Prunella stared. "Nearly midnight! How could I have permitted you to remain so late?"

He staggered when he returned the clock to the mantelpiece, and had to steady himself by grasping the back of a chair.

Prunella could not make out why the hour should shock him so, but it was no time to puzzle over the Sorcerer Royal's eccentricity. Mr. Wythe was grey, his countenance fixed and staring.

"I am sure you are unwell," she said.

"It is nothing," said the Sorcerer Royal in that strange, distracted manner. "A headache, nothing more. You must certainly go back to the school."

But Prunella would not be put off. The look on Mr. Wythe's face as he turned from the mantelpiece had gone to her heart. It was a fleeting look—vanished in a moment, for he composed his features into their usual calm—but the pain and fear could not be mistaken.

"Pray sit down. You look but poorly," she said. "Mrs. Daubeney used to be a martyr to her headaches, till Cook put an end to them with—well, she said it was a tisane, but I am sure it was a spell!"

Years of chivvying little girls to take their baths and finish their dinners had given Prunella a knack for making the recalcitrant bow to her will. She bundled Zacharias unceremoniously into a chair, and it was this that saved him, for the first jet of flame shooting out from the grate was aimed precisely at where his head had been a moment ago.

Prunella fell back with a shriek.

"Good God!" cried Zacharias.

The fire spilt out of the grate, growing with inconceivable rapidity, devouring the carpet and flaring out towards the ceiling. Choking black smoke filled the room. This was no ordinary fire, for it was haloed with an eldritch green light, and the pungent smell of magic—a smell of hot metal and sulphur, and of herbs burning—filled Prunella's nostrils.

"Take care!" she gasped, as another jet of flame burst from the fireplace.

Mr. Wythe was still in his chair, ashen-faced. He managed to evade the jet by slumping out of the way, but he seemed incapable of doing any more, though he grasped the arms of the chair and tried to pull himself up. It was clear he was in no state to defend himself, much less Prunella. She must contrive to look after them both.

She grasped his hand and drew the edges of her ragged invisibility spell together. There was no time to think. Working by instinct, she knitted up the rips and tears in her charm and wound it around them both, thinking it furiously into solidity. It must be a wall—a cool wall—a *freezing* wall—

There were weird inhuman faces in the fire, with tendrils of flame for hair, and mouths open in silent screams of rage. Prunella had not erected her defence a moment too soon. The spirits of the fire surged out of the grate, and threw themselves bodily against her ward.

It held. The fire hissed as it met the ward (*cold as ice, cold as November*). The spirits roared, their faces melting and re-forming within the wall of flame encircling her and Zacharias. Sometimes the spirits looked like people, but sometimes they looked very unlike, having far too many limbs, and far too many teeth.

Prunella was so cold her teeth chattered in her head, but the bubble enclosing her and Mr. Wythe was lit with a hellish orange light. The devouring fire surrounded them. She could not hold it off for much longer.

A tentacle of flame pierced the barrier as she grew weary, and reached towards Zacharias. If Prunella had been thinking clearly she might well have allowed the flame to obtain its aim. She was not thinking at all, however, and she flung out her hand to stop it.

The flame wrapped around her wrist. She was so cold she did not feel the heat at first, but then she did.

Zacharias heard the girl cry out, and that brought him back to himself, through the haze of pain. He grasped her, though he was weak, dangerously weak. He should never have allowed her to stay, so close to midnight.

"Leofric!" he cried. "Leofric, damn you, remember the bargain!"

He felt the weakness leave him. Power rushed in a cool stream down his arm.

Prunella did not know quite what was happening, but the pain eased suddenly, and the fire receded. Mr. Wythe rose to his feet.

She had the blurry impression of her ward being turned inside out, like an umbrella in a storm. But it was no longer the spell she had knitted frantically together—it was transformed into something larger and far more powerful. It enveloped the blaze, cooling it in a trice, and crushed down the fire, till the room was dark, and there was nothing left of the flames or the spirits.

In Mr. Wythe's hand pulsed a ball of crimson light. He flung it into the grate. It hit the wall and burst with a hollow roar, many-voiced. Prunella saw the spirits of the fire escape up the chimney, hissing angrily as they went. A remaining nucleus of flame dropped on the logs, where it glowed for a moment before it expired.

Prunella's last thought was that if Mr. Wythe was *not* unwell, after all, she wished she had not troubled to exert herself. Her wrist hurt very much. But then she did not feel it any longer. A merciful darkness swallowed her whole.

There was no sign of the fire when Prunella awoke. She was lying on the chaise longue, and the Sorcerer Royal was in an armchair opposite, deep in thought.

Prunella looked around the room, expecting to see the walls blackened and the furniture reduced to tinder, but it was as though the fire had not happened at all. The only evidence that remained was the throbbing pain in her left wrist.

A dreadful thought struck her.

"My valise!" she cried.

"It is safe by your feet," said Mr. Wythe. He did not seem ill at all. He bent on her a look of concern. "I am glad you are awake. How do you feel?

"How do I feel?" echoed Prunella.

Her immediate sensation had been of relief that Mr. Wythe had not touched her valise while she was unconscious, but now she had occasion to consider herself, she found she was exceedingly cross.

"That is scarcely to the point!" she snapped. "If you were capable all along of fighting off that fire, why did not you? I should have thought you would be ashamed to take your leisure, leaving me to suffer an injury!"

She sat up unsteadily and thrust out her arm, upon which a livid burn had been branded by the flame.

If Prunella had been less upset it might have occurred to her that upbraiding the Sorcerer Royal might not be the best means of persuading him to take her to London. She was quite out of temper, however, and the apparent collapse of her scheme had removed any reason to check her tongue.

Mr. Wythe looked wretchedly guilty.

"I am indeed ashamed," he said. "I regret extremely that you should have been injured by an attack intended for me. If I had been myself, you should not have suffered the least harm."

Such a ready acceptance of wrong could not but mollify Prunella. Besides, she was intrigued by the reference to the conflagration's having been an attack. It had been clear that the fire was of magical provenance, but she had not considered what the purpose of that magic might be.

"Was it meant for you, then?" she said, forgetting her rancour in curiosity. "Are you often so attacked? Why, it is just like the old stories, with sorcerers continually at one another's throats! I had not thought thaumaturges were still so murderous."

"Neither had I," said Zacharias grimly. "The ashes in the grate still bear the impression of the hex. It was designed to injure a magician, without leaving any trace of its presence. That is why the furniture is unharmed. My enemy, whoever he is, hoped to leave me a charred corpse—to be found sitting at my desk, with my possessions undisturbed where I left them."

"How horrible!" said Prunella with relish.

"The hex was certainly intended for me. No other magician was meant to be staying at this inn," said Zacharias. "Unfortunately for you, Miss Gentleman, my enemy did not account for your presence. If you had been a chair, you would have escaped harm. Since the fire took you for a magician, you were burnt, for which I am very sorry indeed."

"As you should be!" said Prunella, but the reproach was perfunctory. It was too interesting to have been present at an attempt on the Sorcerer Royal's life for Prunella to work up any lasting indignation about her part in the proceedings. "I suppose the spell disabled you, so you should not be able to counter it. That was cleverly done."

Zacharias looked embarrassed.

"No," he said. "I was taken ill, as you observed, but that was merely an unlucky circumstance, unconnected to the attack."

He hesitated, then continued awkwardly:

"I am prey to a recurring complaint whose symptoms are most marked in the evening, and particularly at midnight. It was unfortunate that my attacker struck at precisely that time. I am only glad I was able to summon my strength before it was too late—though not in time to prevent your coming to harm."

The harm was not much worse than the cuts and scalds Prunella had received in the school kitchens, but she was not about to admit that. She drew herself up and looked haughty.

"I call it a disgrace!" she said. "My wrist hurts very much, and I should think it will need a great deal of time and care to heal. I don't suppose it will have either, since I must return to Mrs. Daubeney, who doesn't care whether I live or die!"

This was a wholly speculative play on Prunella's part, for she had given up on Mr. Wythe's doing as she desired. It took the wind out of her sails when he replied:

"Of course you cannot go back to that finishing school. Your talent would be thrown away there. I shall take you to London. If I am to reform the magical education of women, why should not the reform begin with you?"

"Oh!" said Prunella. After a moment she rallied, and tried to look as though this were only what she had expected. "Yes! That is what I have been trying to tell you all along."

Mr. Wythe nodded, but he did not look at her.

"Besides," he said, "I am in your debt, and will do what I can to make a return. I should likely have died if not for you. You saved my life."

"Why, so I did," said Prunella, charmed.

9

Zacharias managed to prevail upon Miss Gentleman to return to the school the next morning: whatever had passed between them, she still owed Mrs. Daubeney a farewell, and if she returned, no one need know she had passed the night at the inn.

He had been thinking of his own reputation as well as Miss Gentleman's. He had no wish for it to be bruited abroad that the Sorcerer Royal was in the habit of abstracting maidens from girls' schools and entertaining them in his rooms. "It is quite enough for them to call me a murderer and an ingrate, without adding the ravishing of innocents to my trespasses!"

But Zacharias was tempted to regret his discretion when he was shown into Mrs. Daubeney's drawing room in the morning. The lady herself was cast down upon an ottoman, weeping stormily into a handkerchief. Prunella hovered nearby with a bottle of smelling salts. She had the air of one to whom such displays were commonplace, but the apprehension in her eyes belied her appearance of composure.

"I am sorry to intrude," said Zacharias. "Shall I return at a more opportune time?"

Mrs. Daubeney dabbed at her eyes and sat up. "What time can be opportune now that my poor Prunella is ruined?"

"I met Mrs. Daubeney as I was returning to my room," explained Prunella.

Mrs. Daubeney had had every intention of snubbing Mr. Wythe when she saw him again. She considered he had behaved very shabbily in failing to be impressed by the Seven Shackles, which she regarded as a prime feather in her cap. And he had been a shocking dinner companion, speaking once in ten minutes if he spoke at all. No, the Sorcerer Royal was quite exploded in Mrs. Daubeney's eycs. She would not be surprised if he had murdered poor dear Sir Stephen after all, and that faithful old dragon of his!

Her plan to treat him with silent dignity was forgotten in her distress over Prunella, however. Mrs. Daubeney's affection might fail so far as to lead her to demote Prunella at her convenience, but Prunella's disgrace was a catastrophe she had neither conceived nor desired, and she was all the more dismayed for that she felt she was in part to blame. Prunella would never have been so reckless if she had not been distressed by the little scolding Mrs. Daubeney had given her. Clearly she had run away in a fit of temper, and thereby come to her downfall.

But Mr. Wythe's was the guilt, and he need not think he would escape it. Any notion of silent dignity was cast aside, and Mrs. Daubeney harangued Zacharias quite as though he were an old acquaintance.

"If you had a heart, you might imagine my feelings when I saw Prunella's bed unslept in!" she said. "My own child, whom I raised ever since her poor father walked into the river! I do not claim my care was a substitute for the affection of her parents. I daresay it was not, but I challenge you to name anyone who would have shown a penniless female such devotion as I gave!"

"You have been very good, Mrs. Daubeney," said Prunella. "To a mere penniless female!"

There was an undertone in her voice that made Zacharias glance warily at her, but Prunella knew her audience. Mrs. Daubeney was too wound up to take any notice of her interjections.

"And then to learn she had fled my roof for yours!" lamented Mrs. Daubeney. "The world may call you a great man, Mr. Wythe, but I say you are the veriest blackguard for preying upon a young female, reared in retirement, and innocent of the ways of the world!"

"Pray do not distress yourself, Mrs. Daubeney," said Prunella. "Even if anything untoward had happened—and Mr. Wythe will vouch that it did not—I haven't got any reputation worth speaking of, you know." Her eyes glittered. "After all, it is not as though I were one of the young ladies."

Mrs. Daubeney drew herself to her full height, the picture of affronted hauteur.

"Prunella, you forget yourself," she said. "Remember your father was a gentleman!"

"But if he drowned himself and left his infant daughter with the landlady, he cannot have been very respectable," argued Prunella.

"Ah! Poor Gentleman," said Mrs. Daubeney, shading her eyes as though she were looking down sunlit avenues into the depths of her past. "He had had a hard time of it, indeed."

Zacharias saw his chance.

"I gather Mr. Gentleman contrived at his own demise?" he said.

"He left a note," said Mrs. Daubeney. "Otherwise I could never have believed it of him. Such a prettily written note! *'Miranda'*—we were such friends, we never stood on ceremony with each other—*'Miranda, I know your generosity will forgive this final trespass, despite the trouble I have caused you.'* Even then, in his anguish of mind, so considerate!"

Zacharias nodded sagely. "It sounds like him."

Mrs. Daubeney's eyes widened. "Did you know him?"

"I owe you my apologies, ma'am. I ought to have told you yesterday, but I did not wish to speak until I had confirmed Miss Gentleman was the object of my search," said Zacharias. He sat down across from Mrs. Daubeney, though she had not invited him to take a chair. He must conduct himself with the utmost confidence, or the game was up. "Mr. Gentleman was a particular friend of my guardian, Sir Stephen Wythe. I saw him often."

"Why, you cannot have been very old then," said Mrs. Daubeney. "Gentleman came here the instant he returned from India. He told me he had no relations and no friends he cared to see in England. If you knew Mr. Gentleman before he left for India, you cannot have been very old."

"Certainly I was not very old, but Sir Stephen told me so much about him, that I feel as though I knew him myself," said Zacharias, inventing wildly. "He—he was not such a man as one easily forgets!"

In Mr. Gentleman Zacharias had hit upon the one subject in respect of which Mrs. Daubeney would swallow nearly anything. Her eyes dimmed. "Yes. You knew him, I can see!"

"Unfortunately Sir Stephen did not hear from him for many years after they parted," said Zacharias, suppressing a pang of guilt. "He then discovered that Mr. Gentleman's fortunes had taken an adverse turn; that he had passed on, and left a daughter in straitened circumstances. My guardian had only sufficient time to discover so much before his own death, and he was not able to help his friend's daughter as he desired. It was his wish that I should locate her, and offer her what assistance I could. It was in accordance with that wish that I came to your school."

"That explains why Georgiana's nephew did not come!" cried Mrs. Daubeney.

Zacharias paused to cast a glowering thought in the general direction of Rollo Threlfall, who was doubtless strolling along Bond Street at that very moment, blissfully unaware of the predicament in which he had landed his friend.

"Yes, I proposed that I should take Mr. Threlfall's place," said Zacharias. "I had heard a rumour that Mr. Gentleman had passed his last days in these parts, and I wondered whether his daughter might not be among the gentlewitches at your school."

"I had wondered! The Sorcerer Royal was never concerned with the education of gentlewitches before," said Mrs. Daubeney. She was enchanted by this vision of her beloved Gentleman as an intimate of the Sorcerer Royal, fondly remembered even upon Sir Stephen's deathbed, and herself the friend who in her nobility of character had preserved his daughter from the workhouse. "But this accounts for all!"

Zacharias nodded, though he felt wretchedly uncomfortable. Having set his hand to the plough, however, he could hardly turn back.

"I was soon certain that Miss Gentleman was the young lady I sought, but I had only time to inform her of the bare fact of my guardian's connection with her father," he said. "Anxious to learn more, she came to the inn yesterday to speak with me. She ought to have consulted you, ma'am, before undertaking such a visit alone, but we will forgive Miss Gentleman her eagerness to understand more of her origins."

"That was very impulsive of you, Prunella," said Mrs. Daubeney chidingly. "But I suppose it was understandable. Goodness knows I have longed to know more of Gentleman's history! He never gave me a hint of what he had endured. He was not a man to complain."

"By the time I had answered Miss Gentleman's questions, it was so late I was reluctant to turn the coachman out of bed to return her to you," said Zacharias. "Fortunately Mrs. Headey was able to make up a bed for her at the inn."

"Well, Mrs. Headey is a mother, and ought to know what she is about," said Mrs. Daubeney. "But it looked very bad—you cannot deny it looked very bad, Mr. Wythe. A man of the world will understand these things. I beg you will recollect that Prunella has not a soul in the world to depend upon, except for me!"

Her eyes welled up with tears. Zacharias looked at Prunella in desperation, but this display of sentiment did not seem to affect her one whit.

"You forget, ma'am, that I have myself," she said. "Should you like the smelling salts?"

"I assure you I am as anxious as anyone could be that Miss Gentleman should come to no harm," said Zacharias. "I wish only to assist her, and would like to accompany her to town, if you will permit it. Lady Wythe will be pleased to receive her there, and we can make such arrangements as Sir Stephen would have wished."

Zacharias had decided upon this course the night before, when he and Prunella had fabricated this tale of Sir Stephen's connection with her father. He could not inform a woman so opposed to women's magic that he was removing her charge so that she could learn precisely that. Besides, his plan to reform women's magical education must remain secret for now, until his position was stronger, and he had marshalled support for his scheme among his colleagues. As for what Lady Wythe would think of her part in the proceedings, that was a complication Zacharias left for the future.

"Lady Wythe!" cried Mrs. Daubeney. "But she is the daughter of a baronet!"

Though she herself had ascended rapidly in her fancy to the heights of intimacy with the current and former Sorcerers Royal, she could not so quickly adapt her view of Prunella. After all, only the day before she had resolved to evict Prunella from her bedchamber in the east wing: some of the schoolgirls slept there, and Prunella would do better in the servants' quarters.

It required a rapid readjustment of her notions for Mrs. Daubeney to absorb the idea of Prunella as the honoured guest of Lady Maria Wythe. In justice to Mrs. Daubeney's heart, however—a genuine living, beating article, even if it was on occasion shouted down by her head—not two minutes had passed before she had assimilated the idea, and began to think it an excellent thing for dear Prunella. There was no doubt it was to Mrs. Daubeney's credit that it had happened, and Prunella ought to be grateful to her for this sudden elevation.

Though Mrs. Daubeney did not admit it to herself, she was conscious of a sneaking sensation of relief, for it was certainly true that Prunella was growing too magical for the school. It was not inconvenient for her to be removed at this juncture, and ideal that it should be done in such a manner as to enable Mrs. Daubeney henceforth to claim a connection with the Sorcerer Royal.

"She is that," said Zacharias. "What is more, she is very kind, and will do her best to make Miss Gentleman comfortable."

"Well, Prunella, it shall never be said that I stood in the way of your advancement," said Mrs. Daubeney. "I always knew you were meant for better things. One does not often meet such men as your dear father."

"I hope to leave today, ma'am, if that does not cause too much disruption in your arrangements," said Zacharias. "I have been delayed longer than I should like, and need to get on as soon as I can."

Mrs. Daubeney looked dazed. "Certainly—that is to say, Prunella will need time to pack."

"I shall not need long," said Prunella. "I have just enough as will fill a small valise."

"I suppose you will have a maid to accompany you," said Mrs. Daubeney, pulling herself together, and assuming the stern countenance of a guardian. "I am afraid I can spare no one at such short notice."

Zacharias opened his mouth, then closed it, feeling foolish. Mrs. Daubeney had overestimated his worldliness: he had very little to do with women on the whole, and it had not occurred to him that Mrs. Daubeney might expect a chaperone for Prunella.

Prunella was not disconcerted, however. She sat up on her heels, brightening.

"Of course," she said. "Lady Wythe sent her maid down. She is waiting outside the door, I think, Mr. Wythe?"

"Is she?" said Zacharias, thoroughly confused.

"Cawley," said Prunella, raising her voice. "Pray come in."

Into the room lurched a nightmarish vision wearing a human form, but neither human nor alive.

Zacharias blinked. No, it was only a woman of about forty. A solid, sensible-looking female, such as any anxious duenna might be reassured to have as her charge's companion. Her hair was brown—no, grey—no, chintz—

"Good morning, ma'am," said the woman, but she had no voice. The words simply appeared inside Zacharias's head.

Zacharias shut his eyes deliberately. When he opened them again, his mind was focused on the effort of sight, and he observed what he had been missing.

Prunella had constructed a chaperone out of cloth. The body was made of linen sheets, rolled and bound together. The head was a yard of chintz, shaped into an approximate sphere. At the bottom of the swaying, bobbing figure was a pair of men's shoes.

It was really very difficult to keep the image clear. Zacharias's mind urgently desired to return to what it was sure was the truth: that before him stood a woman of flesh and blood, who was bobbing and answering Mrs. Daubeney's questions in a voice that was her own, not Prunella's.

This was leagues beyond the invisibility spell Prunella had wrought the evening before. In its subtlety it was even more impressive than the ward she had thrown up against the fire. Zacharias could not have so deceived another magician until he had nearly completed his education, after years of study and practise.

"Thank you, Cawley," said Mrs. Daubeney. When the woman had curtseyed and excused herself, she said:

"That is a good sort of woman. Lady Wythe possesses excellent judgment of character, I am sure. I shall feel quite comfortable leaving you in her care, Prunella. Perhaps"—her voice faltered—"perhaps it is all for the best. You will know what to do for her, Mr. Wythe, as I have never done."

Zacharias," hissed Sir Stephen in Zacharias's ear, "that girl is a humbug!"

Only the strictest habits of self-discipline enabled Zacharias to continue walking towards the door as though nothing out of the ordinary had occurred. Mrs. Daubeney and Prunella had vanished into the upper reaches of the building, to pack what little Prunella planned to bring with her, but it was approaching mid-day, and there was no saying that Zacharias might not meet a maidservant or schoolgirl on his way. Sir Stephen usually exercised more discretion than this.

His importunate spectre continued to hover at Zacharias's shoulder, however, so that Zacharias was compelled to duck into the kitchen garden, and hope anyone who saw him assumed he was addressing a zephyr.

"Sir, much as I am honoured by the privilege of your visits—"

"Call them visitations, rather! For that is what you think 'em, I know," said Sir Stephen briskly. "But I cannot hold back when a timely word might avert folly. I know better than anyone that when you have got a maggot in your head you will rush on regardless, but it ought to be obvious even to you, Zacharias, that that chit has no more idea of studying thaumaturgy than I have of being crowned the Queen of Fairyland."

Zacharias stiffened. "Indeed, sir? And what do you say is her purpose in bearding a strange gentleman in his rooms, and abandoning everything she has known?"

"I do not deny she is a bold-faced hussy," though Sir Stephen spoke more admiringly than not. "I will not pretend to know her purpose. But it is not difficult to see that a pretty, artful baggage like that might desire to go to town for any number of reasons, none of which is likely to include becoming a thaumaturgess."

"Miss Gentleman seems to me a pleasant, unaffected young lady," said Zacharias with dignity. "In any case, whatever might be said of her manners or morals, it is impossible to fault her reflexes. I am in her debt, and I have agreed to instruct her. I cannot very well go back on my word now."

"From the way you go on, no one would think your hearth-fire had attempted to murder you," said Sir Stephen testily. "Have not you better things to be thinking of than the education of gentlewitches?"

"A Sorcerer Royal must take assassination attempts in his stride," said Zacharias. "I had thought something of the sort would happen ever since I succeeded you. We both knew what widespread displeasure my becoming Sorcerer Royal was likely to occasion. What is more natural than that someone should seek to curtail my term of service?"

This observation did not improve Sir Stephen's spirits. He glared at an artichoke as though it had offended him personally. "Did Leofric say whether your enemy was a thaumaturge?"

"It is scarcely likely to be a strolling magician or a cunning man," said Zacharias, evading the question. "What reason does anyone but a Fellow of the Society have to desire my extinction?"

"I should have thought your colleagues would at least submit to the constraints of the Charter of the Society."

"Did you? I was not so sanguine," said Zacharias. "It is just as well they have acted, though unfortunate that they should have struck when Miss Gentleman was present. Yet who knows? She reacted first, before I had even discerned the peril. We might not be speaking now if she had not been there."

"That is another thing," cried Sir Stephen. "That your complaint should have incapacitated you at the crucial moment is another shocking thing. How are you to defend yourself from assassins if you grow regularly faint and aguish? That is contrary to the very principle of the Exchange."

Zacharias hated any reference to his illness, as Sir Stephen ought to have known. Sir Stephen had scarcely begun to say, "I beg you will tell Leofric he must restrain himself," when Zacharias turned away.

"The chaise will be waiting," he said. "I had best have a word with Turrill."

"Zacharias!"

"It will not happen again," said Zacharias, in a voice iced over with a thin layer of frost. "Of that you may be certain."

As Zacharias approached his conveyance, the scope of the undertaking to which he had agreed began to dawn upon him.

The chaise that was to bear him and Prunella to Fobdown Purlieu was indeed waiting. It was doubtful whether it was capable of doing anything else.

Turrill was a good-humoured man on the whole, whose anxieties about driving the Sorcerer Royal had been eased by Mr. Wythe's being as pleasant-spoken and openhanded a gentleman as he had ever met ("Even if he is black as coal, I am sure that is none of his fault, and it would be a dull world if God had cut us all from the same pattern"). It was no wonder he felt hardly used upon this occasion, however, and Zacharias was not surprised to be addressed in terms of reproach.

"You hadn't ought to have done it, sir," said the coachman. "You may turn me into a frog for it, but I must speak my mind, and I say you hadn't ought to have done it. If I had not given satisfaction, you had only to say the word and I should have hopped to it, not wishing to offend any gentleman of such a liberal disposition as yourself, and not being such a fool as to desire to vex a sorcerer besides. There was no call to go a-magicking the chaise—and where you got the squashes for it out of season, I am sure I don't know."

"Neither do I," said Zacharias, bending down to examine what had previously been a wheel, and was now an enormous squash.

All four wheels of the chaise had suffered this curious fate. The body of the carriage rested precariously upon its new bearings.

"Good gracious!" said Prunella behind him, in a peculiar throbbing voice. "Is *that* what has happened?"

Her face worked convulsively, and Zacharias saw that in a moment she would burst into laughter. He glanced at the irate Turrill, who was in no mood to deal with giggling females, and pulled Prunella aside for a conference.

"May I ask what possessed you to wreak such wanton destruction upon my conveyance?" he said in an indignant whisper. "I cannot conceive how you think I will contrive to take you to London in a chaise that has no wheels."

Prunella tried to look solemn, but her delight would keep breaking out. Her countenance was so bright that Zacharias caught a smile tugging at his own lips. He made up for the lapse with a disapproving frown.

"I beg your pardon!" said Prunella. "I did not mean to at all! It was only that I thought I ought to guard against your running off without me, so I cast a spell to secure our conveyance till I had stepped into it. I had no notion it would have such a conspicuous effect. I wonder where the squashes did come from, out of season!"

She was about to tip over into laughter, but Zacharias fixed her with a penetrating glower until she sobered up.

"Pray do not look so cross!" she begged. "Does not it divert you even a little? I have never seen anything so ridiculous in my life! I am glad the spell took effect before we started, for it would have been unfortunate if it had seized upon the chaise when we were coasting along, would it not?"

"I cannot see that we are in a better position to have our chaise put out of action before we have begun," said Zacharias. He hardly knew what to make of such whimsical conduct. Sir Stephen's warning seemed now to assume an ominous significance. Could an anxiety for learning really be the motivation for such pains as Miss Gentleman had taken?

"Of course we are. If it had happened later, we would be sure to be upset, and our horses would have fled, and highwaymen would have set upon us, and we should have been very uncomfortable," argued Prunella. "Whereas now it will take but the work of a moment to reverse it."

She was determined to show not the least uncertainty as she strode up to the chaise. In fact Prunella had no notion whether her spell would comply with the strictures she had imposed upon it. She had thought merely to freeze the chaise in place for a time, as a precaution. She did not really think Mr. Wythe would abandon her, but Prunella had lost a great deal of her faith in humanity over the past few days, and she meant to leave nothing to chance.

The squashes were a piece of absurdity she had not calculated upon. Magic had never been so refractory before. She had always found it biddable, and in any case she would never have conceived that she had sufficient magic to transform matter in such a dramatic fashion. As she clambered into the chaise, helped by a sullen Turrill, it occurred to Prunella to wonder whether this unexpected turn had anything to do with the seven blue stones nestled in the depths of her valise.

"Well! If it was to be fixed so easily I do not know why he did not just say so, instead of putting me all in a pucker," grumbled Turrill's voice by the door. "A sorcerer likes his joke as well as the next fellow, I suppose. I can't say as it amuses me, but it ain't my chaise."

Raising his voice, he addressed Zacharias:

"Seems the wheels have been set aright, sir, so we can be on our way as soon as suits you."

Prunella poked her head out of the window. She was nearly as relieved as the coachman to see that there was nothing of the vegetable about the wheels now.

Zacharias boarded the chaise in foreboding silence, but fortunately they had not enough time to be awkward. Mrs. Daubeney emerged from the building, approaching the chaise at a run.

"You never meant to go away without a fare-thee-well?" she cried.

"Mr. Wythe is in a terrible hurry," said Prunella. Zacharias, who had been opening his mouth to say something civil, cast a look of outrage at her. "We waited quite as long as we could. Did you persuade Cook not to give notice?"

"Oh, she is beyond anything! I am sure the kitchen chimneys are vastly trying, but there is nothing to be done about their smoking, for we simply cannot support any further expenditure after"—after the expense of the Sorcerer Royal's visit, Mrs. Daubeney meant, but she stopped herself just in time. "If we are not all poisoned at our dinners it will be a miracle. What shall I do without you, Prunella? Cook would never attend to me, and now she will be worse than ever, for she knows I will be wholly dependent upon her when you are gone."

"You will do perfectly well," said Prunella, not unkindly. She could afford to be generous, now that she was so close to departure. Her wrongs began to recede into the distance, with the prospect of her escape so comfortably imminent.

To her surprise Prunella found that she was still attached to Mrs. Daubeney. She would never trust her again—no! But one could nonetheless be very fond of someone in whom one had no confidence whatsoever.

"As well as you did before you ever thought to burden yourself with me," she said. "Or my father."

She looked wistfully in Mrs. Daubeney's face, wondering if Mrs. Daubeney might finally impart some insight regarding her father—betray an old tenderness, or reveal a hidden connection—which would give Prunella some clue to her origins.

But Mrs. Daubeney only said:

"I never regarded it in the least, my dear! Remember you are to write to me every day, and pray give my regards to dear Lady Wythe, and thank her for her care of you. And if you should find an opportunity to send me the latest fashions, Prunella, I might find the time to look at them. Not that I am one to peacock myself, but it is just as well not to appear a laughingstock in the parents' eyes. We see some very modish mothers at the school, you know, Mr. Wythe. Oh! You have not forgotten Cawley?"

Prunella sat back. She was grateful for Mrs. Daubeney's ready supply of conversation, for it gave her the space she needed to put away her disappointment. Still, she was not quite natural when she spoke.

"Indeed, no!" she said, her voice quavering. She cleared her throat. "How could we? She is coming out now."

Sure enough, Cawley came, lurching out from the vestibule where Prunella had left the bundle of old linens in preparation. Cawley's gait was imperfect, but it grew steadier as she walked, and she ascended the step to the chaise with hardly a wobble. By the time they reached London, thought Prunella, no one would ever tell what she had been before.

10

THE BORDER WITH Fairyland was not much to look at, being marked by nothing more than a hedgerow straggling along the outskirts of Fobdown Purlieu. The village had been known in former times for its peculiarly magical quality: its visions of hunters and black dogs, its rains of frogs and the regular addition to its population of changelings, who grew into fey children and vanished in various outlandish ways.

Such oddities had fallen off in recent times, however. There was now little to distinguish Fobdown Purlieu from any other village in England, save the curious, pretty customs conducted at christenings and funerals to prevent fairies' stealing the souls of the newly living and the freshly dead.

The border itself had shrunk in proportion to the Fairy Court's affection for Britain, so that though the hedgerow ran along the whole length of the field in which Zacharias stood, the border itself only covered a section no more than twelve feet wide. To those with the sight to see it, the border appeared as a bilious green shimmer above the hedgerow, rippling gently like a sheet caught by a breeze.

"Of course, Fairclough calculated that there were three hundred and seventeen paths to Fairy," said Sir Stephen. "But I do not know that one can rely upon Fairclough's arithmetic. A man of great parts, but if he could tell you he had ten fingers and ten toes that was quite as much as he was capable of."

"Certainly his method has its flaws, but having attempted the calculations myself, I should not have thought there were any fewer than two hundred and fifty ways into the Other Realm," said Zacharias. He shaded his eyes as he looked up, the light of the border imbuing his aspect with an eerie green glow, so that he looked no less the spectre than Sir Stephen. "It is a pity we have not discovered more of them."

This twelve-foot stretch of wavering light was the only formal border between Britain and Fairyland, and one of the few portals to that land English thaumaturgy had discovered. In days past there had been considerable traffic across the border: adventurous villagers and ambitious thaumaturges alike had made regular visits to Fairy, while a continuous flow of familiars had rushed in from the opposite direction, seeking novelty and excitement in the mortal world.

It had used to be that a magician seeking elevation need only scramble across the border and inveigle a magical creature into entering his service, and he would return a sorcerer, covered in glory. Reading of such exploits in his youth, Zacharias had admired their daring, but Sir Stephen had pooh-poohed all this:

"Yes, they believed themselves vastly clever, I do not doubt! I suppose they thought their familiars went with them out of pure good nature, but you may be sure they were disabused of that notion quickly enough. There is a reason sorcerers look such glum fellows in their portraits. And they were not the only ones to be punished for their folly. As if one could rob one's neighbour time and again, and still expect to be invited to dinner! Everyone suffered from their rapacity, in the end."

The days when a thaumaturge could make his career by a single visit were long over—which accounted, in some measure, for the poisonous resentment of Zacharias among his peers. The Fairy Queen and King had in time found their numbers so reduced—so many of their most agreeable courtiers kidnapped (for it was invariably the most amiable that succumbed to the thaumaturges' importunities)—that they had instituted a ban upon mortals' crossing the border from England, unless they did so with a special invitation from the Court.

Such invitations were not precisely uncommon: they were granted to a few goodly young men in each generation, for the Queen could never do without a handsome young mortal or three in her retinue. But the invitations were hardly an unalloyed honour. An invitation from the Queen of Elfland could not be refused, and one's prospects of ever going home again were unpromising. Geoffrey Midsomer was unusual in having returned.

The Court's subjects were also prohibited from crossing into England. As sorcerers died, their familiars left for Fairy and did not return. There had not been a new familiar in England in half a century.

Still, despite the uneasy relations between the two kingdoms, the border remained porous, open to the fluxion of magic, if not to the passage of mortals or fairies. From the border flowed magic to the rest of Britain.

It was not such a setting as was likely to forgive any mistake. A fumbled formula or misspoken verse might have grave consequences so close to the border. Zacharias occupied himself for a time with preparing the ground for his enchantments, casting spells of concealment and confusion.

Sir Stephen was nobly silent for a full half hour, but as the light began to change, and their shadows grew long on the grass, his patience wore out.

"What are you about, Zacharias?" he said. "It is getting late, and you know you ought not to be essaying upon perilous new magics on the edge of Fairy at sunset."

"It would be imprudent to put my plan into effect without taking steps to conceal it. The Fairy Court is unlikely to look kindly upon my endeavours."

"It is imprudent to implement your plan at all," said Sir Stephen sharply. "I could wish you had had time to refine your formulae—I do not like how you have cobbled together Bascombe's declining with Gascoyne's loop. Since your hand has been forced, however, it is best to get it over with. You will hardly wish to be here as dark falls."

Everyone knew there were times of the day that were more magical than others: the deep heart of the night, and the times of transition, at sunrise and sunset. Even twenty years ago thaumaturges would avoid casting their spells at the witching time of night, for the surplus of magic at that time, and the attentiveness of ghosts and spirits, lent any enchantment an unsettling volatility.

This was no longer a concern, however. Nowadays magicians anxious to ensure their success might well wake after midnight to take advantage of the thinning boundaries between the worlds. Sunset was not quite so perilous a time—but so near Fairyland, and with untried spells, it was as well to be cautious.

Zacharias sighed. "I suppose I ought to have a look at the other side before I begin."

"Oh, if that is the reason you have delayed!" said Sir Stephen. "There is no need to be apprehensive. You ought to know the prohibition on entry does not apply to us."

"In principle," said Zacharias.

Zacharias had never been able to get to the bottom of why an exemption should apply to the Sorcerer Royal. If the Court so disapproved of English thaumaturgy as to forbid English thaumaturges its demesne, why should it welcome only the chief representative of that despised body? The nearest Zacharias had ever got to the truth was Lady Wythe's once teasing Sir Stephen about his having made up to the Fairy Queen, and Sir Stephen's responding with an uncharacteristic blush—and *that* seemed too absurd an explanation.

Zacharias knew enough thaumaturgical history to be wary of Fairyland, and he would gladly have forgone the check, but it would be foolhardy to embark upon his enchantments without first surveying the other side of the border. If there were anything unexpected—a passing fairy, who by its presence increased the atmospheric magic on the other side, or adverse weather conditions, which in Fairy might take outlandish forms—it might throw his calculations out, and introduce all the instability he feared.

Approaching the border warily, he leant through the sheet of light, keeping a firm grasp of the hedge as he did so.

After all his deliberations, the border offered no resistance. Zacharias saw on the other side rolling green fields, not unlike those that surrounded Fobdown Purlieu. A grey sky glowered above. There was a lone harpy flying in the distance, with the weary, single-minded air of a Cit hurrying home from his bank.

So much Zacharias saw before the magic rushed up and slammed him in the face. He was shoved backwards by the force of the blow, and landed heavily on the damp grass of England.

"Good God!" cried Sir Stephen. "What's amiss?"

To assist Zacharias to rise required a solidity Sir Stephen no longer possessed, and it was clear he felt his impotence. Zacharias was too stunned from his abrupt ejection from Fairy to respond at once, but as soon as Sir Stephen's anxious countenance had penetrated his consciousness he scrambled up, dusting himself off.

"I am not hurt in the least. Pray do not be concerned," he said.

Sir Stephen's worn face, translucent in the dying light of the day, went to his heart. He looked away, knowing Sir Stephen would prefer indifference to pity. But Sir Stephen did not lack courage.

"What a mother hen I am become!" he said soberly. "If I were my old self I should not start at every shadow, and be alarmed when you stumble, but one's anxiety rises in proportion to one's incapacity to do anything about it. Never outstay your time upon this earth, Zacharias. I am better acquainted with my own weakness now than I ever wished to be."

Zacharias scarcely knew where to look, or what to say. Affection there had always been between them, whatever their disagreements—and there had been more of these than Zacharias had permitted Sir Stephen to know. But their relationship could never have been mistaken for one of equality while Sir Stephen lived. Wealth, influence, age and obligation had separated them, and while never quite pretending to the rights of a son, Zacharias had regarded Sir Stephen with all the respect due a father, a teacher and the chief of their profession.

With Sir Stephen's death, however, the gap between them had closed imperceptibly. It was one of the many embarrassments of being attended by his guardian's spectre, that he should begin to see in the spirit the frailties of the man.

"You could not know what had occurred," said Zacharias finally. It was out of the question for Sir Stephen to venture across the border himself: it was all too easy for a ghost, under the influence of Fairy, to persuade itself it was a sprite, with deleterious consequences for its hope of salvation. "It is nothing that poses any immediate peril."

A disturbing certainty was coalescing within him, however, and he returned to the flexible sheet of light shining above the hedgerow. This time he was more cautious, and only put his hand into Fairyland. He yelped and withdrew it at once.

"What is it?" said Sir Stephen.

"Magic," said Zacharias. "There is a buildup on the other side."

It was only atmospheric magic, no different from the weak stuff that pervaded Britain's ether and made Lady Wythe sneeze. The magic on the other side of the border differed in one key respect, however—its concentration. It was only to be expected that the air should have a magical tang to it in Fairyland, but this force was beyond anything Zacharias had expected.

"How extraordinary," said Sir Stephen. He had not quite recovered from his mother hennish mood. "Ought you to continue your spells now, if merely putting in your head for a look draws such a response? Perhaps it would be better to wait till morning. Indeed, you ought to refrain from doing anything before noon."

Zacharias cast a levitation spell. The top of the border was too high for him to reach it unaided, and he wished to examine its whole breadth.

"That scheme is exploded, I suspect," he said grimly. "I do not think I ought to cast my spells at all."

Sir Stephen had not had the advantage of sensing the magic on the other side, and he was too unnerved to have embarked upon the chain of reasoning that had unfurled in Zacharias's mind. It was only now, as he calmed down, that the questions began to occur to him, that Zacharias had resolved nearly to his own satisfaction five minutes ago.

"How can the creatures be managing with such an excess of magic?" wondered Sir Stephen. Any surplus of magic in Fairy was wont to be attended by disaster. It lent too potent a stimulus to Fairy's excitable peoples, giving rise to numberless feuds, burglaries, love affairs and other misadventures. The Court had formerly rather approved of the traffic to England, because it siphoned off excess magic, and kept Fairy's inhabitants tractable. It was only when the balance began to tilt in Britain's favour, as a result of the depredations of magicians greedy for glory, that the Court had demurred. "How curious that they should be encountering the opposite difficulty from ours."

"Or not so very curious," said Zacharias. "Ha! I have it!"

Sir Stephen floated up to examine the object he had found. It was affixed in a conspicuous position halfway up the sheet of light that marked the border, and had only escaped observation before because it was so small.

"Fairy always delights in an unsubtle jest," said Sir Stephen, after a pause. "Leofric used to perpetrate the rankest puns."

"Indeed," said Zacharias. He tugged at the object, though without much hope of extracting it. It was a cork, firmly lodged in nothing at all.

"So Fairyland has stoppered the flow of magic into England," said Sir Stephen. "And this is how the Court has seen fit to inform us. It accounts for a great deal."

"But leaves much more unexplained," said Zacharias.

He sighed. The enchantments he had prepared were intended to address a natural decline in England's magic, not this unnatural stoppage. With the former his spells would have been chancy. With the latter, they were of no use whatsoever. He might as well have stayed in London for all the good his trip had done—and the Spring Ball was in two days' time.

"There is nothing for it, then," said Sir Stephen. "You must seek an audience with the Fairy Queen."

At Fobdown Purlieu's only inn, Prunella was encountering her own difficulties. The innkeeper and his lady seemed curiously inattentive to their business, though they had welcomed Zacharias with warmth when they observed the sorcerer's silver star pinned to his coat. Mr. Lale had led Prunella and Cawley to a room and abandoned her there with Zacharias's possessions. It was only when Prunella ventured out to remind her hosts that no provision had been made for her, that she was given a little room of her own.

"Did the Lales strike you as being a trifle eccentric, Cawley?" said Prunella as she unpacked. Cawley, of course, did not answer: Prunella had not quite divined the secret of imparting the spark of life to her creation. "She seemed preoccupied, I thought, and he was scarcely civil! They are an unfriendly people in this part of the country."

Prunella had never travelled so far abroad in her life—at least as far as she could recall—and she was enjoying the novelty of being a visitor in regions unexplored.

"I suppose people will be even worse in London!" she continued. "Everyone is vastly more agreeable in the country than in town, Henrietta says. Yet she longs to be in London, and talks of nothing else when she has left it. The metropolis must lend even the bearishness of one's neighbours a peculiar charm. Now, let us put you away, Cawley. There is hardly enough room here for two."

In truth, the effort of maintaining Cawley for the duration of their journey had taken more out of Prunella than she had expected. She had never been compelled to maintain such a sustained outpouring of magic before, and she was glad to leave the folded bundle of linens on her bed when she slipped away to seek her dinner.

There was no one in the dining parlour, and no fire either. Though Prunella rang the bell several times, it seemed a long while that she waited, shivering in a dimming room, before the landlady entered—and then Mrs. Lale started and frowned, as though she were offended by the very sight of Prunella.

"Oh!" said the landlady. Mrs. Lale was a sonsy, comfortable-looking creature, and it seemed as though a smile would better fit her countenance than its angular look of disapprobation. "I had thought perhaps Mr. Wythe had returned."

"No, it is only me," said Prunella pleasantly. "But I am just as capable of feeling cold as Mr. Wythe, so I should be obliged if you would send someone to light the fire. There is the matter of dinner, as well. I should very much like some dinner. I fancy Mr. Wythe will require something hearty when he returns, for magic is tiring work, you know."

She gave Mrs. Lale her best smile, but this enjoyed less success than Prunella was accustomed to having with her smiles. Indeed, it seemed positively to displease Mrs. Lale that Prunella should make so bold as to smile at her.

"And the woman you came with, will she be wanting her dinner as well?" said Mrs. Lale.

"Oh no," said Prunella, eager to be helpful. They were the only guests at the inn. Perhaps Mrs. Lale had hoped for a peaceful evening, and was put out at having customers to tend to. "Cawley is a little indisposed, and has retired for the evening. She won't want any dinner."

"Well, miss, if your companion has retired I think you cannot do better than to join her," said Mrs. Lale. "We shall have Mr. Wythe's dinner ready when he comes. But it would look better, and put everyone at their ease, if you did not wait up for him, and I am happy to tell Mr. Wythe I said so."

Mrs. Lale exited the room while Prunella gaped. She left the door ajar behind her, however, and her voice echoed down the passage, telling a servant to light a fire in the dining parlour.

"But you need not speak to the young female, Mary," said Mrs. Lale. "To think of Mr. Wythe bringing the creature here! Such a thing would never have happened in Sir Stephen's day. They do say as Moors are more liable to be inflamed than ordinary men, and I suppose it's to be preferred to his preying on innocent girls. But it's not what one likes to see in a decent establishment. If it were any other gentleman but young Mr. Wythe I shouldn't have stood for it, but Lale begged me to bear it, for Sir Stephen's sake."

Mary was evidently tenderhearted. She could be heard suggesting that it was hard on Prunella to be denied her dinner. After all, the poor thing had a mother.

"One that could not be decent, or she would be ashamed to see her now!" said Mrs. Lale. "No, you will not have me feeling sorry for her, Mary. You never will persuade me that the creatures do not like it, for if they were decent women they should have done anything rather than come to such a pass."

An indistinct protest from Mary was followed by Mrs. Lale's saying sharply:

"Even if natives feel differently on these points, she ought to have learnt to conduct herself properly if she means to live in England. I do not propose to put myself out on her account, I assure you. We shall see if Mr. Wythe has the boldness to complain on his strumpet's behalf!"

Entering the dining parlour, Mary found Prunella sitting as though she had been turned to stone. The maid was no fool—the door had given way before her hand so easily that it could not have been shut—and she lit the fire in a silence that concealed great agitation of spirits.

The young lady was so very young! What a pity if such a pretty creature were really as wicked as Mrs. Lale said! Mary was sure she saw the poor girl's lip tremble. Of a certainty she had heard every word.

Mary need not have worried. To Prunella, bred in a setting as near a nunnery as any English establishment could be, the notion that she could be mistaken for a fallen woman was so extraordinary that it could hardly offend. In these matters she was almost as innocent as Mrs. Daubeney had alleged, and the loss of her reputation for virtue—a weighty matter for any female who had any part in society—seemed so unreal as to occasion, at first, no concern.

After her first internal exclamation ("Why, that woman thinks me some sort of Jezebel!"), she had been struck by the humour of the situation. While Mary knelt by the fireplace with her tinder, pitying the poor young lady, Prunella had been fighting down giggles:

If I sit here shrieking with laughter, they will pass from thinking me a fallen woman to believing me a lunatic, and it will end in my having to sleep in the stables!

After Mary left, however, hunger began to have its effect in sobering Prunella. Once the first amusement was over she began to see what a shocking position she was in. What a landlady of a village inn believed of her was of little account, but Prunella could not afford such misunderstandings once she reached London. *That* would ruin everything she planned for.

It had not occurred to her before that her olive skin and dark eyes would seem to many an argument for the laxness of her morals. Had she but known it, she might have given serious thought to how odd it would look that she was travelling alone with Mr. Wythe, even accompanied by Cawley.

It is a pity we do not look more alike, or we could have told everyone we were long-lost siblings, and no one could complain of impropriety, reflected Prunella. *How absurd it all is! No one would dream of maligning me so if I were a man. I might go anywhere and do any magic I pleased if I were Peter, not Prunella. Mr. Wythe could present me to the world as his apprentice without occasioning the least remark. Why, there would be nothing to prevent* my *setting up as a sorcerer, once I had contrived to hatch the eggs!*

She spent a full half-minute considering whether she might pass herself off as a man: it would be so very convenient! But she gave up the notion with a sigh.

It might serve for a time, but I could not sustain it for long; indeed, I would not wish to. I must make as good a fist of being female as I can, and secure my position by the means permitted to my sex. What could not I accomplish with the support of an indulgent and monied husband? I fancy I should like patronising a girls' school. I could set up as a rival to Mrs. D, and hire poor Miss Liddiard and the rest, and let the girls work as many enchantments as they desired.

The idea diverted her, but she dismissed it to return to the crucial question: *But how shall I get myself any sort of husband if everyone thinks me a strumpet?* A poor orphaned female—a native, if you please! and inconveniently magical to boot—had little hope of accomplishing her aim, even if she managed to preserve her reputation.

Prunella lingered a while in the dining parlour in hope that she might benefit from Mr. Wythe's appearance to the tune of a mutton joint or cold souse. But when it became clear that he would not return soon from his mysterious errand, she retired to her bedchamber. The Lales' delay in giving her the room was now explained.

They thought I would be sharing his, I suppose! Prunella was glad no one else was there to see her blush. *I ought to have flown into a passion directly when they did not give me my own room; that would have persuaded them of my virtue. My being meek and believing the best of everyone has led them to think me a low trollop. I shall not run into that error again!*

She rummaged in her valise and brought out the treasures, scattering them upon the bed. It was now nearly dark, and the fitful light of the taper lent uncertain illumination to the room, but the blue stones seemed to glow like gems. They were hard as gems as well, nothing of the eggshell about them.

She must persuade Mr. Wythe to teach her about familiars' eggs as soon as she could, thought Prunella. Her interest in the subject could not draw suspicion, for who would suspect such an absurdity as her possessing seven eggs? She must take great care to ensure no one ever did suspect: doubtless Jezebels were not permitted to keep familiars' eggs, even if the eggs were their fathers' by the ancient right of treasure-seekers.

"I suppose I must resurrect Cawley, so that she can lend me countenance," Prunella said to the eggs. "But she is so tiresome, and such a drain on one's magic! I am knocked up from keeping her going for a mere day, and I shall need a chaperone for a great many more days."

It felt natural to be addressing the eggs. Prunella had a hazy notion that the spirits locked within the eggs had thoughts and feelings of their own, dormant as they seemed—that in some way they were awake to all that passed in the outside world. She was sure the squashes were their doing.

If only she could puzzle out the dratted spell that kept them locked in slumber! It was true that Prunella had as yet no clear notion what she would do with the familiars' eggs if she could hatch them, but that they were the key to everything she desired she did not doubt. She knew she should be able to turn them to account once she fathomed the secret of them.

"What *can* I do to awaken you? Could I ask Mr. Wythe when he returns from the border? Perhaps I could pretend I'd read about a similar circumstance in a book."

But even as she spoke, the idea presented itself to her, so simple and obvious that she wondered that she had not thought of it before.

The eggs and the familiars within them were from Fairy—and the border with Fairyland was almost on the doorstep of the inn. Why should not she take the eggs there, and see how they responded to proximity to their place of origin? She might kill two birds with one stone, for where better to find magic than the Fairy border, that ultimate source of England's magic? There would surely be enough resource there to animate a thousand Cawleys.

Mr. Wythe would not like it, of course. Zacharias had held forth at length on the instability of the border, and the delicacy of his proposed experiment, by way of explaining why he did not think it suitable to bring his new student with him on his errand. But if Mrs. Daubeney's school had taught Prunella anything, it was that magical affairs must be conducted in secret. There was no reason Mr. Wythe need ever know of her excursion. She would go that evening, telling no one, and bring the treasures with her.

She tied the velvet pouch containing the eggs under her skirts. Then, on a whim, she drew out from her valise a chain Mrs. Daubeney had given her when she was a little girl, and the carved silver ball that was her only other legacy from her parents. She would wear the orb on her neck, she decided, in remembrance of her poor father.

11

ZACHARIAS SUFFERED ANOTHER attack of his complaint that evening—an acute paroxysm, all the fiercer for the fact that the previous fit had been interrupted by the attempt on his life at the Blue Boar. It was late when the spasm released its hold upon him, permitting him to sleep. It seemed an outrageous cruelty on the part of an unfeeling world to wake him two hours later.

"I am sorry, Zacharias; I should not have woken you if I could have avoided it," said Sir Stephen. "But if you will pick up runaway orphans, you must expect never to have a moment's rest." The humorous tenor of Sir Stephen's words was belied by the anxiety on his face.

"What is it?" said Zacharias.

"Miss Gentleman is going to the border," said Sir Stephen. "And if we do not catch her, I fear she will do herself a mischief."

The fields were eerily still in the moonlight. No villager in Fobdown Purlieu would be abroad at this time for love or money. The witching hour might mean little elsewhere, but next to Fairyland, only a fool did not tread carefully at this most magical time of the night.

"She left the inn with that wicked old case under her arm," said Sir Stephen. "She cannot mean to run away to Fairyland, surely? She seems too modish a young lady for such an old-fashioned yearning."

A doomed longing for Fairy was a magician's affliction—no female had ever been known to suffer it. Even among thaumaturges it was an outdated passion. To the modern thaumaturge magic was too prosaic a thing to move him to indulge in such irrationality.

"It may not be surprising in a young female who has learnt all her magic from old books," said Zacharias. He would certainly arrange a donation to Mrs. Daubeney's library, he reflected.

"There she is!" cried Sir Stephen.

The shimmering light of the border could be glimpsed above the dark mass of the hedgerow. Silhouetted against the light was the form of a young woman. Sir Stephen vanished into the night. Zacharias started forward.

"Miss Gentleman!"

Prunella had begun to regret going to the border.

It had not been difficult to find Fairy. The moment she had stepped out of the inn, magic had gathered like an itch along the bridge of her nose, growing stronger as she neared the source of England's magic.

When she saw the unmistakable glow above the hedge, the stones in the pouch tied to her skirts had suddenly taken on an extraordinary weight, as though they would drag her to the ground if they could.

After that first promising response, however, Prunella's encounter with the border had proved disappointing. She arranged the eggs upon the sward so that they reflected the light of Fairy, in case that might provoke some reaction, but this had no effect whatsoever. She chanted a spell or two—a growing charm all the girls secretly used on their plots in the kitchen garden (a quiet but ferocious competition obtained among the girls as to who might produce the finest carrots), and then an awakening spell she had often employed for her sluggish charges at the school. But the eggs regarded this not at all.

She could feel the presence of magic all around her—every blade of grass, every inch of the sod, had absorbed a prodigious quantity of enchantery over the years—but somehow she could not grasp it.

She took to pressing each of the familiars' eggs, one by one, against the border itself. The light had a surprising solidity: when she pressed a stone against the border she felt a thrill go through the egg and along her arm, and then a surrender, as the wall of light gave way before the pressure. But after the first relaxation it went no further, and the eggs looked exactly as they had before.

Prunella was nearly out of patience when Zacharias arrived, and she was compelled hastily to return the stones to the pouch tied beneath her skirts.

"What are you doing here?" she said ungraciously.

"What am I—?" sputtered Zacharias. "Pray, what are *you* doing here? Have you any notion of the risk you run by coming here at this hour? You would not be the first unwary mortal to be picked up by a roc or kidnapped by a pooka while straying too close to Fairyland."

"I shouldn't have thought anything like a roc or a pooka had been in these parts for a hundred years," said Prunella. "Why, there is nothing in your border! We were told all the magic in England flowed from this source, but there is hardly any magic here at all."

"Did not you observe the cork?" said Zacharias.

It was a challenge to find it amid the glare of the border, but Zacharias located it, and guided Prunella's hand to the cork lodged mid-air. She looked puzzled.

"What is it?" she said.

"A joke," said Zacharias sourly. "The Fairy Court has blocked the flow of magic from its realm into ours, and it has had the goodness to leave this calling card. There is a remarkable buildup of magic on the other side, as no doubt you have sensed. I wonder how they manage!"

"Oh," cried Prunella involuntarily. "So there is no magic to be had here at all?"

Zacharias stared.

"Miss Gentleman," he said, "I beg you will tell me what brought you here—and I would counsel you to be honest, if you still desire me to take you to London."

Prunella had no intention of telling Zacharias about the eggs. She would be powerless to oppose him if he decided to remove them from her, circumstanced as she was in a remote village, far from anyone who might take her part. But she could not think of any convincing falsehood to explain her actions—so the truth, or some of it, would have to do. Glad that the darkness of night concealed the colour in her cheeks, she said:

"It is Cawley, you see! Though you might not think it, she requires a vast amount of resource, and it is beyond me to sustain her for the duration of our journey. I had thought I might retire her once we were away from the school, but—"

She hesitated. Prunella might be a brazen hussy, as the school's cross-grained Cook had told her many a time, but she was not quite so indelicate as to wish to inform a handsome young gentleman that she had been mistaken for his mistress. Since there seemed no alternative, however, she told him what had occurred at the inn, concluding:

"So I thought I ought to try extracting magic from the border. I beg you will not be too vexed with me! You must know how provoking it is to be checked by a lack of resource when one wishes to cast even the simplest enchantment."

"I regret that you have been so insulted," said Zacharias slowly. He felt, with a pang of guilt, that he had not given serious thought to ensuring Prunella was shielded from offence. The vulnerability of her position was as clear to him as it could be to Prunella. "You are certainly right that we must resurrect your chaperone, and I shall see to it. I wish you had expressed your concerns to me, instead of racing off to the border at the middle of the night."

He raised his hand when Prunella opened her mouth, and continued:

"I can quite see why you did not wish to confide in me, of all people! But if I am to be your instructor, and you my apprentice, there must be complete confidence between us. We shall meet with enough opposition from the world—if we are to make a success of your education, we must contrive to be allies, and trust one another. Come, can we agree on that?"

He held out his hand with a slight smile.

If Zacharias's air of melancholy increased his appeal to susceptible young ladies, a relaxation in that melancholy scarcely injured it. His smile, and the warmth and gentleness of his manner, were all the more attractive for forming a contrast to his usual reserve. Prunella dropped her eyes, feeling foolish, but she shook his hand and murmured that she was very much obliged—would do her best.

"Thank you," said Zacharias gravely. "May I see you back to the inn, Miss Gentleman? We have been fortunate to avoid any incident, but I cannot think it wise to linger at such an hour."

Even as he spoke, a shadow appeared behind Prunella. It began as an inky splotch of darkness upon the light of the border, and it grew.

"Mr. Wythe?" said Prunella. At his fixed stare, she turned to look behind her, and gasped. "What is that?"

"A creature on the other side," said Zacharias.

They called this the witching time: magical creatures were at their most unpredictable at this hour. Magicians had been known to vanish forever into the darkness when they were so foolhardy as to venture upon nighttime visits to the border.

Zacharias grasped Prunella's arm and shoved her behind him, cursing himself inwardly. He had learnt the night before that he had enemies whose notions of justice would not stop at murder. At least one of them knew his movements well enough to follow him from London to Hampshire, and had nearly managed to get past his defences. Who knew what other stratagems his enemies might have devised for his confusion?

"Who goes there?" he cried, but he was already bracing himself to attack when a voice spoke in tones of rumbling discontent:

"Mana pintu ni?"

The voice was familiar, though Zacharias could not immediately recall when he had heard it before. On the other side of the border appeared the black shadow of a claw-like hand. It tapped the border three times. The sheet of light swung open like a door, and an aged woman scrambled down the hedgerow.

"Why, it is only a little old lady!" said Prunella.

That the arrival was a foreigner was clear from her brown skin and her manner of dress. She wore a tunic fastened with brooches that sparkled in the light from the border; beneath this a cloth wrapped around her person served as a skirt. Her attire seemed too light for the chill of a spring evening, however. The elderly female shivered. The next moment a cloak appeared out of thin air, and she folded it around her shoulders.

She caught sight of Zacharias, and stiffened.

"There you are wrong," said Zacharias faintly. "She is not merely any little old lady." He stepped forward. "I believe we have met, ma'am."

The matron opened her mouth, frowned, and said a quick spell. It was not too cold a night, but her breath issued in puffs of green mist. When the puffs dissipated, she spoke in fluid English:

"You must have done something very shocking to have incensed the fine ones," said Mak Genggang. "In my country one need merely wander into the jungle to find the spirit realm, but the spirits have erected a perfect forest of wards about Britain. How do you contrive on so little magic? Though to be sure, the punishment is no more than you deserve for your wickedness."

"I am sorry to hear you say so, ma'am," said Zacharias. He paused. "Did the Fairy Queen tell you as much?"

"Is that what you call her? I never saw *her* at all," said Mak Genggang. "I merely went through her country as a shortcut. It takes such an age to travel to Britain otherwise. I had to come, of course, since that ridiculous raja is here begging for scraps from the foreigners' table. I shall not have that young *ciku* stealing a march on me! It is convenient that I have met you, for you will be able to help me."

There must once have been a time when he was not harried on every side by the whims and starts of importunate females, reflected Zacharias wistfully, but that halcyon period seemed very far away.

"Indeed?" he said noncommittally.

"I desire to speak to your King," said Mak Genggang. "You had best bring me to him straightaway—and no dillydallying, if you please, for the fate of the nation depends upon it!"

"Good gracious," said Prunella, staring. "But what dreadful thing is it that is going to befall us?"

"*I* have befallen you," said Mak Genggang. "I was not referring to Britain, however. I was speaking of what is of rather more importance: the fate of *my* nation, which your King seeks to bully!"

"If you will permit me to say so, ma'am, I believe there is a misunderstanding," said Zacharias. "Our King has no wish to alienate you, and I am sure would regret any inadvertent offence."

"If he had no wish to offend, he ought not to have lent his ear to Raja Ahmad!" retorted Mak Genggang. "A sovereign ought to learn better judgment of character. It must be clear to anyone with their wits about them that the raja is a fool. But then again"—her eyes gleamed—"I suppose it serves your King's purpose to treat with fools!"

Zacharias decided he would steer clear of diplomacy. If he was to avoid confusing Britain's relations with Janda Baik beyond repair, he had best keep his lips sealed, and entrust this new arrival to those who understood politics.

"I would be pleased to escort you to town, ma'am, and if I cannot promise you an audience with the King, I can certainly introduce you to his representatives," he said.

Edgeworth would be far from delighted to see Mak Genggang, and Zacharias was likely to lose any credit he still possessed with the man when he produced her. But after all, she could not be left to rampage about the country, and doubtless find some magical means of breaking into Windsor.

"We must hope that the Government will find some means of addressing your grievances," said Zacharias, who thought this very unlikely.

But Mak Genggang was more sanguine.

"I have a suspicion they will," she said, with alarming good cheer. "If they know what is good for them!"

12

ZACHARIAS RETURNED TO London in no mood for the Spring Ball. He had never been fond of a party, and this promised to be an even more dismal occasion than usual, if the Government carried out its intention of orchestrating a humiliating public review of England's atmospheric magic levels.

Lady Wythe was visiting friends in the country, or Zacharias would have brought Mak Genggang and Prunella to her. Since he could not, he borrowed a leaf from Prunella's book, and told his housekeeper that he had been honoured with a visit by a fairy princess and her duenna, which must be kept secret.

Fortunately Mak Genggang's arrival had solved one difficulty, even as it created others. They were able to dispense with Cawley, for as Prunella put it, "Mak Genggang is so old she must be respectable, even if she is a foreigner." She and Mak Genggang were fast friends at once, and Zacharias might have been concerned by the content of their whispered conversations as they talked away the long miles to London, if he had not been brooding over what he had learnt at the border.

He must obtain an explanation for the block on their magic as soon as he could, and the most direct way of achieving that was to seek an interview with the Fairy Court. The Court must be in expectation of such a calling to account, but Zacharias doubted they would welcome the confrontation. He certainly did not.

There was, of course, the Fairy King's rout, which was held every rising of the blood-red moon in the Eastern Reaches of the Draconic Provinces. Zacharias had been aware of the occasion, as a potential factor that might affect the ebb and flow of magic into Britain, and therefore the enchantments he had planned for increasing Britain's magic. He had had no intention of attending the event—the Sorcerer Royal had not been seen at the rout since Sir Stephen had been chased out by a fury wielding a flowerpot (a story Sir Stephen had often told to his own disadvantage, but never fully explained). But in theory the application of any foreign ambassador for an audience with the King would be granted at his rout. There was no reason why Britain's representative should be an exception, uneasy though their relations were now.

When had Fairy stoppered the flow of magic? Not till after Geoffrey Midsomer had crossed the border upon his return to England, for surely he would have detected it then—the Court had made no attempt to conceal what they had done. Magicians were a gossipy race, and any thaumaturge worth his salt would have broadcast the intelligence far and wide. Zacharias must, then, be the only one who knew of the block.

He must prevent the news reaching the Society till he had a better notion of what had moved the Fairy Court to act as it had done. His position was already so uncertain that it could hardly survive such ill tidings, unless he were able to offer a remedy—though what form that remedy would take was not at all clear to him.

With all of this to worry him, Zacharias arrived at the Society in his best silk stockings poorly equipped to take any pleasure in the Ball.

But he was not alone in this. There was a note of unease in the gathering that sat oddly with the gaiety and bustle.

The first Spring Ball had been hosted by the Society at its new buildings in 1376, in celebration of the grant of the lease by the Crown. More than four hundred years later, it remained the prime opportunity of the year for magicians and Ministers to mingle, though the attitude of each body of men to the opportunity had undergone a considerable change within the intervening period.

When the tradition of the Ball had first begun, it had been considered a coup for the Crown that it should have contrived to persuade the intransigent sorcerers to accept its liberality. Now the position was reversed: there were very few English magicians who could claim the title of sorcerer, and the Society was much less sure of its status than it had been in former times.

Zacharias discerned this uncertainty in the strained faces of his blue-coated colleagues and the patient titters of their wives. Everyone was merry, but he doubted anyone was at their ease. No doubt the news of the Government's plans had got out. But the Society's imminent embarrassment seemed to recede in importance compared to what he had learnt at the border.

"What are *you* doing here?" said a voice behind him, in tones of unutterable disgust.

"I could not have stayed away forever, you know," said Zacharias mildly.

"If you think a week is sufficient for your enemies to forget you—!" exclaimed Damerell. "Sir Stephen never had the least regard for his own security, and he has imparted the same recklessness to you, I see."

"I thought I might as well return, since Hampshire seemed no safer than London," said Zacharias.

Damerell eyed Zacharias through his quizzing-glass, then said, "Let us walk on. There is a good spot for confidences up the hall."

They stopped by an alcove in which hung a painting by a past

Sorcerer Royal's sister. Eliza Hamersham must have had more than a *soupçon* of the gift her brother had turned to such advantage in his career, for her portrait of a beloved niece and her terrier had an effect out of all proportion to its innocuous subject. Eliza's way of rendering her subjects' eyes slightly larger than was lifelike, and of imparting to their skin a deathly bluish tint, made any person of sensibility so uncomfortable that few chose to linger there. The other guests gave them a wide berth.

"Now what has Hampshire done to you, that London would not?" said Damerell.

Zacharias gave him a brief summary of the attack at the Blue Boar, though he said nothing of Prunella's part in it. "Since running away did not seem to improve my position, I thought I might see how standing my ground would serve. What is the feeling here? Has there been talk of what the Government is planning this evening?"

Zacharias had confided in Damerell regarding his encounter with Edgeworth: he trusted Damerell as much as he could trust any fellow thaumaturge, and he needed a pair of eyes and ears to attend to what occurred while he was gone.

Damerell shook his head, appearing to examine Miss Hamersham's work closely. "Not one peep from the Government have I heard, though the Society has been a hive of activity in your absence. The object of that is your removal from office. Fortunately, as you know, it requires an Herculean effort to convince thaumaturges to agree. They have just come to a consensus on your successor, but deciding upon a means of unseating you, and installing him, will require a great deal more bickering."

Zacharias observed to his relief that there seemed to be limitations to the concern a man could feel at the burdens loaded upon him. His organ of anxiety was already so exercised that this new complication only provoked irritation.

"I hope that will not interfere with my reform," he said absently. "Though I suppose it will—I suppose it will interfere with everything. Bother! Who is to be my successor?"

"I am glad you take it so coolly," said Damerell. "Your successor is to be the prodigal son, of course. Who else could it be? Geoffrey Midsomer's return has been so neatly timed, it would be a positive waste for him not to be put forward."

Zacharias heard this without surprise. The younger Midsomer was, as Damerell said, a natural choice for those Fellows of the Society who disliked a mere African's wielding the staff of the Sorcerer Royal. Midsomer Senior was more a magician by reason of his birth and connections than for any native ability, but his son was undeniably gifted. Geoffrey Midsomer had invented several ingenious spells in his youth, and of course he possessed the unusual distinction of having sojourned in Fairyland.

It was a bold move to play for the staff of the Sorcerer Royal, but then, why should not Geoffrey Midsomer be ambitious? He basked in the glory of having escaped the Fairy Court; his uncle was Lord Burrow, who chaired the Presiding Committee of the Society; and he could only benefit from having such a rival as Zacharias. He provided a convenient focus for the hopes thwarted by Zacharias's investiture, and so could not want for support.

Zacharias could only think of one thing Midsomer lacked. "He is not a sorcerer."

Damerell nodded. "But neither were you, you know, before you took up the staff."

"Oh, I am a sorcerer," said Zacharias wearily. "Would that I could forget it!"

The silence that ensued then might have been very awkward, for Damerell knew no more than anyone else of what had happened the night Zacharias had been made Sorcerer Royal. The Presiding

Committee had conferred for long, secret hours when Zacharias had emerged the master of the staff, whom none but the Sorcerer Royal could use.

The staff, being famously fastidious, was generally acknowledged to be the ultimate arbiter on the question of who should be deemed the Sorcerer Royal. Still, it was irregular in the extreme for a Sorcerer Royal to lack a familiar. Zacharias himself had been so distressed by Sir Stephen's death (or pretended to be, said his enemies), as to be unable to offer any explanation for the circumstance. It was whispered that the Committee had been compelled to consult the Fairy Court by shewstone in order to reach its decision. But the decision was made: Zacharias was declared the true Sorcerer Royal, the acknowledged successor of Sir Stephen.

Damerell was an intimate not only of Zacharias but of Sir Stephen, and he might justly have expected to be told more. But Zacharias had not confided in anyone. He had assumed his new responsibilities quietly, as though the abuse and suspicion heaped upon him did not exist. Damerell could scarcely ask, since Zacharias had not offered to explain, and he was possessed of too much true delicacy to probe further. He said serenely:

"Very natural, I am sure! I should feel the same in your position. Though I do not much envy your adversaries either. Their difficulty is that you are a most gentlemanlike fellow, leaving aside your colour. Of course, that can't be left aside, but it all makes matters rather awkward for those that would persecute you."

"I cannot say I feel any pity for them," said Zacharias.

"All things considered, you may be the worse off," Damerell allowed. Despite the lightness of his tone, the look he gave Zacharias was worried, and he added abruptly, with unwonted seriousness, "What a predicament you are in, Zacharias! What do you propose to do?"

Zacharias had glimpsed John Edgeworth among the milling crowds.

"No more than what I have been trying to do all along," he said. "My duty. I beg you will excuse me for a moment."

Zacharias thought he ought to break the news of Mak Genggang's arrival as soon as he could. It was an awkward thing to do at a party, but then the Spring Ball had always been an occasion for intrigue.

How Mak Genggang's presence might affect the Government's plans regarding Janda Baik, he would not attempt to predict. If Zacharias were a Foreign Office bureaucrat, he thought he might throw in his lot with Mak Genggang, rather than the fretful sultan. His encounters with each had been brief, but they had been sufficient to decide his views on who was likely to triumph in any struggle for power.

Fortunately, his views were of no importance whatsoever. If those whose decision it was to make would only take Mak Genggang off his hands, Zacharias would be content.

Luck was not with him that day, however. Edgeworth was at the opposite end of the room, but what with the crowd, he might have been a league away. Zacharias had not contrived to cover half the distance when he found his path blocked by a stranger, who was talking animatedly to someone behind her.

Zacharias murmured a courtesy, intending to edge around the woman, but something about her voice caught his attention.

"I must see him! Knowing the face of one's enemy lends such nourishment to one's hatred as cannot be equalled. I am surprised you wish to forbid it!"

Her companion replied in a protesting tone, "I should not dream of forbidding it, Laura. I merely beg that you have patience. There will be time enough to see— Wythe, by Jove! Are you here indeed?"

Zacharias had already recognised the companion's voice, and was attempting to wriggle away before he could be observed, but he was defeated by the crush. He turned to face the one person he most wished to avoid.

"Good evening, Midsomer," he said.

"I had not expected the pleasure of seeing you at the Ball," said Geoffrey Midsomer. "Were not you lately in Hampshire?"

Midsomer wore an awkward smile, as if he were as discomfited by the encounter as Zacharias. They had been acquainted since they were boys, but they had never had much to do with each other. Zacharias could not feel friendly towards the son of a man who had campaigned against him since he was a child, and that the young Midsomer now wished to supplant him was unlikely to be any further recommendation to Zacharias. He bowed, and his reply, though civil, was brief.

"I returned to town today."

"I should not detain you, but my wife has entreated to be introduced," said Midsomer. The woman who had been standing in Zacharias's way went to Midsomer's side and slipped her hand through his arm, looking up into Zacharias's face with unusual directness. "Laura, my dear, this is Mr. Zacharias Wythe, who is the Sorcerer Royal."

"How do you do?" said Zacharias.

Mrs. Geoffrey Midsomer was fashionably dressed, with her curls piled high in a yellow satin turban, but neither her face nor her figure possessed any particular beauty or distinction, save her eyes. These were large and bulbous, and of a hue so pale they almost seemed silver. She stared openly at Zacharias.

"So this is the Sorcerer Royal!" she said. She had a high-pitched, musical voice, with the slight inflection of a foreign accent—a curiously familiar accent, though Zacharias could not identify it. It was this accent that had drawn his attention when Mrs. Midsomer was speaking to her husband earlier. "He is not at all what I expected, Geoffrey."

Zacharias glanced at Midsomer, taken aback, but though Midsomer flushed, and appeared conscious of his wife's discourtesy, he did not reply. It did not seem meet for Zacharias to respond, since he had not been addressed. After a moment's hesitation he said to Midsomer:

"I hope you do not suffer any ill effects from your residence in Fairyland. It has been a considerable time since any thaumaturge has enjoyed such exposure to Fairy and been able to return. I believe the last was Loveday, was it not? I read his journals with interest, but his observations are now fifty years old, and fresh intelligence will be very welcome."

"I am preparing a paper for the Society," said Midsomer. He seemed ill at ease, and glanced around the room as if looking for some means to extract himself from the conversation he had begun.

Zacharias was really interested in what Midsomer might have to say regarding the Fairy Court, and he might have forgotten his own discomfort in pursuit of this subject if John Edgeworth had not emerged from the crowds and approached them.

Edgeworth was accompanied by Sultan Ahmad and his interpreter, though the sultana was absent. Zacharias would have to find some means of dispensing with Edgeworth's foreign guests while they spoke. Edgeworth would hardly desire the sultan to know of Mak Genggang's arrival before he had had the opportunity to digest the news himself.

"Edgeworth! I had hoped to see you here," said Zacharias.

Perhaps he spoke with more heartiness than he felt, in recollection of the unfriendly note on which they had last parted. He was braced for Edgeworth still to be aggrieved, though disguising it with a statesman's politic civility, but he was not prepared for Edgeworth's response.

"Yes, how do you do?" he said, barely glancing at Zacharias. "You have been ruralising, I hear. I hope it has done you good. Nothing like a retreat to the country to set a man up."

Without waiting for Zacharias's reply, he turned to Midsomer. "Geoffrey, I had nearly despaired of finding you in this crowd. I had no notion Parliament kept so many braying donkeys fed—Ministers and magicians both. Pray, will you take me to see the Society's collection of magical artefacts? I believe Uncle Augustine's thighbone is among them. It is an ancient family legend how he was discovered to have been a changeling only after his demise, and I should like to see him."

"I should be happy," said Midsomer, looking relieved at the chance to remove himself.

"Perhaps Mr. Wythe would be so good as to entertain Sultan Ahmad in the meantime, so that we may avoid boring His Highness," said Edgeworth. "I am conscious that these familial relics must have little interest for any but an Edgeworth."

With a nod at Zacharias and the sultan, he strode off with Midsomer and his wife. As they vanished into the crowd Edgeworth could be heard saying:

"Now, Geoffrey, regarding that spell you promised . . ."

The situation was worse than Zacharias had thought. He had expected some coolness on Edgeworth's part, but not this readiness to snub him in public.

That Edgeworth was on such terms with Midsomer as to address him by his Christian name was no surprise—they had probably been at school together. What worried Zacharias more was what it was that Midsomer had promised.

"I must say, this is very irregular!" exclaimed Mr. Othman.

Sultan Ahmad corroborated this with a murmured complaint. He was richly attired in an embroidered gold suit, the look completed by a knotted headdress and a dagger in an elegant scabbard at his hip. His splendour drew admiring glances from the other guests, but any desire to be introduced could not survive the sultan's glower.

Zacharias roused himself. He must consider his position at another time. For now, he had an offended foreign dignitary to deal with.

"I wish you would convey my apologies for what occurred at our previous encounter," he said to the translator. "I had no notion we would be broken in upon in that fashion. I would not have offended His Highness for the world."

"Mr. Edgeworth has explained all," said Mr. Othman grudgingly. "It was a shamefully botched affair, but His Highness is willing to overlook it. He is extremely unhappy that he has not yet received a commitment from your Government, however."

It struck Zacharias that it might have served Edgeworth's purpose to avoid giving the sultan a proper account of the Sorcerer Royal's position. Edgeworth himself knew, or ought to know, that Zacharias was not beholden to the Crown, nor even at the service of the Society. His first allegiance was to the cause of magic itself, and how it could be turned to the nation's advantage.

"His Highness knows, of course, that it could not rightly be called *my* Government," Zacharias began.

"The sultan is not surprised! He thought it strange that a black man should be a representative of the British King," said Mr. Othman. "He is pleased to understand the true state of affairs."

Sultan Ahmad added a stream of lugubrious commentary, which Mr. Othman translated into a fluid particularisation of grievances, much to Zacharias's discomfort:

"Since you, too, are a stranger here, you will enter into the sultan's feelings. He fears the British are as untrustworthy as we have always heard. He suspects they have no intention of giving us ships or guns. The sultan wishes he had never been so injudicious as to abandon his island—he finds England excessively cold and uncomfortable, the food unpalatable, and the people unfriendly. It is all the more unfortunate that the country should be so inhospitable, with the queen in her delicate condition. She could not bear to let the sultan leave her for so long, and insisted on accompanying us. We cannot even leave, for we cannot contemplate travelling until the queen is safe. To think that the prince will be born under foreign skies, and not on the soil of his own kingdom!"

Zacharias tried to break into this flow of confidence, but in vain. When Mr. Othman finally paused for breath, he said:

"I sympathise extremely with the sultan's distress, and am sorry he should be so displeased with this country, but I fear he labours under a misapprehension."

But Mr. Othman was not listening. Both he and the sultan were staring over Zacharias's shoulder, transfixed by a sight that seemed to horrify them. The translator opened his mouth and closed it again, and pointed a trembling finger.

"Witch!" he cried. He shot Zacharias a furious look. "You have led her to us. We are betrayed!"

Zacharias turned, and saw something even more dreadful than Mak Genggang standing at the end of the room with her arms akimbo and her eyes ablaze with the light of war. Next to her, rigged out in a spectacular pink dress and looking around with lively curiosity, was Prunella.

13

PRUNELLA HAD NOT begun the day with any intention of making an appearance at the Spring Ball. Zacharias had departed at noon, leaving her and Mak Genggang at his town house—which was just as well, in Prunella's view, for she had her own plans for the day.

Mak Genggang disposed of herself, declaring that she meant to examine the English sky.

"Surely it cannot be very different from the skies above your country," said Prunella.

Mak Genggang looked pityingly at her. "That shows you have not travelled abroad, child. There is much that can be read from a foreign sky. I shall require solitude, so you need not come with me."

With that Prunella was left alone, which suited her.

The longer she continued in possession of the eggs, the more she felt a strange sympathy with them—but she lacked any language in which to communicate with her treasures. If she was to awaken the eggs, she must learn more about them, and the Sorcerer Royal's library would contain all she could need to know.

The house formed part of the Crown's property, the lease of which was enjoyed by the Society, and it had been inhabited for centuries by Sorcerers Royal conscious of the fact that more rooms meant a greater number of nooks and crannies in which their enemies might conceal themselves. It required only a brief search for Prunella to find Zacharias's study.

She was not an imaginative creature, and she was more amused than daunted by the alchemical sigils on the floor and the skull on the windowsill.

"How divertingly thaumaturgical!" she exclaimed. "I wonder what the symbols signify, and what would happen if one were to string them into a spell. But there, if anything like the squashes should recur, Mr. Wythe would be very cross, and likely send me back to the school directly. I must be circumspect."

She curbed the temptation to rummage in Mr. Wythe's desk, decipher the sigils on the floor, or take a closer look at the unlamented Mr. Longmire. Instead she mounted a step Zacharias kept in the study to enable his reaching the higher shelves (though for Prunella it only served to elevate her to the middling level), and surveyed the books.

Zacharias possessed a tidy mind, but it was not a mind organised on wholly predictable principles. Prunella could not at first make out that the books had been arranged according to any sensible system. She discarded tome after weighty tome of thaumaturgical lore—all prodigiously interesting and philosophical, no doubt, but not at all to the purpose. But when she had pulled out and dismissed six medieval bestiaries in a row, the answer struck her.

He has ordered his books by subject, of course.

She soon divined that there was an underlying alphabetical sequence in accordance with which the books were arranged, for a number of treatises on talking moldiwarpes (a subject which had drawn a surprising amount of scholarly interest) were to be found immediately following the medieval bestiaries. Still, Prunella had a trying time attempting to trace the routes taken by Zacharias's thoughts. The books she desired were not to be found under *familiars* (though there was a great deal on *fairy*, which took her off course for a full hour), but comprised five shelves between *objects, magical* and *pellars, Cornish*. A thin monograph on *Paredros, vulgarly styled Familiars* explained the position.

She began reading the monograph, toying with the silver ball she now wore on her neck. Here Prunella ran into further difficulties. She was no great reader, and her choice was written in so laborious a style that she found herself rereading the same page several times, without absorbing any of the sense.

Not that there is much sense in it, for I believe this man is saying he thinks familiars come from Heaven, not Fairyland at all, thought Prunella. *Which I think must be blasphemy, and I* know *is silliness!*

She was beginning to tire of reaching for books on shelves built for the use of someone considerably longer in limb than she, and she was discouraged by the rows of books which might all—or none of them—contain what she desired. She was therefore not displeased to be interrupted by Mak Genggang.

Prunella put down her book, but made no attempt to conceal the fact that she had been going through the Sorcerer Royal's possessions. Mak Genggang would not mind it.

"What is it you have there? A book?" said Mak Genggang. She thought it clever of Prunella to read, though she was doubtful of its utility: "I do not know if reading is quite natural for a girl. In my day females kept to enchantery and agriculture, trading at market and tending to the children, and that was enough for us."

She glanced over the shelves with a jaundiced eye. "And are all these books the young gentleman's? I do not think much of your sorcerers, if they must rely upon paper for their enchantments! My sorceresses have all their spells *here*."

She tapped a spot on her person below her bosom, but well above her navel. Prunella said, surprised:

"Are there sorceresses in your country?"

Mak Genggang was a puzzle. In manner and appearance she struck Prunella as being little different from an English village witch, of the sort who plied villagers with love philtres and finding charms, far away from the disapproving eye of the Society. Yet she had walked through Fairyland to England; the Sorcerer Royal treated her as an equal; and she was possessed of such a serene and persuasive conviction of her own power that neither fact seemed remarkable.

"Perhaps you would call most of them magicians," Mak Genggang allowed. "There are one or two women that have entered into pacts with familiar spirits, but I have no truck with such irreligiousness."

"But your lady-magicians are able to sustain the connection with their familiars?" said Prunella. "They do not suffer any ill consequences from their pacts?"

"No worse than the men," said Mak Genggang ominously. "To commune with spirits is one thing. Unlike Raja Ahmad, I have no prejudice against lamiae—poor women, most of them, who were ill used in life, and abandoned in death!—or indeed any of the other spirits that inhabit our country. But I could not abide the unholy bondage to which British thaumaturges submit."

Prunella only half-understood this, but what she did comprehend was novel, and not unwelcome. She stored away this tidbit to consider later, murmuring:

"It is shocking, I am sure!"

She rose to return her monograph to the bookcase—conversation with Mak Genggang seemed infinitely more attractive than the author's tortured periods. As she moved, the silver ball on its chain swung out of the collar of her dress.

"I did not know the British had singing orbs," remarked Mak Genggang. "I hope you did not pay too much for that. The foreign traders are always seeking to pass them off on my women. They say the best are as rare as Saktimuna's tears, and vastly powerful, but what I say is my women have as much magic in one of their fingernails as could be contained in any bauble—or any book."

"It was a gift," said Prunella, after a pause. She touched the silver ball at her throat. "Is it called a singing orb in your country?"

"It is called a singing orb in whatever country you are likely to find it," said Mak Genggang, seeing through her nonchalance. "Do not you know how to use it? Give yours to me, and I will show you the way of it."

Prunella unchained the little silver ball from around her neck. Mak Genggang had such force of character as rendered it difficult to deny her anything she requested, and besides, Prunella was curious to see what she might draw from her trinket.

The first results of the witch's experiment were unpromising. Mak Genggang twisted the ball with her bony, strong fingers, but whatever she expected did not transpire. She let out an indignant huff of breath, and murmured a spell, but still nothing happened. She held the orb up to her eye, glaring, then thumped Zacharias's handsome walnut desk with it.

"Oh!" said Prunella, springing up at the cracking noise.

"No effect whatsoever!" exclaimed Mak Genggang, inspecting the silver ball. Fortunately the table, too, seemed unaffected. It was one thing to read Mr. Wythe's books, thought Prunella, but to break his furniture would really be too bad. "How odd to have given you a locked orb! But perhaps it is not odd at all. I suppose you had the orb from some suspicious character?"

"I had it from my parents," said Prunella, surprising herself with the truth. "They died when I was a child."

Mak Genggang looked pleased.

"That accounts for it," she said. "That is one common use of a singing orb, to hold family secrets and convey legacies. The secrets will be chained to your blood, of course. Give me your hand, child."

Prunella hesitated—rightly, as it turned out. Without waiting for an answer, Mak Genggang grasped her hand, picked up a penknife from the desk, and slashed Prunella's thumb with it. Prunella yelped, in startlement as much as in pain.

"Now, don't be babyish!" said Mak Genggang. "I am sure you are too brave to cry out at a little cut, and I will bind it up in a moment."

Prunella had been scolded often enough by Mrs. Daubeney for her wicked obstinacy and her unguarded tongue. How Mrs. D would marvel to see her now, meek as a lamb! she reflected. But Mak Genggang would reduce anyone to silence. Prunella only let out the smallest of squeaks when Mak Genggang held her injured thumb above the orb and squeezed it.

A drop of blood pooled in an indentation on the orb. The blood ran into the grooves of the carvings, filling out the strokes and curls and flourishes. Where it flowed, light shone out of the sphere.

Mak Genggang threw the ball in the air. It described a silver arc, glinting in the sunlight, but when it ought to have begun falling to the ground, it stopped, and hovered mid-air.

"Oh!" said Prunella, forgetting her thumb in her delight.

The light shining out from the orb gave the carvings on its surface the appearance of being traced in fire. The minute flowers and animals, the graceful loops and swirls, all shone forth brilliantly.

The orb began to sing in a woman's voice: a quavering contralto, deep, throaty and rough, as though she had worn her voice thin with shouting. The words were unfamiliar. Prunella did not understand the language, but she thought suddenly: *She is very angry. I wonder why?*

She felt the stones stir in the pouch tied under her skirts. Prunella pressed down upon them with her hand, thinking she must be mistaken—but no, the pebbles which had been so still even at the edge of Fairy were wriggling. It was as though she had a pocket full of beetles.

"Oh!" said Prunella, now in dismay.

"There," said Mak Genggang. "It is the blood that does it. I don't suppose you can make out anything she is singing? The song is an enchantment, that is clear, but she might have had the sense to include a translation spell. Why, child, what are you about?"

Prunella had caught the orb out of the air. She rubbed it against her skirt, and was relieved to see the blood come off. The song began to waver. When she had wiped it clean the voice died away entirely, and the treasures went still in their pouch.

She had found the secret of awakening them.

"I don't wish to alarm the servants," said Prunella hurriedly. "What they would think if they came in to find a flying orb warbling at us!"

"I expect they would not think anything at all," said Mak Genggang. "They seem idiotish creatures. Not a one of them understood me when I desired them to take me to the Society of Unnatural Philosophers."

If Prunella thought her subterfuge had succeeded, however, she was wrong. Mak Genggang continued:

"It is only natural that you wish to keep the secret to yourself. Well, now you know how to call it forth, and may listen to your mother's voice at your leisure."

"My mother?" said Prunella.

"Did not you hear her?" said Mak Genggang. "It was very improvident of her not to have taught you about your singing orb. If she was going to the trouble of enspelling it so it could only be unlocked by your blood, she ought to have enciphered a message within your veins while she was at it, so you would know how to use the orb when you were old enough. It is a mother's duty to teach her daughters about the uses of blood, particularly a magical daughter."

"But why do you say it is my mother?" said Prunella. She could not recall, now, if there had been anything familiar in the weary voice, singing in an unknown tongue.

"Why, only a mother can store secrets in the blood of her children—that is to say, an unscrupulous witch may do anything with anyone's blood, but that is a very evil magic, and attended by all manner of fell consequences. Did not you say you had the orb from your parents?"

"Yes," said Prunella. "But it was my father who gave it to me."

"A man, casting blood magics?" scoffed Mak Genggang. "You may as well say the English King loves Janda Baik, and has nothing but our good at heart! There never was a man but was frightened of blood magic—the magic in a woman's blood, most of all. For what is more potent than a woman's blood? I am sure mine has saved me many a time in my dealings with the spirits!"

Prunella was only half-listening. The idea that the orb belonged to her mother—that it was her mother's voice, and no stranger's, she had heard—was so novel that it was only with difficulty that she abstracted herself from her thoughts. Mak Genggang was repeating her name.

"I beg your pardon, ma'am?" said Prunella.

"I said, since the servants seem not to know whether their heads are in the air and their feet on the ground, or whether it ought rightly to be the other way around, you will have to take me to these thaumaturges," said Mak Genggang. "That is what I came to tell you, before we were distracted by your orb."

"Why do you wish to see the unnatural philosophers?" said Prunella, puzzled.

"I don't give a fig for them," said Mak Genggang. "It is the so-called sultan I wish to see, and the sky says he is with them. At a party, forsooth! I know what he is doing; he is begging from the British, thinking he will return laden with cannon enough to blow me and all my women to paradise. But he will find Mak Genggang is not so easily outdone! I should like to see what spirit he has for merriment once he knows I am come."

Prunella had started to say that she did not know where the Royal Society of Unnatural Philosophers was, but her interest was piqued by the mention of a party. "A party, at the Society? But thaumaturges are infamous dancers, Henrietta says."

But as she spoke she recalled the reason why Henrietta had had an opportunity to see thaumaturges dancing. It had been a great event, *the* great event of the year at the Society. Henrietta had attended it in her first Season, and she had been full of it for weeks afterwards when she returned to the school.

"The Spring Ball!" Prunella exclaimed.

"That is what the sky called it," said Mak Genggang.

Prunella put aside the troubling mysteries of her inheritance with relief. She would return to the orb and the treasures later—for now there were more pressing concerns to be thought of.

"I long to see the Spring Ball!" she said. "Henrietta said it was the prettiest thing she had ever seen, and she has been to dozens of parties. Are you going? What shall you wear?"

"I shall go in what I am standing in," said Mak Genggang. "A witch is always appropriate whatever her attire. It is quite another matter for a young girl, however. We will ask the sky what is suitable for the occasion."

"Cannot the sky tell you where the Society is?"

"I know where it is, but that is hardly to the point. It would be shockingly brazen of me to go alone to a party full of foreign gentlemen," said Mak Genggang. "But if you are with me, there cannot be any impropriety, for we shall look after each other. Are you coming? We ought not to delay any longer, or they will all go home, and my interrogation of the sky will be all to do over again."

"Yes," said Prunella. She stood, and slipped the silver orb under the collar of her dress. It nestled against her breastbone, a cold weight, heavy with secrets. "I shall certainly come."

Prunella's first impression of the Spring Ball was of light. Veritable forests of candles were arrayed around the Society's rooms, their glow reflected within innumerable shining mirrors, till it seemed as though the rooms were ablaze.

The effect had been achieved by mortal art alone. The Society, being composed in large part of gentlemen fond of their food, had chosen to focus its magical enhancements upon the refreshments. But to Prunella, the change from the dark night without was almost magical in itself. She felt as though she had entered another world.

When her eyes had grown accustomed to the light she looked around, ready to take pleasure in everything. But her heart sank as she registered her surroundings.

It had been her intention to avoid Zacharias if she could, since she presumed he was at the Ball, but in fact when she saw him she was so consumed by disaster that she hurried towards him, grateful to see a familiar face.

"Mr. Wythe, what is to be done?" she exclaimed. "Mak Genggang assured me that the sky knew these things, but it is clear to me the sky knows nothing of high society, and I wish I had never come! It was very unwise—indeed, it is nothing less than a disaster!"

"I cannot but agree," said Zacharias. "But if you think so, why did you come?"

Prunella was too troubled to attend. "Only look at my dress!" she said. "To think of wearing hoop skirts and silk taffeta when every other young female is in white muslin! I do not know if the sky meant to be disobliging, or if it is merely ignorant. Surely it must have seen that this is not at all the thing. I look a very guy!"

"That was not quite what I meant," said Zacharias.

The cut of Prunella's gown was absurdly old-fashioned, it was true, but the hue was remarkably becoming, and the dress could not but benefit from being worn by the possessor of such lively dark eyes, and such a small, piquant face. The sky had not gone so far as to suggest that she powder her hair, and her dark curls tumbled over the back of her dress, only just restrained by a pretty bandeau. Altogether the effect was charming—Prunella looked like a china shepherdess, modelled in bronze.

To Zacharias's own astonishment, he heard himself say, "Indeed, I think you look very well." He was no great hand at gallantry, and he felt like a coxcomb the moment his speech was out.

Prunella was nearly as embarrassed. How she would have liked to respond with the elegant coquetry of her imaginings! Instead she flushed, cast her eyes down, and said abruptly:

"Oh, you are being civil!"

Anything less flirtatious could scarcely be imagined. But it was easier to devise witty replies in one's fancy when the gentleman whom one addressed was a fiction: nameless, faceless, and not nearly so attractive as a certain Sorcerer Royal.

Fortunately they did not long have the luxury of feeling awkward. Mak Genggang's path had been blocked by a footman who sought to prevent her from accosting the sultan, and she began haranguing him for his impertinence, in tones that drew the fascinated attention of everyone in the room.

"Wythe," gasped John Edgeworth, emerging from the crowd, "what in Heaven's name is that harridan doing here? Was not it enough to magic her up in your shewstone to affront the sultan? *What* is she saying to Morton?"

Mak Genggang was dressing down the footman with animation and fluency. Her translation spell was still in effect, and her words were comprehensible enough.

"She is telling Mr. Morton that everyone knows the hooting of an owl always presages a death," said Prunella helpfully. "I wonder what she means by prosing about owls at a ball! Oh, I see what she is at. She says she has not heard any owls hooting tonight, but if Mr. Morton persists in his impertinence, she may well do so. How cleverly she has put it!"

Mak Genggang raised her arm. A bony, stick-like limb it was, but there must have been some potent power in her eye and voice, for the footman took a step back. Seizing her advantage, Mak Genggang sailed past him, and pitched straight into the terrified sultan.

"I see Your Highness's royal wife is not present," she said. "I hope she is resting. I was shocked to hear that she should have been dragged across the seas in her condition! But there, it is all of a piece with your want of foresight and consideration! I am sure the poor girl rues the day she was ever compelled to leave Achin and take you as her husband."

Sultan Ahmad made a defiant reply. Unfortunately it was lost on the onlooking audience, since he lacked the benefit of a translation spell, and must needs make his defence in his own language. Nor was he even allowed to complete it. Mak Genggang cut him off, crying:

"I didn't know, he says! I should have thought even a blockhead would guess the likely consequence of bringing his wife along on such a journey. You ought to have checked yourself. But you could never govern your lower passions, even as a boy. What a life you led your poor nurse! They hoped you would improve with age, but your being taken by the Achinese put paid to all of that. We celebrated when the foreigners sent you back to us, but we should have mourned instead, that they took our prince and returned him a tyrant! Oh, your father was a very *syaitan* in his youth, but he would never have done what you do now. God was merciful in decreeing his death before he could witness his own son, puppet of the Achinese kingdom, grovel before the British like a cur!"

The blood drained from the sultan's face. He stood staring, his eyes burning in a rigid countenance. Then he unsheathed his dagger and held it up before him. The crowd gasped and fell away. The dark blade of the creese gleamed like rippling water touched by moonlight.

"Woman, you will rue your insubordination!" snarled Mr. Othman.

"Shall I, indeed?" said Mak Genggang.

She flicked her hand as though she were waving a fly away. The creese was knocked out of the sultan's grasp and went shooting across the room. The swifter of thought and keener of instinct ducked or leapt out of the way, but not everyone was so alert to the danger. The dagger impaled a yellow satin turban crowning the bemused countenance of Mrs. Geoffrey Midsomer.

The ladies around her shrieked as one woman.

"What in the name of Poseidon—!" said Mrs. Midsomer.

"Oh, Laura! Tell me you are not killed!" cried a friend.

Another friend swooned, and this example was followed by several of the other women in quick succession. Mrs. Midsomer stared at them as if wondering what they were about, but then the danger she had been in seemed to dawn suddenly upon her. The change was so comically abrupt it almost seemed as though she had realised all at once how improper it was for her to take an assault upon her person so calmly.

Her eyes rolled back. She collapsed, and was caught by her husband.

"Good God!" cried Geoffrey Midsomer. "Stay away, sir!" Zacharias had rushed over to help. "If you come any closer, I shall not be responsible for the consequence."

"Is Mrs. Midsomer injured?" said Zacharias.

"What a vast fuss for nothing at all!" exclaimed Mak Genggang. She looked more embarrassed than her words suggested, but she continued with obstinate ferocity: "It has only hurt her turban. Surely that ugly woman's head does not go all the way up?"

To Zacharias's relief the weight of Mrs. Midsomer's drooping head, combined with that of the creese, induced the turban to drop to the ground, revealing her ringleted scalp to be unharmed.

"Thank God," said Zacharias. "Midsomer, I cannot say how deeply I regret this accident."

"Regret?" said Midsomer. He rose to his feet, raising his unconscious wife with no very gentle hold as he did so. "Oh, you have not begun to regret this evening's work, sir. But you will regret it, indeed. I shall see to that!"

"How dare you!" shrieked Prunella across the room. "Unhand her this moment, you brutes!"

Zacharias looked up to see his colleagues descending upon Mak Genggang. A few were already unsheathing their wands, but this worried Zacharias less than the way Mak Genggang raised her hands. He strode over, his staff held negligently—but pointedly—at his side.

"What is the meaning of this?" he said.

Zacharias was still the Sorcerer Royal, even if his peers questioned his right to the title. They hesitated, even the more belligerent lowering their wands, but one of the boldest said:

"You saw what she did to that blade. It was magic! A woman, polluting the halls of the Society with rank witchery! She must suffer the traditional penalty."

This received a warm reception among his fellows, but Zacharias said dampeningly:

"Let us have no doubt about what you propose. Do you mean to say you wish to burn her at the stake? An elderly woman, a stranger to us, who has committed no worse crime than that of making a scene?"

The thaumaturge who had spoken first hesitated.

"Yes?" he said, but another said at the same time:

"Do you call attacking Mrs. Midsomer nothing?"

Zacharias saw that this line of talk must be headed off, or the men would work themselves up into a righteous fury, and he would be hard put to it to control them.

"She must certainly be tried," he said. "But let it be conducted in an orderly fashion, by the Presiding Committee. This is hardly the time or place."

He swept a pointed look over the ruins of the Spring Ball. The Society's unmagical guests might have enjoyed the drama of Mak Genggang's confrontation with the sultan, but they had cleared out at the first sign of a magical quarrel.

"I am surprised that the Sorcerer Royal should show such indulgence to a foreigner, and ignore her insult to an Englishwoman," said one of the wand-wielding magicians. "But perhaps I should not be. If we had a Sorcerer Royal that thought of his country first, this evening might have had a very different conclusion."

"If you think it in Britain's interests to antagonise Mak Genggang's nation, I beg you will take it up with the Government," said Zacharias, unmoved. "I have been told the Government is anxious to preserve its relations with her people, and I am bound to act accordingly. Though she may seem a mere common old woman, in her country Mak Genggang is an arch-witch of repute, and rough treatment of her is likely to cause ill feeling."

"Was not the witch's quarrel with her own sovereign?" said a thaumaturge. "I do not know how these foreigners manage their affairs, but in England she would be hung for high treason."

"The sultan has little love for her, but he is not likely to be pleased if we execute his subject out of hand," said Zacharias. "He might well think his opinion ought to be consulted on the point. I cannot condone anything that risks offending him."

Zacharias secretly suspected Sultan Ahmad would be just as pleased to hear Mak Genggang had been dealt with by the Society after he had decamped from the Ball. Any pique would soon be outweighed by the incalculable benefit of never again having to deal with Mak Genggang himself.

But the Society had not the privilege of Sultan Ahmad's acquaintance, and no grounds upon which to gainsay Zacharias's account of the sultan's feelings. He had introduced just enough doubt to render his colleagues uncertain about their course. While they hesitated, he grasped Mak Genggang's arm, declaring that she should be detained in the Society rooms for the night:

"Tomorrow there will be time enough to carry out a full investigation of her offence."

"I shall certainly not be imprisoned, Sorcerer!" hissed Mak Genggang.

"Would you prefer to be hexed by ten magicians at once?" he muttered, steering her away from the crowd. The resistance in the tough old arm within his grasp slackened. "I beg you will have patience. I shall endeavour to ensure you are at liberty again as soon as it can be contrived. All will be well, I assure you."

He spoke with more certainty than he felt. Zacharias suspected Midsomer had only spoken the truth. He would soon have reason to wish he had never gone to the Ball.

14

Zacharias escorted Prunella back to his lodgings after the close of the Ball, adjuring her sternly not to go anywhere, nor do anything whatsoever, while he attempted to resolve the difficulties in which Mak Genggang had mired them all.

It was late and Prunella was weary, but she could not avoid the orb any longer. Part of her longed to know more, even as another part shrank in indistinct fear from learning anything further of her history. Alone in her bedchamber, she took the orb off its chain and looked at it, glinting upon her palm.

"But what is there to be afraid of?" she said aloud. Despite Mrs. Daubeney's attempts to gilt his memory, her father was a suicide who had died in miserable obscurity, and achieved nothing of what he had hoped for. Surely she could not discover anything worse than that.

She shook the eggs out of their pouch, spreading them out upon a directoire so positioned that she could observe them while she worked with the orb.

Squeezing her eyes shut, Prunella bit her lip until the coppery taste of her own blood filled her mouth. She fumbled for the orb, and pressed it against her lips. She opened her eyes, and flung the silver ball in the air.

It hung suspended, shining as before, and the woman's voice issued from the orb—unsteady at first, but gaining strength as she sang.

She might have been singing in Greek for all Prunella understood of the words, but she listened, half-entranced, as though by close attention she might decipher the meaning of the song, and divine some quality in the voice that marked it as possessing a connection to her own.

She was so engrossed that for a brief time she forgot all about the treasures, and was only reminded of them when one of the stones rattled off the directoire and fell on the floor. Prunella leapt forward and scooped it up.

The egg felt as hard as ever, no different from any dull stone, she thought—but then she felt something move within it.

She rose and looked at the treasures. Some of the stones were vibrating, though the directoire itself was still. To her mingled delight and alarm she saw that one of the eggs was beginning to crack. The finest fissure could be discerned upon its surface, growing as she watched.

Magic infused the air; her every breath was haloed with green mist. Prunella felt as though she were standing at the brink of a sea of magic, watching a swelling wave gather force before it crashed upon the shore.

The very walls seemed to grow thin and insubstantial, scarcely capable of holding out against a fearsome world outside. The black shadows in the corners of the room took on a life of their own; they peeled off the floor and danced around her, holding hands. Ordinary things—the grate, the bed, the directoire, the curtains—all took on a dreadful significance.

Prunella found her head hurt badly. The light from the fire was too bright. It was hard to move, for she felt as though with every step she pushed back a great load—a veritable boulder of magic. But she reached for the orb and somehow contrived to grasp it.

Fortunately there was a basin of water not far from her. She dropped the orb into it, heard it splash—for Prunella could hardly see now; her vision was so crowded with lights and vivid colours—and rubbed it with her fingers till it was clean. Her task was hindered by the violent shaking of her hands, but the song began to fade, and finally the voice went silent.

The egg in her hand was no longer anything but a stone. She placed it gently upon the directoire, and took stock of her treasures. Only one had that crack across it, which now looked like a mere fault in the stone—though not a minute ago she had seen a green light shining from it, and known that whatever it was that was locked within the stone was emerging.

A stray line from the monograph she had read that morning returned to her—its only reference to familiars' eggs:

> *It is clear that familiars hatched from the egg have nothing to do with the true, angelic paredrus. Indeed, from the effects of such hatchings as we have seen, there is some ground for asserting that the former are rather creatures of the diabolical kind, but though the argument presents a rich vein worthy of further investigation, it falls without the scope of this work.*

Prunella had dismissed this earlier as nonsense. But she saw the author's meaning now. He meant that familiars' eggs were dangerous, and never more so than when they hatched. She knew this with a bone-deep certainty. She had known, when she saw the egg begin to crack, that she was not capable of controlling the spirit it contained, nor of predicting the fury it might unleash.

That she would—*must*—hatch the eggs, however, she knew without a shadow of a doubt. Her headache was nearly gone, but she would have endured far worse for such a return—such a sense of limitless glory! She could not bear the thought that she might never again stand on that shore, looking out across that vast ocean of wonder. If this was how thaumaturges felt, little wonder they were so jealous of their magic, and begrudged women the most trifling spell! So too should she hoard magic if she had experienced that sensation and feared losing it.

Still, it is unjust of them, she thought. *If Mak Genggang is right, there is no reason a female cannot command a familiar's powers as well as a man. It is shockingly ungallant of men to withhold from us our fair share of magic!*

Zacharias would have warned Prunella to proceed with caution if he had heard her thoughts. Strong magic was not unlike wine in its effect upon the heads of those unused to it, and the intoxication of a first encounter with the powers of a familiar had led more than one thaumaturge into folly. Zacharias might have said that given what one surrendered in the Exchange, no one in his right mind would become a sorcerer if not for that exhilaration—or unless he had some other potent incentive.

But Zacharias was not present to give a lecture Prunella would have found dull. She had not quite made up her mind to become a sorceress herself, but she longed to make another trial with the eggs, if only to experience again that heady taste of power.

Even if she possessed the secret of awakening the eggs, however—even if her mother (if it was truly her mother) had left her the song that would unlock their spell—she could not use it till she knew what was needed to pacify the familiars that emerged.

After all, whatever I do with the treasures, I must know how they are to be hatched safely. I could scarcely sell familiars' eggs that do nothing but give their owners headaches! Perhaps—the disturbing thought would occur—*perhaps what the Society says is true, and I only suffered from the treasures because I am too weak to endure their magic, being a mere female. But there is one person who will know if that is true—one who will tell me what I must do to govern the treasures, if I am capable of it.*

She would go now, before anything occurred to prevent her asking the questions for which she craved answers. Mr. Wythe's lodgings were near the Society, and it would be a short walk, shorter than the one she had taken from the school to surprise Mr. Wythe at the Blue Boar.

If it were ancient, secret wisdom Prunella sought, she must consult that mistress of secrets, that revealer of mysteries, that unparalleled witch, defier of sorcerers and sultans alike—Mak Genggang herself.

Dawn had begun to unfold its silver light over the Society gardens when Zacharias passed through the gate. He was not surprised to see the figure waiting for him by the doors, though he had told no one of his intentions.

"I had thought I would see you here," said Midsomer.

Zacharias bowed, though he was chilled by a premonition of disaster. He did not remark upon the curious circumstance of both his and Midsomer's being abroad so early. Midsomer knew that Zacharias had travelled under darkness in hope of having the chance of speaking to Mak Genggang undisturbed. Zacharias knew Midsomer had hoped to catch him out. It was so unnatural a situation as not to require comment.

"I hope Mrs. Midsomer is recovered from the shock she received yesterday," said Zacharias. "I am glad she came to no lasting harm from the altercation."

"God grant that may be the case. It is too early for anyone who has my wife's welfare at heart to trust that she has indeed suffered no harm," said Midsomer coldly. "I am not here to discuss my wife, however. I had hoped to have the opportunity to speak to you in private."

"I have not much time, I am afraid," said Zacharias. "But perhaps if you came to my rooms later—"

"There is no need. What I have to say will not take much time," said Midsomer. "I intend to propose to the Committee today that the Society take steps to subdue the witches of Janda Baik, whence came the hag Mak Genggang. Will you support this motion, or not?"

Zacharias's sense of foreboding grew stronger. "What steps do you propose?"

"Whatever is necessary to ensure they can no longer pursue their evil magics," said Midsomer. He smiled without mirth. "I admit I have not yet sketched out a plan of attack, but I am sure your imagination can supply any gaps."

"You mean military action," said Zacharias. "Have you forgotten our agreement with the French, sir? The *sorcieres* watch our movements too closely ever to miss such a flagrant breach."

Midsomer looked pleased at this response, though he sought to conceal it, affecting a frown.

"It is as I thought," he said. "You may be so anxious to treat with our enemies that you will swallow any outrage, but I assure you such meekness is not universal. I believe that English thaumaturgy possesses a bolder temper, that will not brook insults to its women, and I intend to test my hypothesis today."

"I believe the Society knows its duty," said Zacharias, though he felt little enough conviction on the point. "It knows, as you should, that we have not the magical resource to contend with France's *sorcieres*, were they to engage us upon the battlefield. The addition of magic to his arsenal could well turn the tide in Bonaparte's favour. Consider, sir, what horrors would await every woman in Britain in consequence. It would be imprudent in the extreme to risk so much for an accident that has given Mrs. Midsomer no more than a passing fright."

But Midsomer was not listening. He had heard what he desired from Zacharias, and had no interest in continuing the argument, but hurried on to his main point:

"So you mean to oppose my motion, sir?"

Zacharias had never liked Midsomer, but he had not thought him so willing to subordinate everything—the good of his country, every dictate of common sense—to his ambition.

"I would consider it my duty to do so," he said.

"Then, sir," said Midsomer in triumph, "I must advise you to resign the office of Sorcerer Royal, and forswear the staff."

Zacharias stared at him, taken aback. Midsomer continued:

"Consider how much trouble your resignation would save. I would refrain from demanding punishment for your failure to prevent the shameful events of last night, and you could hold aloof from our retaliation against Janda Baik, since you hold the hag in such friendship."

"I will certainly not resign, and I am surprised you should ask it of me," said Zacharias, swallowing his fury with difficulty. Would Midsomer have treated with such high-handedness a Sorcerer Royal who was an Englishman? There was no need to ask the question. The answer had been made clear to Zacharias, in a multitude of ways, his entire life.

Midsomer shrugged.

"I had little hope you would agree," he said, with an air of resignation. "I knew we should be obliged to take the staff from you by force, but I had hoped we might be able to resolve the matter peaceably, for everyone's sake."

"And am I to accept that my being replaced by you would be for my own good?" said Zacharias contemptuously.

Midsomer blinked. Zacharias had thought it obvious that his own civility was a polite fiction, disguising very different feelings, but he saw that Midsomer had not recognised this. Midsomer had not thought to receive anything but unwavering courtesy from a Sorcerer Royal he had repeatedly insulted. He had no more expected such plain speech from Zacharias than he would have accepted a pert answer from his black footman.

"Say, rather, for the common good!" said Midsomer, flushing. "What did you do to defend Englishwomen from that hag? As much as you have done to prevent our public humiliation by the Government, and the removal of our privileges!

"Yes," he added, at the alteration in Zacharias's countenance, "you believed you had concealed that! It is fortunate I discovered the Government's intention before the Spring Ball, and did the little required to appease it. That you could not even do so much speaks volumes of your vaunted ability."

"I never laid claim to any extraordinary ability," said Zacharias. He was trembling with anger. "But that I refused to stoop to bribery, or bend to illegitimate pressures, I believe speaks for itself."

Midsomer stepped back, his lip curling.

"I should call you out for that if you were an Englishman," he said. "But I would not lower myself by fighting the likes of you. I have given you fair warning. If you will not give up the staff, you will have to bear the consequence of your obstinacy."

"I do not make out your meaning, sir," said Zacharias, his voice dangerously quiet. "I beg you will explain yourself."

Midsomer met his eye, unblushing. He said:

"Recall that Cecil Hallett was asked to surrender the staff, and refused."

The hairs rose on the back of Zacharias's neck. Every thaumaturge knew of the manner of Cecil Hallett's demise. It had been such a death as was not easily forgot.

"That procedure was outlawed by the Charter," he said.

"The Charter can be amended," said Midsomer. "Good day to you, sir. I would think upon what I have said if I were you."

Zacharias mounted the stairs to Mak Genggang's room in considerable agitation of spirits. He was so distrait that he would not have noticed the servant girl hurrying down in the opposite direction if she did not brush against him in her haste.

He was almost at the door to Mak Genggang's room when he recalled that the Society employed no female servants.

He caught up with Prunella outside the building. She was walking briskly towards the gate, a basket tucked under her arm, for all the world as though she were going to market to buy a fish.

Prunella was in cheerful spirits, though she had slept little the night before. A minor enchantment had sufficed to lead her to the room where Mak Genggang had been imprisoned within the Society. Though the Committee had hedged the room about with wards to prevent the witch's getting out, no one had thought to institute any measure to prevent others from getting in.

They had stayed up half the night talking, and very profitable the conversation had been too. Even after Mak Genggang had nodded off, halfway through a rambling story about a weretiger of her acquaintance, Prunella had been too excited to sleep. She had paced the room, making great plans, till dawn's pale light shone through the window.

They had agreed they would make their escape once it was light: "Else I shall be bumping into things, and like as not be eaten by an owl," said Mak Genggang. Prunella could not help feeling they had contrived it very neatly, till she saw Zacharias on the stairs.

There was just a chance they might still get away, she thought, for it was clear his attention was elsewhere. When she heard determined footsteps behind her, Prunella quickened her pace.

"If your hope is that I will forget having seen you provided you only walk fast enough, I am afraid you will be disappointed," said Mr. Wythe. Amusement and irritation mingled in his voice in equal measure. "Surely you do not think to escape me so easily?"

Prunella resigned herself to discovery. Still, Mr. Wythe need not know everything yet.

"You have an unfair advantage; being such a wretched long creature, you need only take one stride to my two," she retorted, tugging the gingham cloth over the top of her basket. Unfortunately its inmate possessed less discretion.

"He is right, you know," piped a tiny voice. "We ought to have disguised you with a spell. I cannot conceive why I did not think of it before. My wits must still be in disorder from last night's hullaballoo."

Zacharias's eyes widened. Before Prunella could stop him, he pulled away the cloth, revealing what she had hid inside the basket.

The basket itself was a product of magic. It had originally been Mak Genggang's shawl, and had been transformed because Prunella thought a basket looked servant-like. Nestled within it was Mak Genggang, exactly as she had always been, save that she was no larger than a mouse—a cat could have eaten her, if it was so foolish as to try. She sat cross-legged with her palms braced against the bottom of the basket.

"Good day, Sorcerer," she said. "It is a fine house your magicians have, but far too cold. You ought to waste less magic on warding poor old females, and spend more on warming your feet. Mine are as cold as the sultan's heart!"

"What are you doing?" gasped Zacharias.

"She is hiding," said Prunella crossly. "You know we talked about the importance of discretion, Mak Genggang!" She turned down the cloth. "You need not stare at me. It is shocking that the Society should have been so disrespectful as to imprison Mak Genggang for a misunderstanding, when that silly turbanned creature was not even hurt."

"I can see that it seems disproportionate," said Zacharias, striving to keep his calm. "But you cannot simply smuggle out a prisoner of the Society!"

"Oh, but I have," said Prunella. "It was the easiest thing in the world, and it needed to be done, you know, for Mak Genggang could not escape herself. I have never seen such an extravagance of magic, and all to prevent her flight! Now I have seen the Society's profligacy, I am hardly surprised the nation suffers from a lack of magical resource. I only wonder that we have *any* magic left."

"Are you truly unaware of the extreme delicacy of the situation?" said Zacharias. "The Society was all for meting out immediate punishment. It was all I could do to persuade my colleagues to wait for a formal investigation. They have been uncommonly patient, according to their lights, but any wrong movement now may cause an explosion. You must return her."

"I certainly shall not!"

"I should like to see her do it!" said Mak Genggang beneath the cloth.

Squaring her shoulders, Prunella marched off down the street. There could be no thought of abandoning Mak Genggang to the Society now, when the witch had taught her so much. She would stand by Mak Genggang, and she did not mean to look back.

And Prunella would have held to her resolve, if there had not been a great thud behind her, and if Zacharias had not let out such a horrible scream.

Zacharias did not mean to make a play for Prunella's sympathy. He had slipped and fallen: it had rained during the night, and the ground was still wet. He thought nothing of it, but when he sought to rise he found he could not.

He reached out to steady himself, and put his hand down in a puddle of rainwater. He did not mind this either—until claws sank into his hand.

Zacharias screamed. The pain was excruciating, and when he tried to tear his hand away it felt as though his arm would sooner be pulled out of its joint. The puddle grew and transformed.

Zacharias saw a gaping maw made of brown water, with translucent fangs, and leaves swirling down its throat. He took a deep breath despite the prickling of magic in his nostrils, knowing that one inhalation would need to last him a while, and then the monster gulped him down.

Prunella, turning reluctantly around, saw a mass of water consume Zacharias's person. She shrieked.

"What is it?" cried Mak Genggang.

"Mr. Wythe is being murdered!" said Prunella. She thought of the fire at the Blue Boar, and clenched her fists. "Oh, the villain! What shall we do?"

Mak Genggang peered over the side of the basket. Zacharias was fumbling blindly at his coat, perhaps seeking his staff, but he seemed to be fighting against a great force to move at all. His eyes and mouth were screwed shut, and his face wore a look of grim resolve.

"If the water does not hold him long enough to suffocate him, it will poison him first," said Mak Genggang, in the judicious manner of an expert. "Look at how his face twitches—the water is acid, and eats at his skin. It is a clever hex. Must we save him?"

"Mak Genggang! He persuaded his wicked magicians to preserve your life."

"And threw me into gaol!" said Mak Genggang. "Very well, child, I will do it, so you need not make faces at me. He is a well-bred young man, after all. I like a young man who shows a proper respect to his elders."

She held out her arms, and now it could be seen that Mak Genggang was not merely a tiny replica of her former self, for there was a singular new addition: a pair of wings growing out of her back. Mak Genggang had invented these to ease her escape. They were of thin, leathery skin, spread over delicate cartilage, and looked nearly translucent as Mak Genggang took to the air.

She hovered for a moment above the devouring mass of water, then dived into it, alighting upon Zacharias's shoulder.

Zacharias felt a tiny weight settle upon him. He moved his shoulder to try to dislodge it, but then for the first time since he had been devoured, there was an intermission of pain. A cooling protection flowed down his arm, shielding his flesh from the acid sting of the water—extraordinary blessing!

There was a buzzing at his ear, blurred by the water, and Zacharias heard indistinctly the words:

"Listen to the spell, Sorcerer. I am too small to cover you entirely, but you may do it yourself if you attend."

The relief of the pain seemed to return to Zacharias some of his own mind. He focused on Mak Genggang's voice, and though all noise was blunted underwater he discerned the syllables of an enchantment, repeated over and over again. The words were foreign, of course, but one did not always need to understand the words of a charm to cast it: as a youth Zacharias had amused himself by casting spells in Sanskrit to tolerable effect, though he had made only a brief study of the language.

It required an effort of will to open his mouth to speak, for he knew he must swallow the burning water in consequence—but he did it.

As he murmured the enchantment, speaking slowly despite the fiery agony from the water sliding down his throat, the relief began to envelop him. It spread from his arm down his left side, along his leg, and then the effect of the spell began to communicate itself across to the right side of his person. Provided he kept repeating the spell he could preserve himself from this distracting pain, but how would he get himself out of this fix? No exertion of mere physical strength would extricate him from the grasp of the water. Besides, he was beginning to feel faint from lack of air.

"Mak Genggang," he said, or thought—he was not sure which—"if you can but make a hole through the water, and if Miss Gentleman will assist—"

Mak Genggang did not reply, but a gap opened in the water, and Zacharias thrust out a wet hand. Prunella grasped it at once, though she winced at the sting of the poisoned water.

"What can I do?" she said.

"Give me your magic," gasped Zacharias. That meant a gulp of too much water. He coughed, struggling for air, but Prunella's small hand was solid and warm in his. He cast out his drowning consciousness like a net, and drew in magic through her.

Prunella had never experienced such a peculiar sensation. The world was brilliant with colour and light, and everything looked strange, but truer than it had ever been. The monstrous bulk of water turned into a furious woman, with trailing green hair, a lashing serpent's tail and long-nailed fingers throttling Zacharias. Zacharias himself was a silvery salmon thrashing in her coils. Mak Genggang, hovering above the fray, looked exactly the same.

She saw all this in a flash. Then there was no more Prunella: she was one with all the fleeting imps of the air. Magic rushed through her, like water through a pipe, into Zacharias's hand.

Out of the corner of her eye she saw the salmon wriggle out of the woman's grasp. All at once Prunella's bones and muscles seemed to turn to jelly. She collapsed, and Zacharias fell on his knees beside her, brown water showering down on them. He was free.

"A spell for untangling," he gasped. "The water had me in a binding charm. The counter-formula is no more difficult than untying a knot, but it requires force. I could not have done it without your aid."

"I feel very odd indeed," said Prunella.

She no longer saw salmon or water-women, but the world had acquired an ugly patina. The trees stood too close, their branches raised like a threat, and the water upon the road shone like oil.

"It is the reaction to the spell," said Zacharias, looking at her anxiously. "The absorption and release of so much magic is unpleasant for any mortal who is not accustomed to working with a familiar. The ill effects ought not to be lasting, however—"

"I am going to be sick," announced Prunella.

Whereupon she was, at length. When she was done she rolled away from the result and gazed up at the sky, feeling that life was too grim to be borne. Voices spoke above her, but they did not trouble her.

"Don't stand there staring, man," snapped Mak Genggang. "Help the girl up and get her home! Prunella, I am sorry to abandon you when you are so ill, poor child! But my women need me, and you have Mr. Wythe, whereas they have only a poor old woman to rely upon. Remember what I have told you."

Prunella's thoughts were hazy, but she remembered the core of what Mak Genggang had taught her. It was so simple as to be impossible to forget.

"It comes down to blood," she whispered.

"Did you speak, Miss Gentleman?" said Zacharias. His worried countenance hove into view. "Mak Genggang has flown, I am afraid. If she stayed she would have been caught, for the Fellows will be arriving soon. However, I have sent a zephyr for a hackney coach, and we shall be gone before anyone sees us. I should have arranged for transport by magic, save that you ought not to have too much to do with magic till you have recovered. How do you feel?"

"It stings a little," said Prunella. This was an understatement, hardly capturing the overwhelming sense of disillusionment that had swamped her the moment the magic was gone. "Are you hurt?"

Zacharias smiled. "You need not worry about me."

As she lay upon the street, furious, impotent and distressingly inelegant, Prunella discovered two things about herself.

She liked Zacharias very, very much—perhaps better than she had ever liked anyone in her life.

She loathed being weak with a passion. She had always known that she could not endure a fool, but it was not till this moment that Prunella realised how much less she liked weakness in herself.

It could not be just, she thought, that Zacharias should be so good, and so persecuted. And that *she* should be exposed to such peril and discomfort was not to be borne. But why should a possessor of seven familiars' eggs have any anxiety about defending herself, and those she . . . liked very much?

The situation could not continue. Something must be done. And who better than Prunella Gentleman to do it?

15

A STRANGE SONG entered Zacharias's dreams that night.

He had harboured some doubts regarding the propriety of Prunella's remaining at his residence, since Mak Genggang had flown. But there seemed nothing for it, for Lady Wythe was not due to return till the morrow.

"I shall certainly present her to you tomorrow, however," he said to Prunella. "Until then, the discretion of my servants may certainly be relied upon."

The Sorcerer Royal's servants had formerly been bound by a geas against disclosure of any detail of his household affairs, breach of which was visited by the most terrible revenge. That tyrannical practise had been discontinued by Sir Stephen, but the strict code of secrecy continued. The housekeeper still insisted on sending a footman to collect the household's meat from the butcher under a disguise, so that no one might know whether the Sorcerer Royal had had a boiled fowl or roast beef for his dinner.

Zacharias had thought Prunella might protest, recalling her

encounter with outraged propriety in Fobdown Purlieu, but in fact she made no complaint. She seemed distracted, and Zacharias had only just embarked upon an explanation of the mechanism of the geas—a strikingly innovative formula for its time—when Prunella said she was tired. She thought she would retire.

Zacharias suffered no recurrence of his complaint that evening, and he slept remarkably well considering the stresses of the day. He roused reluctantly as the song became harder to ignore. There was something in it that compelled him to consciousness. The music held within it an exhilarating promise; it flooded his being with a sense of—

Magic.

Zacharias sat bolt upright in his bed. The song was a spell. Magic was being done under his roof, and no small magic either. His first thought was that he must be under attack again. His second, when this proved not to be the case, was that Prunella must be in danger.

The scent of magic grew stronger as he hurried to the bedchamber where she had been lodged, at a decorous distance from his. With the morning's sortie still vivid in his recollection, he scarcely hesitated at her door, though Zacharias was not generally given to entering the bedchambers of young ladies.

Bursting into the room, he found Prunella crouched on the floor, one hand pressed against her breast. The song seemed to come from her, though her mouth was shut, and she gazed down with an air of absorption. Within a small circle of candlelight lay the object of her gaze: three blue stones lying upon a black cloth.

A layperson might have wondered at Prunella's fascination with a few pebbles. Zacharias saw the stones with a sorcerer's eyes, and knew them for what they were. Familiars' eggs—vessels containing the spirits of magical creatures who, weary of their lives in Fairyland, had volunteered for service in the mortal world, and been locked within stone, to be reborn in the earthly realm.

One egg would have been wealth beyond a magician's wildest

dreams. Three eggs were more than Christendom had seen at one time for a hundred years.

This was a shock greater than any other, in a week of surprises.

"Those are familiars' eggs," he said.

Prunella was so intent that she did not even look up.

"And they are just about to hatch," she said.

Prunella had confided in Mak Genggang regarding her treasures the night before, though she had had to overcome a lingering hesitation to do it. To possess such a treasure was very tiresome, reflected Prunella, for it made one distrust everyone—and she could not rid herself of the recollection of Mrs. Daubeney's faithlessness.

But Mak Genggang was a foreigner, and would soon return to her own country; she had helped unlock Prunella's singing orb, and asked for nothing in return; and there was no one else who could give Prunella the counsel she needed. She would give Mak Genggang an egg for her services, and for her discretion: that should be reward enough, if all Prunella had heard of the value of familiars' eggs was true.

In the event, the reward proved unnecessary.

"So you have inherited spirits from your father!" exclaimed Mak Genggang when all was explained. "Poor child! That is unfortunate. However, all is not lost. They are locked within these stones, you say? We must hope none of them have secreted themselves within your person: spirits are wicked, ingenious creatures and always select just the parts where they may best torment you. How far are we from the sea? I should fling them upon the waves if I were you, and hope that was the last I saw of them."

"But I do not want to throw them away," protested Prunella. "I want to hatch them and make use of them. That is what English thaumaturges do, you know, when they have the good luck to come upon a familiar's egg, and they are much admired for it."

"So I have heard, but you ought not to pattern yourself after such reprobates," said Mak Genggang, frowning. "Do not you know it is a sin so to employ djinns and spirits? We ought only to depend upon the graciousness of God, in magic as in life."

Prunella was alarmed. She could all too easily envision being compelled by Mak Genggang to dispose of her familiars' eggs for her own moral and spiritual good.

"But surely God created the spirits and djinns," suggested Prunella, "and it is no more wicked to use their services than it is to ride horses or eat meat. And you know, dear Mak Genggang, we cannot trust to a steady supply of magic, as you do in your country."

"Very right too. It is a just punishment for your officious interference in other people's affairs."

"But in consequence we are restrained from doing a great deal of good for want of magic," argued Prunella. "I may not be able to do all I desire to rescue you, for instance."

This point could not but hold some weight with Mak Genggang, imprisoned as she was by the Society. Despite her pious objection it transpired that she was not unfamiliar with the intricacies of such sacrilegious dependence upon spirits, for after further argument she declared:

"If you insist, it is better that I teach you than that you should blunder along and be devoured for your pains. The employment of familiars is all very well for infidels, I suppose, and you are a godless creature enough, Prunella."

Prunella acceded to this description of herself cheerfully: "I had no one to teach me better, you see."

"So you have found someone to teach you worse!" said Mak Genggang. "Well, you are a pretty, insinuating child, and you will come to a bad end, no doubt."

But she spoke with grudging approval. Mak Genggang might decry Prunella's ways all she liked, but the same disregard of order and authority which Prunella possessed animated Mak Genggang's own heart. Even if she thought the appearance of reproof due to her age and status, she rather relished a measure of lawlessness.

"I warned Abdullah in just the same way when he came to me with his *bajang*. He did not listen, of course, and what was the consequence? He vanished, never to be seen again, and his wife was left to provide for seven children!" said Mak Genggang. "Salima remarried soon enough, and I expect she likes her new husband better, since he does not beat her. But it was a bad lookout for Abdullah. At least you are better equipped to manage your spirits than any man could be."

"Am I?" said Prunella, pleased. "But why is that?"

"Why, all the greatest magic comes down to blood," said Mak Genggang. "And who knows blood better than a woman?"

WHAT Mak Genggang told Prunella had solidified her resolve to wake the familiars. She could not afford to wait, and let Zacharias continue another month exposed to attack by every fireplace and puddle he encountered. Such constant disruption could only interfere with her plans—and what would become of her if one of those attacks should succeed?

But Prunella found she did not like to contemplate the possibility of Zacharias's being injured, or worse. He could take care of himself, of course; he was Sorcerer Royal, after all. But it was clear she needed magic. London was too dangerous to do without. With such an unassailable ground for tasting the intoxicating power of the treasures again, Prunella saw no reason to put off her trial.

Emboldened by the consciousness of doing not only what was right, but what was necessary, she met Zacharias's shocked gaze with composure.

"I am sorry to have woken you," she said. "There is no need for concern, however. Everything is proceeding just as it ought."

"Proceeding just as it ought—!" cried Zacharias. "Did not that school teach you the dangers of hatching a familiar from the egg?"

It was possible to acquire a familiar by different means: one could inherit a familiar upon the death of its previous master; one could persuade an inhabitant of Fairyland to settle in the mortal world; or one could seek to command the loyalty of a familiar from the egg.

The last method was the most perilous. Familiars hatched from the egg with the intellects of an infant, and no recollection of their past selves. They must be hatched with great care, in the presence of warding spells and other measures of restraint, as might be required by the moods of the familiar once it was hatched.

If the familiar could not be tamed, it must be killed. Zacharias remembered stories of familiars that, in hatching, had left towns and villages in ashes, devastated lands, and killed the magicians that sought to restrain them.

One could not predict what would emerge from a familiar's egg. It might be anything. It might be angry.

The three eggs were vibrating, their surface covered with fine branching lines, and a tiny wet face emerged from a gap in the eggshell. The sight gave Zacharias the impetus to grasp Prunella's arm, pulling her away from the eggs.

"Go," he said urgently. "Wake the servants, and get out of the building. I will contain them." He had no notion how he would do it, but at least he could try to limit the damage, even if he were destroyed in the attempt.

Prunella was not at all grateful for this display of nobility, however.

"Don't be ridiculous!" she said crossly. "Why do not *you* go, and take the servants with you?" She wrested herself from Zacharias's grasp, and went to kneel by the eggs. "There is nothing to be alarmed about, only I wish you would go back to bed, and not trouble yourself about my business. I cannot deal with the treasures in your presence. It would be very improper!"

The familiar farthest advanced in its hatching crawled out from among the shards of its egg. It was a tiny, naked homunculus, hairless and sexless, with pallid skin and glowing eyes. Zacharias had never before seen an immature fairy in the flesh, but it corresponded exactly to the drawings he had studied. The strange, inhuman face screwed up; the mouth opened and let loose the protesting wail of an infant. Prunella caught the creature up in her hands.

"*Please* leave the room," she cried. "I do not at all wish to do what you will compel me to!"

Zacharias started forward to help. He was recalling to his memory everything he had ever learnt about fairies, and his attention was so fixed upon the elvet that Prunella's hex took him unawares. It was a simple cantrip for confusion—naughty girls at the school had used it to deceive the mistresses on their nightly rounds of the dormitories—but it hit Zacharias full in the face.

He tripped over a chair and fell on the floor, noting as he went the clever design of the spell. It was devised to achieve not only a confusion of the limbs, but a bewilderment of the senses, and his were tangled quite successfully. His vision went dark. The elvet's wail was suddenly quieted. He heard the tread of tiny feet upon the carpet, an "Oh!" from Prunella—and then he could see again.

Prunella rose, cradling the elvet, her face flushed, and her dress in disarray. Eggshells lay scattered upon the floor. The feverish light of magic, which had so distorted the appearance of the room, faded away.

The two other infant familiars stretched and yawned. One was a garuda, or Malay simurgh, with the black-curled head of a baby and the body of a chick, its feathers wet and plastered to its body. The other was a wobbly-legged colt with a broad leonine face and tiny antler buds—an Oriental unicorn, of the kind called *ch'i-lin* by the Chinese and *kirin* by the Japanese.

The elvet was crooning in a soft, loving voice to Prunella, and the others reached for her. They seemed content, well fed—but a familiar could only be tamed at birth by the liberal application of fresh blood, the blood of the magician who wished to be its master. It was this that made taming familiars from the egg such a chancy venture, for the sorcerer was rendered vulnerable at the time when he most needed his full strength.

"You are wounded?" said Zacharias. Prunella must be hurt, though she looked unharmed; there could be no other explanation. "I will go for a physician—no, that will not do—we must make shift to tend you here. Permit me to examine the injury."

Prunella had gone a brilliant scarlet.

"There is no injury," she said pettishly. "I beg you will not make a fuss over nothing. I have settled it all."

"If it would not be proper for me to examine it, the housekeeper could assist, I am sure," said Zacharias anxiously. "Pray do not allow reserve to expose you to any risk."

"Mr. Wythe," said Prunella, with indescribable hauteur, "I beg you will not take offence when I say that a gentleman would not persist in this line of questioning!"

Her face was averted, but her cheek was still flushed with high colour. Little though Zacharias had had to do with women, Sir Stephen—believing there was no area of knowledge that should be withheld from an unnatural philosopher—had taken care to acquaint him thoroughly with the workings of the mortal frame, male and female. It became evident to him what the source of Prunella's mastery of the familiars must be.

"Oh," Zacharias said, stricken with embarrassment.

Prunella did not dignify this with a reply, but busied herself with her new familiars. The elvet still cradled in her arms, she drew a shawl over the chick, and knelt by the unicorn, cooing, "What a sweet creature you are! And will you grow into a great horse, truly?"

It was a charming scene. It was also unprecedented in the history of Britain. In one fell stroke Prunella had become the most powerful sorcerer who had ever lived.

16

Zacharias's trials had revealed within him an unsuspected core of unflappability. He passed almost immediately from shock to applying himself to practicalities.

"We shall have to take Lady Wythe into our confidence," he said. "It will make everything easier, for she will be able to prepare a space for our lessons, and get the servants out of our way. We must be discreet. No one else can know. The Society is no more kindly disposed towards female magic than Mrs. Daubeney, and I shall need time to change its mind regarding your education."

Prunella was not really attending, she was so blissfully absorbed in her familiars. She looked up with the start of someone waking out of a lovely dream.

"My education?" she said. "Need I any instruction now? Surely my familiars will teach me all I need to know."

"Your familiars know scarcely more than you about the operation of magic—certainly not the principles of mortal thaumaturgy," said Zacharias. "Recall that they are newborn, and will have forgotten much of their former lives in Fairyland. They will rely upon you for guidance and restraint—and you will pay dearly for any lapse. Even under Mrs. Daubeney's scheme of instruction you must have heard of the perils of excessive magic ungoverned by learning."

"Say, rather, *especially* under Mrs. Daubeney's scheme of instruction," said Prunella. The infusion of potent magic had had much the same effect upon her spirits as a bottle of champagne, and Zacharias's sobriety could not dampen her. "If she had her way the girls would hardly have been taught anything else. Miss Jellicoe used to have to pretend she was lecturing them on the evils of magic, when they were only conning their figures. Poor thing! I believe algebra was all she ever thought of."

Zacharias paid this diversion little regard. Giddiness was to be expected in a new sorceress.

"There is no time to lose," he said. "Your familiars are young: it will be some time before they reach the peak of their powers, and for the time being they are pliant. We ought to start right away."

He had expected that the prospect of beginning her studies would delight Prunella, but to his surprise she said doubtfully:

"Oh, if you think we must! I should not like to take you from your work. You must have a great deal on your hands now that Mak Genggang has flown, and that wicked Society is rampaging about demanding your head on a plate. I am sure you ought not to concern yourself with my instruction when matters of such importance require your attention."

"Your instruction is a matter of great importance," said Zacharias severely. "The education of Miss Prunella Gentleman may have been of concern only to herself before. Now that she has acquired three familiars, her education is rightly a matter of concern to the entire nation, little though it knows it!"

"Why should that be?" said Prunella, bemused.

"Miss Gentleman, you represent what English magic has been

seeking for half a century," said Zacharias. "With three familiars, you need do nothing else but learn enough to avoid either destroying them, or being destroyed by them, to ensure the whole kingdom's advantage. Three familiars will bring with them magic enough to supply a generation of thaumaturges. The better you understand them, the better for all of us."

"Good gracious," said Prunella. A gleam of naked ambition lit her eye. "But that means I am terribly important!"

"And you will have a great deal of work to do in consequence," said Zacharias. "We will start tomorrow, once you are settled with Lady Wythe. I suppose your introduction will take up the whole morning—she will need to find you a room, and instruct the servants—but we may begin in the afternoon. There should be no obstacle to your devoting all your days to study."

Though Zacharias had much to worry him, he could not contemplate the prospect of weeks of devotion to the study of unnatural philosophy with indifference. Even if he lacked the time to engage in such delightful work himself, to superintend the studies of another was nearly as good, and he looked forward to it with every expectation of pleasure.

If he had not been so pleased himself he might have noticed the perceptible lengthening of Prunella's face. As it was, he was taken aback by her response.

"It all sounds most improving, I am sure, and I am obliged to you for your pains," said Prunella awkwardly. "But I do not know that I will have time for such a very comprehensive course of study. How shall I achieve anything if I am forever at my books?"

"What else can you wish to achieve?" said Zacharias. "You are a sorceress three times over! That is an achievement no other woman in history can equal."

"Which is delightful, I am sure, and I intend to take full advantage of it," said Prunella eagerly. "We may feel perfectly comfortable now, for

Nidget and Youko and Tjandra will see to it that your wicked assassin is thwarted in any further attempts upon your life. But do you see, Mr. Wythe, I hatched them to *save* trouble, not to make it. I could scarcely establish myself if I was running about after my familiars all day!"

"But what more do you require to establish yourself?" said Zacharias, bewildered. "Any of my colleagues would say they could do no more if they had but accomplished what you have done."

"But all of your colleagues are men, and have some means of getting a living," said Prunella. She felt Zacharias was being obtuse. "What shall I live on while I am cultivating my familiars as you desire me to do?"

The question had occurred to Zacharias already. He said:

"While you are my apprentice you need not be concerned about finding a living. We could not of course apply for the bursaries to which a gentleman in your circumstances would be entitled; yet I am so positioned that we may contrive very comfortably without." Sir Stephen had approached the getting of a fortune with all his usual enterprise, and fortunately he had no nearer relations to dispute the will in which he had left a considerable portion of that fortune to Zacharias.

"And after I have completed my apprenticeship, what then?" said Prunella.

Zacharias hesitated. A gentleman thaumaturge in need of funds might tutor the sons of the wealthy, serve the Society, or advise the Government on magical affairs. A gentleman sorcerer would hardly need to seek opportunities, but could wait at his leisure to be sought out. It was a puzzle to know what a female in the same position could do, however, since history offered no precedent.

"You understand the difficulty," said Prunella. "I could hardly be beholden to your charity forever. That would not do at all! Since I have neither connections nor money, the only means I have of acquiring either is to marry." She paused, but she could not continue to mislead Zacharias if she was to have his help in achieving her purpose.

"To own the truth," she said, "that was my chief aim in coming to London. I should never have met anyone who would do if I had stopped at the school."

Prunella's assertion would have scandalised neither Mrs. Daubeney nor Lady Wythe, though they might have thought her rather bold to set out her aim so plainly. Zacharias was not accustomed to thinking of marriage in such mercenary terms, and he was shocked.

"Surely you do not mean to tell me that your purpose in coming to London was to marry a wealthy lord?" he said.

"Oh no! What can have given you that notion?" said Prunella. "I should be happy with a tradesman, provided he had a respectable competence. Though of course, a fortune would be even better, and you know, I am so pretty that really I think I ought not to settle for anything less! But you see why I could not devote myself to the course of study you propose. If I am to marry, and marry well, I shall have to enter society, and spend a portion of my days being introduced to gentlemen, and dancing with them, and affecting to take a great interest in what they say, and all that sort of thing."

"And what of your familiars? Are they to languish away? Does magic mean so little to you?"

Prunella flushed in indignation. "No, indeed! Of course I will give my familiars all the care they need. But neither they nor magic can feed me. What has magic done for anyone at Mrs. Daubeney's school, save in the suppression of it?"

"You could not be more concerned than I regarding the injustices perpetrated against your schoolfellows," Zacharias began, but Prunella, feeling her candour had been ill rewarded, shot back:

"I think you will find that I can! What might not I do for feminine magic, with wealth and position? But I cannot do anything useful until I have established myself. Else I could be a sorceress seven times over, and still only hope to be some afflicted girl's governess, tasked with scolding her out of her magic!"

It was impossible for Zacharias to refute this. His own example showed how little magical talent alone could do to secure one's position in society. His colleagues could deny his ability, and indeed often did, but Sir Stephen's influence, his wealth and position, were harder to ignore, even after his death. Little as Zacharias liked it, he knew well enough that these were the most potent argument for civility among his peers, and had often moderated their treatment of him.

"If you truly had any concern for Miss Liddiard and Henrietta and all the rest of them, you would help me," said Prunella into a tense silence. "All I need is to be introduced into society upon a respectable footing. The rest I could contrive myself."

Zacharias sighed.

"Miss Gentleman," he said, "I beg you will look here." He rolled up his sleeve, holding his arm out.

"It is your arm," observed Prunella, after a moment's puzzled contemplation.

"You will not, I am sure, have failed to notice its colour," said Zacharias. He rolled down his sleeve again, conscious of Prunella's intent dark eyes, waiting for a conclusion.

"Certainly society has not," he continued. "My colleagues are compelled to deal with me, however much they may dislike it. But in the circles to which you aspire, I am of no account whatsoever. A magic-making African might serve as a diversion in high society, but never more than that. Society would never consent to be influenced by such as I."

"But you are the Sorcerer Royal," said Prunella. Her cheeks warming unaccountably, she added, "If *you* wished to be married to anyone, you would never be refused on account of your colour."

Zacharias stood for a moment gazing down at his own hands. He could not say whether he agreed. Lady Wythe would have dismissed his doubt, even as she allowed that not every family would be delighted to own such a son-in-law:

"But you should not like such illiberal connections yourself! There are a great many sensible people who will know how to value you even as you deserve. You need not shut yourself off from the world for fear of the few who might be so little-minded."

But the world had given Zacharias little reason to believe that the sensible, as Lady Wythe termed them, outnumbered the little-minded, though he had not sought out opportunities to test the truth of her statement. He needed no further reminder of the peculiar loneliness of his position—of the fact that, but for the intervention of fate, he might never have known the ease he now enjoyed; might never have had even the few friends he possessed.

"Perhaps not," he said. "I have never made a trial. It is not within my power to make you respectable. I cannot even do that for myself."

"Lady Wythe could," said Prunella. "Anyone to whom she lent her countenance could not but be respectable."

She clasped her hands. Zacharias had never seen her so serious.

"You know what it is to be on the fringes of everything—to see that others have what you lack, for nothing more than an accident of birth," she said. "I suppose my scheme sounds wild enough, and perhaps no one will marry me after all, for fear of what *my* colour might signify. But I must try, or spend the rest of my life a lady's maid, working petty magics as it suits my betters—and that would not suit me at all!"

Zacharias looked at the elegant hands wound together, the head crowned with cloudlike dark hair.

"I doubt you need have any worry of that," he said, feeling the blood rise in his cheeks, though he spoke in the driest manner he could manage.

"Not if you will help me," said Prunella. She was so engrossed in what she was about to say that she did not notice Zacharias's embarrassment. "And if you do, as I know you could, I shall study as many tomes as you like, and what is more"—she flung back her shoulders, raising her head—"you may have an egg!"

Zacharias did not at first understand what she meant. Then he went still. "You have another?"

"I have four more eggs, besides the ones I hatched," said Prunella. "But I should think one would be sufficient to pay for the expenses of my coming out, do not you agree?"

Zacharias could tell she was not nearly so confident as she pretended, but Prunella was not in fact wrong. He could think of several thaumaturges who would pay a great deal more than she could spend in a year for a familiar's egg, and count it a bargain.

"How did you acquire seven familiars' eggs?" he demanded.

"Why, I found them while I was rummaging in the attic."

"Pray be serious," said Zacharias, frowning. "It is a matter of greater consequence than you know."

"Never mind where they are from, for there are no more to be got from that quarter," said Prunella firmly. "All you need know is they are mine, to do what I will with them. What do you say to my offer?"

Zacharias hesitated, hardly knowing what to think, or what to do. "I am not sure it is not my duty to take them from you, if only for safeguarding."

"As if you would!" said Prunella. She looked at him, and her brow clouded. Doubt, and a touch of fear, entered her eyes.

For a moment Zacharias saw how fully sensible Prunella was of the weakness of her position. Even with three familiars, an untrained female, alone in the world, could not resist the Sorcerer Royal if he chose to compel her compliance. But defiance lit her eyes: she squared her shoulders and tossed her head, as though she would fling off any uncertainty.

"Even if you did, the eggs would be no good to you," she said. "They are bound in an ensorcellment, a vastly strong one, and they will never be anything more than four dead stones unless the spell is lifted. I have the secret of unlocking the charm, but no one else knows it."

Zacharias said drily, "I can quite see why you do not feel the need for education, since you possess such a number of magical secrets!"

Prunella did not smile. Her face was composed, her mouth a determined line, but she could not altogether conceal her uncertainty. Zacharias recalled the look of alarm that had passed fleetingly through her eyes.

"Come," he said gently, "are not we friends? I do not think we are so far apart. You will wish to learn as much as you need to, to be able to govern your familiars, and I understand that you require some assurance regarding your future. I do not say you have convinced me that a London Season is the best means of achieving it—"

"You have not proposed any alternative!" exclaimed Prunella.

"But," continued Zacharias, "I can hardly proclaim myself an expert in this regard. Lady Wythe will know better. Shall we ask her if she will do as you desire, and see how she replies?"

Prunella blinked, taken aback. Then she rallied, saying with a businesslike air:

"Do you mean to say you accept my offer of an egg?"

"If you agree to training," said Zacharias. "And I should very much like to see all the remaining eggs, if you have no objection."

"Perhaps you may," said Prunella. "Since we are friends."

Before anything could be asked of Lady Wythe, Prunella must first be accounted for to her, and Zacharias found this as difficult as he had feared. In Lady Wythe's sitting room the next day, he attempted to explain that the girl he had produced was not his mistress, without ever lapsing into such indecorousness as to say the word.

"I am conscious of how this must appear," he said. "But I assure you, I should never seek to—should never involve you in any sort of— I hope you believe I should never require you to countenance anything approaching impropriety."

"Zacharias," said Lady Wythe, "I am not a schoolgirl, that you should stammer so. I was married thirty years, and have hardly led a sheltered life. I beg you will tell me your trouble."

"You are very good, ma'am," said Zacharias, but he still looked worried. "I scarcely know where to begin."

Though she had sworn she would let Zacharias manage the affair, Prunella had been growing rather restless, and at this she could no longer contain herself. She interjected:

"Mr. Wythe means, ma'am, that I am not a courtesan, but what is even worse—a witch!"

This elicited a forbidding look from Zacharias.

"Say, rather, a thaumaturgess," he said. "Or perhaps we might call you a *magicienne*. Witches practise a type of petty or folk magic, very different from our thaumaturgy, and your village witch is just as likely to be a man as a woman. It is a loose usage to describe every female who practises magic as a witch, much to be decried."

"Mr. Wythe has been so good as to offer to teach me, ma'am," said Prunella, ignoring him. "I used to be at a school for gentlewitches, where of course they taught no thaumaturgy, and it seems it is a very shocking thing to be magical and taught nothing but how to restrain it."

Lady Wythe looked bewildered.

"Age must be scattering my wits," she said, looking to Zacharias. "I had thought the teaching of restraint was precisely what must be done with women who are afflicted by magic. I do not, you know, refer to the household magics the servants do—there is no harm in enchanting a pot to prevent its boiling over, or a broom to sweep a floor, but is not unnatural philosophy a different matter altogether? I had always understood it was forbidden to our sex."

"So it is," said Zacharias. "But if you had seen what I witnessed at that school, ma'am, you would agree that far more harm is done in preventing the natural exertion by women of their abilities than could ever be done by training them up as thaumaturgesses. I believe a thorough reform is required."

He inclined his head towards Prunella. "Miss Gentleman has kindly acceded to my testing the principle upon her. If all goes as we hope, we shall have in Miss Gentleman an example of success to present to the Society when I propose my reform. But my scheme requires your participation, ma'am. Miss Gentleman knows no one in London. I should be grateful if you would take her in. I would provide for her expenses, and her stay need not be of long duration."

Lady Wythe looked from Zacharias to Prunella. Such quixoticism from Zacharias was not wholly unexpected to Lady Wythe—she was accustomed to his fits and starts—but it was clear she was concerned about the young stranger. She leant over to Prunella and took her hand, to Prunella's alarm.

"I hope you will forgive me, Miss Gentleman, but do you truly grasp the scale of the undertaking to which you have agreed?" she said. "Magic is a perilous practise, you know—strenuous for men, and it must exact an even greater toll upon a woman's frame."

"Miss Gentleman is—" began Zacharias, but Lady Wythe forestalled him.

"My question was addressed to the young lady," she said firmly. "You need not be afraid to tell the truth, my dear. Simply say what your wishes are regarding yourself, and I shall see that they are respected."

Prunella hesitated, glancing at Zacharias, but he had retreated into his chair at Lady Wythe's reproof, and looked haughtily unconscious.

"I am obliged to you for your solicitude, ma'am," said Prunella slowly. "But I have been devising spells and cantions since I was quite a little thing, and was never the worse for it. It was never part of my plan to become a thaumaturge, but—" She paused, and looked at Zacharias again.

Lady Wythe looked anxious.

"You must not let him persuade you to do anything you dislike," she said.

An extraordinary noise issued from the long-suffering Zacharias. "I, compel Miss Gentleman to do what she would not like to do!"

"You are very kind, ma'am," said Prunella earnestly. "But indeed, I am happy to submit to Mr. Wythe's instruction. Mr. Wythe and I understand one another, I believe."

"Well, it is an extraordinary situation," said Lady Wythe, keeping her thoughts to herself. "But I do not doubt Zacharias's judgment in thaumaturgical affairs, and I should be happy for you to stay with me."

"I am obliged to you, ma'am," said Zacharias. "That will render our course a great deal smoother." He coughed, and went on, more awkwardly than ever:

"There is another favour I must beg. Miss Gentleman has travelled to London because she wishes to be—I believe the term is 'brought out.'"

Lady Wythe stared at him.

"Into society," Zacharias added.

Prunella thought it right to intervene.

"As I said, I never thought of being a thaumaturge till I met Mr. Wythe," she said. "But I should very much like to enter society."

"Heavens," said Lady Wythe blankly. "But why on earth—?"

"Because I should like to have a husband," said Miss Gentleman, surprised to have to explain the obvious.

"I understand Miss Gentleman will venture to find herself a husband, and only desires assistance in gaining access to the best society, so that she may begin her efforts at the highest level," said Zacharias. Miss Gentleman nodded approvingly. "If you would be so good as to introduce her into society, she has agreed to submit to a moderate regimen of thaumaturgical training."

"Oh, there is no question whatsoever," exclaimed Prunella. "I would read a thousand grimoires if that was what it took."

An awful silence descended.

"I cannot seem to make sense of the situation, despite your explanations, Zacharias," said Lady Wythe finally. "I cannot make out why it is so necessary that Miss Gentleman should agree to training. Of course, my dear"—this to the young lady—"you must be married, if that is what you wish. But it seems to me that the best means of achieving that would be for you to return to this school. I should be happy to exert my influence with the headmistress to see that you obtained a good place, and in time I am sure a young woman of your charm cannot fail to find a suitable husband."

"But a *suitable* husband is not what I want at all," cried Miss Gentleman.

"With respect, ma'am, we have not yet told you the whole," said Zacharias. "Miss Gentleman has recently come into the possession of three familiars. They have consented to travel within her valise to evade detection."

Lady Wythe had not taken notice of the valise before. It loomed suddenly large in her vision: a small brown case, much the worse for wear, resting on Miss Gentleman's knee.

There was no disbelieving Zacharias. His authority on such matters could not be gainsaid, and he spoke with total conviction.

"You see my position," said Zacharias. "There is no alternative. Miss Gentleman must be trained."

"Indeed," said Lady Wythe faintly.

Lady Wythe insisted on Zacharias's staying the night in her house. It was so late, and still so cold in the evenings, she was sure he ought not to be venturing out again, and it would be the easiest thing in the world to make up a bed for him.

She suspected, rightly, that despite the late hour, Zacharias intended to go from her house to his office, for his fortnight's absence had stored up for him a great deal of work. When he began to suffer the symptoms heralding one of his attacks, however, he thought it wise to submit, recalling his misadventure at the Blue Boar.

He was not surprised to find Sir Stephen waiting in the spare bedroom for him.

"You must certainly inform the Society," said Sir Stephen.

As he sat down to take off his boots, Zacharias was conscious of a sense of relief. Even if they were bound to quarrel on the subject, he could at least be frank with his former guardian. It was not possible to confide in anyone else, for Prunella had bound him to secrecy regarding her four remaining treasures.

"If you mean I should tell the Society about the familiars' eggs," said Zacharias, "they are Miss Gentleman's property, and she has only agreed to make one over to me once she has succeeded in contracting a marriage."

Sir Stephen disregarded this.

"Of course, there are the creatures that have hatched!" he exclaimed. "What a wretched coil it is—for if you bring the Society the eggs they are bound to ask where they came from, and if it were to come out about the girl's familiars, you could hardly survive the scandal. Your position is already precarious, and that hag's antics have not helped."

They both knew that this was such news as would rock the halls of the Society. On every previous occasion of the discovery of a new familiar's egg, the conferral of the egg had been the subject of protracted negotiations, of the furious jockeying of talented men of birth, of Machiavellian political manoeuvrings—even, in less enlightened days, of war.

It would not signify, to the thaumaturges who would sit in judgment upon Zacharias, that Prunella had such talent as Zacharias had never seen before in an untrained magician. Nor would it signify that he had scarcely been in a position to prevent her bonding with the familiars when they hatched. The familiars, in hatching, might well have destroyed the inn if not for Prunella's swift action, and no thaumaturge—no *male* thaumaturge—could have predicted what she would do to pacify them. Precious few thaumaturges had ever encountered a familiar freshly out of the egg, and what Prunella had done went against every piece of received wisdom Zacharias had acquired in the course of his excellent education.

But he was the Sorcerer Royal, and he had stood by when half the largest crop of familiars the kingdom had ever seen was thrown away on a magician with no family and no training—above all, a magician who was female.

"Yet would not the gift of the eggs make up for the lapse?" argued Sir Stephen. "Such a gift as the nation has not seen in centuries! The girl could be dealt with. She need not pose any difficulty. The thing is to make a clean breast of it, Zacharias."

"The eggs would not be much of a gift without Miss Gentleman's cooperation," said Zacharias, rubbing his temples. "Miss Gentleman allowed me to examine them. They are bound by an enchantment that locks them in stasis—a spell of wholly unfamiliar working. She knows the secret of the counter-spell, and without it the eggs are no good to us."

"Cannot she be made to reveal the secret?" said Sir Stephen. "You need not stare at me so. What are your fine scruples against the interests of the nation? You must certainly tell the Society, and surrender the eggs. It is your duty."

"We disagree as to where my duty lies," said Zacharias. Any relief he had felt about being able to discuss the problem had dissipated. His head was pounding, his breath came short, and the air was full of light and colour.

"Zacharias," said Sir Stephen. His voice vibrated with frustration;

it was clear he would like to raise it, but he strove to govern himself. "Listen to me, Zacharias: you think me unscrupulous, no doubt. You think I am ruthless; you pity the girl. You know there is truth in what I say, however. Every circumstance is conspiring to remove you from your office, and should that happen, who knows what might be the result? Recall your agreement"—he lowered his voice—"your pact with Leofric!"

"Miss Gentleman has trusted me," said Zacharias with difficulty.

"She deceived you! She imposed upon you for her own purposes, and now you are burdened with a brazen nobody, who has no family, no resources—"

"And three familiars," said Zacharias. "You know that if I were to surrender her to the Society, they would not be content with the four eggs. They would seek to wrest her familiars from her."

He did not need to elaborate upon what the consequences of that would be. It had happened not infrequently in centuries past, when England still had sufficient sorcerers to quarrel with one another, that a sorcerer would have his familiars forcibly removed from him. The effects varied, but they were without exception horrific. Some former sorcerers ran mad. Some lost all their magic, which to many magicians seemed a worse fate. A few continued for days or even weeks as though nothing were amiss, until they died suddenly where they stood. Their corpses grew instantly withered and grey, and turned to dust at a touch.

"That would be very bad," assented Sir Stephen reluctantly. "Still, I am sure you could persuade the Society to show restraint."

"Why should it, for a female of no account?" said Zacharias. "You are quite right. Miss Gentleman has nothing—neither principles, nor connections, nor money—nothing but her magic and her absurd effrontery." Zacharias half-smiled, though he had been vexed enough by that effrontery. "She has only my good will to rely upon, and I—I owe her my life. I could not betray her. I will abide by our compact."

He had to stop, for the old agony began to tear at his bowels. He staggered to the bed and collapsed heavily upon it, nightmare shapes figuring in his blurred vision. Before him extended a long, grim night, for the worrying at his vitals would not permit sleep.

"Oh, Zacharias," said Sir Stephen. His voice seemed to come from a great distance, weighted with sorrow and reproach. "When will you stop striking these ill bargains?"

Zacharias did not answer, and Sir Stephen said no more. His cool, insubstantial hand brushed Zacharias's head, and its touch bestowed relief.

Sir Stephen drew a spell across his temples, filling his troubled head with cloud and shadow. Zacharias smelt rain. His vision cleared, and he saw the dark expanse of a night sky, soft and starless. Finally he slept, forgetting pain.

17

Rollo Threlfall was having an excellent day.

Rollo did often have excellent days. The youngest son of an indulgent father, he was never burdened by any graver responsibility than that of making up numbers at ambitious hostesses' dinners, or deciding whether to purchase a likely piece of horseflesh. The unclouded skies of this particular day were rendered all the bluer by the reflection that if not for the nobility of his friends, he would at that very moment be at his aunt Georgiana's, providing an account of the speech he had given at her friend's school.

As he had not, after all, given the speech, he had been not been called upon to visit his aunt, for Aunt Georgiana's affection for her nephew was as moderate as his fear of her was acute. Rollo had passed the previous evening at the Theurgist's instead, winding up an excellent dinner with wine and pleasantries, and he had awoken in the morning to a throbbing head the approximate size of the Stone of Scone.

By noon, however, Rollo was out of bed, as lively as the day he was born, and swathed within a neckcloth whose points could not be faulted by the most exacting Pink of the *ton*. He was in great good humour as he sallied forth to meet Damerell at the Theurgist's, and his mood was only improved by the sight of Zacharias Wythe, sitting with Damerell at their accustomed table.

"Halloa! This is a piece of good luck!" said Rollo. "I had not thought to see you so soon, Zacharias. I must congratulate you upon your success. I had a letter from my aunt last week, and it seems you went down a treat. Mrs. Daubeney was excessively obliged—said the handsomest things about your speech."

"I am happy to have given satisfaction," said Zacharias. Mrs. Daubeney's letter had clearly withheld more than it disclosed, he reflected.

"Not half so happy as I am," Rollo assured him. "Of course it was nothing to a clever chap like you, giving a speech to a pack of ravening schoolgirls, but if I had had to do it I expect I would have jumped into the river before the week was out."

"It will be a source of unending gratification to me, that I should have been instrumental in averting that fate," said Zacharias gravely. He inspected his cup of coffee, apparently lost in thought. "However, it was not an unrewarding visit. I encountered a few interesting characters at the school."

"Oh?" said Rollo. "I thought it was only girls."

"Yes. But even girls may be characters, you know," said Zacharias. "Still, I cannot say I enjoyed the experience. I nearly turned tail and fled when I mounted the stage before all those eyes. What is the Queen of Elfland to an assembly of schoolgirls? At least she is not given to giggling."

Rollo shuddered. "Giggling!"

"Such devotion on my part, I think, merits some recompense."

"It is beyond anything," said Rollo fervently. "If there is any service I can render, Zacharias, you have only to say the word!"

Zacharias nodded, as if this was what he had been waiting to hear.

"Very good. You will be pleased to know I have hit upon the very thing," he said. His entire manner changed: he sat up, steepled his hands and continued, in a crisp, schoolmaster-ish voice:

"You will oblige me by prevailing upon your aunt Georgiana—and indeed upon any and all of the respectable women you know—to introduce Miss Prunella Gentleman to unmarried gentlemen of eligible prospects, so that she may find a husband."

Rollo goggled. Damerell was apparently seized by a fit, but when a footman rushed up, desiring to assist, Damerell waved him away.

"Have some sense, man!" he gasped. "Don't *interrupt*!"

"What can you mean?" said Rollo.

"I gave a speech at a girls' school in your stead, and in consequence I find myself burdened with a new apprentice, a female of overweening ambition," said Zacharias. "We have agreed that I shall facilitate her introduction into society, in return for which she will apply herself to the study of magic. I have nothing to do with the *beau monde*, but you do. It seems only just that you should take over the task."

Rollo gazed at Zacharias in wild surmise, before turning piteous eyes upon Damerell.

"Why, Robert, it is clear as daylight," said Damerell. "A girl has followed Zacharias to London, and she wishes to find a husband. Zacharias desires you to manage the business. And I must say, Rollo, it would only be gentlemanly to step up, considering what he's done for you."

"But, dash it—"

"I don't desire you to marry her yourself," said Zacharias reassuringly. "I gather she hopes for something better than a younger son, though I confess I have no clear notion of the income she seeks. You should certainly speak to her about her requirements, however."

"It is best to be clear on these points," Damerell agreed.

"Dash it, Zacharias," Rollo burst out. "I am amazed! I never would have thought it of you, of all people. I *can't* introduce your barque of frailty into society. Why, it is out of all reason—it is—I don't know what it is!" He paused, choked with emotion.

"What Rollo means to say is that he thinks the proceeding unprincipled in the extreme," translated Damerell.

Rollo nodded. Breath returning to him, he added, "And what's more, it just ain't the thing!"

"There is nothing of that sort between me and Miss Gentleman," said Zacharias sternly. "I propose to tutor her—there is nothing more to our connection. Lady Wythe has agreed to have Miss Gentleman to stay with her, and to lend her countenance. But as you know, Lady Wythe has not been much in society of late, and I would spare her what I could. She has never been very fond of crowds."

"She is staying with Lady Wythe?" said Rollo. "I must say, it seems a dashed racketing way of going on. Lady Wythe always strikes one as being such a model of propriety!"

"How many times must I tell you that Miss Gentleman is a perfectly respectable young lady?" said Zacharias in a terrible voice. "Will you or will you not do it, Rollo?"

"My dear fellow, anything to oblige, but—but anything decent, you know!" begged Rollo. "Anything *plausible*!"

"I fail to see what is either indecent or implausible about my request," said Zacharias freezingly.

"Zacharias, with the best will in the world—!"

Damerell dabbed at his eyes with a handkerchief and put it away. He seemed to feel that Rollo had suffered enough.

"It's no good, my lad," he said to Zacharias. "Rollo's aunt ain't good *ton*. She's not a maternal aunt, you know. She is connected to the other side of the family. Haven't you ever met her?"

Zacharias, still rather wooden, said, "No. But I had understood she was received by all the best families."

"Oh yes. When Rollo's aunt Georgiana knocks on one's door, one doesn't bar it and hope she goes away," said Damerell.

"Doesn't do any good," said Rollo morosely, with the conviction of one who had tried.

"Quite. Rollo is of the best sort of family on his mother's side, but his paternal relations are a different affair altogether," said Damerell. "For your real influencers you must look elsewhere. *I* know them—and they owe me a favour or two. But first I must know what lies I am to tell them. Who is this girl? Tell your uncle Damerell."

Zacharias explained something of Prunella's history, and the position she had occupied at Mrs. Daubeney's school.

"I gather that her father was a gentleman, though he seems to have been an elusive character," he said. "Of her mother Mrs. Daubeney knew nothing. Mr. Gentleman spent time in India, and it seems likely that the mother was a native of that country. There is no suggestion that there was any irregularity in the connection, however. Miss Gentleman speaks as prettily as any fineborn girl, and she has as much education as any of Mrs. Daubeney's gentlewitches."

"Well, the mother need not be an insuperable obstacle," said Damerell, considering the matter. "There is no other family in England? That is all to the good. We need not fear the appearance of disreputable relations upon the scene. Is the girl pretty?"

Zacharias spilt his coffee, and was too busy mopping up the result to meet Damerell's eyes.

"Quite astonishingly so," he said.

Damerell governed his features with his habitual composure, but his delight was evident to one who knew him as well as Zacharias did. The damnable thing about Damerell, thought Zacharias, was that he never failed to observe precisely what you would conceal.

"Very good," said Damerell. "But why is it necessary to help Miss Gentleman to a husband?"

"I intend training her in the thaumaturgy, and she has promised to apply herself if I arrange for her to be introduced into society," said

Zacharias. "She seems confident that she will be able to obtain a husband of means, if she can only contrive to gain access to the right people."

"She sounds a female of considerable resource. I admire her already. But now we come to the vital point: why is she to be trained?"

Zacharias was prepared for this.

"It has become clear to me that it is necessary to reform the thaumaturgical education of women," he said. "The system that currently obtains is injurious to those women and girls who must do violence to their own natures to conform to it. Mrs. Daubeney's school supplied ample proof of that. It proved, too, that there is a store of magical ability among women, which we would be foolish to disregard. A number of her students have obvious talent—talent that will otherwise be wasted in clandestine enchantments in the drawing room and kitchen, in charms to beautify a table or amuse an infant."

"Miss Gentleman is to be your first example of what may be done with feminine magic, then," said Damerell.

Zacharias bowed. "Even without training, her abilities are striking. With instruction, what might she not achieve?"

He knew this was a poor explanation. If his purpose was to demonstrate the desirability of reforming women's education by training one talented female, why not select one who would not make such strange demands? But further Zacharias dared not go. He must conceal the existence of Prunella's familiars for as long as he could.

"Far be it from me to find fault with so noble a scheme," said Damerell contemplatively. "But you will forgive a friend's impertinence, Zacharias—have you considered the Society's likely reception of it, when we have recently had such an alarming lesson in what may be done with feminine magic? I refer, you know, to the Malayan vampiress who nearly killed Mrs. Geoffrey Midsomer."

"She was a witch, not a vampiress," said Zacharias. "And if Mrs. Midsomer was bruised, that is the most I have heard she suffered in the way of injury! If I were to wait until the Society liked the notion of teaching women magic, my reform would never come to fruition."

"Still, could not you wait till your position is stronger, before you quite upend all of the Society's beloved prejudices?" said Damerell.

Zacharias shook his head. "Who knows how long I will be Sorcerer Royal? I may never again be in such a position to effect good."

"But that is just what I do not like. It is such an unfortunate time for you to announce a scheme that is bound to be unpopular, with Geoffrey Midsomer wooing half the Society and bribing the other half, and the Treasury eyeing our coffers, and above all, our magic running dry."

"That, at least, is a difficulty the Society will no longer be able to throw in my face," said Zacharias, relieved to be able to supply good news for once. "I am confident we will see a marked improvement when the results of the next inspection of atmospheric magic levels are published in the *Gazette*." The introduction of Prunella's three familiars was bound to give rise to *that* benefit, at least.

Damerell blinked. "But that is excellent! Did your efforts at the border succeed, then, Zacharias?"

"After a fashion," said Zacharias guardedly. The block on England's magic was another matter best kept secret for now. The Fairy King's rout was that very evening, and Zacharias would have a better notion of the reason for the block soon enough.

Damerell sat in silence for a while, no doubt turning over the various holes Zacharias could discern in his own account.

"You are grown very sorcerous, Zacharias," he said finally. "You never used to be so mysterious. But I will see what I can do for your apprentice. The girl will need to be dressed properly, of course. Lady Wythe will obtain her admission to Almack's, I presume."

"Yes," said Zacharias. "We have agreed that Miss Gentleman is to have everything that is suitable. You may call upon my bankers for any expense."

"Then I think I can contrive a splash for your Miss Gentleman," said Damerell. "But—you will allow me to say it once—it is a singular deal you have struck, Zacharias! One would think anyone would be pleased to be apprenticed to the Sorcerer Royal."

"Unfortunately, Miss Gentleman is not just *anyone*," said Zacharias glumly.

WHEN Zacharias returned to his study there was a small brown leaf on his desk. It looked as though it had blown in through the window, but Zacharias knew it for what it was at once.

A closer inspection proved it to be no ordinary leaf: its veins glittered with gold, and gold edged the blade. The Fairy King's signature was on the other side: an inky hoof-stamp, redolent of earth and smoke.

His application for an audience had been accepted. Zacharias slipped the leaf into his pocket, feeling unwontedly nervous. It was what he had wanted—but the encounter must be managed carefully if it was to bear fruit.

That evening he laid the leaf on the floor of his study, and paced around it counterclockwise. The leaf would work its own magic. All he needed to do was circle it till the path was open.

As he trod his circumscribed round he found himself murmuring a little rhyme, which his nurse had used to sing to him, in his nursery days:

Ride a cock horse
To Banbury Cross
To see a black man
Upon a black horse—

"But no, I have confused it. How went it?"

A ring on his finger
A staff in his hand
The queerest magician
Ever seen in the land.

But that did not seem right either.

Zacharias stopped his pacing to puzzle it out, and saw that the gold veins on the leaf had spread out and multiplied, so that golden light lay in shining intersecting lines upon the floor. When he set his foot upon one of the lines, it widened into a shimmering path. He followed the path, and went through the walls of his study as though they were not there.

He ought to have found himself in the air, for his study was on the second floor, but instead he was walking down a dark tunnel. He felt as though he was asleep and dreaming, though his eyes were wide open. The only light was the golden glow from the path beneath his feet; the only sound that of his own voice, as he fumbled for the lyric:

As I was going to Charing Cross
I saw a fine lady upon a white horse
Runes at her fingers and spells at her toes
And she shall have magic wherever she goes—

"But that is all nonsense!

"There is," Zacharias said, "a great deal in nursery rhymes. I wonder that there has not been a proper study of them. I must propose it to the Committee."

"Mr. Zacharias Wythe," announced the liveried eel at the door. "Sorcerer Royal, and ambassador of the mortal kingdom of Great Britain!"

Zacharias stood in a great gilded hall, lit with a profusion of candles, and filled with people—if they could be called people. For a moment he stood blinking in the dazzling light, and the guests stared at him. A brief hush fell.

Then the noise rose again, the chatter as lively as ever. It had been several decades since a Sorcerer Royal had been seen in Fairyland, but time held a different meaning for the inhabitants of Fairy, and given the Queen's predilections, mortals were not so uncommon a sight as to provoke any lasting astonishment.

Zacharias was only one of many ambassadors waiting to be shown into the antechamber where the King held audience. He wandered around, still dazed by the strong magic by which he had been whisked to Fairy, narrowly avoiding stepping on the toes, flippers and tails of his fellow guests.

His anxiety about his upcoming audience was suspended for the moment, forgotten in the glory of Fairy. He had always hoped one day to see it, and this was such an opportunity as he would not soon have again.

In the mortal realm, *Fairyland* was used loosely to describe a number of magical nations which acknowledged themselves subject to the Queen and King of Elfland. The non-thaumaturgical might be even more imprecise, and use the term to describe all magical realms, whether connected to the Fairy Court or not. But of course, strictly only a creature of Elfland could be called a fairy: a being capable of changing its shape, but in its true form a sexless homunculus, pale-eyed and hairless.

Dragons, griffins, phoenixes, cockatrices, unicorns and the like were not native to Fairyland. It was a curious fact that in days past a familiar was more likely to encounter magical creatures of other species in England, in service to its master's associates, than it was to have met such creatures in Fairy. For in Fairy could be discerned all the divisions of nation and class which subsisted in mortal society.

Though at least Fairy prejudices did not reflect those of English society, and here Zacharias was no more conspicuous than any other foreign ambassador. He was not even the only person in the hall wearing the form of a dark-skinned man: a novel incident to Zacharias, which felt all the odder for the fact that he knew his mortal sight could not be trusted to discern the true face of things here in the land of illusion. The various beings crowding the hall likely bore a very different aspect at home, and in their own eyes.

Though some were less disguised than others. Zacharias leapt back as a platter of sweetmeats clattered upon the floor before him, brought down by the sweeping movement of a dragon's tail. A school of piscine footmen rushed to clean the mess, but the offender was unabashed.

"The Court might make better accommodation for its guests!" she exclaimed. "I declare the room grows smaller every year! Do not you think so, sir?"

Zacharias was taken aback to have criticism of his royal host so boldly demanded of him. He replied, in some confusion, that as this was his first visit, he was unable to judge.

"Your first visit?" said the dragon. She raised between two imposing talons a monocle the size of a dinner-plate, and peered through it at Zacharias. "Why, you are a mortal—a mortal English thaumaturge! You are never the creature who came and left us? I thought you might return, but not so soon."

"I think you have mistaken me for another, ma'am," said Zacharias. It was no great surprise, perhaps, that a black man and a white should appear much of a muchness to a dragon. "The thaumaturge you are thinking of is settled in England, and I believe has no intention of returning to Fairy. I am a different man altogether."

"Oh!" The glowing topaz of the dragon's eye swung closer to Zacharias. The pupil was a narrow black slit like a cat's. "Why, you are the new Sorcerer Royal! How very droll! I must say you are much handsomer than I expected. Some of the Sorcerers Royal I have seen *I* would have eaten in the egg." She let out an unexpected donkey's bray of a laugh.

"Magical ability does not always correspond with physical perfection in mortals," said Zacharias. "We differ from dragonkind in that respect."

For reasons quite unclear to Zacharias, an image rose in his mind of Prunella, kneeling on the floor and playing with her familiars, one dark lock slipping out of its restraints to curl around the shell of her ear. He dismissed the image, feeling unaccountably embarrassed.

"Oh, that is to understate the case entirely!" declared the dragoness. "I can never make out why mortal thaumaturges should be so ugly—puny, pale creatures, with scarcely any whiskers, and nothing in the way of scales. And as though it were not enough to be disagreeable-looking, they are shockingly bad behaved. You might do a great deal more to govern your thaumaturges, sir."

"I am sorry to hear you say so," said Zacharias warily. The dragon could only be speaking of Geoffrey Midsomer—it had been too long since any other thaumaturge had entered Fairy for her to be complaining of anyone else—but he had not heard that Midsomer had caused any offence at the Fairy Court. "I have not received any complaint regarding my colleagues' conduct."

"I suppose it is not only your people that are to blame," acknowledged the dragon. "He ought not to have asked her, but then, Lorelei ought not to have gone. If I had been summoned to the mortal realm by an upstart magician, you may be sure I should have resented it. She is a designing creature, however, and there is no knowing what plans she has laid. She was betrothed before, you know, and her tears and sighings over the previous fellow were beyond anything. And then to up and run away with a mortal! Oh, she is a deep one!"

"I beg your pardon," said Zacharias. His voice was calm, betraying (he hoped) none of his dismay, for he could not afford to show anything that could be taken as an admission of mortal guilt. "Do you mean to allege that a thaumaturge summoned a magical creature to England, to serve as his familiar?"

"Allege? Why, it is only the truth," said the dragon. "Everyone knows it!"

Spells to summon familiars had been unlawful since the Court had closed the border to traffic from England. This was part of the contract between the two nations, by which outright conflict had been avoided, and it was a compromise for which Englishmen should be more grateful than they were. Fairy had first proposed resolving their differences through war.

"But was not the thaumaturge prosecuted?" said Zacharias. Surely he would have heard if the Court had punished the illicit summoner. Relations had not deteriorated so far that the Court would not have mentioned such a breach to the Sorcerer Royal—had they?

"Well, no one has liked to decide what is to be done," said the dragon. "What with the Queen being away on her tour of the subject realms, I believe the King plans to overlook it as long as he may—Lorelei is such a favourite of Her Majesty's. They say Lorelei always intended to follow the mortal, and the whole thing was cooked up between the two of them."

"Indeed?" said Zacharias.

That meant there was an extra sorcerer at large in England—one so consumed by ambition as to be untroubled by the possibility of igniting a war with Fairyland. It could only be one man. No one else would have had the opportunity to become acquainted with the Queen's relations, and to prevail upon them to follow him to the mortal realm.

Midsomer would, of course, have concealed the existence of his familiar, since he had obtained it by a breach of their treaty with the Court. He would have required considerable resource for a summoning spell powerful enough to draw out a subject of Fairyland contrary to the Court's prohibition, and that must have disguised the first influx of fresh magic associated with the new familiar.

In time Midsomer's familiar would grow more powerful, as its understanding with its new master improved. There must already have been a perceptible upswelling in England's atmospheric magic, attributable to his familiar. Midsomer could not have concealed *that* forever—but he might have hoped to take the credit for the increase as part of his campaign to oust Zacharias.

"Do you recall the name of the gentleman in question, ma'am?" said Zacharias, in his most drearily official tone. "He should certainly be punished, if what you say is true."

"Do you know," said the dragon ingenuously, "the name has quite gone out of my mind. I would try to remember it, only I will begin to bore you with all this gossip." A knowing glint flashed in her eye. "I am sure you will have heard it all before, in any case. Leofric is well, I hope?"

Zacharias stiffened.

"We speak but infrequently," he said coldly.

The great halls where the guests mingled suggested that the King's own chamber would be correspondingly grand. Yet the dark earthen tunnels through which Zacharias was led seemed to fit with a more ancient tradition of Fairy architecture. Before the fairies had built, they had dug. As Zacharias wriggled through the narrow opening into the King's antechamber, he half-expected to emerge into a burrow.

In fact he might have been in any fashionable town house in London. The Fairy King's antechamber was decorated with velvet draperies slung over high windows, elegant carpets and furnishings all in the most modish style. There was only close-packed earth beyond the windows, however, and that, along with the pervading smell of fresh-turned soil and wood smoke, gave Zacharias the disconcerting feeling that he was in an ordinary mortal house that had been buried in an earthquake.

Flanked by fish-faced guardsmen, the Fairy King lounged upon his throne, marvellously made up, and dressed in a pink watered silk waistcoat that would have made Damerell blanch. His Majesty was quite the complete dandy, equal to any Pink of the *ton* riding in Hyde Park or loitering in White's, save that his attire was a decade behind the mode. Nor could the heavy perfume he wore entirely drown out his native scent—the scent of nighttime, wilderness and the hunt.

Zacharias made his leg, grateful for the fact that the courtesy excused him from speaking just yet. He had already discerned the gleam of intelligence in the heavy-lashed eyes behind the quizzing-glass. The King might be a strange whimsical creature, and the Queen the acknowledged power in the Fairy Court, but it was clear that only a fool would dismiss His Majesty on that account.

"We hope you do not mean to talk about familiars, Mr. Wythe," drawled the King. "That was all the last fellow ever spoke of. One might think England cared about nothing else. Indeed, now we think of it, have not the English just received a familiar from us? That fellow took her. What was his name—autumn, winter?"

The King peered at Zacharias expectantly.

"I am afraid I do not know his name myself, sir," said Zacharias. He almost wished he had not just learnt of Midsomer's crime. It was an awkward piece of intelligence to have hanging over his very first encounter with the Fairy King. He could not, of course, accuse a fellow thaumaturge of summoning himself a familiar before the Fairy Court, however little he liked the thaumaturge in question. "As a matter of fact, I was not aware that we had received a new familiar until today."

Before the King could answer, a lobster-headed courtier leant over to whisper in his ear. The King's eyes widened, and he coughed.

"Well! Never mind that. At any rate, England may have no more familiars from us. You will do very well without."

"Of course," ventured Zacharias, "I am delighted to hear that the Court has relaxed its policy so far as to permit a new familiar to cross to our realm. May I ask—"

"You may ask nothing!" snapped His Majesty, in one of the startling shifts of mood that characterised the fairy race. His brow darkened. A small grey rain cloud, grumbling with thunder, appeared above his head. "I call it a damned piece of impertinence, do not you?" This was to the lobster courtier, who nodded solemnly, his antennae twitching with disapproval. "Was not it plain that we had no wish to speak of familiars? If you persist with your tedious questions, we shall be compelled to dismiss you. There are quite enough bores in Fairyland as it is!"

"I beg your pardon, sir," said Zacharias, alarmed. "I cannot say how much I regret causing any offence. It is the last thing I should wish to do."

His Majesty sat back in his throne, still rather huffed, but as Zacharias conscientiously piled repentance upon remorse, the storm cloud above His Majesty's head grew paler and paler. Finally it dwindled to a white wisp, and a courtier blew it away. The King gestured to his courtiers to pass him a snuffbox, and inclined his head to show Zacharias might stop.

"We will pass over it," he said graciously. "What shall we talk of instead? I presume you came with a request for some boon or other?"

It was hardly an ideal time to draw the block on Britain's magic to the Fairy King's attention, but Zacharias could see no alternative. He might not have the opportunity again.

"I merely wished to apprise Your Majesty of an irregularity which has come to my attention," he said.

Zacharias had no doubt the Fairy Court was behind the block. The obstruction could not have been erected or maintained without the contrivance of the Queen and King, and the cork was as good as a royal seal. But he could hardly accuse Fairy outright of conspiring against Britain's interests. The only way he could raise the subject, and avoid drawing down upon himself a royal tantrum, was to feign earnest innocence.

"It appears there is a stoppage preventing the ordinary flow of magic through the border between our realms," he continued. "I sought this audience in order to inform Your Majesty, knowing what a deleterious effect the obstruction to the natural circulation of magic is likely to have on your country, as much as on mine."

The King had been in the act of taking a pinch of snuff when Zacharias began, and his speech was seen off by a thunderous sneeze from His Majesty. This was followed by a prolonged silence while the King buried his face in an enormous handkerchief.

A full five minutes passed before the King emerged from behind his handkerchief—a fraught five minutes for Zacharias, for he had no notion how the King would respond, though it was clear enough what the King was about. First one, and then another fish-faced courtier was drawn behind the screen of his handkerchief to confer in whispers. His Majesty's countenance wore rather a sullen cast when it finally reappeared.

"We do not see that you have any reason to complain," said the King without precursor. "It cannot make any difference to you that the flow of your magic has been diverted. England's magic has been declining for so long that you ought to have grown accustomed to it by now."

"Diverted?" said Zacharias. "I had understood that the magic remained in Fairyland."

"So it did at first, but the accumulation of magic made things so very awkward that we were compelled to pump it out elsewhere," said the King. "You need not look so alarmed. Our surplus did not go to France—we do not like them any better than you—for greed and sanguinariness there is nothing to choose between the two nations. No, we sent the excess to a few more docile mortal kingdoms, and they were very grateful. It was really rather gratifying to have given such pleasure."

Zacharias was conscious of how vital it was that he should tread carefully; he had no wish to provoke the King again, but the idea of Britain's magic being funnelled to other nations was one he could not endure in silence.

"Your Majesty, I must protest," he said. "Surely this is inconsistent with Fairyland's policy never to favour any mortal sovereign over another—an ancient policy, and a judicious one."

"And one we should like to hew to, if we could," said the King. "But the realities of government do not always permit the unobstructed application of principle. Besides, it would be easy enough for you to resolve the difficulty. The power to remove the block lies in your own sovereign's hands. All your nation needs to do is put an end to its shameful mistreatment of the vampiresses of Janda Baik."

Zacharias gaped. At his expression, His Majesty said: "Did those wretched lamiae not tell you? We declare, they are the most block-headed creatures that ever died! How is a threat to take away your magic meant to influence your conduct if you do not even know of it?"

Zacharias cast his mind back over everything he could recall of Mak Genggang, wishing now that he had troubled himself to attend more closely to her whispered dialogues with Prunella. It was true Mak Genggang had remarked upon the block on magic when she had arrived at Fobdown Purlieu, but she had not seemed to know the reason for it. Or had she indeed known, and sought by circuitous language to inform Zacharias? Perhaps he had merely failed to understand her meaning, cloaked as it was in Oriental inscrutability.

But that will not do, thought Zacharias. Mak Genggang had not been inscrutable about anything whatsoever. She had expressed her sentiments towards Sultan Ahmad with a clarity and directness adapted to the meanest understanding.

"No," said Zacharias finally. "We did not know it was the lamiae of Janda Baik who desired our magic to be stopped." He hesitated. It was difficult to know what he might say without trying the King's patience too far. But surely it must be permitted to raise the question. "May I ask, sir, why you acceded to their request?"

"It is all the fault of that blasted sultan, of whom your sovereign is so fond," said the King. "He was making it so damnably hot for the vampiresses that they threatened to return to Fairyland unless we did as they asked. Just when we thought we were rid of them forever! They are distant cousins of Her Majesty—Her Majesty abounds in pestilential relations—so they cannot be denied, but you can have no notion of what an appallingly uncomfortable neighbour an Oriental lamia makes. Tracks in blood everywhere, smells continually of vinegar, has not the decency to wear her feet the right way around, or to put away her innards, but leaves them dangling out in the open for everyone to see."

His Majesty paused to brood over the iniquity of his wife's relations.

"It would be an end to all peace if they returned," he said, with a sigh. "We should give them our first-born child if that would persuade them to stay away. Indeed, we made the offer, but they would not look at poor Cuthbert. No, you will have to make do without fresh magic, Mr. Wythe, unless you can persuade your sovereign to refrain from interfering with the lamiae. He must take his chances if he intends to continue this uncertain business of Empire-building. You never know what may come of it, or whose third cousin you may offend."

This was clearly intended for a dismissal. The King said to a courtier:

"You may send in the next fellow. Good day to you, Mr. Wythe."

Zacharias bowed. He did not say what every thaumaturge in Britain knew—that the Sorcerer Royal's word now had little weight with his sovereign. He lacked the influence even to dissuade his Government from requiring the Society to pay its rents, much less to discourage it from adopting any course it desired regarding other nations.

The royals of Fairy were wont to adopt diverse guises, and it could not be supposed that such a trifle as skin colour would be of any account to them. But perhaps they were aware of mortals' peculiarities in that regard, and had some notion of how easily the staff might be wrested from Zacharias's grasp. Why should the Fairy King comply with the requests of a temporary Sorcerer Royal? His Majesty might believe he would be replaced soon enough. Thinking of the forces arrayed against him, Zacharias could not bring himself to disagree.

18

"AND HAVE YOU seen this Miss Prunella Gentleman, of whom so much is said?" said Lady Throgmorton, as she sat supping a cup of black bohea with her friend Alethea Gray. Their intimacy was of but two months' duration, but that it was a true friendship was evidenced by the enthusiasm with which each spoke of the other:

"A most fascinating woman!" said Mrs. Gray of her friend. "Truly beautiful! Truly gracious!"

"A very good creature indeed," said Lady Throgmorton of hers.

"Miss Gentleman? Oh, I have not met her above half a dozen times," said Mrs. Gray airily.

Mrs. Gray would not have dreamt of omitting to meet Miss Gentleman a day before everyone else had discovered in themselves a desperate desire to see her. Mr. Gray had made his considerable wealth in trade, and Mrs. Gray's parents had been no one in particular. She was well aware that her intimacy with the leaders of high society rested upon her talent for being in the right place at the right time—for always guessing the piece of news everyone longed to know, and having the acquaintance of every person worth knowing.

"A delightful girl," she said. "So original! Her manners so wild and unaffected, and yet so pleasing!"

"She is pretty, of course?"

"Oh, she is well enough. I do not admire dark women half so much as fair," said Mrs. Gray. Lady Throgmorton and her three daughters were all as golden-locked as china shepherdesses. "But she certainly shows to advantage among the Season's debutantes. It seems impossible these days to find any truly pretty girls; it makes even a dark little thing like Miss Gentleman seem a phoenix. Your girls are an exception, of course. How I long for their coming out! What an occasion that will be!"

"My daughters certainly never needed magic to improve their complexions or curl their hair," said Lady Throgmorton with asperity. "What we see in our ballrooms is not so much a falling off in the general level of beauty, Alethea, but an undeceiving—a *disenchantment*, I might say—of a public that has grown accustomed to the illusions of vain chits."

Mrs. Gray had more intriguing news to impart of Miss Gentleman, and she was reluctant to be diverted from the subject by the deceptions practised by young ladies. "I doubt Miss Gentleman is party to any such sophistications. It seems she was raised in some out-of-the-way little village—never came to town, and was kept ignorant of who she was. She is being brought out by Lady Wythe as a favour to her father."

Mrs. Gray spoke these last words with such an air of mystery that Lady Throgmorton's eyebrows rose.

"Her father?" said Lady Throgmorton.

"You will already have guessed his identity, of course," said Mrs.

Gray in a conspiratorial whisper. "It is a great secret, but it is obvious to anyone who has spoken with the girl. No similarity in appearance, mind you. It is clear she is the likeness of her mother. But she has such a way of holding her head, and using her hands, and saying droll things, that—in short, one only wonders how the family contrived to conceal the connection for so long! Blood will out, after all."

"It does, indeed," said Lady Throgmorton. She had not the least idea who Mrs. Gray was referring to, but Mrs. Gray nodded and winked so, it would be too embarrassing to admit ignorance in the face of such knowingness. She would get the truth of the matter from her lady's maid, Lady Throgmorton resolved.

"She is his natural child, of course," said Mrs. Gray. "They are being very close about who the mother was. Of course, *what* she was anyone can see from the girl's complexion—but he is not the first gentleman to contract an undesirable connection with a native! The indiscretion is years old now, and he has no wish for such an ancient scandal to be dug up again."

"Quite," said Lady Throgmorton, her mind racing through the list of noble gentlemen who could possibly be meant by Mrs. Gray's mysterious allusions.

"Poor child! I can find it in my heart to pity her!" sighed Mrs. Gray. "To know nothing of her own mother! And in the circumstances, she could not wish to know more. Her father has not been ungenerous, however. I am told he has settled upon her—"

She named to Lady Throgmorton such a sum as made that estimable woman nearly spill her tea.

"That is generosity indeed! I suppose he has no other children?"

"Oh, it would be a mere trifle to such a one as he!" said Mrs. Gray.

In truth she could not have said if Miss Gentleman's father had one child or five: she knew no better than Lady Throgmorton who he was. From her enquiries, however, she was confident that neither did anyone else. The risk that her ignorance would be discovered was as low as the rewards of appearing to know the truth were high—and after all, Mrs. Gray reflected, she was bound to discover the truth sooner or later. She always did.

"Little wonder the men are all madly in love with her! She could be black as coal, and still have every gentleman in London at her feet with that fortune," said Lady Throgmorton, who cultivated a bluntness that her friends described as stimulating, and her detractors as vulgar tactlessness. "Is she a nice sort of girl, would you say, the mother aside?"

"Quite unspoilt," Mrs. Gray assured her. "I do not think she is so very brown—you would hardly know she was not English by candlelight. And her manners cannot be faulted. She showed me every attention, and seemed scarcely to regard the gentlemen, though some of them were very desperate to be noticed."

"I have no notion of such affectation," sniffed Lady Throgmorton. "The girl has simply concluded that the best way of holding a gentleman's attention is to pretend not to value it, you may be certain."

Despite her skepticism, Lady Throgmorton was not disinclined to take an interest in Miss Gentleman. She had a nephew who was getting to the age for marriage—a nephew whose conduct might be restrained if he had a wife, and whose numerous creditors would be pacified by the sum Mrs. Gray had named as being the extent of Miss Gentleman's patrimony.

"Still, if she is a pretty-spoken sort of girl, she might do for Percy," continued Lady Throgmorton. "You may introduce her to me, Alethea. Catherine longs to see Percy settled. He is not in want of a fortune, of course, but a pretty, modest, dutiful sort of girl would make just the wife for him."

"I will certainly introduce her to you. What an excellent thing it would be for the girl!" cried Mrs. Gray, though not without an inward observation that Percy's previous inamoratas had not been remarkable for either modesty or dutifulness. "You will be delighted with her."

"With all of London in ecstasies, I could hardly be so contrary as to disagree," said Lady Throgmorton drily.

For Damerell had acted according to his word, and brought out Prunella with *éclat*. The great thing about the rumours he had spread abroad, said Damerell, was how easily they might be denied.

"I may have suggested that her noble father had not left Miss Gentleman a prey to want, but I never breathed a word about who he might be, or how much he had given her," he said to a disapproving Zacharias. "Every such detail is a vulgar addition, made after the story left my hands. However, as no one has named her parents, it will be difficult for anyone to explode the tale, and even if it is discredited, Miss Gentleman can always disclaim any knowledge of it."

Zacharias could not like this. "Surely it can only cause her embarrassment once it is discovered there is not a shred of truth in the tale."

But Prunella thought Damerell's scheme a capital one.

"All that is needed is for a gentlemanlike creature of independent means to fall violently in love with me," she declared. "Then he will not give a fig if I have a duke for a father, or no father at all. And I do not see why I should not persuade at least one gentleman to fall in love with me—indeed, I hope to persuade several!"

She was a protégé after Damerell's own heart. Prunella took to the ballrooms of London in the spirit of ruthless calculation of a general entering a battlefield. Within a week she had marked out the Lady Jerseys and Countess Esterházys of the world, who wielded the most influence among the *ton*, and she laid herself out to please them. She took no notice of the numerous gentlemen who promptly lost their hearts to her.

"I shall not soon stop being pretty and saucy," she explained, "so I need not worry about losing the interest of the gentlemen. But I must have the good opinion of the women, for their word is all the capital I have, and I am lost if they take it into their heads to disapprove of me."

Zacharias might tut, and Lady Wythe look anxious, but Prunella was in her element. She was a complete success, and had never enjoyed herself so thoroughly. As Damerell said complacently, she paid for dressing: the drab serge dresses and absurd pink satin of the past were banished, and Prunella was attired in diaphanous muslin and jewel-hued silks instead. The simple style of gown in fashion set her off to admiration, and her dark colouring meant she could support the most vivid hues. There was a crimson velvet pelisse in particular, trimmed with white fur and worn with a white beaver hat crowned with a nodding plume of ostrich feathers, which filled Damerell with solemn pride.

"If I am remembered for nothing else, I shall die content," he said to Zacharias. "I should say Miss Gentleman was in a fair way to gaining a proper understanding of dress, save that her eye is not quite unerring. She has conceived an inexplicable affection for a wicked green bonnet in particular, that makes her look as though she were expiring of the yellow fever. I wish you would advise her to burn it."

"If I had any belief that Miss Gentleman would attend to anything I said, I would not talk of hats," said Zacharias. "She ought to pay less attention to frivolity, and more to her studies."

Zacharias was far from pleased with the whole business. Though he was busier than ever with his duties, he appointed a time every day when he visited Lady Wythe's house, and sat with Prunella at her lessons. She remembered everything he taught her, and he had no complaint to make of her practical ability. Still, he could not help but take offence when she started nodding off over her books, and he was almost cross when this occurred a second time at one of their sessions.

"Though I should not presume to advise upon your conduct in society, I could wish you would not stay out so late," he said. "Surely it would not injure your matrimonial prospects to leave a ball at ten, instead of half past one?"

Prunella started awake.

"Oh, I am sorry! Did I doze off again?" she said, stifling a yawn. "How shockingly uncivil of me. But to leave a party so early would not be civil either, you know. It is likely to offend one's hostess, and then one could not be sure that one had met all the eligible gentlemen, for some of them arrive quite late. Mr. Damerell says he never arrives at a ball before eleven."

"I should not recommend modelling yourself upon Damerell," said Zacharias, frowning. "He is an excellent fellow, but I never knew a sorcerer that did less magic. Indeed, Prunella, neither your familiars nor your studies are receiving the attention they merit. There is a great deal for you to learn, to know how best to serve both your familiars and yourself, and what with all your distractions you are in danger of neglecting them."

"I am sure they do not think so," said Prunella indignantly. "Do you, my darlings?" The familiars were slumbering in a pile at her feet, and showed no sign of hearing her. "They are with me all the time, and they understand me perfectly. After all, there is little purpose in forgoing balls for books if I must conceal my abilities, and pretend I know nothing of magic, and was never taught the difference between a witch bottle and a hag stone. If I am only going to be married at the end of it, I may as well devote my energies to ensuring I dance the best quadrille at every ball."

Zacharias felt the reproach in this, and said gravely:

"I can see that your education may seem purposeless to you, since it must be kept secret for now. That is not to say you shall never use it, however, and indeed it is my aim that you will use it, for your own benefit and others'. Magicians are obstinate creatures, but they can be persuaded, and they esteem power above all things. Three familiars are as effective an argument for feminine magic as they will ever have heard."

"You have the staff of the Sorcerer Royal, which is just as good an argument, and they still do not like you," pointed out Prunella.

Zacharias felt suddenly weary. His complaint disrupted his sleep, and he was so busy with the duties of his office that he had scarcely had time to think of what was to be done about Midsomer's schemes and Fairyland's block on magic. He had proposed to John Edgeworth a meeting to discuss the Janda Baik affair, but Edgeworth had supplied one excuse after another to avoid him. Zacharias doubted the same excuses were offered to Geoffrey Midsomer.

Lady Wythe's servants had built the fire conscientiously high, and the room was too close and hot for thought. Zacharias rose to open a window and, looking out, saw London sharply delineated in a thin golden light. It was a day of clear blue skies and crisp air, mingling winter and spring in equal parts.

"What do you say to a walk?" he said abruptly. "We will have to practise certain spells outdoors, in time, and I have prepared a space in the Park for the purpose. It is hidden from view by an enchantment, which only I can unlock. Let us see if you are able to find it. That will be a useful test of my magic, and a practical lesson for you."

Prunella brightened. "Certainly! Let me put away my familiars"—they had agreed the familiars should be hidden in her valise when she was out, to avoid their detection—"and I shall be with you directly."

It was unfashionably early to be visiting Hyde Park, and there was no one to be seen. As Zacharias and Prunella trod along the path, it was as though they were the only two people in the world.

"I see you have a new hat," said Zacharias.

Even to Zacharias's untutored eye Prunella's dress was an improvement on the plain attire in which she had first appeared to him. This particular bonnet was curiously unbecoming, however: it was a bright pea green, and seemed to draw out from her dusky cheek some of its glow.

"It is my favourite hat," said Prunella. "Damerell will have it that it is unbecoming, but one does grow curiously attached to such things sometimes, does not one?"

"Indeed," said Zacharias. Now that he thought of it, had not Damerell said something to him about hats? There was something peculiar about this one, as well—something he did not at first identify, and then could scarcely believe when he saw it.

His hand flashed out, but he was just a second too late. The bonnet lifted off Prunella's head, morphing into a green-feathered bird with a wide-eyed face—the face of a human child, save for the golden beak in place of the nose and mouth. The simurgh sought refuge on Prunella's shoulder, chirping in alarm.

"Appear as you are not!" snapped Zacharias. As the glamour dropped over the simurgh, the child's face vanished, replaced by an ordinary bird's head. A vivid-hued parrot on the popular Miss Gentleman's shoulder would draw attention, but not nearly so much as the simurgh would have done.

"How could you tell?" cried Prunella.

"Your reticule is the unicorn, and as for your pelisse—"

"It is I," piped a tiny voice. The elvet was the only one of Prunella's familiars that had learnt to speak in a human tongue. The unicorn and simurgh spoke only their own languages, and communicated with Prunella in thought.

"What are you doing?" said Zacharias. His spirits had begun to improve the moment they were out of doors, but now his voice sharpened, though he strove to keep it even. "Did not we agree upon the importance of keeping your familiars hidden?"

Prunella tried desperately to look solemn, but a smile would keep breaking through her gravity. The elvet's high-pitched giggle could be heard in the vicinity of her pelisse.

"But that is the clever thing about it! They are completely hidden," she said. "They have been so longing to see the world, and I could not think of a way to contrive it, till Nidget hit upon the notion. Nidget is the one who understands shape-shifting, for unicorns and phoenixes do not as a rule, but it taught the others as a favour to me. They have learnt remarkably quickly, though the bonnet is not quite right. Tjandra refuses to be red, though it would be so much more becoming. He likes being a hat very well, however—it gives him an excellent vantage point for looking about himself."

"Is it not possible to make you aware of the danger," said Zacharias, "the *terrible* danger, of the familiars' being detected? I have explained what public outrage it would cause if it were to be discovered that you possessed these familiars. Every effort would be made to separate you from them. And if you will not consider yourself or your familiars, consider me. My position would be untenable if it was revealed that I knew of your familiars, and did nothing to prevent their attachment to you."

Prunella's face grew stormy. "As if you could prevent it!"

Zacharias held her gaze until the colour rose in her cheeks, and she dropped her eyes.

"I know I could not. That would not signify to the Society," said Zacharias. "They would consider the responsibility for the disaster mine. And it would be a disaster, Prunella—a disaster for which I would be called to account."

Prunella rolled her shoulders as though she sought to shrug off the burden he had placed upon them. She said ungraciously:

"I am sorry."

Zacharias looked at the small head still held defiantly high. He was shaken by a pang of he knew not what emotion—whether it were pity or admiration, he could not tell. His anger dissipated.

"It is my first concern that you—all of you—should be safe," he said gently.

Prunella nodded, though she refused to look at him. In a low voice shorn of bravado, sounding quite unlike herself, she said:

"I like to have them by me. One feels less out of place."

This took Zacharias aback. "Do you feel out of place?"

"Why, of course," said Prunella. She paused. "I have never been among my own people, you know. At Mrs. Daubeney's I did not quite belong with the girls, and the servants would not have me. I was not even Mrs. D's, though I was there on her sufferance. Even now, when I am received with such cordiality, and scarcely go anywhere in London without meeting someone of my acquaintance . . . it is strange to know you would be cast off by the people who greet you so warmly, if they knew the whole truth about you."

"There are advantages to being outcast," said Zacharias. "One is set at liberty from many anxieties. There is no call to worry about what others will think, when it is clear that they already think the worst."

"I suppose you ought to know," said Prunella. "But you do not seem to benefit much from *your* liberty. Damerell says you are the most nice-conscienced, duty-bound fellow he knows."

Zacharias smiled without mirth. His chief aim had always been that he should stand beyond reproach in word and deed, since his colour seemed to prove a ground for any allegation. He was content—or at least resigned—but he needed no reminder of how he was circumscribed.

"I am held by bonds of gratitude," he said. The words were bitter on his tongue. "I was born a slave, you know, and should have passed my days in backbreaking labour if Sir Stephen had not taken notice of me. It was by the merest chance that we met. He was travelling on the *Minerva* in the West Indies, conducting a study of maritime magic levels. He purchased me from the captain, brought me home to England, manumitted and educated me. He was persuaded that with instruction I would be capable of attaining the highest peaks of thaumaturgical achievement—that I might, in time, even become Sorcerer Royal myself."

A curious sympathy had existed between Zacharias and Prunella since the day they had first met, despite their differences in temperament and disposition, but there had also been constraint. Prunella was always on her guard, and Zacharias could not be completely easy around her—for more reasons than one, not all of which he wished to articulate to himself.

But today the restless energy that usually animated Prunella was tempered; the tension in her quick movements and ready speech was blunted. Zacharias realised that he had seen her calm and collected, speaking audacities with composure, but he had not seen her truly at ease. Perhaps she began finally to trust him.

"You must have been very young when you met Sir Stephen, for Lady Wythe is always talking of what you were like as a boy," said Prunella.

"I was but an infant," said Zacharias. He added, with some awkwardness, "I was travelling with my mother and father, who belonged to the captain of the *Minerva*."

A fine line appeared between Prunella's eyebrows. "Did not Sir Stephen purchase your parents as well?"

"No," said Zacharias. "Presumably he did not discern the same potential in them."

The statement brought up the old anger and confusion, followed by the accustomed guilt, that he should be so ungrateful as to resent the man who had rescued him from bondage. And yet he did resent Sir Stephen, even now.

"I don't see why you feel obliged to him at all," said Prunella. "What right had he to part you from your parents when you were so young?"

Her words seemed to echo Zacharias's own thoughts, thoughts he had suppressed many a time, striving to feel the unclouded gratitude expected of him. What might his life have been, with a father and mother? It could not have cost Sir Stephen very much to purchase them as well—certainly not enough to strain his ample resources.

How could his benevolence have extended so far as to move him to free Zacharias, but no further?

But it had been impossible to ask these questions of Sir Stephen or Lady Wythe, whose affection could not be doubted. That Zacharias's own love for them was leavened with anger was best left unsaid; he tried not to know it himself.

"Very probably I would have been separated from my parents in any event," he said. "What assurance can I feel that my parents were not in time separated from each other, against their will, and they powerless to prevent it?"

The answers to these questions were too painful to pursue to their conclusion, even in thought. They had only ever served to increase the complicated unhappiness that lay in wait whenever he thought of his parents.

Prunella cast her eyes down, her face troubled. The simurgh nestled close to her and nipped her ear.

"It would be terrible not to have anything of your mother and father," said Prunella, speaking half to herself. "Not to have anything at all . . . Have you ever tried to find them, Zacharias?"

Zacharias stared at her. "Find them?"

"It is not such an extraordinary notion, surely," said Prunella. "If I had money, as you do, I would go and look for my mother and father. Why, you do not even know they are dead. They might be alive! Just think, perhaps you could meet them—you could speak to them!" She clenched her fists, but fell silent.

They walked wordlessly together for a while, but when Zacharias spoke after a long pause, it was as if he was merely continuing a conversation they had been having all along.

"I would not have been rescued from my bondage if not for Sir Stephen's conviction that he could make of me something extraordinary. I was not told that I must prove the African's ability to English thaumaturgy, and Sir Stephen never said in so many words that he wished me to succeed him as Sorcerer Royal. But that these were the purposes for which I was educated was clear. Many men and women have lived and died desperate for the advantages I have been granted by a capricious Fate. How could I not perform as expected?"

"Zacharias," said Prunella. "Did not you *want* to be Sorcerer Royal?"

She sounded astonished, as if the alternative had never crossed her mind before.

"I have found that opportunity brings with it its own set of chains," said Zacharias, after a pause. "That power generates demands which cannot easily be gainsaid—as you are learning now, I think."

"Yes," said Prunella. She raised earnest eyes to his face. "I know I am a shocking burden to you, Zacharias, but I do wish I could help. I should like to be a friend to you, if I could."

For some reason she blushed. Zacharias felt a corresponding warmth rise in his own face. He pressed her hand lightly, and found he would like to retain it. Discerning this inclination in himself alarmed him so much that he dropped Prunella's hand, and assumed his most businesslike manner.

"There is one thing you could do," he said. "I need to speak to Mak Genggang. Do you know where she is?"

19

PRUNELLA'S CONVERSATION WITH Zacharias in the Park had left her in a thoughtful mood. Though she was meant to attend a card party that evening, she was just as glad when Lady Wythe declared herself too indisposed to go.

"I am sorry to spoil your fun, my dear," said Lady Wythe, blowing her nose. "Could not that charming young friend of yours, Mrs. Kendle, go with you? She is a flighty creature to chaperone anyone, but you are not likely to get into any sort of scrape at Mrs. Cornwallis's."

"Sophia is engaged tonight, I believe," said Prunella. "I shall not mind a quiet evening. Mr. Wythe has reproved me for my want of industry, so I mean to make a great advance in my studies, and amaze him tomorrow with the perfection of my formulae."

"I hope you will not overwork yourself," said Lady Wythe. "Zacharias drives himself so hard that he is not properly conscious of the toll he is likely to exact by demanding the same of others."

Prunella promised to exercise restraint, though she said ruefully, "I think there is little danger I shall do too much!"

She began the evening's work with the best of intentions, but the elvet picked a quarrel with the other two familiars: the unicorn and simurgh possessed placid tempers, but Nidget was a jealous, spiteful creature, and objected to sharing Prunella's affections with the others. It was necessary to separate them, and placate Nidget. And then Nidget was so amusing, and told her such curious things about Fairyland, though it had only partial, confused memories of the place, that somehow Prunella had not got past the second chapter of the book she was reading when Lady Wythe's butler announced a visitor.

"Why, Sophia," exclaimed Prunella. "I thought you had gone to your party. You have come at an awkward time, I am afraid. Lady Wythe is unwell, and has retired for the evening."

Sophia Kendle was a pretty young creature, vastly proud of having been snapped up in her first Season. She had fallen madly in love with Prunella the moment they met: "I am sure you are destined to marry a duke, you are so pretty and clever, and then your not knowing anything of your family is so romantic," she declared.

She had just turned twenty-one, but looked younger as she danced up the hall to take her friend's hands. She formed a curious contrast with her husband—a contemporary of Sir Stephen's and a middling thaumaturge, possessed of a considerable fortune.

"We did not come to see Lady Wythe, save to request a favour of her," said Mr. Kendle.

"What Kendle means to say is that he is a cruel beast, and has decreed that we must go to a stupid party of thaumaturges, where I shall know no one, and be bored to death," said Sophia. "I plagued him to stop here, so that I could beg you to come with me. Pray say you will, darling."

Prunella hesitated. She did not know Mr. Kendle well, but he did not look as though he desired Prunella to join the party.

"I do not know that Lady Wythe will like it," she said, but Sophia cut in eagerly:

"But she can have no objection, for I shall chaperone you, and that will be ever so droll! The party is a very respectable one, only you know thaumaturges are such tedious creatures, my dear Kendle excepted, I *could* not endure a whole evening among them without a friendly face to look upon. I meant to go with Amelia, but my sister is unwell, and I do not expect it will make any difference to our hosts if we exchange her for you."

"Miss Gentleman does not wish to go, Sophia. It is uncivil to insist, and we ought not to keep the horses standing," said Mr. Kendle.

Sophia drooped, crestfallen. Mr. Kendle looked so self-satisfied that Prunella was suddenly possessed by a spirit of perversity. She had not intended to accept Sophia's invitation, but she should like to discomfit Mr. Kendle: Prunella disliked a man who would crow over his wife. Then, too, Mr. Kendle's odd manner kindled her curiosity. What reason had he to dislike her?

"Not at all!" said Prunella. "I should be pleased to go, and it is kind of you to ask, Sophia dear, for I should have been dull here by myself. Let me run up to Lady Wythe to beg her leave, but I am sure she will not mind, and we need not keep your horses waiting any longer."

Lady Wythe had no objection to Prunella's accompanying her friend ("Though it is curious I should not have heard of a thaumaturgical ball!" she remarked), and they were soon off in the Kendles' carriage.

The mystery of Mr. Kendle's manner was satisfied sooner than Prunella expected. It was dark when the carriage drew up outside a town house. The windows were blazing with amber light; carriages lined the street outside; and altogether it seemed a very considerable party. Prunella was glad she had worn her primrose silk, though it would have been a trifle grand for Mrs. Cornwallis's party (Mrs. Cornwallis had a wealthy bachelor cousin, who had already declared his fondness for a pair of snapping black eyes).

Prunella had not contrived to catch the hosts' name amid Sophia's chatter. She had prepared an expression both charming and apologetic as they entered the house. When she saw the hostess she forgot her preparation altogether, however, and gaped.

"May I introduce my wife's friend, Miss Gentleman?" said Mr. Kendle.

Mrs. Geoffrey Midsomer did not seem to know the name, or to remember Prunella from the Spring Ball. But then there had been a great many people at the Ball, and Prunella only recognised Mrs. Midsomer because of her part in its spectacular close.

"Delighted," said Mrs. Midsomer. "How do you do, Miss Gentleman? How kind of you to come, Mr. Kendle. Geoffrey values your support beyond measure."

Mr. Kendle glanced nervously at Prunella. "We look forward to the evening, indeed."

Indeed, thought Prunella. She did not at all regret coming.

IT was clear the Midsomers were not aware of Prunella's connection with the Wythes, which suited her perfectly. It was a detail they might easily have missed, as Mr. Kendle had done. Prunella doubted he had known that his wife's friend had any connection with Lady Maria Wythe until Sophia had insisted on going to her house.

She contrived to put Mr. Kendle at his ease by disclaiming any acquaintance with the Sorcerer Royal: "Oh, he frightens me to death! Lady Wythe wonders that I am never to be found when he visits!" When he had left her and Sophia to speak to his friends, Prunella took care to ensure they were lost in the crowd, well away from their hosts.

She wished she had asked Zacharias about Geoffrey Midsomer. He was the ill-tempered man who had been so uncivil to Zacharias at the Ball, but she knew from stray snatches of conversation between

Zacharias, Damerell and Lady Wythe that that was not all. Whatever the trouble was, it must account for Mr. Kendle's being so froward about her accompanying Sophia.

"What a fascinating party!" she said to Sophia, looking about with unfeigned interest. "But this is not an official Society event, is it, Sophia?"

Sophia was not sure. "There does seem a vast number of thaumaturges! I never saw so many in my life. Kendle said it was to be a gathering only of Mr. Midsomer's friends, but it seems he has a great many friends. What a curious creature that Mrs. Midsomer is! Did you think her pretty, Prunella?"

"I did not."

"Nor I. Yet the Midsomer family is an old one, much esteemed in magical circles, Kendle says, though not wealthy. Mr. Midsomer could have had anyone he liked."

Prunella thought of the broad, potato-like face of Mrs. Midsomer. It had neither charm nor beauty, but there had been a curious power in those restless, searching grey eyes.

"Perhaps he likes her," said Prunella.

"People have the oddest tastes," said Sophia. "What are you looking at?"

Prunella's eye had been caught by a painting, an unremarkable daub in oils of a brownish-grey landscape. Anything less appealing could scarcely be conceived, and yet the painting was housed in a gorgeously worked gold frame, with a spray of hothouse flowers set beneath it like an offering. She pointed this out to Sophia, who exclaimed:

"But that must be the picture that prophesies! Kendle told me of it. It is a family heirloom. The Midsomers have had it since the Conquest, and they are sinfully proud of it."

There was a dark smudge in the corner of the picture, which closer attention revealed to be a cloaked figure huddled under a ledge of rock.

"That must be the oracle," said Sophia. "Kendle says the painting is an enchantment, and the oracle speaks prophecies when the mood takes her."

"'Her'?" said Prunella, looking at the smudge with fresh interest. She would have questioned Sophia further, if she had not seen the gleam of silver on the small table beneath the painting.

There was a singing orb on the table. It might have been the twin of the one she wore around her neck.

"Is something amiss?" said Sophia.

"No, why should you ask?" said Prunella. She picked up the singing orb, remarking casually: "What a pretty trinket! But you were speaking of this prophetess, Sophia. I thought women were not permitted the practise of magic?"

"Oh, the oracle was not a mortal!" said Sophia, laughing. "What a diverting notion! No, she was a sibyl, Kendle says, which is a fairy, you know. She was trapped within the picture by the artist, a thaumaturge who had been attached to her, but was betrayed in his affections."

As Sophia spoke Prunella examined the singing orb. Their arms were still linked loosely together, and she hoped Sophia would not feel the rapid beating of her heart, or the trembling in her hand.

The orb was not quite the same as her own. It was of a different, darker metal, from which the candlelight struck bluish green sparks. It was carved with different marks, too: minute pinpricks, forming lines and flourishes that intertwined across the surface of the orb.

"What a tragic story!" said Prunella. She was wondering whether, if she could only distract Sophia for a moment, she could conceal the orb within her reticule. It was wicked to steal, of course, and Zacharias would be cross if he discovered it, but surely there was no harm in borrowing the object for a time. A comparison with her own orb might enable all sorts of instructive experiments.

"Yes, isn't it? I adore a tragedy!" said Sophia. "Kendle tells such gruesome tales of the attachments between mortals and fairies, and they are invariably tragical, for the fairies' caprice is beyond anything. You should hear how the Fairy Queen treats her mortal paramours when she tires of them! They are turned into mantuas and half-boots, transformed into newts, and who knows what else besides. I am sure *her* poor swain wished he had never taken it into his head to fall in love with a fairy!" She gestured at the painting.

"Why do you say so?" said a new voice.

Prunella hastily returned the orb to the table, and turned to face the lady who had joined them.

"Mrs. Midsomer!" she said brightly. "Mrs. Kendle and I were admiring your lovely painting."

"It is an ugly piece, but Geoffrey likes it," said Mrs. Midsomer. Her strange eyes seemed almost to glow with their own light. "And the sibyl serves her purpose. You do not seem to admire her, ma'am?"

Sophia was crimson. It was awkward for her to have been overheard speaking of the Fairy Queen's discarded beaux by the wife of one such.

"One feels sorry for the poor man, you know," she stammered. "To have his confidence so betrayed!"

"But he died of old age, whereas she is doomed to pass the rest of her life trapped betwixt gilt frames," said Mrs. Midsomer. She turned to Prunella. "I saw you were interested in my bauble, Miss Gentleman."

Prunella preserved her composure. Mrs. Midsomer was a whimsical creature, it was clear, but she need not think she would intimidate Prunella Gentleman.

"It is a pretty thing!" said Prunella. "I was wondering, ma'am, what it is for?"

Mrs. Midsomer gave her such a penetrating look Prunella almost wondered whether she was able to discern Prunella's own orb, concealed beneath the bodice of her dress. But instead of replying, Mrs Midsomer leaned over, and said to the painting:

"How are you keeping, sibyl?"

Her loud, harsh voice plucked at a memory in Prunella's mind. Had not Zacharias said something about the voice one must use when casting spells?

"Magic hates a whisper," he had said. "The forces of the supernatural respond best to a good strong bellow."

The huddled figure in the painting rose, revealing a lined, weary face.

The sibyl had once been beautiful, but age and isolation had worn her down. The hair under the rough fabric of her hood was silver, the face seamed with lines of sorrow.

"What d'you want of me?" she snapped. Her voice issued from the canvas clear and curiously full-bodied, in contrast to her flattened form. "When Ormsby locked me away I thought I should at least profit from some peace, but no—it's pester, pester, pester, all the day long. 'What's my fate, sibyl? What's to become of me?' Surely that's clear enough—death and the ruin of all your hopes, the same for all mortals."

"Not me," said Mrs. Midsomer.

The sibyl pursed her lips. "I would not be so cocksure if I were you. Death and despair are hardly the preserve of mortalkind, as you'll find soon enough."

"It is not my fortune I wish you to tell," said Mrs. Midsomer. "I shall make my own. But tell me of this woman." She gestured at Prunella. "Who is she? Have I anything to fear from her?"

The sibyl raised her great hollow eyes, and Prunella felt Sophia's arm quiver in hers.

"The mortal woman has love, but she will lose it, and know the bitterness of despair," said the sibyl. "Which is to say, she likes her husband now, but will soon stop when she knows better."

"That," said Sophia, trembling in indignation, "is exceedingly impertinent!"

But Mrs. Midsomer overrode her protest, snapping at the sibyl:

"It is the other mortal I meant! What do you see of her past and future?"

Prunella had been trying to make herself scarce, stepping sideways so that Sophia hid her from the sibyl's view, but she did not move quickly enough. The sibyl's gaze fixed upon Prunella, and her eyes widened. *"You!"*

It was a large, busy, noisy room, and the press of the crowd had been such that their curious interchange with the sibyl had gone unnoticed till now. At her cry heads turned in their direction, and conversations broke off in exclamations.

"I do not need my fortune told, thank you," said Prunella hastily.

"What do I see?" cried the sibyl in a voice that to the unfortunate Prunella sounded like a foghorn. "I see the Grand Sorceress, her palms embroidered like a bride's in mortal blood! I see the Keeper of the Seven Spirits, mistress of the four points of the realm. I see the past and future of English magic, converging in one. I see the Undersecretary of Wonder and the Queen of the Five Boroughs of Magic (the last merely an honorary title, of course). Hail to thee, Lady, who brings such visions with her—hail and well met!"

"Hail to thee, too, I am sure," said Prunella.

"But you are talking nonsense!" said Mrs. Midsomer crossly. "What has she to do with my beloved?"

"She has nothing to do with your beloved," retorted the sibyl. "No one cares for your beloved half as much as you do! This girl is a fine creature, for a mortal, and she will make their wicked Society so cross I am delighted to have seen her."

"Oh, if that is all!" said Mrs. Midsomer, losing interest. "Then you may be quiet!" She walked off without a second look at any of them.

"Good gracious!" said Sophia. "What a very odd woman! As for that sibyl, well!" They looked at the sibyl, who had returned to her downtrodden pose, and looked like nothing more than an ordinary picture.

"I do not know what Kendle will say! And to have subjected you, my dear, to such a diatribe! I could not make out a word of her speech, could you?"

"Not a word," echoed Prunella. "She must have been driven mad by her long imprisonment. I pity her, do not you?"

"I think she is too impudent to be pitied," said Sophia, who was still pink with vexation. "I declare I was never so put out! How I wish Kendle were something sensible, like a Member of Parliament. I have said as much to him, but he will not contemplate giving up magic for a moment."

To Prunella's relief, Sophia was so taken up with the sibyl's incivility to her that she said nothing of the creature's speech about Prunella. The sibyl had not spoken so very loudly, and the general hubbub had been such as almost to drown out her voice. Prunella could not trust that Sophia or Mrs. Midsomer would not pass on enough of the sibyl's speech to betray her, however, even if they did not understand the whole. Prunella had hardly understood it herself, but it had all sounded decidedly magical, and was bound to cast suspicion on her.

Dared she conceal the incident from Zacharias? He would be excessively vexed to hear of it. But he might be able to explain the meaning of the sibyl's speech. The Seven Spirits were the treasures, of course, including the four unhatched eggs, but who was the Grand Sorceress, and what were the four points of the realm? The Undersecretary of Wonder rather lacked elegance as a title, reflected Prunella, but the Queen of the Five Boroughs sounded well.

"Oh, what a bore!" exclaimed Sophia.

"What is it?" said Prunella.

The guests had gathered at the end of the room. She and Sophia were swept along with them, but there was nothing to see—only Mr. Midsomer standing at the centre of the crowd, looking about with an air of complacency.

"I believe he means to make a speech," said Sophia. She pulled her mouth into a pretty *moue*. "I am sure these magicians are vastly clever, but do not you think, Prunella, that they do not know the first thing about a party? Fancy forgoing dancing for speeches!"

"Gentlemen, I am honoured by your presence here tonight," said Midsomer in a carrying voice. "Honoured by your support of my endeavours to restore dignity to our profession. Too long have we been compelled to silence—but soon we shall speak with one voice, and our words will decide the destiny of English thaumaturgy."

"There is Kendle!" whispered Sophia.

Mr. Kendle stood with a group of other magicians close to Midsomer. Their countenances were grave, but their eyes were fixed on Midsomer with a fierce, bright look that made Prunella uneasy.

Midsomer held up a scroll.

"I have here that for which you have waited," he said. "Our amendment to the Charter of our honourable Society is approved. The Hallett procedure, which has so long been prohibited, has been restored. We have now a means by which the staff of the Sorcerer Royal may be removed from the unworthy. No longer need we abide by the dictates of a Committee that has acceded to the usurpation of our profession's noblest office. No more are our hands tied!

"I have invited you here today as a sign of my gratitude—but also to remind you that our work has just begun. On Thursday I shall stand before the Society and propose a motion for the procedure to be undertaken to remove the pretender. I require your support, colleagues, for a vote that will alter the history of English magic!"

"Never fear, Midsomer, you have it!" and "Hear, hear!" cried his audience.

Midsomer swept a triumphant look over the crowd.

"Now, gentlemen, since you are of my mind," he said, "I come to my third reason for arranging this gathering. I have long desired to take you into my confidence. I have hidden my secret only for fear that it might put our enemy on his guard. But now the time is ripe. English thaumaturgy is assembled against him. And you, sirs, the mainstay of English magic, merit nothing less than the truth. When I returned from Fairyland, I returned with a gift for England—a pearl beyond price, hidden till today. I returned with a familiar!"

The guests fell silent, as though in one stroke they had been deprived of their faculty of speech. But in a moment their voices rose again, the whole room talking excitedly at once.

"But then, sir," cried one man, "you are a sorcerer!"

Midsomer inclined his head, as much as though the title were a royal one. "I have not claimed the title before this day, but I hope I am as worthy a sorcerer as ever sprung from English soil."

He said no more, but he did not need to say anything else, to call up in his colleagues' minds the man for whom he was such a natural replacement—a man who had *not* sprung from good English soil.

"I think we know, sir, who may be called upon to receive the staff when it is removed from he who so little deserves it." It was Mr. Kendle who spoke, and Prunella lowered her eyes, in case he should notice her looking daggers at him.

"This crowns all our efforts," cried another thaumaturge. "It is such a triumph for English magic as we have not seen in decades. Will you tell us more of your familiar?"

"I will do better than that," said Midsomer, smiling. "I will show her to you."

Turning away from his astonished audience, he said to his wife, standing demurely behind him:

"Laura, my dear, will you come forward, and be introduced?"

"Why, Prunella, your hand is like a vise!" whispered Sophia. "What is he saying?"

Prunella loosened her grasp. She said, striving for calm:

"He is saying that Mrs. Midsomer is a fairy, though I ought to have known it without his telling us. Those eyes alone proved it! And her shocking manners, and knowing how to call forth the sibyl!"

But the excitement vibrating in her voice was owed in largest part not to the revelation of Mrs. Midsomer's nature, but to what it meant regarding Mr. Midsomer. For if he intended to become Sorcerer Royal, and sought to enact this mysterious procedure upon Zacharias—if he had even gone so far as to get himself a familiar, and demand the allegiance of his colleagues—then there could be no question about it. Mr. Midsomer must be the assassin.

Sophia found Prunella rather a distracted companion for the remainder of the evening: her conversation was not so sparkling, and her laughter not nearly so ready as usual, and both ladies were united in desiring an early retreat.

Mr. Kendle would have liked to stay and concoct plans with his colleagues, now that their triumph seemed so near at hand. But his discontent was moderated by the thought that it might be no bad notion to remove Miss Gentleman from the scene. It was unlikely she had understood enough of what had passed that evening to carry tales—though Mr. Kendle indulged his pretty young wife, he had little opinion of her intelligence, and Miss Gentleman seemed no different from any of the other flighty young creatures Sophia called her friends. Even so, he made sure to slip a charm for forgetfulness into her mind when he handed her down from the carriage.

Prunella disposed of the charm by feeding it to Youko, as Nidget and Tjandra objected to the taste. She was in a considerable tumult of spirits, and it seemed intolerable that she would have to wait an entire night before warning Zacharias.

She wished she knew what the Hallett was. Despite attentive eavesdropping at the party, she had not been able to obtain any clarity on the point, for everyone seemed to assume that everyone else knew what it signified. The name Hallett was a familiar one, but where had she heard it before?

Though she racked her mind, pacing her bedchamber, no answer presented itself. But that the Hallett represented another of Mr. Midsomer's attempts to remove his rival, Prunella did not doubt.

How could anyone think he might make a better Sorcerer Royal than Zacharias! she thought. *When Zacharias is so good and clever, and would not hurt a fly! Whereas Mr. Midsomer is little better than a murderer. Indeed, he is only prevented from being a murderer by his incompetence. The horrid little ginger-haired man*—"Oh!"

She had exclaimed aloud, and Tjandra fell off the bed in startlement. He righted himself at once, and flew to the mantelpiece, but it was necessary for Prunella to spend some time petting him before he would condescend to be friends again.

"It was only because I was surprised," she explained. "Mr. Midsomer is related to Clarissa, of course—you did not know her, Tjandra, but she was at the school. I remember she had a brother, and it must be he. It accounts for all. I could believe anything of a relation of Clarissa Midsomer's! She pinched the littler girls when she was cross. I thought it an unchivalrous habit."

Since she could neither wake the household with her news, nor, in her agitated state, go to sleep, Prunella resolved that she would review all the spells she knew for warmaking. *If Mr. Midsomer means to attack Zacharias, he need not think Zacharias's friends will sit quietly by and let him!*

Though few of the schoolgirls had been as vicious-tempered as Clarissa Midsomer, a life passed amid the feuds and rivalries of a girls' school had left Prunella not wholly unprepared for battle. She found she knew six hexes, some of them quite highly finished pieces of devilry, and Nidget said that it was sure it could invent others:

"We were always quarrelling in Fairyland! I am sure I killed dozens of my kinsmen, and other enemies besides."

"I declare, Nidget, sometimes you frighten me," said Prunella, gazing at the elvet in dismay. "I beg you will not say such bloodthirsty things in Zacharias's hearing. I am sure he would not like it. But if your experience helps us defend him, that is all to the good."

Nidget was not overly fond of Zacharias, for it suspected Prunella of allocating too large a share of her affections to the tall reserved mortal who made her such regular visits. It said crabbily:

"And what has he done for us that we should defend him?"

"Why, what would become of me if his enemies should succeed?" said Prunella. "I have not received a single offer of marriage yet, and if Zacharias loses his staff, or worse, before I am able to establish myself, we may find ourselves on the streets! We are only here at his sufferance, Nidget, and it would behoove you to remember that."

Both she and Nidget knew self-interest was not her chief motive for desiring Zacharias's safety, but Prunella could comfort herself that at least none other than her familiars had reason to suspect she felt anything for him but a perfectly decorous gratitude. To be in love was so inconvenient, so—missish! Particularly when Zacharias, she was certain, would never see her in that light. It was nothing more than a passing fancy, she told herself, and fortunately there was such a lot to think of that she scarcely had time to dwell on her feelings.

"You ought not to risk yourself for that milksop," said Nidget jealously, but Prunella snapped:

"You are a fool if you think Zacharias is a milksop! But I know you are not really so foolish. The longer we stay up, the more we shall quarrel, so we had better go to bed, and we will all be better-tempered tomorrow."

With that Nidget had to be content, for she climbed into bed and put her head under her pillow, by way of signifying the conversation was at an end.

20

SCARROW," SAID DAMERELL.

"No, no, he would never do," cried Lady Wythe.

Their heads were bent over a piece of paper, but Lady Wythe started when she saw Zacharias. A blush overspread her countenance, and her look of lively interest changed to reserve.

"Why, what possible objection can there be?" said Damerell. "He has a substantial establishment, and he is far less stupid than some of the others." He only looked up when Lady Wythe failed to respond.

Damerell had traded his usual quizzing-glass for a pair of round spectacles, which did little for his manly beauty, magnifying his eyes to an alarming degree. "Halloa, Zacharias, are you here? We are considering Miss Gentleman's prospects after our fortnight's work."

"It is very improper to gossip so about our acquaintance," said Lady Wythe, attempting to look severe. "I do not know how you inveigled me into the exercise, Damerell."

"What are acquaintance for, if not to supply the pleasures of gossip?" said Damerell. "Besides, you know, ma'am, it is only to help Miss

Gentleman, for if she is to bring off a good marriage she must direct her energies along the channels most likely to produce a satisfactory result. You would not wish her to entertain any unsuitable offers."

"That I should not like," said Lady Wythe decidedly. "What with her looks, and these unfortunate rumours of her wealth, she attracts a great deal of attention she would be better without."

"London's bachelors should rejoice that Lady Wythe has no daughters to guard," said Damerell to Zacharias, in a confidential aside. "I have never known so strict a judge of character. We have dismissed Oliver for his want of conduct, Potier for his want of feeling, and Sargent for his want of conversation. I declare, ma'am, if you had your way, I believe no one would marry at all."

Zacharias was about to tell Damerell what he thought of him when Prunella burst into the room. There were violet circles under her eyes, as though she had slept poorly, but she exclaimed, with even more than her usual energy:

"Zacharias, what can have kept you? I have been practising my spells all night and morning, though I hope you know a killing spell or two, for none of mine are murderous. Mr. Midsomer means to do something very wicked, I am sure of it, and those tedious thaumaturges are all in it together, and they must be stopped!"

Zacharias was taken aback, though not so much that he did not regret Prunella's freedom in using his Christian name. They had fallen into the habit of addressing each other so, and its being an unusual circumstance only struck him now that they were in the company of others. Lady Wythe and Damerell both looked unconscious, but he could trust that neither of them had failed to mark the liberty.

"Did you say you saw Midsomer?" said Damerell.

"Did you say you were *practising*?" said Zacharias.

Prunella poured out her tale of the Midsomers' gathering the day before, only omitting to mention the sibyl's prophecy regarding herself.

"And Mrs. Midsomer is Mr. Midsomer's familiar, and not his wife at all!" she concluded. "At the end of his speech Mr. Midsomer went about shaking every gentleman's hand and thanking him, and it seems they are all planning to vote at this Society meeting for the Hallett to be carried out. Fortunately Mr. Midsomer took no notice of the females, and Sophia and I evaded Mrs. Midsomer for the rest of the evening. I did not wish her to remember me, and Sophia, I know, thought her a horrid bore."

That Midsomer had a familiar was, of course, no revelation to Zacharias, and it explained a great deal that she should have been hidden in plain sight as his wife. It was sensible of Midsomer to reveal his familiar to his followers now, for it made it obvious who should replace Zacharias. There was no earthly reason why he should feel blindsided by how far Midsomer's plans had advanced—he ought to have foreseen this after his visit to the Fairy Court.

"I doubt Midsomer would have been overly concerned even if he had seen you," Zacharias said in a measured tone that he hoped disguised his internal turmoil. "He has not concealed his desire to oust me from my office. I have known for some time what he has planned."

Lady Wythe was not troubling to conceal her internal turmoil at all.

"Zacharias," she said, her voice unsteady, "do you mean to say you have known for some time that Geoffrey Midsomer intended to invoke the Hallett against you? And you told no one?"

Zacharias said warily, "Midsomer indicated he had thoughts of reinstating the procedure. It seemed so outlandish—at the very least, so disproportionate a response—that I did not credit it. That was foolish of me, of course."

"But what is the Hallett?" cried Prunella.

"It is an obscure procedure, and has not been repeated since its namesake was done away with," said Damerell. "Traditionally, of course, the Sorcerer Royal was replaced when he was murdered by his successor. That is a piece of savagery we no longer practise, I am pleased to say; instead, the Fellows of the Society vote to elect a new candidate. Unfortunately, the staff of the Sorcerer Royal is no democrat. There is no guarantee it will submit to being transferred to another while its holder still lives and disagrees. The only means of ensuring the staff complies with the vote is to undertake a ritual sacrifice of its master. If his successor is anointed with his blood, the staff may well decide there has been no material change."

"The ability to move for the procedure was removed from the Charter of the Society after Cecil Hallett was killed," said Zacharias. "But it seems it has been restored."

"That is what puzzles me," said Damerell. "The Charter may only be amended by the Committee by leave of the Crown. How has Midsomer managed to hurry the Government along? Do you recall our application to keep a cat in the Society gardens, by way of preserving the levels of atmospheric magic? We submitted our proposal to the Government last year, and the kitten we identified for the purpose is now a tomcat with an evil temper. An excessively magical creature—it could pass for a Fellow if it were able to hold a pen."

"I knew it was Mr. Midsomer who has been trying to murder you!" said Prunella to Zacharias. "I suppose he is tired of failing, and is seeking to achieve his purpose by this means."

"Trying to *murder* you?" said Lady Wythe.

Zacharias shot Prunella a furious glance. She subsided, looking contrite, but it was too late.

"I am sorry, ma'am. I had hoped to keep this from you," said Zacharias. "There have been certain attempts—magical attacks—"

"Have there been more attacks?" said Prunella. "I declare Mr. Midsomer is a perfect nuisance! Were not the fire at the inn and that wicked puddle enough?"

Zacharias had hoped to pass over the topic lightly, but Lady Wythe's eyes had gone round with alarm, and he could not avoid answering without increasing her anxiety.

"He would be a poor sort of assassin if he did not try again, since it is common knowledge that I am still alive," said Zacharias irritably. "There has been nothing worth mentioning, however: an asp disguised as a sausage at my dinner; invisible obstacles magicked onto my staircase, in the hope that I may trip and break my neck. I assure you"—this to Lady Wythe—"there is no need for concern. Considering the extreme tension that has subsisted within the Society since my investiture, it was only a matter of time before something of the sort happened. I consider myself fortunate that my enemy has so far been easily dealt with."

"But is it truly Geoffrey Midsomer who has been conspiring against you?" said Lady Wythe. "He must be denounced to the Presiding Committee—put away in a gaol. I shall speak to Lord Burrow, and demand that he put a stop to these tricks—"

"By speaking to his nephew?" said Zacharias. Lady Wythe fell silent.

"Besides," said Zacharias, into a depressed silence, "I do not know for certain that Midsomer is behind the attacks."

"It does not seem unreasonable to suspect Midsomer of having something to do with them, however," said Damerell, examining his fingernails with a contemplative air. "Rollo and I will investigate his goings-on. It is clear an eye ought to be kept on the fellow, and Rollo has a remarkable nose for secrets, though you might not think it."

This generosity embarrassed Zacharias, and he spoke with rather more impatience than he intended in trying to disguise this. "I do not see that there is any need for you or Rollo to trouble yourselves with my affairs. It is absurd! As if I needed to employ a troop of intelligence agents on my behalf!"

"On the contrary," said Damerell coolly, "it is tradition. Every Sorcerer Royal who survived more than a few months in office achieved his longevity by the judicious employment of spies."

Chastened, Zacharias said, "I am conscious of your goodness, and

I know you receive little enough reward for it. But then your kindness to me has always exceeded anything I could return."

"If you wish to thank me, you would oblige me by leaving off such talk," said Damerell crossly. "You need not flatter yourself that I am helping you on your own account. How could I do less for the connection of an old friend?" He bowed to Lady Wythe.

"It is not very civil of you to call Lady Wythe old," said Prunella.

"Oh, Damerell may take any liberties he desires, you know. *He* can never be uncivil," said Lady Wythe. She tried to smile through her distress. "It is a great comfort to me that you and dear Robert are taking up Zacharias's cause."

"We will do our best by him," promised Damerell. "We shall be unflagging in our endeavours, despite ingratitude, mutterings, complaints. Never let it be said that Zacharias Wythe wanted friends in this world or any other."

THERE was still work to be done, even when the threat of being sacrificed upon the altar of a rival's ambition hung over one's head. Zacharias returned to his study at the end of the day determined to continue his work. He thought he should make a start on a report to the Society of his audience with the Fairy King, though he felt hardly equal to the task. He sat chewing on his quill, various anxieties tumbling tiredly about in his head.

He did not yet know what he ought to tell, and what he should withhold. Prunella had not known where Mak Genggang had gone, though she had promised to send a message. If only he could contrive to come to an understanding with Mak Genggang, perhaps—

He had not completed the thought when the window shattered. With an energy Zacharias had not known he still possessed, he vaulted across the room, snatching his staff out of the umbrella stand. But what came through the window was no monster or assassin. It was Mak Genggang.

She had returned to her ordinary size, but retained the bat-wings she had invented to enable her escape from the Society. She fluttered into the room and landed on the floor, folding her wings up behind her.

"Good day, ma'am," said Zacharias, after a pause.

He could not decide whether to thank her for coming, or upbraid her for ruining his windows. The former would be more politic, of course, but the latter would be such a satisfaction to his feelings. Whether he intended courtesy or reproach, however, he was prevented from continuing by Mak Genggang.

"So much for the soft words of the foreign sorcerer!" she cried, trembling with passion. "I will say nothing of ingratitude. It is the deception, the cowardly dishonesty in seeking to put a frail old woman off her guard, which is what I cannot endure. You will regret your mistake, however. You will find it is a fool who seeks to impose upon Mak Genggang!"

Zacharias was alarmed by the furious resentment in her voice.

"Mak Genggang—" he began, but she cut him off.

"Do the British think us children, to be daunted by shadows and smoke?" she said. "We have sought only to live in peace, and you have sent an army into our country. Very well! If you wish us to believe you are ready to attack, we shall take you at your word. We may not be experts in war, but you have not heard, perhaps, of the venom of a woman's curse. Our enmity, once earned, survives even death."

In the same bitter voice, the matriarch began reciting a curse. The language was unfamiliar, but the syllables dropping like poison from her lips were pregnant with a tremendous evil power. The wood of Zacharias's desk warped and turned black. A noxious miasma rose from her person, and the floorboards shuddered beneath Zacharias's feet.

"Ma'am, I beg that you will not be rash," cried Zacharias. "I assure you, whatever offence has been perpetrated, I have no knowledge of it. I would be very anxious to remedy any wrong committed against your people."

"You regret your perfidy now that you see the extent of my power, but you ought to have considered it before you betrayed Janda Baik!" snapped Mak Genggang.

"I beg you will believe I have no knowledge of this betrayal," said Zacharias. "I have been quarrelling with my Government to stay out of the affairs of your island. My first wish is to prevent magical conflict, which would be so detrimental to both our nations."

"Of course you deny your wickedness," said Mak Genggang. "The British are all alike—cheats, traitors, villainous blackguards!"

She looked uncertain, however, and Zacharias sought to press his advantage.

"Did not I defend you from my colleagues when they wished to punish you after the Spring Ball? Was it not my apprentice who then freed you from your imprisonment?" he said. "Till now I was not aware of anything that might endanger the accord between our nations. I would regret anything of the sort extremely."

"Do you truly not know?" said Mak Genggang, eyeing him with misgiving. "This evening an attack was mounted upon my women in Janda Baik. They looked to the east, and saw ranks of British soldiers, fearfully armed and ferocious. They looked to the west, and saw British ships lining the harbour, ready to fire broadsides upon their houses. The British demanded that my women surrender and leave the island peaceably, but I am proud to say they took the British representative captive and beat him for his impertinence."

"Good God!" said Zacharias.

"Oh yes! The women of Janda Baik are not mild. Blood, and not milk, flows in our veins," said Mak Genggang. "My women were shot at for their noble response, but that did not deter them. They are not so poor-spirited! They barricaded themselves within their huts and cast spells for truth-telling and the finding of lost objects, until finally the guns were silenced, and they emerged to see the illusions dispelled—no ships, and scarcely any soldiers. My women have captured all ten men, and I believe your soldiers are being taught a salutary lesson. It was foolish of your King to have sent so few to take the witches of Janda Baik, but not nearly so foolish as seeking to overbear my women with trumpery illusions."

"Our sovereign is no magician," said Zacharias slowly.

Edgeworth must have found a thaumaturge to provide his knock-down spell. A thaumaturge who required assistance, perhaps; who desired the Government's prompt attention to a minor matter—the mere adjustment of a provision in the Charter incorporating the Royal Society of Unnatural Philosophers.

But Midsomer had miscalculated badly. He could not have dreamt that this play would result in British subjects being held hostage by a foreign power—a power admittedly small, but confoundedly magical, and now extremely angry. Why should Midsomer or Edgeworth have suspected that the witches of Janda Baik would see through Midsomer's illusions? Neither had seen Mak Genggang amble out of Fairyland as though she were taking an evening stroll, nor felt the virulence of her curse.

But what could have possessed Midsomer to do what was sure to vex the Fairy Court, given its sentiments towards Janda Baik's lamiae? Zacharias no longer doubted that Midsomer knew of the block upon England's magic: if his familiar had not told him, he must have discovered it himself during his sojourn in Fairyland, and he must be aware of the Court's reason for withholding its magic.

Still, Midsomer had shown himself willing enough to risk the good of the nation in pursuit of his own interest. He had already put at naught the Court's prohibition on the summoning of familiars, though he knew Fairyland was likely to include the whole of England in its resentment of any offence. It was the Society's opinion he cared for, for it was only the Society that could help him to the staff of the Sorcerer Royal.

It would be an unattractive office by the time he came to fill it, but what cared Midsomer for that? Perhaps he believed he might do anything with such a convenient scapegoat as Zacharias to hand.

"I think I know who your enemy is, who has made such trouble for you," said Zacharias. "I will put a stop to his schemes directly—if you will have the goodness to do me a favour in return."

Mak Genggang bristled up. "You dare make demands, when your nation has acted so shamefully towards my people? If you think I will grovel to your sovereign, or permit Raja Ahmad to run roughshod over my women—!"

"I think you know, ma'am, that your people have not been altogether just to us," said Zacharias.

"I am sure I do not know what you mean," said Mak Genggang. The lie was so transparent Zacharias almost laughed.

"Why did not you tell me our magic had been stopped at your countrywomen's request?" he said. "If I had known it before, I could have advised you on how best to make your case to our King. Your enemy might never have had the opportunity to ingratiate himself with our Government—might never have been granted the licence to attack your island."

Mak Genggang glared. Zacharias answered this with an unflinching gaze, though he was by no means as calm as he hoped he looked.

To his relief, after a moment Mak Genggang said pettishly:

"It is hardly to the purpose to lament your ignorance now! I did not know anything of it myself till my women told me of the attack. It was only then that they confessed they had been inciting the spirits against the British. They feared they had overreached themselves—that their ploy was discovered, and instead of agreeing to their demands, the English King had responded by this attack. They were reassured when I told them that it was Raja Ahmad's wicked influence that had moved the British to act against them. But perhaps I spoke amiss. Perhaps, indeed, the attack was in revenge for my women's dealings with the spirits?"

Her dark eyes gleamed with suspicion.

"Perhaps," said Zacharias. When Mak Genggang looked outraged, he added:

"I do not know for sure. But you must see that your lamiae's scheme would scarcely have increased my Government's good will towards you. I cannot make out why they did not tell you earlier, so that you could convey the message to us. How could they hope to blackmail Britain if Britain knew nothing of their threat?"

"Of course they did not tell me," said Mak Genggang. "I should never have permitted it if I had known what they planned. Such a small nation as ours cannot afford to offend others, and nothing would be likelier to bring the wrath of the British down upon our heads than stopping their magic."

"Did they tell no one, then?"

Mak Genggang eyed Zacharias, as if she were wondering how much he knew, and considering how much she could tell him. Finally she said:

"It seems there was an acquaintance of theirs in the spirit world, who planned to remove to Britain. She was going to live with a great magician, who had many powerful acquaintances. She promised he would convey the message to the King. That was my women's mistake, of course. They should have known better than to put any stock in an English magician's word."

"It is necessary to choose the right English magician for the purpose," said Zacharias ruefully. "I wish I had known of this sooner."

"Oh, I do not deny my vampiresses have mishandled the affair," said Mak Genggang. "They feared I should tell them to go to their relations if they confessed to any. Absurd creatures! As if I did not know one might disagree with one's relations, and wish to live apart from them! They are my women, however. I am bound to defend them, however stupid they are. Any offence to them must be furiously resented!"

Mak Genggang was well on the way to working herself back up into a passion. Zacharias saw he must intervene if he were to avoid another curse.

"I am not proud of my nation's conduct towards yours, if your account is true," he said. "But I am bound to defend it, as you are bound to defend yours. If the block placed upon our magic could be removed, I might see my way to helping your people, and perhaps we would not need to quarrel. For my veins do not contain milk either, Mak Genggang, and we have still sufficient magic in England for my staff to draw upon."

The matriarch was angry, but she was a leader as well as a witch, and she understood power. Zacharias saw a grudging esteem in her eyes.

"My women would happily persuade their cousins to let the British have their magic, if they could be sure they would not be injured by it," said Mak Genggang. She rose and went to the window, the wings unfurling from her back. "But if, in a week's time, the erring magician has not been found and punished, and assurances of our security given, I shall return. *My* army will not be an illusion, and it will not be easily overcome. We may be mere women, but the dead walk with us. We will give you a week, Mr. Wythe."

"I doubt I will have so much time," said Zacharias grimly.

I have left you no very comfortable office, I find," said Sir Stephen.

He had just appeared by the fireplace, but it was likely he had been present throughout Zacharias's conversation with Mak Genggang, and had heard the whole.

"At least I begin to trace my troubles to a singular source," said Zacharias.

"Yes, that sandy-haired Midsomer lad!" said Sir Stephen. "Who would have thought he was capable of such enterprise? It shows how little there is in blood. If his father ever held two thoughts together in his head at the same time, it was the most he ever did."

"Midsomer is much more beforehand than me," said Zacharias, with a sigh.

"If you devoted all your time to plotting divers villainies, I am sure you should soon outpace him," said Sir Stephen. "It is continuing to attend to your duties as Sorcerer Royal that hobbles you. Well, it is never pleasant to play the informer, but it seems to me there is nothing to be done but to report Midsomer to the Presiding Committee. It was one thing when you could only accuse him of seeking to get rid of you one way or another—that I can see Midsomer's friends and relations would happily ignore—but if he is interfering in foreign affairs, that is something the Society will have to take seriously, no matter how many uncles he has."

Zacharias had already considered this course, and dismissed it. "At the moment I have no proof of my allegations. Mak Genggang would hardly be deemed a credible witness by the Society. And by making this new accusation, I would implicate others. John Edgeworth must have been involved in this attack on Janda Baik, and he is not easily accused."

Sir Stephen frowned, standing before the fire with his hands clasped behind his back, rocking on his feet as he thought.

Zacharias experienced an unlooked-for pang. The sight was so familiar, the scene so much like what it had been when Sir Stephen was still alive, that for a moment Zacharias could not credit that the world was so utterly changed. In some respects their relationship was easier, their respective positions more equal. Yet Zacharias must always regret the shift that had so transformed the footing on which they each stood.

"You have not informed the Society of the block on our magic?" said Sir Stephen.

"I had almost done so," said Zacharias, "but I fear the intelligence that Mak Genggang's vampiresses have been conspiring against Britain is likely to incite another attack on Janda Baik. The situation there is so delicate that anything of the sort must be avoided. We cannot afford to be entangled in a magical conflict—we have not the resource for it, and there is our treaty with the French to consider."

"I tell you what, Zacharias," announced Sir Stephen. "What you need is evidence of Geoffrey Midsomer's wrongdoing—solid evidence, such as even that miserable old Committee could not deny. Who better to supply you with such evidence than me? There is nowhere I cannot go, nothing I cannot see—"

"Nothing you can touch or move," Zacharias reminded him. "I am obliged to you for your offer, sir, but Damerell and Rollo are already at work investigating Midsomer."

Sir Stephen waved away both Damerell and Rollo, and the minor matter of his incorporeality. "Paget Damerell is a good enough fellow, but he is not likely to get very far with that addlepated creature to help him. No, it is a task for me, and I shall contrive some way around the inconvenience of my being unfleshed. At worst, Zacharias, we shall have to engage in a spot of necromancy, and I shall appear to give evidence to the Committee in person. It is what I could not wish, of course—Maria would so dislike it—so we must regard it as a last resort. Yet I should very much enjoy the looks on their faces!"

Zacharias did not continue to argue. If Sir Stephen could discover some means of overcoming his inability to interact with the material world, he would be the ideal investigator. It remained only to thank him, but Sir Stephen scoffed.

"There will be time enough for thanks when I have found something! Though even then I would only be making amends for the wretched legacy I have left you," he said. "Do you know, I fancy I shall enjoy myself. I was never a man to hold a grudge, but if it is put in my way to serve Julian Midsomer out for the trouble he has given me and mine, why! I am not an angel yet!"

And Sir Stephen's blue eyes glinted with a most uncelestial light.

21

PRUNELLA WAS INDIGNANT to be roused early the next morning for her lesson.

"Surely you have better things to concern yourself with than my instruction," she protested.

The same thought had, of course, occurred to Zacharias. Prunella's education was a demand upon his time and energy that he could ill afford. But the thought had followed quick upon its heels that he ought to make the most of every opportunity he possessed to teach Prunella, if she were to govern her familiars safely. It seemed increasingly likely that very little time remained to him to do it.

Then, too, this lesson had required special preparations. It would not be nearly as convenient to repeat it on any other day; indeed, to seek a postponement might occasion offence. Therefore Zacharias insisted.

"Let us resolve to complete five formulae today," he said. "They shall culminate in a spell with which I think you will be pleased. It is beyond anything we have done before, and requires us to be outdoors.

I have reserved a tolerably large space for us at the Park, but I beg you will have particular regard to my concealment charms. It is early for anyone to be about, but we cannot be too careful to avoid detection."

"I think it is all silliness, and you ought to be spending your time thinking of ways to defeat Mr. Midsomer, not teaching me tricks," said Prunella. The mention of a great spell had piqued her interest, however, and she followed this with:

"But since you are set upon it, I suppose I must comply, and the exercise will be good for the familiars."

Prunella insisted on her familiars attending all her lessons. She vowed she could not learn half as well without them, and since the purpose of her education was to enable her to understand the creatures, Zacharias permitted it, despite the risk of discovery. The familiars made poor students, however—they were discourteous, inattentive and quarrelsome; insisted on exploded theories in the face of Zacharias's polite reasoning; and often disrupted the lesson with their squabbling.

They arrived so early in the Park that there was not a soul to be seen, but Prunella kept her familiars within her reticule until they had reached the concealed grove where the lesson was to be conducted. She set the reticule upon the ground and opened it so that the tiny heads of the familiars—shrunk for the occasion so that each creature would fit upon the palm of her hand—could peer over the side.

"Now mind you behave yourselves. We shall have time to talk later, but if you are always interrupting I shall never learn all the things Zacharias says I must learn," said Prunella. "Nidget, I beg you will attend, and not abandon your notes halfway through, as you did before. It is so very useful to have a record of each lesson."

"If Youko had not distracted me, the blackguard, you would have the most perfect record the world ever saw."

"Blame attaches to no one, I am sure," said Prunella hastily. "Pray do not fight, or wander off, and under no circumstance must you leave the reticule. I must go, my darlings, or Zacharias will be cross."

"I thought we might consider the enchantments for summoning today," said Zacharias. "We shall begin with the simplest example of such spells, a charm for drawing upon atmospheric magic—ours is thin stuff, but it is as well to know how to get at it if ever you need it. Then we shall work our way up to the greater summoning spells. We will restrict the scope of our endeavours to this realm—*you* have no cause to do it, but to seek to summon oneself a familiar from Fairy is both unlawful and exceedingly dangerous. Summoning within this realm is not necessarily unethical, however, and if one agrees it in advance with the person to be summoned, it need not even be annoying."

"Will I be summoning a person?" said Prunella.

"Oh yes. One can summon anything capable of being acted upon by magic," said Zacharias. "The gentleman I shall ask you to summon is a colleague of mine, whom I met at a council of the world's magicians last year. We have since corresponded by shewstone, and he has agreed to assist us. I beg you will not mention your familiars, but he knows I have been instructing you in the principles of thaumaturgy. We may trust him to be discreet: he is a reformer himself, though something of a skeptic as regards female magic, and he has some notion of the difficulties we face."

Prunella thought very little of the charm for drawing upon atmospheric magic, but the summoning formulae were a pleasing contrast, more complex than any of the spells she had learnt before, and she soon grew absorbed. The fourth formula was the most difficult. Prunella was so little satisfied with her performance that she would have begun at once upon a second trial, seeking to correct the inelegancies of the first, if Zacharias had not stopped her.

"The summoning has taken, and you will saddle us with someone probably very cross if you repeat it," said Zacharias.

"After all your demands for practise—" Prunella began, but then she saw the dark spot upon the horizon speeding towards them.

It came on swiftly, skimming above the trees, until it resolved into the figure of a gentleman, dressed in foreign costume and travelling astride a cloud.

Prunella only had time to exclaim a pleased "Oh!" before the gentleman's insubstantial conveyance drew up in front of them. He dropped to the ground, landing on his feet, and bowed.

He was of Oriental extraction, with a high, broad expanse of forehead, amused narrow eyes, and greying hair in a queue. He was dressed with great elegance in silk robes, his feet clad in neat boots, and his appearance was so completely that of the foreigner that Prunella was astonished when he said, in impeccable English:

"A most effective enchantment: I congratulate you, Wythe. However, did not the second verse go awry? My journey was unaccountably bumpy for a stretch."

Prunella flushed and said, "It was only my first attempt."

"Miss Gentleman," said Zacharias, "may I introduce my colleague, Mr. Hsiang Han? Mr. Hsiang is a magician renowned in his native China for his great learning. Mr. Hsiang, Miss Prunella Gentleman, the lady I have been instructing in the magical arts."

"Did you cast that spell, indeed, Miss Gentleman?" said Mr. Hsiang, bowing. "When Wythe explained his plan to reform women's education, I told him he was a mere visionary—I called him any number of bad names—but now I see the reason for his resolve. Such a protégé, uniting beauty with genius, must fire any magician's reforming zeal."

"That is all very gallant, but I wish you would explain where I went wrong in the second verse," said Prunella, too vexed by her mistake to be civil.

Zacharias looked reproachful, but Mr. Hsiang laughed.

"You expended too much power at the outset, so that too little remained for the conclusion," he said. "In magic, as in all else, balance must be preserved. Let me send my cloud away, and you can execute the formula again to require its return."

The second attempt proved satisfactory.

"I am obliged to you for your help," said Prunella, looking at Mr. Hsiang with candid friendliness. "Would you be so good as to name your translation spell? It must be a very clever one, for I can scarcely tell that there is an enchantment at work at all."

"She has found me out!" exclaimed Mr. Hsiang, looking at Zacharias.

"I said nothing," said Zacharias. "That was Miss Gentleman's own discovery."

"Why, it was not very difficult to find it out," said Prunella. "Your words sound green."

"Are you able to describe the mechanism of the spell yourself, Miss Gentleman?" said Zacharias. "You should have sufficient understanding of basic thaumaturgical principles to deduce its workings."

"I am very happy to provide an explanation," said Mr. Hsiang. "I understand the lady has only recently begun her studies in our field."

Prunella was on her mettle. It was one thing to complain privately to Zacharias that he demanded too much of her, and their lessons ran on for too long. The ironic eye of a learned foreign magician was another matter altogether, however. Prunella was in truth proud of her magical ability—though she had little fondness for thaumaturgical books and dry theory, magic itself she loved—and she was determined not to make a poor show before a stranger.

"There is a binding element, for otherwise one would hear two voices," she said, thinking aloud. "The Culpeper solution would not do, for it only applies to solid objects, so it must be Starr's entwining that is at work. But that is only the combining element. I shall say it is Horner's spell for interpretation, with Starr's entwining, bound together with Crashaw's preserve. Do I have it, sir?"

"I require Wythe's assistance to make sense of your answer," said Mr. Hsiang, laughing. "Wythe, this Horner, this Starr and Crashaw, are they—?"

He spoke in quick succession a series of foreign names, fluid sounds that dropped unchanged through the translation spell.

Zacharias nodded. To Prunella he said:

"The translation spell is one indigenous to the Chinese, and there is an additional element—a mind-reading element, the enchantment for which I shall teach you in due course—but yours is an ingenious solution, and very close to the truth."

Prunella made a *moue* of discontent, but the two thaumaturges seemed better pleased with her success. Zacharias's satisfaction was obvious, and Mr. Hsiang's manner altered. Prunella's dissection of what was really quite a cunningly disguised little formula had put her up sufficiently in his estimation that he dispensed with gallantry, and adopted the manner of a scholar addressing a student.

"That was not a bad analysis," he said. "Since I have answered your summons upon my cloud, Miss Gentleman, should you like to take a turn on it? It is the most delightful means of transport—nothing so comfortable as a well-conditioned cloud—and cloud-riding is a useful spell to have in one's arsenal. I have had cause to thank Heaven for my cloud more than once."

"I should be pleased to learn to ride it," said Prunella. "Though we have only completed four formulae today, this will make the fifth, so Mr. Wythe can have no objection."

She shot him a saucy glance, which extracted a half-smile from Zacharias.

"I have no fault to find with your arithmetic," he said. "It will make an excellent lesson in controlling the elements of nature, and I am obliged to Mr. Hsiang for offering to teach you the formula. I will take the liberty of reminding you both of the concealment spell, and beg that you will take care not to go beyond its bounds. The boundaries should offer some resistance to your approach, but if you happen to stray beyond them, you must turn back at once."

"Let me call myself a new cloud," said Mr. Hsiang.

He stuck two fingers into his mouth and emitted a shrill whistle, at which a wisp detached itself from the snowy white cumulus heaped in the sky, and flew to his hand.

"Now, Miss Gentleman, if you will submit to being helped onto my old cloud—a steady, good-tempered mount, who will show you the way of it—you are quite balanced? You must *think* yourself into equilibrium. Cloud-riding is an act of disciplined imagination. Splendid. Away we go!"

Cloud-riding was indeed delightful: the sensation of height, of delicious liberty, was beyond anything Prunella had ever experienced. In a few moments they were above the trees. Prunella might have been nervous if she had not been absorbed by the effort of controlling her cloud. It was necessary for them to fly in small circles if they were not to breach the bounds of Zacharias's hiding spell, and directing the cloud required her close attention.

They rode standing upon their clouds, and Prunella realised that she needed to lean forward in the direction she wished to go if she was to move at all. The cloud itself made a soft rest for her feet, but the posture required of her body was uncomfortable in its novelty, and surprisingly difficult to maintain.

"After a period of time the cloud will begin to believe itself as solid as you think it," said Mr. Hsiang. "A cloud makes a fine pillow as well—smells pleasantly of rain—though we do not, of course, rest our heads on the same clouds as those on which we plant our feet. Still, one must never forget that a cloud is a wild thing. It requires a continuous, determined exertion of will to maintain your conviction, and spread the conviction to your cloud, that it is a solid thing, capable of bearing your weight, and happy to do it."

"You speak as though the cloud were a conscious being, sir, capable of thought and feeling."

"But of course it is. What can Wythe have been teaching you?" said

Mr. Hsiang. "Do not you know that magic can only issue from, and act upon, that which contains an intelligent or feeling spirit? Fortunately such spirits are present in almost everything, even the apparently inanimate.

"This shred of cloud, for instance"—he tapped it with his foot—"is a tuft of the Jade Emperor's beard. Of course, it is not intelligent in the sense that anyone would account it a brilliant conversationist. It will never pass for a licentiate. But in some foggy, inhuman way it knows itself: it wishes ardently to return to the beard of which it is a small but noble part, and focused thought is needed to keep it under heel."

"How extraordinary," said Prunella, peering at the cloud beneath her own heel.

"No less extraordinary than that the insight should be new to you," said Mr. Hsiang severely. "I suppose Wythe has been training you in the strict Occidental tradition. For a European he is learned, but he is still prey to many of the curious prejudices that bedevil your people."

"A European?" Prunella exclaimed. Her cloud bucked a trifle, but she stamped down, and it seemed to quiet itself.

"That was gracefully done," said Mr. Hsiang, observing this. "As you can see, even the slightest disturbance in one's emotions may disrupt the progress of one's cloud. It is clear you possess the willpower to master your cloud, however—it is all down to willpower, you know. But to return to Wythe, certainly he is a European, in upbringing, education, habit of mind—even, for all I know, in his religion. Let us not be misled by such a trifle as an accident of birth or colour."

"You would not call it a trifle," said Prunella in a low voice, "if you knew how his fellow Europeans use him."

This embarrassed Mr. Hsiang. He said, with an attempt at lightness:

"I suppose I could not expect *you* to agree that birth is of no account! I could not think why you seemed so familiar, and your name led me astray, Miss Gentleman, but it is clear which family you belong to. It is many years since I last saw the Grand Sorceress, but I could not mistake that profile! I hope she is well? I did not think to see her relations in lands so farflung, but to one of her powers, the distance between England and Mysore must be nothing."

"The Grand Sorceress?" said Prunella.

"The Keeper of the Seven Spirits," said Mr. Hsiang, surprised. "She whom Tipu Sultan named the mistress of the four points of the realm. The Grand Sorceress of Seringapatam, I mean. I hope I did not speak amiss? You look so much like her, that— But I am mistaken. My mind is going with age. I beg your pardon, Miss Gentleman."

Prunella had gone pale. She stared fixedly at the foreign magician, her cloud forgotten. She was remembering a voice—a weary voice, singing the words of a potent spell—a voice unlocked by her own blood. Her mother's voice.

"Miss Gentleman, have a care!" cried Mr. Hsiang.

While Prunella's attention was elsewhere, her cloud had begun to question whether it was, after all, content to bear this strange weight. It seemed to the cloud that it had been happier in a previous life, when it had been as thin as the air, as free as the sky, and united with its kin.

By the time Mr. Hsiang's urgent voice penetrated Prunella's consciousness, her cloud was bucking so outrageously it took all her attention to avoid being thrown off. The cloud sped off in a straight line, headed for the mountainous white drift in the distance.

Zacharias's ward proved a minor obstacle, but it needed only a little straining before the cloud succeeded in puncturing the invisible membrane of the spell. Prunella found herself sailing through a clear blue sky above Hyde Park, unprotected by any disguise, and in full view of anyone who might be there at ten in the morning.

Which—alas for Prunella!—today included Mrs. Alethea Gray and Mrs. Sophia Kendle, driving about the Park in a barouche, their heads bent close together.

Part of Prunella's mind observed that Sophia gave a guilty start when their eyes met. The rest of her was too sunk in horror to wonder at Sophia's starts. Sophia might dismiss the sibyl's speech as nonsense, but neither she nor Mrs. Gray needed to know anything of thaumaturgy to understand that there must be something decidedly magical about Prunella for her to be soaring above Hyde Park on a cloud.

There was no hope of escaping undetected. Mr. Hsiang was pursuing her, shouting:

"Do not look down, Miss Gentleman! To look down would be fatal. But do not fear, we never lose more than ten students a year to cloud-riding."

Prunella put away the past, and the sibyl's words, and her mother's voice, and the guilty surprise in the faces of the women below. There would be time enough to puzzle over these things later.

There was only one thing to do to remedy the situation. Prunella did it.

THE first Zacharias knew of the disturbance was Prunella's reticule falling over. The familiars landed on the grass in a wriggling heap, squeaking: "Prunella, Prunella!"

Then the storm descended out of the blue sky.

It was as though a wrathful god had snuffed out the sun. A precipitous darkness fell, and the world was blotted out by rain. The roar of the tempest was inconceivable.

Zacharias groped his way towards the familiars, hustled them back into the reticule, and shut it on their protests. In the illumination of a brilliant flash of lightning, he saw Prunella swoop down out of the turbid sky.

"You have my familiars safe? Good. Come up on this cloud, Zacharias. We must be away at once."

Prunella's urgency lent her an irresistible authority. Zacharias was swept upon her cloud before he could think to protest. As they lifted off into the air, she said, in a half-shout necessitated by the howling wind and crashing thunder:

"I have summoned a monster."

"What?"

"Not a real monster," said Prunella hastily. "I did not forget what you said about its being a terrible evil to summon creatures from other realms. I used the first formula you taught me—the one for atmospheric magic—to draw upon the thunder hiding within the clouds. Did *you* know spirits populate all things, Zacharias?"

"That old canard! I told Hsiang not to fill your head with outdated hypotheses," said Zacharias.

He did not like heights, and though the cloud, turned a stormy grey, had expanded to accommodate him, it was a tight fit for two people. The cold and wet and noise of the tempest combined with the embarrassment of his unavoidable proximity to Prunella to make Zacharias ill-tempered.

"That idea was debunked in 1660 by the unnatural philosopher Gregor Fähndrich, as Hsiang would know if he read the essays I sent him," he said. "But what has happened? Where is Hsiang?"

"Oh, my cloud went too fast for me, that is all," said Prunella, with a wholly unconvincing nonchalance. "It is a willful creature, but we understand each other now. Mr. Hsiang is quite right about spirits, you know. It came to me in a flash when I saw those wretched females. I cannot conceive what possessed them to go driving in Hyde Park at such an outlandish hour of the morning! Especially Mrs. Gray, who never does a thing unless it has been done by a duchess first. And when did Sophia become a confidante of Mrs. Gray's? It is all a great mystery!"

The storm followed them, concealing them from view, as they flew above the rooftops and chimney-pots of London. The air was so thick with rain that Zacharias could not see farther than an arm's length away.

"I wish you would explain about the monster, instead of indulging in this ill-natured gossip," said Zacharias plaintively.

"Oh, it was the easiest thing in the world! The thunder came ever so meekly to hand when I called it. At first I thought of casting it at Mrs. Gray—like Jove, you know—but I thought better of that, for it might have hurt them, and I only wished to cause a distraction. So I turned the thunder into a monster instead. I told it in the strongest terms that it must leave off once it had its fun, however, and Mr. Hsiang promised he would restrain its worst excesses."

Zacharias opened his mouth, but there did not seem to be language strong enough to condemn Prunella's conduct. He had not managed to hit upon the right phrase when they began to descend.

They landed in a narrow alley not far from Lady Wythe's house, which was emptied by the rain. Prunella tapped the cloud affectionately as she alighted.

"Off you go to the Jade Emperor, good cloud," she said. "What a dear creature it is, though it has led me into such trouble. It would be unjust to blame it, I am sure. I don't suppose clouds have any *moral* sense, do you?"

"Prunella," said Zacharias, with deep feeling, "I should be obliged if you would tell me what, exactly, you intended to achieve by loosing a thunder-monster upon Hyde Park?"

"I would not have dreamt of inventing a thunder-monster under ordinary circumstances, of course, but there was nothing for it," said Prunella. "Mrs. Gray is the most notorious gossip in town, and she and Sophia knew me at once. I could not afford to let them go away, having seen me flying around on a cloud, particularly after what that infuriating sibyl said."

"What sibyl?"

"Of course, I did not tell you," said Prunella guiltily. "I meant to, indeed, only there has been such a great deal to think of! There is no time for it now, however. When we arrive at Lady Wythe's I shall go up to my room and swoon upon my sofa, and you must discover me and call for salts. When I am awakened, I shall explain that I was kidnapped by a foreign sorcerer while I was taking my morning exercise in the Park."

"Kidnapped by a foreign sorcerer?" said Zacharias blankly.

"Yes, is not it clever? The story is such a pretty one, and I thought it up in a moment while I was flying to you. He caught sight of me as he was passing on a cloud and fell instantly violently in love, and nothing would do for him but that he should snatch me up and whisk me away to his native country. I protested, however, and to frighten me into submission he summoned a thunder-monster. But it did not answer, for the monster turned on him, and in the confusion of battle I was able to escape."

"And what did Mr. Hsiang say to your extraordinary story?"

"Well, he is a consummate gentleman, you know, and he was so good as to agree to remain and duel the thunder-monster," said Prunella. "Though to be sure I do not know that he understood the details of the story. However, it is of no consequence, for he will go back to China once he has seen the monster away, and will not be around to be questioned. I must say it has all fallen out charmingly."

Zacharias had been listening in increasing perturbation.

"My dear Prunella," he said, "do you realise what a diplomatic disaster your story will cause if it is believed? Unnatural philosophers are not on the whole known for their chivalry, but the Society could hardly disregard such an affront as a foreign magician's attempting to run away with a young lady. The Society is already incensed by Mak Genggang's escape, and this on top of it will occasion cryings out against all foreign magicians. I have no doubt the Society will propose a motion to break our treaty to refrain from magical war. I will have it on my desk tomorrow morning, wickedly ungrammatical and ill-spelt."

"Oh," said Prunella. She was only temporarily deflated, however.

She brightened and said, "Then I shall tell everyone it is a *dead secret*, not to be told to anyone."

"In that case the whole town will know of it by the evening."

"Yes, but not officially, you see," said Prunella. "It will only be a rumour. I shall confide in everybody, and allow them to believe that there is a part of the secret I have told only them, because I trust them so particularly."

She paused for reflection. "And perhaps I shall suggest to the women that I wish the story to be kept quiet because I have fallen a little in love with Mr. Hsiang, and rather regret my defence of my virtue. With the men, of course, I shall have to take a different tack."

"Your amoral ingenuity in the pursuit of your interest is perfectly shocking," said Zacharias severely.

"Yes, isn't it?" said Prunella, pleased.

The rain had slackened to a thin drizzle when they approached Lady Wythe's residence.

"I think after all you had best arrive a little later, and ask Lucy for me," said Prunella, with the air of one who had been thinking deeply on the point. "We shall let her discover me unconscious. I am sure that will be much more convincing."

"It is an excellent way to drive Lucy into hysterics, but I suppose that is only a slight disadvantage."

"Oh, fiddle!" said Prunella. "Lucy is not such a poor creature. Likely she will try to slap me awake, so I will be the one to suffer!" She put on a melancholy expression, but could not quite preserve it, for the glee of the scheme would keep breaking through. "Do wait here, Zacharias, and follow in ten minutes."

Zacharias saw her peer down at the servants' entrance beneath the street, leap back, and steal up the steps to the front door. She peeped into the window, nodded, laid her hand upon the door, and went into the house.

Her scream cracked in Zacharias's ears like a whip.

Zacharias was across the road before he had begun to think. He bounded up the steps and burst into the hallway. He would have been swept away on the flood if he had not grasped the doorframe in time.

The hallway had turned into a river. It rushed away past Zacharias, flowing along the steps and down the road. Prunella was flailing along determinedly. The waters surged above her head, and the dark curls vanished. Zacharias's heart stopped—but she emerged at the end of the hall, struggled up the stairs and clung to the banister, panting.

"I am well," she said, though her appearance contradicted her. She was wild-eyed, her lips pale. "Oh, I could not bear to drown! It must be quite the worst way to die!" A fit of coughing overtook her, but when she was able to take a breath, she said:

"Zacharias, open my reticule, if you please!"

Zacharias had almost forgotten the familiars. He had secreted Prunella's reticule in his coat. He fumbled for it, and the familiars spilt out, squawking, neighing and swearing respectively.

"What shall I do?" said Prunella.

"Find the source," said Zacharias. The water continued to mount, though he could not tell where it came from. He tasted salt on his lips. "The puddle and the fire were pure magic, using merely the semblance of the elements, but this is real water, drawn from elsewhere. The source must be here—find it, and we can stop it up."

The unicorn had struggled through the water to the stairs. Prunella released the banister and climbed onto its back. It had grown enough to be able to support her, though Prunella looked as though she were sitting astride a large dog.

"Darling Youko! Nidget, Tjandra, find us the source of the hex, if you can, my dear ones."

The simurgh was already dipping in and out of the water, swooping down like a seagull sighting fish, and sneezing and shaking its child's head vigorously when it emerged again. Nidget clambered on top of the clock that stood in the hallway—a handsome antique that

Lady Wythe preserved more in memory of her grandparents than because it kept the time particularly well. This incident was likely to spoil its beauty and ruin what remained of its accuracy, for the clock was half-submerged.

Zacharias was busy casting spells to stop the water from rising any further, and to identify its source, but he was distracted by an indignant chirp from Tjandra.

"It is unkind to call Nidget a coward, Tjandra!" replied Prunella. "I am sure Nidget is doing as much as it can, and neither of us would wish it to drown. You can fly, but if Nidget were to fall into the water it could not swim— *Oh!*"

For Nidget had leant out over the side of the clock, and dropped abruptly into the waters.

"Nidget!" cried Prunella.

The unicorn reentered the waters, though it looked none too pleased to do it. It had hardly taken two steps, however, when Nidget leapt out of the water, clinging again to the clock like a bald white monkey.

"I have it," it said.

It held a metal ball, in which shifted hues of green, blue and grey. Water was still dripping from it, but Nidget gave it a shake:

"Now stop that, wicked curse!"

The water began to drain from the hallway. Zacharias lowered his staff, and saw Lady Wythe standing at the top of the stairs.

"Good gracious," she said.

Zacharias and Prunella had just been settled before a roaring fire, each with an ample portion of negus to finish, when they were interrupted by an incursion—Damerell, looking for once harassed, and trailed by an apologetic Rollo.

"I beg your pardon, ma'am, to have broken in upon such a

charming family scene," said Damerell, making his leg to Lady Wythe. "However, we have received such news as I thought you would wish to hear at once."

He looked expectantly at Rollo, who said:

"I am sorry to be the bearer of such wretched news, Zacharias, but I walked Midsomer's dreams, and he means to move for the Hallett to be undertaken tomorrow. They intend voting upon the motion in the morning, and going straight from the Society to take you up. They have already set up the table at the Society, and the pots."

"Pots?" said Prunella.

"For the blood," said Zacharias. He was keenly conscious of Lady Wythe's dismayed gaze, and he exerted so much effort to conceal his anxiety in consequence that his tone was peculiarly flat, as though he spoke of something that did not concern him at all.

He had known this was coming, of course, but he had thought he would have more time. Perhaps, too, some part of him had thought it would not really happen—had denied, despite all evidence, that his colleagues could bring themselves to carry out such an atrocity. Did he loom so large in their hatreds? Or was it the reverse—did they account him of so little value, that they thought nothing of treating him as they would not treat a dog? What was the death of a black man, after all, against Midsomer's elevation?

"You had best leave town as soon as you can, Zacharias," said Lady Wythe. She rose, composed despite her pallor. "Indeed, I do not know that there is any reason why you should not go now. Lucy can pack what clothes you have here, and you may travel in my carriage. Prewitt is the soul of discretion, and will take you as far as you need."

Her voice steadied Zacharias: it was so calm, so familiar and beloved. He did not respond at once, however, but sat with his head bowed.

He could flee, but he would be easily pursued. Even if he were to disguise himself it was impossible for him to be inconspicuous anywhere in Britain. And it stuck in his craw to think of running from Midsomer: whatever familiars he had summoned, the man was not half the sorcerer Zacharias was, and all his schemes and conspiracies could not alter that fact.

But worthier than pride, and weightier than pragmatism, was duty. Duty required that Zacharias stand his ground. He had too much work to do, and too many promises to keep, for him to give up being Sorcerer Royal quite yet.

"I am sensible of your goodness," he said finally. "But I shall not go anywhere. I have assured Mak Genggang that I will resolve her dispute with our nation, and I would leave far too much else unsettled were I to flee. I do not think the circumstances so very desperate. Midsomer has yet to succeed in getting rid of me, and there is no reason why his endeavours should begin to bear fruit now."

"I commend your courage, Zacharias, but I beg you will not be foolhardy," said Damerell. "Midsomer's supporters are not all of the Society, but they are numerous, and he has chosen for his allies those most irrational, most furious, most immovably opposed to your existence. You may find yourself facing down a mob."

"I still have sufficient resource to face even a mob of irate thaumaturges, I believe," said Zacharias. He picked up his staff, and inspected it as though to check its sturdiness.

"It all seems a vast deal of pother for a position you dislike," remarked Rollo. "Of course Midsomer is a scrub, but if he is so eager to be Sorcerer Royal, why not let him? I thought you never liked it."

Zacharias hesitated, glancing at Lady Wythe. He might have spoken more frankly to Damerell and Rollo, who knew his true feelings regarding his office. But he was loath to expand upon his dislike of it in Lady Wythe's presence, since it had been Sir Stephen's dearest wish for Zacharias to succeed him.

"I would not surrender the staff to Midsomer," said Zacharias. "His conduct has given me no confidence in his suitability for the office. I would not be worthy of my title if I conceded so readily to the loss of my staff to him."

"It all seems perfectly absurd to me," said Prunella. "To think of enduring hexes and floods and politics for a staff, when your only reward is to labour unendingly, and be abused by the Society for it!"

"Floods?" said Damerell.

"Did not you see the state of the hallway when you arrived?" said Prunella. She hesitated, then opened her palm, showing the orb Nidget had found. "It was caused by this."

"Oh, we did not come by the hallway," said Rollo, but Damerell let out a long low whistle.

"What is it?" said Lady Wythe.

"Either someone is so fond of Zacharias as to wish to spare him being sacrificed," said Damerell, "or he despises Zacharias so much he cannot bear to wait for the Hallett to be carried out. That is a curse."

"It is not a curse," said Prunella. "That is to say, I thought it was used to convey messages—is it not, Zacharias?" She held the orb out to Zacharias, who took it.

"I have not seen anything like it before," he said.

"I have never seen one used to convey anything but malice," said Damerell. "They are hardly to be found in this country; we have yet to discover the secret of producing them ourselves. All those I have seen were from India."

The orb was unexpectedly heavy in Zacharias's hand. He inspected the pinpricks upon its surface, ordered in regular patterns.

"This is writing," he said.

"Curses are commonly inscribed with a glorification of their owner, or a description of their intentions," said Damerell, joining Zacharias in his study of the orb. "That looks like a Fairy language to me. The cantillation marks are very similar to those one sees in certain dialects of Banshee. Can you read it, Rollo?"

Rollo made the attempt, but was unable to make out the words.

"I had a governess who was a Banshee, and she tried to hammer it into my noggin," he said. "The governor chased her off in one of his rages, more's the pity. But perhaps it's just as well. The curse brought a flood down upon you, did you say, Miss Gentleman? You may keep several spells in one of these what-d'ye-call-'ems—*we* say secretkeepers in my family. Reading the inscription aloud unlocks the other secrets, and like as not all the secrets in this one are unpleasant. The best thing to do would be to get rid of the writing, would not you say, Poggs?"

"I am of your mind, Rollo."

"Surely we ought not to remove the writing yet," said Prunella, recovering the orb from Rollo's loose grasp. "We ought to learn all we can of the orb's secrets first." She brought it close to her eye. "I do not know how we would remove the writing in any case. It is engraved upon the metal, and I am sure it is magical."

"Oh, that is the easiest thing in the world," said Rollo. "A jet of dragon's flame would do it!"

22

Prunella had once thought life in London would be all flirting and balls and dresses, hitting attentive suitors on the shoulder with a fan, and breakfasting late upon bowls of chocolate. She sighed now for her naïveté. Little had she known life in London was in fact all hexes and murder and thaumaturgical politics, and she would always be rising early for some reason or other!

She could not help feeling a twinge of guilt as the latch clicked shut behind her. The orb that had flooded them out sat in her reticule, along with the familiars, shrunk for ease of transport.

Yet why ought she to feel guilty? She had left a note to explain her purpose. Zacharias would likely be unhappy that she had gone by herself, but he could scarcely accompany her. He had been overtaken by another of his paroxysms the evening before, and had retired, grey with suffering, at Lady Wythe's insistence.

Prunella had recognised the strange orb at once. It was identical to the one she had seen at the Midsomers'. She thought it must be the same, but she knew so little of singing orbs that she could not be certain. There could be no harm in going quietly to Mr. Midsomer's house, however, and seeing if the orb she had noticed before was still there. If it was not, that was a piece of the evidence Zacharias needed to be able to accuse Mr. Midsomer of his crime.

Prunella had a mission of her own as well. She had examined her singing orb the night before, in the solitude of her bedchamber, and it was clear to her now that what she had thought to be mere ornamental carvings—the loops and swirls engraved upon the surface of her orb—were writing, though in a script so unfamiliar that she had not recognised it as such.

As for what script it was, she had her guide in the name of Seringapatam, which Mr. Hsiang had mentioned. The spectacular fall of Tipu Sultan's court at Seringapatam had been such a victory as no one would soon forget—a victory that had secured his vast kingdom of Mysore for Britain.

It all fit together. Her father had returned to England from India, and her mother . . . But Prunella would soon know more of her mother. She might discover something useful about her own singing orb while she investigated the Midsomers'. Perhaps she might even have an opportunity to interrogate the sibyl, whose mysterious reference to the Grand Sorceress Prunella now understood.

When Prunella approached the Midsomers' house, an air of stillness hung over the building. Its facade looked like a solemn white face: "Of someone rather unhappy, I think," said Prunella to her familiars.

It was not too difficult to locate a window looking into the room where the sibyl's painting was hung. It was on the first floor, as Prunella recalled, but this proved no obstacle. Murmuring the formula she had learnt the day before, she summoned a wisp of cloud, clambered atop it, and floated up to the window, Nidget under her arm.

A brief examination of the room through the window satisfied

Prunella that no one was there. Another minute's spellcasting opened the window, and Prunella scrambled into the house, Nidget following her.

"Why, that was simple enough," she said, dusting herself off. "I declare I do not know why more thaumaturges are not burglars. If I cannot find a wealthy gentleman to marry, Nidget, we could always resort to burglary for our livelihood—though I suppose Zacharias would disapprove."

"I cannot say I disagree with him," said a voice that was decidedly not Nidget's.

Prunella jumped and clutched Nidget, staring. A woman rose from a sofa at the other end of the room. It was placed at such an angle that her person had been blocked from Prunella's view when she had surveyed the room through the window.

"So you are a sorceress," said Mrs. Midsomer sourly. "Midsomer swore there were none in England."

Prunella straightened. It was an awkward position in which to be detected, but there was nothing for it. Denial was fruitless. She could only put a bold face on the matter, and be grateful that Tjandra and Youko had not come in with her.

"I am the first, and have not chosen to reveal my powers to the Society," she said. She could not resist adding, "Though it is no surprise Mr. Midsomer should be mistaken. He is wrongheaded in every respect!"

"There, too, I must agree," said Mrs. Midsomer, taking the wind out of Prunella's sails. "If I had known he was so remarkably stupid, I would never have come away with him. However, I am sworn to his service, and since we are now bound together, I suppose I am obliged to take offence at your insult."

"There is no insult I can fling at Mr. Midsomer which he would not deserve," said Prunella. "He shall hear them all, and defend himself, if he can! Where is he?"

"Do not you know?" said Mrs. Midsomer, with a curious half-smile. "And Geoffrey was so worried when he heard you had been at our party! I told him you were of no account, and he ought to focus his attention on the Sorcerer Royal. Geoffrey has a silly habit of seeing enemies wherever he looks."

"He is right to be worried about me," declared Prunella. "I *am* his enemy, and I know what he is about. Tell him I have found this!"

She presented the orb with a flourish.

"Where did you get that?" said Mrs. Midsomer sharply. "It is not yours!"

"It certainly is not," said Prunella, closing her hand around the orb. "I am not in the habit of trying to murder Sorcerers Royal. But Mr. Midsomer is—and he shall account for it!"

Mrs. Midsomer's grey eyes widened, and she stepped forward, actually reaching out to clasp Prunella's arm.

"It worked?" said Mrs. Midsomer. "Zacharias Wythe is dead?"

Prunella withdrew her arm in disgust. "I am not sorry to disappoint you, but no, he is not. He is a great deal more difficult to kill than your master seems to believe, and I must say your master is an absurdly ineffectual murderer!"

"My master!" sniffed Mrs. Midsomer. "He knows nothing of it!"

She snatched the orb from Prunella's grasp, moving so quickly that Prunella had lost it before she knew what was happening.

"You ought not to take things that are not yours," said Mrs. Midsomer.

She spoke always with a slight, charming accent of indefinable origin. It was stronger now, and her voice itself seemed to change. It had deep tones in it that were not altogether human, but recalled the clash of thunder and the deep-chested roar of the sea. Mrs. Midsomer's shadow grew, expanding so rapidly that it filled the room.

Prunella took a step back, and then another. Nidget was taut in her arms, waiting to spring. She could feel the presence of her two other familiars outside. She had been striving to restrain them, but if she did not suppress her increasing fright, they would soon burst in. She bumped into a table and looked around. The painting of the sibyl was behind her.

"You have been remarkably foolish, chit!" said Mrs. Midsomer in a booming inhuman voice. "Zacharias Wythe may have escaped me again, but you need not think you will be so fortunate!"

"Sibyl," said Prunella. She was glad to hear her voice ring out, hardly trembling at all. "Pray tell me, who is Mrs. Midsomer?"

"Lorelei," said the sibyl behind her. "Monstress, siren and mermaid—murderess in desire if not in truth—and a paltry hussy if I ever knew one!"

"Be quiet!" snarled Mrs. Midsomer. She lobbed her orb at Prunella.

Light burst forth from the orb in an array of colours—green, purple, blue and red. Each ribbon of light was a curse, and they scythed through the air towards Prunella.

"Nidget! Youko! Tjandra!" cried Prunella. "To me!"

Zacharias's temples throbbed as he hurried down the stairs. He had passed the night in Lady Wythe's spare room, and overslept in consequence. This invariably happened when Lady Wythe was present to overrule his orders to be awoken at such and such a time:

"Nonsense!" she would say. "Zacharias ought to rest. It would be the height of wickedness to wake him. Do you but try it, Lucy, and you shall have to look for another place."

Yet it had been Lucy who woke him in the end, at Lady Wythe's behest. Lady Wythe rose when he entered the sitting room, wringing her hands. Damerell was there also, pacing a groove into the carpet while he muttered a formula under his breath.

"Oh Zacharias," cried Lady Wythe. "The poor motherless girl! I feel culpable, truly. I ought never to have lent countenance to her pursuit of an establishment. I should have done more to bring home to her the folly in proceeding as she did. And this is the result!"

The note she thrust into Zacharias's hand bore a few lines in Prunella's round, ungainly handwriting.

Dear Lady Wythe,

By the time you read these words I shall be gone. I beg you will not be alarmed—I shall be back before you know it—but pray tender my apologies to Mr. Wythe if I should miss our lesson today. When I return I think I may promise a GREAT SURPRISE! What I mean I cannot tell you now, only wait and you shall see. You may tell Mr. Wythe I have taken my <u>case</u>, and plan to put to use my acquaintance with his friend Mr. Hsiang.

I am, your humble and
affectionate servant, &c.

"Now what does this mean?" said Zacharias.

"Dash the girl, cannot she stay still?" exclaimed Damerell. "The enchantment will never get a fix on her if she keeps flitting about."

When Zacharias looked at him, he said:

"I came prepared to fight off a magical ambush, but find myself embroiled in a domestic melodrama—and what is worse, striving with Murchie's wretched locationary, which is a spell I have never liked. Indeed"—turning to Lady Wythe—"I think it unlikely Miss Gentleman has done what you fear, ma'am. She is surely too sensible to run away with a man upon a single day's acquaintance, when she has no assurance regarding his income."

"You believe she has eloped?" said Zacharias.

Lady Wythe hesitated.

"It is a dreadful thing to think of her," she said. "But I cannot make any sense of Prunella's note unless it is that her abductor reappeared and repeated his offer. I did think that she seemed to regret refusing him, when she was telling me of him yesterday. It would be imprudent of her to accept, of course, but she is so young, and has lacked the guidance of firm principles, and it is so easy for an unscrupulous man to impose upon a giddy young female! Zacharias, *are* you acquainted with the gentleman who wished to run away with her?"

Zacharias murmured that they were acquainted, but he believed there was a misunderstanding. Mr. Hsiang was a very gentlemanlike man, not given to the abduction of young ladies—apart from anything else, he already had three wives.

"And he is so plagued by them that he has often expressed regret that he was not contented with one," said Zacharias. "No, I cannot think she has run away with Hsiang."

He was worried, but for quite a different reason. Zacharias did not know why Prunella had taken the familiars with her, but he suspected it meant Prunella had a plan. The thought filled him with apprehension.

The pale, frightened face of a footman peered around the door.

"Beg pardon, ma'am," he said. "I have said you are not at home, but they have marched all the way from the Society, and they say they will not be put off whatever we do."

For once Damerell relinquished his self-control so far as visibly to lose his patience.

"Oh, what now?" he cried.

Zacharias opened the door to an illusion of magicians on Lady Wythe's doorstep. Midsomer was among them.

"Zacharias Wythe, you are summoned to appear before the Presiding Committee of the Royal Society of Unnatural Philosophers to surrender your staff," said one of the men. He handed Zacharias a scroll. "At a meeting called this morning, it was proposed that the Hallett procedure should be undertaken today. The vote was passed by a majority."

Zacharias took the scroll silently.

Damerell swept the group of thaumaturges with a look of supreme contempt, ending with the man who had spoken. "Why, Cullip, you ha'penny conjurer, Wythe gave you your step!"

Cullip drew himself up to his full height.

"I was elected Secretary to the Committee because it was believed I should do my duty," he said. "And I am doing it now, I hope."

"Quite right," said Zacharias composedly. "Gentlemen, I shall be with you directly. Damerell, if you would have the goodness to tell Lady Wythe—"

"I shall tell Lady Wythe nothing," said Damerell. Damerell did not often lose his temper, but he did nothing by half measures. "They used to say that a man became a magician who was too scheming for Parliament, too bloodthirsty for the Army, and too much of a bloody sodomite for the Navy. But these are not quite the end times. We must still attempt to merit the name of civilised people. On what grounds is it proposed to strip Mr. Wythe of his staff? Even Hallett was deposed for a reason, however factitious. What fiction have *you* invented, pray?"

Cullip had gone a deep pink.

"It is a matter of common knowledge that Zacharias Wythe murdered Sir Stephen Wythe—his predecessor, his benefactor and the man who gave him his name!" he said. "And if it is possible to do worse than that, he has done it, for he also murdered the familiar Leofric, who had served the Sorcerers Royal of England since time immemorial. Now Wythe seeks to rob honest Englishmen of our magic, and give it over into the hands of women and foreigners!"

"What an extraordinary series of accusations," said Zacharias. "On what basis am I said to have committed such wrongdoing?"

He strove to keep his voice light, but his heart sank when he saw the look on Midsomer's face. This was the opportunity for which his enemy had been waiting.

"Do you deny, sir, that the Fairy Court has deliberately withheld magic from Britain at the behest of a parcel of Malayan vampiresses?" said Midsomer. "And was it not you who received their chieftainess when she came to England to further her scheme of revenge? You who defended her, and contrived at her escape when she was confined for her violent assault upon an Englishwoman?"

"I have not heard that Mrs. Midsomer suffered any greater injury than in losing a turban," said Damerell. "Indeed, having seen the headdress in question, I am inclined to believe the witch rather did her a service."

Zacharias shot Damerell a warning look. To Midsomer he said:

"I only recently discovered the block on England's magic, and the reason for it. If you were aware of it before, sir, I am surprised you did not report it sooner. A solution might have been arrived at by now if the circumstances had been explained to the Society. But it seems you have preferred to foment dissension among our colleagues instead."

"I have been working to ensure the removal of a murderer, a thief and a traitor from the highest office in English thaumaturgy," said Midsomer coldly. "It is hardly for you to judge the value of the exercise. If you wish to defend yourself, however, you may do so before the Presiding Committee. The Committee will doubtless give due consideration to any pleas you wish to submit in mitigation."

"Yes, it will all be perfectly aboveboard, I am sure," said Damerell, eyeing him. "You certainly do not lack perseverance, Midsomer. I would not have expected less than that, having failed in all your attempts to assassinate Wythe, you should resort to knocking on his door and demanding that he put his neck in your noose."

"You call me an assassin, sir?" said Midsomer. He tried to smile.

"But the Hallett is a legal device, as I think you will find, and one of great antiquity."

"Oh no," said Damerell, his eyes gleaming. "I call you a sad incompetent, and your toad-eaters a pack of cowards, to seek to murder a man by committee."

Midsomer's face grew stormy. Cullip leapt forward, unholstering a wand from beneath his coat. Behind him an angry chant rose, many-voiced.

Damerell held up his hands. The sky grew dark, though it was morning. The lamps lining the street took on a lurid purple glow. Every man was haloed with green light, and the thick smell of magic washed into the nostrils with every breath.

"Gentlemen, I beg you will be calm," said Zacharias, but he was already scrabbling for the counter-formula.

It was by pure chance that he looked up while searching his memory for the right syllables, and saw Prunella in the sky, speeding towards them upon a cloud.

She was shouting as she came, and when she leapt off her cloud he saw that she was soaking wet, her hair plastered to her head and her dress clinging to her form.

"She has run away," she gasped. "She has hid herself in the sea, the coward, and she will not come out whatever names I call her. I had her—oh, I had her by the tail! I have searched an age, but the longer she is hidden, the more likely it is that we shall never find her. It is her realm, you know, so she will know all the best places to hide. You must come directly and find her out. There is not a moment to lose!"

"Prunella, my dear, you are soaked through!" cried Lady Wythe. She burst forth to the startlement of the assembled thaumaturges, who had not observed her lurking behind the door. "Where on earth have you been? But let us have no explanations now. We must get you dry as soon as we can. Oh—how do you do, sirs?"

The ominous chanting had fallen silent upon Lady Wythe's appearance. Cullip stuck his wand back into his coat and muttered:

"Very well, ma'am, how d'you do? Ahem! I regret the necessity of disrupting your morning with Society business."

"Not at all," said Lady Wythe, smiling. "But you will forgive me if I ask whether the Society's business could not be transacted somewhere other than my doorstep? I have here a young lady who will catch cold if swift measures are not taken, and Zacharias has not yet had his breakfast. These domestic contretemps will seem of little consequence to you, sirs, but you will humour a mere female, I know."

The thaumaturges wavered. Lady Wythe had a great deal of natural authority; she was still held in considerable esteem by the Society; and she knew how to handle magicians. She had resisted the temptation to rush out and make a scene, showing herself at precisely that moment upon good advisement, and she would have brought it off if not for Prunella.

"Zacharias will have to delay his breakfast, ma'am," Prunella said firmly. "We must go and kill the fairy who has been trying to murder him."

Midsomer had begun to speak, but he clamped his mouth shut. Zacharias stared at Prunella, taken aback.

"The fairy?" he said.

"We have had it all wrong, Zacharias," said Prunella. "It is not Mr. Midsomer who set those horrid traps for you, but his familiar! I saw the orb at the party, you see—the curse, I mean—so I went to his house, thinking I might discover if it was the same. But there Mrs. Midsomer attacked me! I routed her, however, I and my fa—" Prunella broke off, glancing at the thaumaturges. "That is to say, I suppose her guilt overcame her, for she turned into a mermaid and fled to the sea. I pursued her, but when I could not find her I thought I ought to return and seek assistance."

"Where is Midsomer?" said Damerell abruptly.

The man was nowhere to be seen. His accomplices appeared no less bewildered than Damerell.

"Oh, was he here?" said Prunella, looking around. "You might have said. He will have gone to help her, of course. I should not be surprised if the creature were halfway across the Channel by now, with her husband in tow."

"Where did you leave her?" said Damerell.

Prunella was already climbing back upon her cloud.

"She was just off the coast at Lyme when I left," said Prunella. "It is a great distance to traverse even by cloud, but we—that is to say, *I* have worked out a modification of Mr. Hsiang's spell that closes the leagues with singular speed."

"We will follow by another method," said Zacharias, who disliked heights. "Damerell, do you think it wise, perhaps, to call—?"

"It is already done," said Damerell. "Gentlemen, we will take our leave of you."

Cullip spluttered: "The Committee's summons—!" But before he could complete his protest, Zacharias and Damerell had vanished.

"If you are so concerned about what the Presiding Committee will think, may I suggest that you summon a conclave to discuss the matter?" said Lady Wythe. A dangerous light shone in her eye. "I shall have something to say to the Committee myself, for it seems to me there has been a great deal of impropriety in these proceedings, which would never have been permitted in Sir Stephen's day."

Even if Cullip had wished to comply with Lady Wythe's suggestion, he would have struggled to assemble an adequate quorum for a Committee meeting. Zacharias was received at Lyme Regis by a group of thaumaturges assembled upon the Cobb, comprising Lord Burrow, most of the members of the Presiding Committee—and Geoffrey Midsomer.

"Mr. Wythe," said Midsomer portentously. "The Presiding Committee has been summoned here to witness, in person, your many breaches of your duties as Sorcerer Royal."

"This is most irregular," said Damerell. "Could not this have waited for a proper trial at the Society?"

Lord Burrow glanced at Midsomer. The Chairman of the Presiding Committee was generally esteemed for his integrity, though he had never much liked Zacharias.

"It is unusual," he said, "but not unprovided for by the Charter. We were informed that we would receive evidence of Mr. Wythe's alleged misdeeds here."

"It is just as well," said Zacharias before Damerell could respond. "For I have an allegation of my own to put to the Committee."

It was clear he could no longer wait for the evidence he had hoped for, which Sir Stephen was still struggling to unearth. Zacharias must put his case, and hope the public and unusual setting would compel an admission from Midsomer.

"I should have preferred to discuss this with you privately, before putting in action the formal machinery of the Society," he said to Midsomer. "But you have left me with no alternative. Do you deny that two months ago you performed an unlawful summoning, thereby depleting London's atmospheric magic, and acquiring a familiar—a mermaid who until recently you have passed off as your wife?"

Midsomer's eyes widened. Lord Burrow looked from Zacharias to his nephew, frowning. Whatever Midsomer had told his supporters, it seemed his uncle had not heard of this.

"Is this true, sir?" said Lord Burrow to Midsomer.

"Oh, why fixate upon such a trifle?" said Damerell maliciously. "Who among us has not dreamt of summoning himself a familiar? Midsomer is to be congratulated upon having become, in one stroke, a husband and a sorcerer. Let us not condemn him for his inattention to such a minor detail as the law."

Midsomer seemed to lose his head at being so transformed from accuser to accused. He said, wild-eyed:

"Will you take the word of a bastard and a negro over that of your own nephew, sir?"

"Why, if they tell the truth, yes," said Lord Burrow, but his voice was drowned out by a growling roar from above.

"Dash it, you contemptible mountebank! You are not to speak so to Poggs. You are not to call him such names!"

A vast shadow had fallen upon the roiling seas. In the sky a golden dragon came arrowing towards them, his wings spread wide and smoke rising from his jaws.

A groan of recognition rose from the Committee. Lord Burrow, looking quite human in his trepidation, turned to Damerell and said:

"Pray tell me that is not Robert of Threlfall."

"Am I not to be permitted the assistance of my own familiar?" said Damerell haughtily. "I *am* a sorcerer, if I am a bastard. If the Society wishes me to forget it, it ought not to insist on sending me so many circulars."

To Rollo, wheeling in the sky, he called: "Do not lose your temper, Rollo. It is foolish to expect a Midsomer to conduct himself like a gentleman. Never mind him, but see if you can find this mermaid Prunella has told us about. She is hid within the waters."

"There you are!" cried Midsomer, with such triumph that Zacharias and Damerell stared. "There is the evidence I promised you, sirs. Mr. Wythe has sought to deprive Britain's thaumaturges of their birthright of magic, and to pass that power to the undeserving. To this end, in secret, he has been educating a female in the unnatural science of thaumaturgy. And here she comes—the witch he has been training!"

Prunella dismounted from her cloud, seeming not to notice the startled gaze of the Committee.

"Have you still not found her?" she said disapprovingly. "Really, I have no notion how you managed before we met. It seems as though nothing can be done without me."

Rollo's massive scaly head appeared above the waters. He was paddling in the sea, looking for all the world like a gigantic dog.

"The mermaid is here somewhere, for I can sense her," he panted. "But I believe she has made herself invisible. Oh, have you arrived, Miss Gentleman?"

"How do you do, Rollo?" said Prunella.

Prunella and Rollo had become fast friends in the course of Damerell's shepherding of Prunella through *ton* society, but as far as Zacharias knew, Rollo had never appeared before her in his true shape. He preferred the human form, it being better suited for such pursuits as inspecting the horseflesh at Tattersall's and playing whist at White's. Yet Prunella did not seem disconcerted by encountering a dragon in the place of the dandy she had known.

"If you would have the kindness to continue searching beneath the waters," she said, "I shall see what I can do to assist."

She spread her hands, and lightnings flashed between them. The waves rose like children in a schoolroom, shoving and grumbling as they came to their feet. Prunella's dark hair streamed out behind her on the salt wind blowing off the sea, and she spoke in a clarion voice.

"Bring her to me," said Prunella. "The siren-singer; the murderous mermaid, fish-tailed and silver-eyed; she of the scale-feet and webbed fingers; she of the many names—Lorelei—Laura Lee—she who is called Mrs. Midsomer!"

"Ha!" said Rollo's voice from the watery deeps. He rose from the sea, liberally sprinkling the magicians arrayed upon the Cobb.

He held something within his jaws. Rearing up, he dropped it gently on the ground, where it lay gasping like a beached fish.

It was Mrs. Midsomer.

23

IT WAS NOT a situation in which even the most elegant woman would have appeared to advantage. Laura Midsomer (*née* Lee, *alias* Lorelei) suffered further from having had insufficient notice of her marine excursion. She was still clad in the everyday attire of a mortal woman, dressed in expectation of encountering nothing wetter than the British spring. Her top half was clothed in a spencer, whose hardier material hid the curves her sodden dress could not fail to display. The whole shining, sinuous length of her tail emerged from her dress below.

The men soon thought better of staring, however. This was Mrs. Midsomer's native environment, and her anger rendered her incandescent with power.

"Blackguards!" she spat. "Fools! Weaklings! Is this how you defend me, Geoffrey, your wife whom you promised to protect, your familiar who pledged you her service? Are these your friends indeed the finest magicians in England, who have permitted a jumped-up chit and her pet beast to manhandle me?"

The pet beast in question peered over the side of the Cobb. An expression of astonishment overspread his countenance.

"Why, what's this?" cried Rollo, but no one paid any mind to him.

Prunella was haloed in green light, the remnants of the power she had expended in her spell still clinging to her frame. The glow reflected in her eyes made them appear lightless and deep, giving her the remote look of a vengeful goddess.

She held out her hand, and a metal ball floated out of the wreck of Mrs. Midsomer's dress. It was wreathed in the same eldritch light that outlined Prunella's form. Within the depths of the orb was reflected an image of the sea, small but wonderfully vivid. Waves crashed against the shore, and white flecks of seagulls wheeled around the grey curve of a minute sky, their lonesome cries echoing in counterpoint to the voices of the birds in the skies above.

"Our conversation was interrupted, Mrs. Midsomer," she said. "This is yours, I think."

"You know perfectly well it is," snarled Mrs. Midsomer. "What business had you to take it?"

"Oh, I am always poking my nose into things that are not my business," said Prunella. "But on this occasion, I had better grounds than usual for doing so. I exercised the rights of an apprentice—" She lifted her eyes to Zacharias, and smiled. "The rights of a friend. Are you the author of the attacks upon Mr. Wythe? That is all I wish to hear from you."

"This is beyond anything," cried Midsomer. "Gentlemen, do you mean to stand by and permit my wife to be interrogated by this—this—"

"Chit?" said Prunella helpfully.

"Magicienne," said Zacharias.

The Presiding Committee stared at him.

"Do you require any further evidence of her abilities?" said Zacharias. "As you have witnessed yourselves, Miss Gentleman has been trained in the strictest principles of thaumaturgical practise, and can justly be called no witch, but a *magicienne.* Though indeed I hope we can one day overcome this unreasoning dislike of witches—fine craftsmen and women, on the whole—no worse, taken as a body, than any illusion of thaumaturges."

"Really, Zacharias, this is not the time to be lecturing the gentlemen," exclaimed Prunella. "Cannot you tell that we are on the brink of extracting a confession from Mrs. Midsomer that she has been conspiring to murder you?"

"These accusations are baseless," said Midsomer, crimson. "I admit I moved for the Hallett when it became evident that Mr. Wythe was unfit to hold his office. That seemed to be my clear duty. However, the notion that I or my wife should have made any attempt upon a brother thaumaturge's life is ludicrous!"

"I say nothing as to *your* involvement. I can well believe you had little to do with it," said Prunella graciously. "Your wife, however, is certainly a murderess."

"You had better say: not a murderess yet!" said Mrs. Midsomer. "If my efforts to kill Zacharias Wythe have failed, it is only because I could not draw upon my full powers. My puling master insisted I refrain from wonder-working, lest I reveal my nature. Now I am in my true form, however—!"

"There, you see," said Prunella to Midsomer. "She *has* been endeavouring to kill Mr. Wythe. She says so herself."

To Midsomer's credit, he looked as astonished as everyone else.

"I knew nothing of this, Laura," he said.

"That is because you do not attend," said Mrs. Midsomer waspishly. "If I have told you once, I have told you a thousand times. I did not come to your realm for my health. I came with one motive: to discover the sorcerer who murdered my beloved, and avenge his death. Once I am done we shall return to my home—to the glorious caverns my aunt the Queen has bequeathed to me, and their mysterious underground seas—so there was no need for you to be in such a pother about your silly Society. Even if you did become Sorcerer Royal you could not remain one for long."

"But I had no notion your beloved had anything to do with Zacharias Wythe," protested Midsomer.

"You would know if you had only listened!" snapped Mrs. Midsomer. "My beloved was not called Leofric when I knew him. A mortal gave him the name—the first Sorcerer Royal. How he loved that mortal! 'Twas for his sake that he went away from me, and lived out his life in exile from Fairyland. To serve the Sorcerer Royal was the only desire of his heart, and Zacharias Wythe killed him, the traitor—the villain—the murderer!"

Her voice rose to a shrill pitch that blended with the wind, whipping the waves into a frenzy. The magicians clapped their hands over their ears. Mrs. Midsomer planted her palms on the ground and flipped herself backwards off the Cobb with effortless strength, splashing into the water.

Midsomer shouted, "Laura, what will you be at?"

"She is growing," said Zacharias, as the wind howled, and thunder cracked the heavens open. It began to rain, big fat drops falling out of a darkening sky.

"I think she has lost her temper," said Prunella composedly: her aura was keeping her dry.

For a brief period after Mrs. Midsomer vanished, there was nothing to be seen amid the surging steel-grey waves. Rollo hauled himself onto the rocky end of the Cobb, and thrust his head over the wall, seeming to have something of great importance to communicate.

"I say—" he said, but he was not permitted to finish his sentence.

Mrs. Midsomer burst out of the waters behind him and rose into the skies, growing with inconceivable rapidity.

Her bulk seemed to fill the world, blocking out the horizon and casting a shadow over the magicians huddled on the wall. The enchantment appeared to encompass everything upon her person, for as she grew, so did the fronds of seaweed draped over her, and the pretty amber pendant on her breast expanded till it was itself the height and breadth of a grown man.

"Midsomer!" roared Lord Burrow. "Look to your wife!"

"He can hardly miss her," remarked Prunella.

"Think of our fishing—our ships—they will be overturned if her antics are not stopped," said Lord Burrow. "Exert your influence, man. Govern your wife!"

"If you think, sir, that is within my power to restrain Laura," said Midsomer wearily, "then all I can say is, you must not have been attending."

"Murderer!" howled Mrs. Midsomer. She drew from the amassed storm clouds a bolt of lighting and flung it at Zacharias. It split the air with an almighty crack, and would have smashed the wall had Zacharias not fended it off with a spell. The bolt went into the sea, and steam rose from the bubbling waves.

"This is outrageous!" said Prunella. "The creature ought to know when she is beaten."

She leapt nimbly off the Cobb before anyone could stop her, and was borne up by a white horse—a steed shaped from the froth on the waves and animated by magic.

"Hup hup!" cried Prunella, driving her heels into the creature's flanks, and off they went, cantering over the heaving seas, while Prunella shouted impertinences at Mrs. Midsomer.

"Damerell, pray persuade her to return," gasped Zacharias. Staving off Mrs. Midsomer's hexes required all of his attention. They were wicked spells, fiendishly complex and prickly with malice, stinging his hands as he disenvenomed them.

"Miss Gentleman will do very well," said Damerell, scarcely

sparing a glance for the small figure vanishing into the grey murk of sky and sea. "You, however, want aid. Watch your head, there!"

Zacharias escaped being exploded only by Damerell's intervention. The chantment ricocheted off Damerell's counter-spell and detonated a pile of rocks at the end of the Cobb, where Rollo sat with his shoulders up around his ears. He jumped, and bawled out:

"Poggs!"

"Rollo, cannot you see that we are busy?" said Damerell. "If you wish to make yourself useful, you might go and find Miss Gentleman, and shield her from the attacks of that sea-woman."

"But that is what I have been trying to say, only no one would attend," said Rollo, injured. "She ain't a sea-woman. She's Lorelei, my own third cousin twice removed."

"You don't mean to say you are related to the wretched creature?" said Damerell.

"Known her since I was out of the egg!" said Rollo. "Lorrie had a frightful temper even then. She ate one of my brothers on a rampage, and he was a mere dragonet, not more than a week old. He had broken her favourite doll, but I don't call that a meet response, do you? Still, that is Lorrie all over! My aunt gave her a right set-down over it. Aunt Georgiana was the only creature Lorrie would ever listen to.

"I had forgotten she was engaged to Leofric," he added musingly. "I could never account for his liking her, though she is my own cousin. Do you know, the most astonishing thing is, 'twas she who cried off! He only came to the mortal world after, but I don't believe the two things were connected, for it is my belief he intended to leave Fairy all along. He was always a great one for insects, and we haven't many in Fairyland—they have a dashed peculiar habit of growing minds, and turning into fairies."

Damerell said dangerously, "Rollo, you may not have observed that Zacharias is striving to contain a fireball, and I am in imminent danger of having my best pair of top-boots ruined by a hex. We are not at leisure to discuss your family's eccentricities. If you are so well acquainted with the lady, however, may I suggest that you ask her to desist? She might take it better from her cousin than from any of us."

"She never liked me above half," said Rollo, unconvinced. "The only reason I was not ate was because I was too old and tough, for I am sure I broke half a dozen of her dolls."

Still, he spread his wings and flapped up towards the upper air where Mrs. Midsomer's head was shrouded by mist and rain. His uncertain voice could be heard through the clamour of the storm:

"Lorrie? I say, Lorrie!"

"Rollo Threlfall?" boomed Mrs. Midsomer, in a voice mingling the crash of the waves and the howl of the wind. "What business have you here?"

"Go for her throat, Rollo!" bellowed Prunella, galloping along on her sea-horse. "Rip it out and ha' done with it!"

Rollo gave Prunella a look of terror.

"I shan't pay her any mind, of course," he said earnestly to Mrs. Midsomer. "Dashed unpleasant way of carrying on. It don't seem quite maidenly to be so bloodthirsty, does it? Is it a mortal thing, do you think, or are the modern females of Fairyland like that too? Leaving aside lamiae, of course. Not but what I have known some very agreeable lamiae in my time. There was a good sort of girl who used to live near my father's cave, Delphyne her name was, I think—unless it was Daisy?"

"Robert," said Mrs. Midsomer, "I am engaged in very important business at the moment, and if you have nothing better to say than to ask me whether I ever knew a lamia named Daisy . . ."

Rollo had been turning loops in the air, sunk in thought.

"Now I think of it, her name was Sybaris," he exclaimed. "But she terrorised the town of Delphi, of course, which accounts for the confusion. Aunt Georgiana could never stick her."

"Cousin Georgiana?" Mrs. Midsomer stiffened. The turbulence of the waves subsided. "Is she here?"

"Good God, no!" said Rollo, horrified. "I was only recollecting that she did not like Sybaris, which is as good a testimonial as anyone could desire. Though to be sure, Aunt Georgiana does not like you above half either—but never mind all that! What I meant to say, Lorrie, is that you ought not to be rampaging about like this. It ain't good *ton*! We are not in Fairyland, you know, where everyone enjoys a good magical fisticuffs. In the mortal realm there are things like ships and fishermen and picnics to think about."

"What have picnics to do with anything?" said Mrs. Midsomer.

"I am surprised at you, Lorrie," said Rollo. "It stands to reason no one can have a picnic if it is raining cockatrices and dragons. A hugeous mermaid don't improve the view, either."

"Do you really mean to defend your friend's villainy to me by such shifts?" roared Mrs. Midsomer. "That mortal murdered my Leofric!"

"But if you would only listen, I am sure Zacharias would be able to explain himself," pleaded Rollo.

"What excuse could there be for such faithless conduct?"

"I am not altogether sure," Rollo admitted. "But Zacharias is a vastly clever fellow, and I am sure he could explain everything to your satisfaction if you would only be so good as to allow him ten minutes—"

Rollo was not allowed to finish his own explanation, however, for Mrs. Midsomer, losing patience, swatted him away. With a piteous yelp, Rollo vanished into the clouds.

"Rollo!" shouted Damerell.

"Pray come out," said Prunella's voice through the storm, "for you are needed."

The storm clouds heaped in the lowering sky merged together to form the shape of a man, large and powerful, and lying prone upon the horizon. He rose, opening eyes of yellow lightning, and said in a rumbling voice:

"If it isn't that blasted girl again!"

"If you are annoyed to see me, that is all the more reason to do your work quickly," said Prunella. "I should be excessively obliged if you would kill this mermaid for us. Once that is done you may go back to being insensate clouds as soon as you wish."

The thunder-monster gave Mrs. Midsomer an unimpressed look.

"It will require a tempest," he said.

"Go to it!" said Prunella.

With Mrs. Midsomer's attention distracted, Zacharias was freed from the necessity of defending himself. He was putting his liberty to good use, and constructing another spell, when a freezing hand gripped his arm.

It was Lord Burrow. Upon his wet countenance was an expression composed in equal parts of fear, fury and plain discomfort.

"Damn it, Wythe, these are conditions calculated to bring on an inflammation of the lungs if there ever were such," he shouted. "Lady Frances will be in such a taking she will not be fit to live with. She has just nursed me through a fever, and found it so tedious she has strictly forbidden my contracting any further illness. Cannot you stop them?"

"That may be within my power," said Zacharias. "I have a notion I know what will calm Mrs. Midsomer's fury. Miss Gentleman will likely subdue her thunder-creature if Mrs. Midsomer can be persuaded to leave off trying to kill me. Though I have Damerell to deal with as well, of course, since Rollo Threlfall has got himself involved."

Damerell was striding up and down the Cobb, chanting curses of such ancient, complex wickedness as to raise the hair of the assembled thaumaturges.

"Do what you can," said Lord Burrow urgently. "I have organised the men in a chanting circle to drain that blasted mercreature of her power, but since this is her native environment, her power is replenished faster than we can draw it."

"But stay!" said Zacharias thoughtfully. "The reason for all this disturbance is that Mrs. Midsomer has been so intemperate as to threaten my life. Does not that show a very creditable loyalty in my friends? I am not sure, after all, that it would be wise to prevail upon them to stop."

Lord Burrow gave him an incredulous look, but with the advent of the thunder-monster the sea had been thrown into even greater tumult. The sheets of rain falling unbroken from the sky seemed as though they would cause a second Flood. The strivings of Mrs. Midsomer and the thunder-monster so infused the place with magic that every wave bore a crest of green foam, every magician was outlined in light and the opaque vault of the sky was a livid green, reflecting the unearthly glow of the battle below.

"Damn your impudence!" said Lord Burrow. "Do you mean to blackmail me at such a time as this?"

"You and Mr. Midsomer both," said Zacharias.

Midsomer was huddled in a corner, watching his wife and familiar in terror. He looked up at the sound of his name.

"If Providence permits us to survive this calamity, it will behoove me to report an unlawful summoning to the Society," said Zacharias. "I understand Mr. Midsomer proposes that the Hallett be undertaken. It could be done at the same meeting."

"We will not survive," said Midsomer, with a slight improvement in his spirits. "So the point is moot."

"It strikes me that my report could cause some awkwardness for so well-known a family as the Midsomers," continued Zacharias.

"My sister Polly would not like it, if that is what you mean," said Lord Burrow. "So you will keep quiet about this business of summoning a familiar—a froward familiar at that; you ought to have chosen a more peaceable creature, Geoffrey—you will keep quiet, will you, Wythe, and sort out this business, at a price?"

"I only desire your support at the next Society meeting," said Zacharias. "I require no more than that you and Mr. Midsomer should vote as I vote, second any nomination I make, and shout down any proposal contrary to my wishes."

Lord Burrow glowered at him. "And we are to lend our names to any harebrained policy arising from your proposals, I suppose?"

"If you think it right to do so. I hope you will, but my price is your support for the space of one meeting only," said Zacharias. "For what I intend, a single meeting will suffice."

A fisherman's hut close to the shore burst into flames, despite the extreme wetness of the weather. Lord Burrow said:

"If you can stop them, you may have whatever you want, and be damned to you! The Hallett will be withdrawn, and we shall vote on whatever blockheaded reforms you desire.

"It is the sorcerer's way to gain his point by main force, after all," he added bitterly. "But you will have to perform your side of the bargain first!"

"It shall be done," said Zacharias.

Damerell was about to put the finishing touches upon a convoluted curse implicating even the neighbours and casual acquaintances of Mrs. Midsomer's descendants unto the seventh generation when Zacharias interrupted him.

"Come, man, pull yourself together," said Zacharias. "There is no need for this. If you are concerned for Rollo there is a simpler way to put a period to the scene, and she will help you recover him, I am sure."

Damerell stared at him, bemused at having been pulled so suddenly out of his incantation. "What?"

"I have begun the spell, but it requires more work, and I should be grateful for your assistance," said Zacharias. "We must make it a watertight chantment, else it will be bound to fail—for she is not what anyone would call complaisant."

24

GEORGIANA WITHOUT RUTH had been having a lovely day. She had passed the morning in visits, gossiping and testing her wits (and in one case, her claws) against her friends and enemies. She had then engaged in some light exercise, hunting down her dinner—a white hart with a blood-red star on its forehead, which wailed in a human voice as she devoured it.

Since creatures of like strangeness were so often to be found in the forests of Fairy as to have lost all their novelty, this impaired her appetite not a jot, and Georgiana returned to her cave in an excellent humour. She curled up on her hoard of gold, but as she was about to float away on billows of sleep, she was rudely torn from her slumbers.

The geas laid upon her could not be gainsaid. The spell was devilishly well constructed, and despite all her efforts Georgiana was borne irresistibly along by it, hurtling along secret ways across the worlds, growing crosser and crosser with each unwilling wingbeat.

The originators of the enchantment had not even bothered to disguise their identities, and by the time Georgiana descended upon

Lyme Regis, she had prepared some rich words for Paget Damerell and that upstart Sorcerer Royal. She would not quietly endure the insult of being summoned to attend to a magician's pleasure, as though she were any trumpery fairy or slubberdegullion spirit, so greedy for power that it was willing to pledge itself to a mere mortal. Oh no! They would soon discover why she was named Without Ruth.

The sight that greeted her upon her arrival was sufficiently appalling to distract her from her wrongs, however.

"Lorelei," she trumpeted, "do I indeed find you in a tantrum? For shame! To be two thousand years old and still so naughty!"

Mrs. Midsomer's churning tail ceased its operations with comical abruptness. The whirlpool it was working up died down abruptly. The mists veiling her form were blown away by a gust of wind, and the sun shone out of the clouds, illumining her abashed countenance.

"Cousin Georgiana!" she exclaimed. "I—I thought you never visited the mortal realm."

"That shows how much you know," said Georgiana snappishly. "I come and go as I wish. You surely did not think *I* was subject to the Court's restrictions upon travel?"

"Oh no, no," said Mrs. Midsomer. She had already begun to shrink.

"Put a stop to this rain, for pity's sake," said Georgiana. "I have just had my scales polished, and the wet will ruin my shine. Pray, who has permitted this thunder-monster to run amuck?"

"I have not run amuck," said the thunder-monster peevishly. "I am only trying to murder this sea-woman, so that I may go to sleep again. I should be happy to wash my hands of the business if the sorceress would only release me."

"Well, never mind this sorceress, whoever she is, but go away," said Georgiana. "You will not soon kill Lorelei. If it were as easy as all that, one of her relations would certainly have pipped you to the post. I beg you will not try to argue. I do not at all like the taste of an elemental."

The thunder-monster faded out of existence, muttering imprecations. An outraged Prunella opened her mouth to object, but she was quelled by a glare from Zacharias.

"As for you, Lorelei, it was all very well for you to make mischief while the Queen was away, but what do you think she will say to your antics when she returns?" continued Georgiana. "Was that a mortal town on the shore? And now it is nothing but a bundle of sticks and damp sand!"

"Oh, you will not tell her!" cried Mrs. Midsomer. "It was never much of a town anyway—spinsters contriving on a hundred pounds a year, and sixpence assemblies. Besides, I acted upon the purest of motives. I was wreaking vengeance for my dear Leofric. Perhaps"—a touch of acid tinged her voice—"you do not recall Leofric?"

"Everyone knew you called off the engagement, so spare me your airs, I beg," said Georgiana. "You were not overly broken up when he left for the mortal world. Why, scarce a fortnight had passed before you were parading your new mortal beau about, though *he* did not long survive the expiry of your affections! I should tread carefully if I were you," she added as an aside to Midsomer.

"But that was before I heard the news," protested Mrs. Midsomer. "Then I knew I had never loved anyone so well, and never would again. Only then, when I finally knew what I had lost, I swore to revenge myself upon the mortal who could so cruelly betray him."

"You cannot have loved him so well if you have not even troubled to discover what he is about now," said Georgiana.

"Mamma never approved of necromancy," said Mrs. Midsomer, with dignity. "She thought it a low habit, fit only for ghouls and mortals."

"Necromancy indeed!" said Georgiana. "From the way you go on, one would almost think Leofric was dead."

Mrs. Midsomer stared at her. "But he is!"

Georgiana had turned her attention to the damp, shivering thaumaturges on the Cobb, however.

"What have you to say in your defence, interrupting the slumbers of an old female for such a trifle? If you could not put up with Lorelei's freaks you ought not to have brought her over the border. She has a tantrum regular, once every other day, and twice on Sundays."

Damerell said, "I do not understand you, ma'am. I see no old female here—only a queen among dragons, ageless and eternal, of matchless elegance and unsurpassed majesty."

"We apologise for our temerity in calling you," said Zacharias. "But we were in desperate straits, and you seemed the only person who would be able to influence Mrs. Midsomer. We hoped you would be so good as to condescend to exert your influence on our behalf, and persuade Mrs. Midsomer to listen to our explanation."

Georgiana snorted, but she had always had a soft spot for Damerell, who was looking up at her with unmistakable admiration. His flattery had the desired effect.

"She will listen, though much good will it do you," said Georgiana. "A more obdurate creature than Lorelei I never knew. However, you will attend, Lorelei, and discover what became of your precious Leofric—not that you were very kind to the poor fellow before he left Fairy."

"You believe I killed Leofric, is that correct?" said Zacharias. He turned to the Presiding Committee, who stood in a soggy huddle, stunned by the storm, and staring in dull amaze at Georgiana Without Ruth. "And I stand accused before you of having, on the same night, murdered my guardian, my mentor and manumitter, Sir Stephen Wythe.

"I have not sought to deny the accusations before, knowing that those who wished to believe them would do so even in the absence of evidence, and not wishing to discuss what was so painful to me. But I did not kill Sir Stephen. Nor did I kill Leofric. How could I have encompassed such a design, even supposing I were so unfeeling as to desire to injure my protector? Sir Stephen was the Sorcerer Royal, Leofric a familiar of great power and cunning, and I was but a journeyman thaumaturge. I was wholly unequipped to do battle with either of them and survive unscathed, much less defeat them."

"You ate Leofric, of course," spat Mrs. Midsomer. "You need not think you will fool me so easily! I see his mark upon you. Your every enchantment smells of him. Oh, I know you have devoured him, poor Leofric—"

"And he has devoured me," said Zacharias.

This put a stopper on Mrs. Midsomer's rant. She gaped at him. Georgiana chuckled.

Damerell said, in the voice of a man enlightened, *"Ah!"*

"What do you mean?" cried Midsomer, but his wife spoke over him.

"Leofric lives?" she said. She placed her webbed hand on her heart, her eyes blazing. "Tell me."

Zacharias told her. It was the first time he had spoken to any living person of the night Sir Stephen died.

A log had tumbled out of the grate. It sat, charred and smoking, by the carpet, and Zacharias knelt to retrieve it. He thought Sir Stephen had nodded off over his work, his familiar's head resting upon his shoulder.

Sir Stephen was growing older, loath as they both were to admit it. He worked as hard as ever, travelling tirelessly between worlds and passing long evenings in his study, but there was no escaping the fact that he no longer possessed all the vigour of his youth. It was not uncommon for Zacharias to walk into Sir Stephen's study to find him drowsing over his papers.

Zacharias did what he could to relieve his burden. There was still considerable discontent within the Society over his appointment as Sir Stephen's secretary. Every unnatural philosopher in London had a son or nephew they believed better suited for the role than a charity case plucked from a slave ship.

But Zacharias was to ignore all such murmurs, said Sir Stephen. "We understand each other," he said. "Such confidence exists between us, as makes you more useful to me than any sorcerer's son could be."

Zacharias had his own doubts as to the perfection of their mutual understanding. Sir Stephen had grand ambitions for Zacharias—fine visions of his future, for which he had been preparing the ground since Zacharias was a child.

But Zacharias knew himself to be unfitted for public life by both disposition and inclination. The role of secretary to Sir Stephen suited him perfectly, for it comprised what was, in his judgment, the most interesting parts of the work of the Sorcerer Royal: research, the invention of new formulae, and the working out of technical problems presented by the Government and the Society, all carried out with minimal intercourse with the outside world.

Sir Stephen's position, which kept him so much in the public eye, tempted Zacharias not at all. But he kept his own counsel, not wishing to provoke an argument. The disagreement was bound to arise at some point, but he would do nothing to hasten it. He was as happy as he had ever been—contented with his work, of real use to his benefactor. Perhaps it was no wonder that he had no premonition of disaster that evening—that, upon entering Sir Stephen's study, he had seen nothing amiss but a log.

It was only when he had retrieved the stray faggot that he rose and saw what Leofric was about. The dragon's serpentine form was curled around Sir Stephen's chair, his forelegs propped up on the armrest. His head was bowed over Sir Stephen's immobile form, and he had already commenced upon his meal.

For a moment Zacharias did not understand what he saw. He had known Leofric nearly all his life, but they had never been on intimate terms. Leofric was not only magical and ancient, but something of a snob: in common with many familiars, he thought all mortals other than his master beneath his notice.

"Leofric," said Zacharias, "do you think that wise? You may wake Sir Stephen."

The dragon's jewelled eyes met Zacharias's without alarm.

"Nothing will wake him," said Leofric. He licked his chops.

Zacharias saw that Sir Stephen no longer had a left hand. That was why Leofric's jaws were red. It did not trouble Sir Stephen, for he was dead.

The strength went from Zacharias's limbs, and he grasped at the table to avoid falling over. He was trembling with horror. He already knew what had happened, but his mind would not admit the truth.

"Sir Stephen has been taken unwell," he heard himself say. He must not leap to conclusions. Something might yet be done. He must unloosen Sir Stephen's neckcloth, get a glass of brandy down his throat. "You must go for a doctor—inform Lord Burrow—"

"Stephen is dead," said Leofric. He spoke with a horrible matter-of-fact detachment, though he had seemed fond of Sir Stephen in life. Leofric had accompanied him everywhere; had told him, with apparent sincerity, that Sir Stephen was his favourite of all the Sorcerers Royal he had served.

"What have you done to him?" said Zacharias. That missing hand could not be denied, however his mind strove to reject the image. He looked down and saw that his own hands were shaking.

"I? I did nothing. It was his heart that killed him," said Leofric, speaking still in that intolerable, unfeeling voice. "I told him he would not last if he did not take care. He killed himself with overwork, as I said he would. He might have had many more years of sorcery."

He looked down upon Sir Stephen's still face, and for the first time a trace of regret entered his voice.

"Now look how he has served himself out," he said. "Dead before sixty, with your position as yet unassured, and so many of his plans unrealised. And I at liberty to exact my reward prematurely."

"Your reward?" said Zacharias.

"I pledged myself to Stephen's service, body and soul, for his lifetime," said Leofric. "In return for which, he agreed he should be mine upon death. Body and soul."

This was the first Zacharias learnt of the Exchange, for no sorcerer willingly spoke of the grim deal he struck with his familiar—the price demanded by every magical creature before it would submit to bondage.

He had often complained to Sir Stephen of the opaqueness of the field of thaumaturgy. There was so much that was not known, or only half-known, because magicians were so jealous of their secrets. Each generation took some of its discoveries with it to the grave.

"What learning may not we be losing by this foolish attachment to mystery?" Zacharias had argued. "Surely transparency would serve us all better, and none could lose by it."

Sir Stephen had not been convinced. "After all, the very essence of magic is its inscrutability. No one could become a sorcerer without one great secret."

And this was the great secret. Zacharias had not conceived that it could be so horrible.

"You need not look so distressed," said Leofric. "Stephen was prepared for his end. The Exchange really only poses difficulties for those sorcerers who believe in salvation. Stephen was always in two minds about heaven. Forsaking it did not come so hard to him as it would to others."

"I thought you loved him," said Zacharias.

He was surprised at how calm he sounded. His voice seemed to have its own separate life, which had nothing to do with the rest of him. The weight of a terrible sorrow pressed against his ribs, but he would not let it crush him yet.

"Who would render such service as I have purely for love?" said Leofric. "It is no more than the bargain every sorcerer strikes. I have performed my end of the contract. Now it is come time for my remuneration."

"Do not take him," said Zacharias, the words seeming to flow from him without his volition. Surely the anguish could not continue. It was intolerable. "Pray—pray do not."

"It was agreed," said Leofric. He bent his head again.

Zacharias could never explain the impulse that overtook him then. When he reflected upon it later, in the cold light of day, he was not persuaded that he would make the offer again.

But at the time, his shock, the unreality of the scene, and the vivid memory of Sir Stephen—the near-conviction, impossible to contradict, that at any moment he would open those bright blue eyes, with their usual look of pride and affection—all combined to rob Zacharias of his instinct of self-preservation.

"Would not you consider a substitute?" he said.

Curiosity glinted in Leofric's amber eyes. "What do you propose?"

Zacharias swallowed.

"You may have me," he said, "in replacement for Sir Stephen."

Leofric hissed with laughter. "You! Child, for six hundred years I have served the Sorcerer Royal. No lesser magician could satisfy me."

"It was not my intention to suggest that you should devour me only when I was dead," said Zacharias. He was familiar with the cuisine of Fairyland, having read the memoirs and travelogues of adventurous thaumaturges. In these civilised times the Fairy Court only served at its banquets courses which were no longer alive, but that had not always been the case. "Could not you satisfy yourself upon me while I was yet alive? Would not that please you better than a corpse?"

He faltered over the last word. It seemed so hideous to be referring to Sir Stephen as such.

"What a very interesting proposition," said Leofric. His head was arrested in its downward swoop, the scales upon his neck gleaming dully in the candlelight.

For the first time Zacharias realised what extremely sharp teeth Leofric had, and how numerous they were.

"It would hurt you," said Leofric. "You would survive—but not for very long."

"You would have all of me, upon my death," said Zacharias. "And you would have had the pleasure of a living meal before then."

Leofric abandoned Sir Stephen's body and dropped down on his haunches, the better to consider Zacharias.

"It could be done," he said. "I should have to enter you. You will find the enforced intimacy a trial. I am no garrulous enthusiast, no chattering blockhead, as you know, but you would be aware of my presence at all times. You would never be alone—never wholly yourself—again."

He paused for reflection, and a shiver went along his wings. "If I occupied your person, that would make you a sorcerer. One soul for two sorcerers is a bad bargain, you cannot deny."

"Then it is fortunate, is it not, that I would not be a sorcerer for very long?" said Zacharias.

"Do you truly wish to sacrifice yourself for your guardian?" said Leofric. "Recall: Stephen was ageing, and you are yet young. He understood the deal he struck. You do not owe him so much."

"I owe him a great deal," said Zacharias. "But what I offer, I offer for the great affection I bore him. And for the love he bore me."

As he spoke, he knew all he said to be true. Love and grief bore him up. He looked unwaveringly at the dragon, bolstered by the courage they lent him.

Leofric was silent. Then he lifted his head, his eyes glowing.

"It would be churlish of me to reject such a gift," he said. "There is a final point to settle, however."

He coughed, and continued with a touch of primness:

"There is my reputation to think of. My acquaintance in Fairyland sneer because I have elected to pass my days at the service of a mortal magician. The only reason they have not thrown me off altogether is because the mortal I acknowledge as my master is the supreme magician of magicians—the chosen of all sorcerers in Britain. I can be familiar to no lesser personage than the Sorcerer Royal."

Zacharias stared. Yet there was a nightmarish logic to it. He knew, as well as Leofric, that Sir Stephen had intended that Zacharias should be his successor, when old age or death should have put it out of his power to continue to perform his duties.

"The staff is in the stand," said Leofric. "You need only take it up. It will know you, I promise."

Zacharias thought of what Sir Stephen's life had been. He had had influence, yes—he had been esteemed by his colleagues, had mingled with the good and great of the land, and enjoyed the many fruits of his labours. But thirty years ago Sir Stephen had been one of the most lauded young innovators in unnatural philosophy, who by his researches had promised to deepen humanity's understanding of magic, and strike out fresh paths untried by any thaumaturge before him.

What discoveries had he made since he had taken up the staff? What time had he had to pursue his own researches? He had been consumed by the neverending work of managing his wayward flock of thaumaturges, ingratiating himself with the Fairy Court, and appeasing a Government that thought Britain ought to be able to conquer magic by main force, as they did other nations.

Zacharias had hoped for a different life. But he had been given so much—far more than most thought he deserved—far more than he might otherwise have had. He had known all along that he would have to pay for it.

"If I take up the staff, you will leave Sir Stephen be?" he said.

"He will be left to go his own way, to salvation, or damnation—whichever he merits," said Leofric. "And I will serve you as familiar until the end of your life, whenever that may be, by the terms of this new Exchange."

"Well," said Zacharias. "You cannot say fairer than that."

He stepped across the room and took up the staff.

Leofric vanished, and the room filled with thick black smoke. Zacharias choked on it, coughed, and struggled to breathe, but he could only draw in lungfuls of smoke, which coalesced into a deadweight within his chest. Power ran through his limbs. His vision became suddenly, almost painfully keen.

Sir Stephen's body lay limp and undisturbed in his chair. Sir Stephen rose from it, his ghostly countenance drawn with horror. He said:

"Zacharias, what have you done?"

Zacharias did not answer.

The pain had begun—an agony that clutched his stomach like a vise, and gnawed unbearably at his vitals. It would not always be so bad, for he was usually granted a remittance during the day. Wishing, probably, to prolong his feast, Leofric reserved the worst attacks for midnight. At times Zacharias could almost believe himself unaffected, save for the feeling that dogged him, that he had lost something the night Sir Stephen died, and would never recover it.

He did not see Leofric again, for Leofric was always with him. The dragon had only spoken the truth. Zacharias was never wholly himself again.

25

Whether it was the exertion of battling Mrs. Midsomer that had worn him out, or whether disclosing the burden he had borne since Sir Stephen's death had imparted some much-needed peace, Zacharias slept soundly that night. He roused at the first knock and lay for a moment gazing at the rays of morning's first light stealing past the drapes. He felt perfectly relaxed, and the accustomed headache was notable for its absence.

Prunella was at the door when he opened it. Zacharias was so used to tempests and disasters that he did not even recoil at this breach of etiquette, but said:

"I shall get my staff."

"Do, for we may need it," said Prunella. She was dressed, though it was early, and her face was unwontedly grave. "It is no emergency, but with this meeting at the Society today I do not know when we shall next have the chance to speak alone, and I could not endure the mystery for much longer."

She refused to say any more till they were in her sitting room, and she had secured the door.

"Are you in great pain at the moment, Zacharias?" she said abruptly.

"Not at all. I am very well," said Zacharias automatically, but then he recalled that she knew—indeed, everyone knew. It felt unnatural to say more, but Prunella would assume he was dissembling if he did not. He added, with difficulty:

"Leofric tends to feed at midnight. He knows I must have energy for the day. In any case, he did not trouble me last night. He is not unreasonable."

"I think he is disgusting," said Prunella. "You need not frown at me so, Zacharias. I hope he hears me! It is only the truth. My familiars will want their reward in time, but they would never hurt me while I was capable of feeling it."

"It is the nature of the Exchange. We struck a bargain, and he has abided by it," said Zacharias. He would have liked to abandon the unhappy subject of bargains and exchanges altogether, but it was his duty as her instructor to discuss it with Prunella. "That is why I would have prevented you from bonding with so many familiars, if I could. You benefit from it now, but at the end of your life . . ."

"Never mind about the end of my life," said Prunella briskly. "We have sorted it out amongst ourselves. Nidget is to have my head, and Youko and Tjandra will have the rest of me, divided equally, and whoever is fastest may have my soul—though I doubt I have much of one. There will not be much left for a funeral, but when I am dead that will not worry me, and I plan to make old bones. But we must not be distracted, Zacharias; we have not much time. Did not you wonder that I knew Mrs. Midsomer's orb for what it was?"

The question had not occurred to Zacharias. It struck him that this was a shocking oversight. He said, embarrassed: "There was so much else to worry about that I did not think to be surprised."

Prunella nodded. "I had seen something like it before, you see."

She held out a small silver ball, very similar to Mrs. Midsomer's orb, save that it was wrought of a paler metal, and etched with different carvings. It was attached to a long silver chain.

"I wear it always," said Prunella. She was still for a long moment, gazing down at the orb. "I found it in the attic at the school, along with the eggs. They were among my father's effects. I believe they belonged to my mother."

"I thought you did not remember your mother."

"Nor do I." Prunella looked up at Zacharias, her eyes luminous with unshed tears. "But she remembered me."

She wiped her eyes with the back of her hand, and continued:

"Mak Genggang showed me how to awaken the orb. I might have told you of it before, but there was not time—and I suppose, Zacharias, I did not altogether trust you. I have been so much in your power that I thought it wisest to reserve a secret or two to myself, in case I should need it. And you are so conscientious, I thought you were bound to report it to the Society. I had no notion you were as capable of keeping a secret as you have shown yourself to be."

"There is no need to explain yourself to me," said Zacharias, adding drily, "You will embarrass me with all these compliments."

A gleam of humour flashed through Prunella's face in response.

"Well, in truth, if I did not think you might be able to help, perhaps I would not be confiding in you now," she said. "But I had not realised before that it was writing—the carvings upon my orb, I mean. I thought perhaps you might be able to read it, for you told me you made a study of the Indian languages, did you not?"

"The Sanskrit only," said Zacharias. He held out his hand, and after a moment's hesitation Prunella passed him the orb.

"I recognise the script, however," he said, examining it. "I believe it is Hindustani, though I am no expert. Shall I sound out the words?"

"It will have no effect unless I supply the core of the spell," said

Prunella. She could not conceal the significance this held for her, and there was an unmistakable quaver in her voice.

Zacharias knew he must tread carefully, but he knew nothing of these orbs, and his thaumaturgical training rendered it impossible to leave this be. "And what is that, if I may ask?"

"You ought to know by now, Zacharias," said Prunella. A smile ghosted across her lips. "It comes down to blood, of course. What else could it be?"

A fat pincushion on the mantelpiece held all the needles a witch could require, but Prunella paused with the needle resting against her thumb.

"Do you promise to keep anything we see a secret?" she said.

Zacharias hesitated, but with Prunella's steady gaze upon him, he said, "I give you my word."

She nodded, and in one swift, sure movement, stabbed herself in the fleshy base of her thumb.

"Now, Zacharias," she said, and held her thumb over the orb. The drop of blood spread rapidly along the lines of the engraved words and pictures.

Zacharias saw the script vanish in light as he stumbled over the unfamiliar syllables. By the time he finished reading the words out, the orb was ablaze. Prunella took it from his hand and threw it in the air.

The light blossoming from the sphere took on substance and form. An image coalesced before them of a dark-skinned woman kneeling on the ground, very lovely, though past her first youth. She wore a gorgeous silk saree and gold jewellery. These, and her carriage and bearing, spoke of wealth and power.

"Oh," said Prunella in a strangled whisper, and then she was silent.

The woman spoke in a low, fierce whisper that resounded through the room.

"My daughter, the spell I have cast will kill your father," she said.

The language was foreign and the words she spoke entered the ear as mere liquid syllables, but their significance entered the mind. This was another translation spell, one Zacharias had not encountered before, but elegantly designed.

"Listen well, for he will not survive to tell the tale," said the vision. "You are my daughter, the heir of a line of great magicians, and I am the greatest of these, the Grand Sorceress of the Court of Seringapatam." She said this with the simplicity and directness with which Prunella made her own most outrageous statements—with an unselfconscious arrogance that was utterly convincing.

"Your father has betrayed us, and will suffer for it. He came to our court claiming to be a scholar of European magics, who wished to advance the understanding between magicians of different nations. He professed to love me, and I, believing him sincere, permitted his attentions. For two years he concealed his true intentions within his treacherous heart, waiting for his chance. We discovered I was expecting you. In my loving folly I confided our family's most precious secrets to him, he being the natural protector of their heir—so I thought. Fool that I was, I revealed to him the treasures of which I am guardian—the treasures I preserved for you, and my granddaughters.

"I do not believe, now, that he was ever truly attached to me. I do not believe he intended to become attached to you, but he could not help himself. You were born, and he found he loved you. He took you from me—the coward, the liar, the thief! He fled the country with you, and worse, he has taken the treasures with him.

"Attend! The treasures are seven, each a portal to a realm of wonder, disguised as stones. They are subject to an enchantment that preserves them in dormancy, but when the charm is broken a spirit of great power will inhabit the stone and be hatched into the world, like a snake from an egg. My blood will preserve the secret of unlocking the treasures for you, and your blood will reveal it, for the same ichor runs in our veins. When you are of an age to profit from the treasures—when you are ready for your inheritance—the spell I have laid on you will open the path for you to find this message.

"Unlock all the treasures, when you have learnt the secret of it. Bind the spirits to you with your blood. Now that you are lost to me there is no call to preserve them. Now that you have gone over the black waters the line of our family is broken. I shall not know my granddaughters, and you shall not know me. Feed the spirits—love them—learn from them—they will be grandmother, mother, aunt and daughter to you. The foreigners will not touch them. I have enchanted the stones so that even should a foreigner contrive to hatch a spirit, it would turn instantly upon him and tear out his throat.

"Nor will your father profit from his treachery. He will be tormented by nightmares; his food and drink will turn to ashes in his mouth; he will be served out for the wrong he has done you and me. But I cannot come for you."

The woman looked away. Light fell across her face—the harsh sunlight of a foreign land, striped with black shadows like prison bars.

"I am your mother, but I am Grand Sorceress first, and my word cannot be forsworn. I must accept my punishment for allowing the treasures to be taken from me—for my foolishness in trusting your father.

"My beloved, I discharge you from any need for revenge. I have murdered enough for the both of us. When you have the spirits' loyalty, learn, wait and survive. With the seven spirits by you, you will be the greatest magician the world has ever known. Your fame will spread across all the nations of the earth; your name will be fragrant in the thirty-one worlds. Wield your power wisely and well—and live!"

The woman leant forward, her eyes flashing, a smile both triumphant and tender curving her mouth.

"You are *my* daughter," she said. "Can there be any doubt that you will be brilliant—audacious—and free?"

The vision disappeared. She had been so vital, so overflowing with life and energy, that her going seemed to leave the room dark.

Prunella reached blindly for a chair and collapsed in it, burying her face in her hands. Zacharias was anxious to be discreet, and for a while he absorbed himself in the study of her bookshelves, noting with disapproval the number of novels and frippery magazines with which they were laden. But Prunella was silent for so long that he grew concerned.

"Are you quite well?" he said.

Prunella raised a startled dark gaze to his face. Her eyes were dry. "She looks just like me!" she said.

It was so prosaic an observation Zacharias was tempted to laugh, but it was only the truth. The resemblance was remarkable: the shape of the eyes, thin lips and decided chin were all the same, but the most striking similarities went beyond the physical. Prunella's mother had looked the great woman. So, too, would Prunella appear when she was older, refined in the fire of an indomitable will.

"Your mother's ability accounts for yours," said Zacharias. "The Grand Sorceress of Seringapatam! I suppose it is hardly a surprise she did not pursue you to England," he added absently, though he regretted his words at once.

If Prunella's mother had been at Seringapatam at the time of its fall then it was, indeed, no surprise that she had not come to recover her child, even a decade after the conquest. But it had been neither kind nor tactful to say so.

"I expect she has had a great deal of business to attend to," he said hastily. "I do not wonder that she has not had an opportunity to get away."

"Oh, indeed!" said Prunella, with an appearance of nonchalance. "I expect she has been busy."

She went to the window. It was a transparent enough device to prevent his seeing her face, and Zacharias was not surprised that when Prunella spoke, it was to change the subject.

"I suppose Lady Wythe will have risen by now," she said. "I ought to return to my room, or Lucy will think I have eloped again. Will you be quite safe at the Society today? Ought my familiars and I to come, in case those wretched thaumaturges take it into their heads to carry out the Hallett after all?"

"I hope you will come, though I have no concerns regarding my safety," said Zacharias. "Lord Burrow is opposed to the Hallett, and Midsomer need not worry us overmuch. Now that Mrs. Midsomer is gone with Georgiana Without Ruth, I cannot think him capable of anything great in the way of magic. As for his intrigues, I fancy I have a surprise that will throw anything he might try into the shade. I shall need your agreement to carry it out, however."

"Oh, certainly!" said Prunella. "I should be glad to help. I am very much obliged to you, Zacharias. I could not have deciphered my mother's message alone, and I knew I could repose the utmost confidence in you. I knew *you* would never betray my secrets."

Prunella's gratitude was wholly sincere, but she spoke, too, out of careful calculation. Zacharias did not blame her. They both knew what a secret it was that he now possessed.

YOU cannot now deny where your duty lies," said Sir Stephen.

Zacharias had stopped by his study to collect his thoughts and pick up some papers before the meeting at the Society. He was not altogether surprised to find Sir Stephen lying in wait for him.

"No, indeed," said Zacharias. He had not had much time to consider the morning's revelation, but its implications had been immediately obvious to him.

Sir Stephen was so excited he did not notice the tone of Zacharias's voice, but continued:

"To think that England has been in such want of familiars for decades, when a single kingdom in India has been hoarding seven eggs! Their magicians are famously close, but I had no notion how much they concealed. What the Society will say when you tell them!

Who knows what other wonders lie hid in that vast subcontinent? And where else might we not find similar riches? Why not the deserts of Araby, the steppes of Mongolia, the Malay archipelagoes? We must begin the survey at once. It will take time, ingenuity, perseverance. If Miss Gentleman's mother is an example of foreign magicians, we will have considerable difficulties to contend with—deceptions to penetrate, evasions to circumvent, defiance to overpower."

"I gave Miss Gentleman my word I would not tell anyone," said Zacharias.

Sir Stephen had been pacing the room in his flurry of spirits, but this stopped him in his tracks. He turned on Zacharias a look of amazement.

"If I did not know better I would accuse you of being bewitched by a pair of snapping black eyes," he said. "Even you must admit the girl has not a right to all the familiars of India. Indeed, it is bad enough that she has three; it is a breach of the Society's rules for any magician to possess more than one familiar, as you very well know. The girl will pay for it if ever the Society discovers her crime."

"I know it," said Zacharias.

"But you may save her by this revelation, Zacharias," said Sir Stephen. "And yourself, for it would be such a stroke as no Sorcerer Royal has ever managed. What are Miss Gentleman's three familiars to a continent's worth of familiars' eggs? It overturns all our assumptions."

Zacharias shook his head. He was calm, quite calm, and yet his pulse beat high in his throat. He had grown practised in disagreeing with Sir Stephen since his death, but they had never diverged so far before.

"Did not you hear the Grand Sorceress?" he said. "'*The foreigners will not touch them*'—and so Mrs. Gentleman murdered her husband, and enchained the secret of unlocking the eggs to Prunella's very blood. She foresaw what would occur if Europe were to discover her people's wealth: the interference in their affairs; the miserable increase of bloodshed and oppression."

Sir Stephen went white, then red.

"Need I remind you that you are England's Sorcerer Royal?" he said. "Your title will on occasion demand the exercise of power—even, where necessary, what you are pleased to call oppression and bloodshed. But that is the nature of the office. You are called upon to advance the good of this nation, and none other. Your allegiance is not to magic alone, nor to all humanity, but to your own portion of humanity, to the country that nurtured you—"

"And enslaved my parents?" said Zacharias.

That silenced Sir Stephen. He sat down in the chair that used to be his, moving, for once, like an old man.

Pity and affection strove within Zacharias against implacable truth. But they could not triumph forever. Nor could Zacharias's loyalties ever be as clearly delineated as his guardian's. He had always understood this. Sir Stephen, he knew, had not.

"You know I have always been grateful to you and Lady Wythe," he said into the ringing silence. "I can never make a sufficient return for your goodness. You could not have been kinder to a blood relation."

"We could not have loved you better had you been our own son," said Sir Stephen heavily. He passed his hand over his eyes.

"I believe it," said Zacharias gently.

He was conscious of a sensation of relief, as though he had laid down a burden he had been carrying, all unconscious, his entire life. Till that moment he had not known what a trial it had been to be compelled to hide his true sentiments from his closest connections.

Sir Stephen lowered his hand, and met Zacharias's eyes.

"You may not have chosen England, but England has chosen you," he said. "I would never have said Zacharias Wythe owed any debt to her. The Sorcerer Royal, however, does. What is at stake is more important than your conscience, Zacharias. If you were not prepared for that, you ought not to have taken up the staff."

"You know why I took up the staff," said Zacharias.

He felt no resentment—he had made the decision and he must live with it—but the words, spoken by him to Sir Stephen, could not be anything but a reproach. Sir Stephen's steady blue gaze was unwavering, though he must have felt the words as a blow.

"Your reasons do not signify," said Sir Stephen. "What matters is that you did it. You are Sorcerer Royal. Now what do you propose to do about that?"

Zacharias picked up his staff and weighed it in his hand.

He did not think he would miss it. There was very little, indeed, that he would miss.

It was true Prunella could not escape punishment if her familiars were discovered. It was growing increasingly difficult to conceal their existence; it would soon be impossible, now that the Presiding Committee had witnessed her in the act of magic-making. Zacharias had always known they would come to a point at which he must present her to the Society, and brave the consequences. It had come sooner than he would have liked, but he knew now what he must do.

"Come to the Society with me, and you shall see," he said.

26

A MEMORY STIRRED within Zacharias as he entered the Great Hall among a sea of pale faces: a memory of being small and anxious, wishing very much to please, but fearful of being weighed and found wanting.

Time and use had overlaid the memory with fresher impressions. He was no longer intimidated by the vaulted ceilings, the ancient wood-panelled walls or the portraits of sorcerers past, gazing down upon the proceedings in eternal displeasure. He now knew the measure of those around him.

The Society was hard put to summon a quorum at most meetings, but today the Hall was uncommonly crowded. Curiosity about how the Sorcerer Royal proposed to defend himself against the Hallett proved an irresistible draw. Thaumaturges were packed so close in the Hall that sparks of magic flew in the narrow spaces between their bodies.

They were due to be disappointed, as the sharper-witted among them had already deduced. Zacharias Wythe was so composed one might have thought he had never heard of a ritual sacrifice in his life, and Geoffrey Midsomer sat huddled at the back of the room in a fit of the sullens.

Lord Burrow, rising to speak, put paid to any remaining illusions that the meeting might involve anything other than the usual tedious periods.

"I must apologise for this breach of protocol, but Mr. Wythe has kindly surrendered his precedence today to permit me to make an announcement on behalf of the Committee," he said. "It has come to the Committee's attention that a purported amendment was made to the Charter, to remove the clause prohibiting the Hallett procedure. This was done in a highly irregular fashion, and we shall be taking measures to withdraw the amendment. There is no longer any intention to undertake the Hallett; the Presiding Committee deems it unnecessary."

At the disappointment that rippled through the audience, Lord Burrow raised his voice.

"I might add that the Committee considers the attempt to make use of the procedure ill-judged, and regrets that certain elements within the Society should have gone to such lengths to revive its availability. We are satisfied of Mr. Wythe's claim to the staff, and no allegation against him has been proven that would render it necessary for him to surrender it."

So far as this went, this was perfectly satisfactory from Zacharias's perspective, and he experienced a faint pang of regret at Prunella's timing when Lord Burrow paused, staring.

Zacharias had bribed a servant to smuggle Prunella into the building through a side-door, but Prunella had decided to disregard the discreet entrance he had painstakingly orchestrated for her. She wafted down the centre of the room on Damerell's arm, appearing splendidly unconscious of the looks and murmurs she drew.

Midsomer glared. Josiah Cullip clearly longed to speak, but he had been given a stern talking-to by Lord Burrow after the events of the day before, and to draw attention to himself now was to risk his position as Secretary to the Committee. It was another supporter of Midsomer's who took up the gauntlet.

"At least one accusation requires no proof, for he has admitted it himself," said Mr. Kendle in a strident voice. "Zacharias Wythe has been teaching women magic, and has even invited one here! Is not that a breach worthy of consideration, or is the immunity of the Sorcerer Royal to shield even that folly?"

"There is no provision in the Charter either for or against the practise of magic by females," said Zacharias. "The general prejudice against it is founded merely in convention. Of course, even if there were such a prohibition in the Charter, the Charter can be amended, as some of my colleagues will be aware."

Kendle looked rather foolish.

"I do not deny having trained a woman in the principles of thaumaturgy," Zacharias continued. "She is, as Mr. Kendle observes, here today. And I so dispute any contention that I have done wrong, that I shall declare now, that I hope my instruction of Miss Gentleman will be only the first phase of a comprehensive system of education of women with magical abilities."

An outraged murmur rustled through the audience. Zacharias spoke over it. He was conscious that very little time remained to him to say his piece. Once he had achieved his purpose—the great, improbable design he hoped to effect at this meeting—it would be too late, and he would have lost his chance.

"It is my hope that we shall soon have schools for the instruction of *magiciennes*, as useful and esteemed as our schools for boys," he said. "Since it will require a considerable outlay before any such establishment may begin its operations, however, I would suggest in the meantime that the Society sets up scholarships to fund the instruction of talented magic users who could not otherwise study thaumaturgy.

"Nor should the scholarships be restricted to women. Mine is only one of many voices that have decried the recent practise of demanding that magicians pass for gentlemen before they may pass for thaumaturges. Why should not thaumaturgy be open to the poor? Who among us has not seen the lad on the street, barefoot and ragged, entertaining his friends with a cantrip? The farmer who shields his crops from the frost with a spell, and the coachman who speeds his carriage by magic?"

Zacharias was prevented from continuing by the hubbub of his colleagues' voices, as his audience vociferously denied ever having seen anything of the sort. Before either he or they had said all they wished, however, they were interrupted in the most spectacular manner conceivable.

The glass of a high window shattered, and a second woman entered the Great Hall—one whose presence Zacharias had *not* counted upon.

Mak Genggang glided around the Hall above the openmouthed thaumaturges, landing finally on her feet beside Zacharias. She had not come alone.

Sultan Ahmad and Mr. Othman seemed shamefaced about the wings they had sprouted, and were inclined to hang back, but the sultana was not at all discomposed. She was the only one of the curious party who remained wingless. There was nevertheless a subtle difference about her whole person, but Zacharias had little time to contemplate the change. An eerie yowl pierced the air, of such an extraordinary pitch that the magicians in the Hall clapped their hands over their ears.

"Good God!" cried Lord Burrow. "What in Heaven's name is that?"

"Who is that, if you please!" said Mak Genggang. "He has not a name yet, but he would thank you to be civil all the same, would not he, the precious little creature?"

The infant cradled in her arms did not seem amused by her coaxing. It glowered. In a baby of its diminutive size, this should have been more endearing than intimidating—and would have been, if not for the fact that the tiny mouth contained a complete set of fangs, and the eyes shone a lurid red.

"Mak Genggang!" exclaimed Prunella. "Why, what are you doing here?"

"We are going home, but I thought it would only be civil to bid you good-bye," said Mak Genggang. "You may give me a kiss, child."

When Prunella had complied, the witch nodded at the indignant magicians, saying:

"And *you* may assure your sovereign that he need not worry about us any longer, since he has taken such a kind interest in our island. Sultan Ahmad and I have settled our differences—you will see that I have given him and Mr. Othman wings, so that we may fly home together. The queen is coming to stay with me and my women for a time, so that we can look after her and the little prince."

Zacharias murmured confused felicitations, which the sultana ignored, and the sultan scowled at.

"Is the baby ill?" said Prunella, inspecting the child with open fascination. "Why does it look so queerly?"

"Oh, he is in fine fettle," said Mak Genggang, bouncing the creature while it glared around with eyes like red lamps. "Such a child as any mother would be proud of. It is only that he arrived in the world a little late, after his mother had already died.

"Yes," she added, at Zacharias and Prunella's exclamations of horror, "the queen had an uncomfortable time of it, poor soul. She was brought to bed of the dear boy last night, but she perished in the process, alas. Fortunately she was transformed instantly into a lamia. That was a piece of great good luck, for it does not happen to all poorly mothers, you know. But it could hardly be expected that her son should be anything but a vampire after that."

The thaumaturges who had approached to peer at their unexpected guests stepped back as one man, leaving a space around the sultana. Zacharias, looking at her with new eyes, saw the signs of the transformation she had undergone. The nails on the slim brown fingers were long and yellow; the lips were blood-red, and she licked them from time to time with an unnervingly long tongue.

"How extraordinary!" said Zacharias, feeling this did very little to describe the situation.

"Oh, certainly!" Mak Genggang agreed. "I have never seen a male vampire! To be sure, it is uncommon for the child to survive—usually it dies, or is eaten. Fortunately the sultan had the sense to seek me out at once, and I contrived to prevent his royal wife from devouring the poor babe. When a lamia first rises from her deathbed she cannot very well control her instincts, you know, but we have managed to make her understand. However, mother and child still require a great deal of attention, and the sooner we are home, the better."

"There I certainly concur," said Lord Burrow. He turned to Zacharias. "Mr. Wythe, this is a meeting of the Fellows of the Society, and there are certain rules to be observed. If you wish to entertain visits from every passing witch, might I suggest that the Great Hall is not the place to do it?"

"But this is not merely a personal visit, sir," said Zacharias on a sudden inspiration. Mak Genggang was already tucking the babe under her arm and looking about for an exit. "I believe Mak Genggang intends to make an announcement of particular interest to the Society.

"Ma'am," he said to Mak Genggang, "we had an agreement, as I recall. The thaumaturge who caused your coven such inconvenience has been punished. His familiar has been taken from him."

"I am pleased to hear it," said Mak Genggang. "It is no more than he deserves. I should advise you not to stop there, but set fire to his house, too, and sell his children to pirates. That is the only way he will learn to abandon his wicked ways."

"I am sure he has already begun to regret his wrongdoing," said

Zacharias, keeping a stern eye on the furious Midsomer. "But I think you promised a favour in return for his punishment, Mak Genggang. It was to do with the block upon our magic?"

"Well!" said Mak Genggang, hesitating. "As to that, it seems to me the less magic the English possess, the less likely they are to send magical armies to menace us."

"Oh, pray remove the block on our magic, Mak Genggang," Prunella interrupted. "It is so provoking for our magicians to be forever running out of magic. Of course they are tiresome creatures and do not deserve anything better, but it puts them in such horrid tempers, and they take it out on Zacharias."

"Which is very bad for him, I am sure," said Mak Genggang. "However, if it is a question of whether he is to suffer, or my women—"

"But I am thinking of you and your women," said Prunella earnestly. "For you must know that our King still has any number of ships and guns and soldiers, and he is probably quite wicked enough to use them if you vex him."

"Miss Gentleman!" sputtered Lord Burrow.

But however treasonous it might be to malign one's own sovereign to the representative of a foreign power, it seemed to have the desired effect.

"Perhaps you are right," said Mak Genggang begrudgingly. "We shall see. I will ask my women to intercede with the spirits on Britain's behalf, and perhaps they will permit magic to enter your realm again."

"We should be very much obliged if you would," said Zacharias.

"You must not expect immediate results, however," said Mak Genggang. "My women have been in a continual twitter since the attack. You might not think it, but lamiae are the most high-strung creatures in the world! But I will tell them they have nothing to fear from the foreigners. The Sorcerer Royal himself has extended his protection to them, and the Sorcerer Royal can be trusted. Is not that so?"

The bold black eyes met Zacharias's, and in them he read a threat that rendered their gaze rather more frightening than the baby's.

"I certainly hope so," he said.

Zacharias's colleagues had not followed all of the conversation, and after Mak Genggang departed through the window she broke, it was necessary for him to explain that he had (he hoped) remedied the problem of the decline in Britain's magic, without employing a single spell.

The thaumaturges were inclined to think he ought simply to have put the foreign witch under lock and key until her followers had promised to remove the block on England's magic.

"After all, there is nothing to say she will keep her word," said Kendle. "Like as not she will not. No foreigner ever does." He gave Zacharias a look pregnant with meaning.

"I do not know that I credit this cock-and-bull story of vampiresses bribing the Fairy Court to deprive Britain of magic," said another thaumaturge. "I have taken the measure of our atmospheric magic myself this past fortnight, and it is on the rise for the first time in years—each week higher than the last."

"Indeed," said Zacharias. "That brings me to another announcement I wished to make today."

"Another announcement!" said Lord Burrow: he had begun to think of his dinner.

"I think I can promise it will be my last," said Zacharias.

"I beg you will be quick about it," said Lord Burrow. "If it is about those scholarships, we shall take the notion under consideration, so you need not belabour the point."

"I hope you will," said Zacharias. "I believe it is a scheme that can only benefit the nation. I hope my successor will agree, but as I am resigning, it would be overstepping my place to say any more."

The room went still. Damerell looked up, alert as a hound that had caught the scent.

"You are not allowed to resign, man," cried Lord Burrow.

"I think you will find that I am," said Zacharias composedly. "But I am conscious of the importance of avoiding any gap in succession, and I have already considered who should take the staff after me. I believe the staff will concur, for Miss Gentleman is the best-equipped of any magician living to adapt to the peculiar demands of the position."

For a moment a fragile silence reigned over the Hall—a quiet composed of pure astonishment. It was broken by a deep, bubbling, delighted laugh, issuing from Damerell's corner of the room.

"I have never been so happy to have risen before noon," said Damerell.

Prunella stared at Zacharias as though she had never seen him before. But no one took any notice of her, for everyone else was having his say.

The general feeling was that Zacharias had lost his mind, and was almost as much to be pitied as censured.

"You have perhaps been working too hard, Wythe," said Lord Burrow. "Perhaps you should take a sabbatical. A holiday will set you up."

"It is not such a bad idea," said Cullip, who looked in better spirits than he had since Zacharias had left him shivering upon the Cobb. "Since the Sorcerer Royal proposes to forswear the staff, we should put his successor to the vote. Mr. Geoffrey Midsomer—"

"Has withdrawn himself from candidacy," said Zacharias, fixing his gaze upon Midsomer, who squirmed. "Besides, you forget, Mr. Cullip, that magic is not a democracy."

With this he picked up the staff and, pitching low, threw it to Prunella. She caught it, looking as startled as any of the men around her.

"For the sake of the Seven Spirits, Miss Gentleman, and in the name of the Grand Sorceress," said Zacharias. "An enchantment, if you please. I would suggest a summoning. I believe your interpretation of the old formula will greatly interest the gentlemen present."

Recognition entered Prunella's eyes, followed by a glow of pride. She lifted her chin, holding up the staff.

It was a risk. The staff of the Sorcerer Royal was not known to be kind to the magicians whose mastery it rejected. But Zacharias was not afraid—or so he told himself, over the deafening thump of his own heart. The mistress of three familiars could justly claim precedence over any thaumaturge in the Hall, including himself.

Prunella spoke the formula for summoning in ringing tones.

For a dreadful moment nothing happened. One of the gentlemen standing by Prunella sought to take the staff from her. She offered to knock him on the head with it, before Damerell intervened:

"You will have the courtesy to permit Miss Gentleman the trial, sir, or have me to answer for it."

"Is this some sort of joke, Wythe?" Cullip began to bluster, when a gargoyle came to life behind him.

Nidget somersaulted off the wall, knocking the astonished Cullip off his feet, and it was followed by the others.

Tjandra blossomed from the bosses above—the dear familiar bosses, which had been so helpful to Zacharias in days past. The simurgh's brilliant green wings seemed to block out the light as he flew to his mistress.

Youko made the most conventional entry. She trotted in through the door, pushing thaumaturges out of the way with a jerk of her horned head, till Prunella was surrounded by her familiars—a small, indomitable figure, with the staff glowing in her hand.

IT is not a point that admits of debate," said Mr. Plimpton. "The rule cannot be circumvented."

The private room to which the Presiding Committee had retired was too small for the number of people crowded into it, and Mr. Plimpton had been growing hotter and more disgruntled in the course of the meeting. He was a large, bald man, in appearance resembling nothing so much as an irate infant, and his temper had reached such a pitch that Damerell was moved to suggest in a whisper that Prunella summon a nurse to put baby down for a nap.

He spoke in jest, but Prunella secretly thought it no bad idea. It seemed absurd that the Committee should be so perplexed by a minor point of protocol, when her three familiars sat around her feet, proving her the most powerful magician in the room.

"The command of the familiar Leofric has been a precondition of the office since the time of Roger Hayes," said Mr. Plimpton. "The staff is not sufficient."

"It was sufficient with me," said Zacharias. He was wrinkling his forehead in a manner that signified he had a headache, but did not intend to let anyone else know it. It was a look with which Prunella had grown all too familiar.

Mr. Plimpton glanced at Lord Burrow, who coughed.

"We had received confirmation from the Fairy Court that Leofric had submitted to your control," he said. "They would not be drawn on the details, but they were unwavering on that point. We could scarcely have permitted your accession to the office without that assurance."

"I cannot see what is so terribly special about this old dragon," said Prunella. "My familiars could match him any day, I am sure."

"Admittedly a practitioner that has the benefit of three familiars must be reckoned an extraordinary force," said Lord Burrow, not quite addressing her.

The Presiding Committee had not made up its mind as to how it stood on Prunella, and had fallen into two camps: one that glared at her, and another that pretended she was not there. Prunella found both equally diverting.

"But the office of Sorcerer Royal is not merely reserved for the magician that can prove himself most powerful," said Lord Burrow. "One of its purposes is to preserve our traditions of magic, and the

Sorcerer Royal's familiar is not the least of these. The Sorcerer Royal must have Leofric as well as the staff. Since it appears Mr. Wythe retains Leofric as his familiar, he cannot simply relinquish the staff and expect to be divested of his office."

"I assure you," said Zacharias wearily, "if I could be free of Leofric, I would."

Prunella was not particularly interested in the discussion. It was clear to *her* that she was Sorceress Royal, and if the Society wished to quarrel with the fact now, they would soon think better of it. Leofric, however, was a subject in which she had considerable interest, and she felt no compunction in interrupting the Committee's ditherings for this.

"Have not you tried persuading Leofric to leave you, Zacharias?" she said. "I think we ought to have it out with him, ought we not? He seems a wretched inconvenience. I am sure we could find you a better familiar."

"There is nothing to have out," said Zacharias shortly. "Our agreement was clear. In any case, even I am unable to converse with Leofric. Our communication takes place by other means."

"I suppose you mean your midnight visitations!" said Prunella. "It all sounds very unpleasant. I think we ought to speak to him by ordinary means."

Zacharias opened his mouth, doubtless to object, but Prunella's familiars had explained his arrangement with Leofric, and it did not seem to her that it would be difficult to extract the dragon. The procedure might cause Zacharias some discomfort, but if she acted quickly enough, he would scarcely notice it. Since his mouth was already open, she decided to take time by the forelock, and plunged her arm down his throat.

"Good God!" cried Damerell.

Zacharias was choking around Prunella's arm—a horrible sensation—but she resolutely ignored it, and rummaged about. Leofric did not, of course, occupy Zacharias's physical insides, much though it might feel like it to Zacharias. He inhabited instead a magical space that happened to overlap with Zacharias's vitals. Fortunately Leofric was the only inhabitant, and Prunella soon found what she was after: a bony limb, covered with scales. She grasped hold of it.

Prunella withdrew her arm in triumph. Zacharias was clutching at his chest, his face twisted in a grimace. He bent over, his hand pressed to his heart, and let loose an enormous sneeze.

"Is this he?" said Prunella.

A dragon sat on the floor, looking astonished. It was far smaller than Rollo, and not half as attractive, for its skin was leathery with age, and its amber eyes had a hardened, cynical look.

"Good day, Leofric," said Zacharias. He looked somewhat dazed. "May I present to you the Sorceress Royal?"

Leofric had clearly not been attending to the goings-on outside Zacharias, for he said:

"A Sorceress Royal? I agreed to serve you only upon the condition that you held the staff."

"Your agreement is precisely what I wished to speak to you about," said Prunella. "What good does your bond do Zacharias, if you are forever gnawing away at his insides and making him indisposed?"

Leofric gave her an incredulous look.

"Zacharias has access to the profoundest depths and most exalted heights of magic," he said. "I have bestowed upon him the gift of an ageless wisdom, and an understanding of the mysteries of sorcery surpassing the ken of ordinary mortals."

"If ordinary mortals can do without, I cannot see why Zacharias should not be content with a comprehension only of those mysteries that fall within their ken," said Prunella. "Would not you consider terminating the agreement? You could return to Fairyland. I am told it is a prodigiously agreeable place."

"The agreement will only be terminated when I have received my payment," said Leofric, with hauteur. "I accepted Zacharias's soul in exchange for Stephen's, on the understanding that I could begin to exact payment while he was still alive. As matters stand, I have rendered service to two sorcerers, and have enjoyed the benefit of only a portion of one soul."

"But," argued Prunella, "if Zacharias were to live till he were seventy—which let us say he will, because the Bible says so, though it would be no surprise were he to be killed off earlier, living as he does in a nest of snakes and scorpions in human form—if, as I said, he were to live to a ripe old age, defying assassins, and being Sorcerer Royal all that time, that would require of you forty-six years of bondage. You have only rendered Zacharias a few months of service. Even if we were to be generous and allow it to be a year, you would only be entitled to one sorcerer, in compensation for your service to Sir Stephen, and two percent of another."

Prunella was delighted with this calculation, which she had invented as she spoke, and thought rather clever. Leofric seemed less pleased.

"I am not sure I like your purported successor, Zacharias," he said.

"Nor do any of us," said Mr. Plimpton.

"You will have to recover the staff," said Leofric to Zacharias—speaking as though Prunella were not there at all! "It was shockingly careless of you to have lost it."

Prunella saw that she was losing her audience's attention. She had hoped to avoid what she must do—what she had planned since she had heard Zacharias's account of how he had come to be Sorcerer Royal—but there was nothing for it. The alternative was to permit Leofric to continue tormenting Zacharias, with the certain result that Zacharias would be bound for an early grave, and that was not to be thought of.

"You have not heard me out, Leofric, but I think you ought," said Prunella. She must be calm, and keep her mind clear as glass, or the familiars would begin to suspect her intentions. "Zacharias promised you one mortal in exchange for two. But what if I were to offer you something else entirely? Another type of feast, far better, far finer, not to be compared with mortal flesh or spirit? Would not that settle the balance?"

A gleam of interest lit Leofric's eyes.

"Speak further," he said—but then her meaning struck him. He reared back, squealing, a noise that startled the thaumaturges, and sent Tjandra fluttering up to the ceiling.

Prunella did not take her eyes off the dragon.

"Which would you offer me?" growled Leofric.

"The oldest. It is best," said Prunella. Her hands were trembling. She clenched them into fists. She would need them soon. She would need to act at once, quicker than thought. "But you must release Zacharias from his bond. Say it now."

"Yes," said Leofric, and Prunella's hand flashed out. She seized Nidget by the scruff of its neck, and, with a strength she had not thought she possessed, threw the elvet at Leofric.

Leofric darted forward. A snap of his jaws, a heartrending wail from Nidget, and Nidget vanished.

Zacharias sat down abruptly. The other magicians were pale with shock.

Prunella observed that the trembling in her hands had spread to the rest of her person. She felt as though she had been hollowed out.

But it had had to be done, and she had her mother's own capacity for ruthlessness. The daughter of a Grand Sorceress—the heir to the Seven Spirits—could not hesitate to act for fear of any consequence.

"Tjandra, Youko—to me," said Prunella quietly.

There was a moment of doubt, when it was not clear what the simurgh and the unicorn would choose: loyalty, or rebellion. Out of the corner of her eye, Prunella saw Zacharias reach for his staff, before he recollected that it was no longer his.

She was not afraid. And her lack of fear—her certainty that her familiars would come to her—communicated itself to them. The familiars valued fidelity, but above all, they esteemed power.

They came to her hand, as she had never doubted they would: first Youko, bowing her head to be stroked, and then Tjandra, perching on her shoulder, and burying his face meekly in her hair.

Lord Burrow collapsed into his chair. Damerell swore in a low voice.

Prunella raised her head and looked at Leofric.

"It suffices?" Her voice was rough, as if she had been weeping, though she had not made a sound. She touched her cheek, and saw that her hand was wet. She had not noticed the tears rolling down her face.

Leofric swallowed and let out a contented sigh.

"The debt is discharged," he said.

Damerell was clearly shaken, but he said:

"It strikes me that a fairy, in return for one and a bit of a mortal, goes far beyond an equal exchange. Indeed, it seems to me that you are somewhat in Miss Gentleman's debt."

"The agreement—" began Leofric.

"Oh, leave off your rules-lawyering, pray," said Damerell. "Rollo always said this was why you were so disliked at Court. You may call it a fair bargain, and perhaps it will suit Miss Gentleman to agree, but how will the Fairy Court view your devouring one of its subjects?"

"You would never tell the Court. It would make Miss Gentleman too unpopular," said Leofric—but this line of talk seemed to make him nervous.

"The honour of mortals is not much esteemed in Fairyland anyway," said Damerell. "It may even be said that a fairy that submits itself to the indignities of mortal service deserves whatever it gets. But the Court is likely to take a very different view of a dragon who eats its own kin."

He lowered his quizzing-glass and began to polish it.

"Of course," he continued, "if the, ah, devourer in question were a familiar of Miss Gentleman's, I should not dream of breathing a word to anyone. Miss Gentleman is a friend of mine. A ravening dragon to whom one has no connection may be criminal, but the familiar of a friend can only be eccentric."

"I am at Miss Gentleman's service, of course," said Leofric, bowing his head towards Prunella. "Now that the debt is paid, and the staff has acknowledged her its mistress."

"I am obliged to you," said Prunella, "but I do not want your service. Tjandra and Youko are enough for me—and without intending any offence, I could not bear to replace Nidget with its devourer. Why do not you return to Fairyland? I expect you have not seen your friends there in ever so long."

"It does not seem to have occurred to you that there is a reason for that," said Leofric grimly. "However, if that is your wish, I shall abide by it. I am at your disposal—summon me as you wish—so long as our agreement subsists."

"I shall be silent as the grave," Prunella assured him. "And so will these other gentlemen be, if they know what is good for them."

"Am I correct, then, in understanding that you have acknowledged your subservience to Miss Gentleman?" said Damerell.

Leofric was poised at the open window, but he paused to say, "Oh yes, if that is how you wish to put it," before he leapt out into the air.

"Gentlemen," said Damerell to the room, "I think that addresses the last of your concerns. May I be the first to congratulate our nation's first Sorceress Royal?"

Prunella curtsied and managed to smile, though she hardly felt like it. She was already learning the price of power. For that moment at least it was small comfort that she knew herself capable of paying it.

"I do not know that I have ever been more shocked," said Sir Stephen.

"Yes," said Zacharias. "Prunella has a gift for occasioning shock."

They were walking in the Society gardens. The Presiding Committee had disbanded in confusion, and Damerell had escorted Prunella home.

"It is because she lacks any scruples whatsoever," added Zacharias. "She will make a good Sorceress Royal—far better than I ever was."

"And is Leofric truly gone?" said Sir Stephen. There was a trace of wistfulness in his voice. "He had his faults, I know. He was determined he should be acquitted according to his merits. But who is to say he was not entitled to his reward? He rendered faithful service for many years, and to me, at least, he was a true friend."

"He held you in esteem, I know," said Zacharias gently. "Do not think that I resent him. Magical creatures live by a different code. He did me a favour in accepting the substitution I offered—though I cannot say I regret him."

"The pain is quite gone?"

"It ceased the moment he ate Nidget," said Zacharias. "If nothing else, Leofric is a dragon of his word."

"So he always was," said Sir Stephen.

They passed under rustling canopies of pale green leaves, their measured tread bringing them along the shrubbery which screened off the outside world.

"Well, there is no need to explain anything to you, Zacharias," said Sir Stephen. "You always knew me and Maria as well as we did ourselves. Never was there such an observant child. Your nurse said she never knew such a feeling little creature. Why, you will not recollect this, but when you were quite a little boy, no more than three or four years old, you used to take my hand when I visited the nursery, and ask if I were very tired, in such a solicitous manner as, combined with your imperfect pronunciation, was quite absurdly moving."

Zacharias did, in fact, remember this. He had been instructed to ask the question by his nurse, who considered that, as a charity case, he should make special efforts to win his guardian's affections.

"It stands to reason they will find it harder to love a little black creature like you, than if you had dear Lady Wythe's blue eyes and golden hair," Martha had said.

She had meant to be kind. Martha had been attached to him notwithstanding his blackness, and had wept to leave him when she went away to be married. It had all happened long ago, in any case, and there was little purpose in disillusioning Sir Stephen now.

"May I hope, sir, that you are finally acting in accordance with my wish that you should move on to your final home?" said Zacharias. "You know it was never any part of my intention to bind you to this world."

"Then you should not have sacrificed yourself for the good of my immortal soul," said Sir Stephen. "You are not the only one capable of feeling beholden to his friends."

"If we are to enter into the question of which of us owes the greatest debt to the other—" Zacharias began.

"I beg we will not," said Sir Stephen mildly. "I chose to take you on, you know. Since the decision to become a parent is invariably self-interested, it is my belief that a parent's obligation is to the child, and the child's obligation is to itself. However, let us avoid such old ground, or we will fall to quarrelling again. I have always said I would consider myself at liberty only once you were relieved of the burden you assumed upon my death. Now you are free, it is clear that my duty no longer calls me to tarry. I have known for a while that I am awaited elsewhere, and have only delayed because you had the better claim upon me."

Zacharias could not speak. Sir Stephen's continued presence had not always been convenient, but he had, Zacharias now realised, come to rely upon the certainty that Sir Stephen would appear when he was needed. It was curious to think that he had been present at Sir Stephen's death, but was the only person for whom his death had not been real—until now.

"Whatever they have in the worlds beyond this one, I will miss these gardens," said Sir Stephen, looking around. "So many memories are associated with them. Still, memory is not enough to linger on. Maria may eventually succumb to the attentions of that impudent fellow Barbary, and then where would I be? Better to pass on—to leave you mortals to the business of living, and concern myself with the business of dying."

Rather shocked, Zacharias said: "I cannot conceive that Lady Wythe would dream of entertaining inappropriate attentions so soon after your death."

"Oh, they are not inappropriate," said Sir Stephen. "Daniel Barbary would never do anything inappropriate, damn him. He has vouchsafed only the most delicate civilities—the kindest consideration. He would make an excellent husband if Maria were inclined to risk marriage again. It would doubtless be for the best if she did: she was not made for a solitary existence, and though I know you would do what you could, you could not provide anything like the companionship of a husband. It would be greatly to Maria's advantage to contract another union—and so I had better move on. Doubtless these matters will seem of little consequence in the next life."

"You have been very good to me, Sir Stephen," said Zacharias unsteadily. Now that the loss approached, it seemed to him that it came too soon. There still remained far too much to say—far too much left undone, to permit of their parting.

"What, now, will we speak of obligation again?" said Sir Stephen, smiling. "I have proscribed all such talk, remember. I have heard enough of duty from you, Zacharias. Now you are liberated from your office—which I know you entered for duty's sake—I hope you will concern yourself much more with what you desire. With what would give you joy. You have given me such joy, my dear boy. That I shall remember, wherever death may take me."

At the gate Sir Stephen paused and laid his hand upon Zacharias's shoulder. A light pressure—a last look, full of affection—and he departed. He walked along the street, his image fading as he went, until even by straining his tear-blurred sight to the utmost, Zacharias could not descry any trace of his oldest friend.

27

ZACHARIAS WAS AT a loss for what to do about the caterpillars. He had taken the lease of the cottage in large part for its charming garden. The trim flowerbeds and vegetable patch had captured Zacharias's imagination. He had envisaged himself kneeling upon the earth, digging in the soil, making every day small, tangible contributions to flourishing.

He had not conceived of the multitude of afflictions that threatened vegetable kind, however. Every evening he pored over weighty tomes on gardening lore, and he rose every morning prepared to do battle, but in vain. His endeavours bore no fruit, of the metaphorical or physical kind, and each day he confronted the reproachful attitude of a garden struggling to retain its grip on life.

It eventually dawned upon him that he was going about the business in the wrong way. He had taken up gardening as a diversion from his primary occupation, the magical researches that took up the main part of his days, but he saw that he could not continue this strict division between work and leisure if he were to make any sort of success of the garden. If he desired it to thrive, he must apply to it what skills he had.

Once he had worked out a suitable formula, the garden did indeed begin to do better. Zacharias had hopes of roses soon, and he thought he might even venture to eat one of his cabbages.

This was to run a real risk, for it was not clear what the full effect of the spell had been. In ingesting the cabbage, would he also be consuming the magic that had grown it? What would be the consequence of that? He would not feed the cabbages to anyone else, but for himself he thought he might make the trial.

It was an advantage of living alone in the countryside that it enabled one to lead the uninterrupted life of the mind. Cut off from London, he could afford to ignore the bickering, the intrigues, the grandstanding and shufflings for position that had bedevilled his former life. Provided he did not, by leaving out any excessively magical equipment, alarm the villager who visited once a day to cook a hot meal and tidy the cottage, he was left in peace to pursue truth—even if that involved the occasional ingestion of a dubious cabbage leaf.

The caterpillars were a problem, however. Fat, fuzzy and complacent, they sat upon his vegetables in veritable hordes, ignoring him until he addressed one directly.

"Good morning, sir," he said.

The caterpillar paused the busy movement of its jaws to reply:

"Pleasant weather, this, eh?"

It was an ideal summer's day. The skies stretched out in endless blue overhead, unmarred by a single wisp of cloud; the fresh scent of greenery and earth rose into the nostrils, imparting a lively pleasure in being alive and outdoors.

"You seem troubled, sir, if you don't mind me saying so," said the caterpillar.

Zacharias experienced a brief internal struggle, but decided upon candour.

"I am simply at a loss to account for the preternatural intelligence of you and your brethren," he said.

"I thank you for the compliment, but I am not certain my brethren are so very intelligent," said the caterpillar cheerfully. "They seem tolerably addlepated to me!"

"Oh pipe down, Gilbert," said one of its fellows, without rancour.

"The formula I devised was intended to encourage the development of this garden and its inhabitants," said Zacharias, thinking aloud. "It was designed to seize upon the urge for life at work within each living being, making use of that natural force, so that magic would have little to do but expedite what would in any event occur in nature. Is the urge for life, at its base, a desire for understanding? Will my cabbages begin to compose minuets if I leave the formula to work itself through them? Indeed, what strange transformations might not I undergo if I pass too much time within the garden? I too am a living being, and presumably subject to the influence of the formula."

"Your period of rusticating would appear to have made you an eccentric, Zacharias," said a voice over the hedge. "Does conversing with your vegetables aid their development?"

Prunella stood in the lane outside the garden, her hand on her unicorn's flanks. It looked as though she had ridden there on Youko, for she was dressed in a smart nankeen riding habit, and a flush glowed in her cheeks. The simurgh Tjandra was perched upon her shoulder, giving her something of the appearance of a fetching young piratess.

"I was addressing the caterpillars, not the cabbages," said Zacharias, after a pause.

His heart was beating absurdly fast. It was the lack of prior notice, of course. He was no longer accustomed to society.

Prunella nodded. "I suppose you do not often have the opportunity for rational conversation. You must be very dull, living so out of the way. I have not seen a soul since I left the village."

"There's us," said the caterpillar Gilbert.

Prunella blinked.

"I contrive to occupy myself," said Zacharias. "Would you like a cup of tea?"

Prunella wandered around the cottage, examining the books on the shelves and commenting unasked on the notes scattered on every available surface: "That formula will never work; there is a glaring error in the first verse, and besides, the spirits of the earth will only attend if you speak Anglo-Saxon."

"There is pen and ink on the desk, if you are moved to correct any errors you observe," said Zacharias. "I hope you have not been brought here by any untoward circumstance? From Damerell's letters I had believed that only a minority within the Society continued unpersuaded of your claim to the staff, but I fear he may have sought to spare me anxiety."

"Oh, I do not give a fig for the Society. It may engage in all the hysterics it desires—they do not make me any less the Sorceress Royal," said Prunella. "But I must say, Zacharias, it was shocking of you to have foisted the staff on me and gone haring off to the countryside. Why, I had not even completed my studies when you absconded."

"I did send you the necessary texts," said Zacharias, looking at her with concern. "I knew it would be a trying time for you, but I believed it the lesser of two evils for me to leave at once. Though I was never a very popular Sorcerer Royal, I feared there might be a movement to reinstate me if the alternative was you. If I removed myself from the scene, however, I believed the Society would soon be brought to recognise your eminent suitability for the position—if only because there was no other eligible candidate, since Midsomer had agreed not to make any attempts to oust you."

"Oh, Geoffrey Midsomer is quite exploded," said Prunella. "He has gone back to Fairyland, and we do not expect his return in this mortal lifetime. He is not the only wicked thaumaturge in the world, however. I have had three attempts on my life in as many months. Tjandra and Youko insist on sleeping at the foot of my bed, and I am continually tripping over wards—Damerell sits spinning them in a corner of my study. Just you think on that, Zacharias. You have exposed me to the impertinence of every ha'penny magician who thinks he would make a better Sorcerer Royal than a half-caste upstart."

"You still continue alive, however," said Zacharias heartlessly.

"They make as unhandy assassins as they are incompetent magicians," allowed Prunella. "Still, it is a tiresome way to live. It was very unkind of you to have put me in the way of it."

"I believed you the best candidate," said Zacharias.

"And it was the only means by which you could prevent my being hauled up before the Presiding Committee and executed as a felon," said Prunella. "*I* know."

Zacharias was taking the teacups out of a cupboard, and he would have smashed his best china if Youko had not nipped out and caught two teacups neatly upon the points of her horns.

"Oh, did not you think I would discover your reasons?" said Prunella. "I was bound to find out, you know. Indeed, I ought to have known it sooner. You were always going on about what a shocking thing the Society would think it, that I had so many familiars. Once I learnt that the Sorcerer Royal could not be prosecuted for any crime, save as the Charter provides, it was all perfectly obvious."

"That was not my only motive," said Zacharias. He drew out a small table, set out the crockery, and poured the tea, allowing the ritual to calm him before he spoke again.

"I had for some time been wrestling with a dilemma," he said. "The duties of my office seemed to require that I render up your treasures to the Society, despite the trust you reposed in me. I told myself that since the eggs belonged to you, and I had promised to keep the secret of their history, I could not betray your confidence. I felt no security in that position, however. If I had continued for much longer in the office, I suspect I should have found it untenable. It was necessary for me either to forswear the staff or surrender the eggs: I could not both remain Sorcerer Royal and keep faith with you."

Prunella stared at him over the rim of her cup.

"That would never have occurred to me at all," she said, with candid astonishment. "Of course I would never tell the Society about the treasures. They would want to take them away from me. I have not made up my mind to use them myself, despite my mother's instructions—Youko and Tjandra suffice for my purposes, and after what I had to do to make Leofric leave, I am not inclined to take on a new familiar. It would be like a second betrayal. But I shall certainly preserve the treasures for my daughters, and their daughters. And if *you* told the Society, I should very likely have to kill you, for I could not permit my mother's pains to be so thrown away."

"I suspected you would have a different view of what your duties required," said Zacharias. "As a private citizen, I might well agree. In my public role, I should have found it difficult to sustain such a view."

"How extraordinary," said Prunella. She uncovered the teapot and cast a quick, professional glance over its contents, saying, "I am due another assassination attempt, I see. I must arrange for this wretched Bloxham to be sent away. He is not an ill-looking creature, despite his inability properly to orchestrate a murder. I might see if the Fairy Queen desires an addition to her retinue."

"Is it so bad, being Sorceress Royal?" said Zacharias.

"Assassins aside, you mean?" said Prunella. "It is not so *very* bad. I am very good at it," she added, speaking as of a matter of fact. "It has made me wholly unmarriageable, but I cannot lay all of that at your door. Do you remember that shocking gossip Mrs. Gray, and the day she caught me flying about with dear Mr. Hsiang? I could not make out why she should be driving about the Park so early in the day—with Sophia Kendle, too, who was never friends with her before. It seems that Mrs. Gray had made inquiries about my family, and she contrived to discover an ancient relative of my father's, an unpleasant old uncle who disowned my father when he married my mother. Of course, the first thing Mrs. Gray did was spread the news about town, starting with Sophia, because she was a particular friend of mine. That's spite for you!"

"Your mother's identity is known, then," said Zacharias, watching Prunella closely. She did not seem overly distressed, however.

"Only that she was a black woman. No one in England seems to have heard of Seringapatam's Grand Sorceress, and I have no intention of teaching them," said Prunella. "It is quite absurd what a fuss there has been about it. So long as they thought me the offshoot of a noble family—my mother a *bibi* abandoned by my father—I was acceptable, it seems. But now that they know my father was a nobody who was married to my mother—and more to the point, neither of them left me any money—all my suitors have abandoned me. Sophia will not even speak to me—though that may be because I named her husband to the Presiding Committee. She would rather he were a Member of Parliament."

"You nominated Kendle to the Committee?" said Zacharias. "I thought he disliked you."

"He dislikes me extremely," said Prunella agreeably. "It is ever so diverting to see him sitting in Committee meetings, gnashing his teeth because I gave him his step. He is tremendously useful: because he will insist on openly regretting Midsomer, everyone else is terrified of agreeing with him in anything. All I have to do to ensure a motion is passed is persuade Kendle to vote for the opposite course."

"It seems you are having a salutary effect upon English thaumaturgy."

"They all quake at my approach, if that is what you mean," said Prunella. "It is that I caused the death of my familiar that frightens them the most. Everyone considers my want of feeling perfectly appalling."

"Does that surprise you?" said Zacharias.

Prunella lifted her chin in the defiant gesture so familiar to him. "I cannot regret it, though I miss Nidget, and I know I used it barbarously. It deserved better of me. But I sacrificed it to help you, and I would do it again."

Zacharias cast his eyes down, his cheeks warm. He was surprised, looking inward, to find that his decision had been made, almost unbeknownst to himself. It remained only to gather his wits and courage for the attempt. He had not expected to be brought to the point so soon, and he could not tell if this were the perfect time, or the worst. But he must do it now, or spend the rest of his days in regret.

"Have you any wish to marry, in the circumstances?" he said. "I myself doubted, as Sorcerer Royal, whether my duties would not prevent my enjoying any domestic happiness."

"I never thought of that, you know," said Prunella. "I only wished to have my own establishment, and not have to teach, like Miss Liddiard and all the rest of them, and be snubbed by my betters, and abused by my charges. Now, however, I have the stipend, and since Lady Wythe has kindly insisted that I remain with her, that suffices for my needs. But I do regret the prospect of children. I can hardly bequeath the treasures to my daughters if I do not have any daughters at all. However, there is no purpose in worrying about it, since it is unlikely anyone will ever offer for me."

"There, I think, you are wrong," said Zacharias.

"You know what I mean," said Prunella impatiently. "I suppose I could always call upon the butcher's boy who used to linger in Mrs. Daubeney's kitchen, but I had grander ambitions. I did not only wish to be married, you know. I desired to wed someone wealthy, who was excessively in love with me, and would let me do whatever I wished."

"That is still open to you," said Zacharias. His throat constricted, and for a hideous moment he thought he would not be able to get it out, but by some miracle he managed to continue. "I inherited an ample provision when Sir Stephen died. I have been contented with a simple life, but if you—that is to say, if I were required to live in a higher style, my income could easily support it."

Prunella looked blank. "I have not the least idea of your meaning."

"I only meant to say that I would marry you," said Zacharias's voice, seeming to come from very far away, and not from himself at all. "That is, I would like to, if you would take me. I fulfill the conditions you specified, though I do not presume to believe that that alone is a sufficient incentive for you to accept my offer."

Prunella shot out of her chair as if the cushion had burst into flames beneath her, and scuttled to the other end of the room. Youko, peacefully at work on a piece of seed cake, looked up in alarm. Tjandra flew to the chimneypiece, squawking.

"What can have possessed you to say that?" she rapped out.

Now that the thing was out, Zacharias felt more comfortable. "It seemed the right time. I am sorry to have alarmed you, however."

"Oh, it does not trouble me at all," snapped Prunella. She started pacing around the room in her agitation. "It simply came into your mind? You had no reason to think your offer would be welcome?"

"I can see I have surprised you," said Zacharias. He hesitated. "Perhaps it would have been better to have given you some warning—to have built up to it. Courtship is not an area in which I can boast any expertise, however. My work, my experiences—indeed, my inclinations—have been such as to put it out of my power to make a proper study of the practise."

"What did you go for to do it, then?" said Prunella belligerently. "When we were talking so pleasantly!"

"When you were haranguing me for having made you Sorceress Royal, you mean?"

Prunella was not listening.

"I suppose my talking of my prospects led you to believe I am desperate for an offer," she said. "I do wish to be married; I have made no secret of that. But I have also always made it clear, I hope, that I will only accept a *real* offer. No, you are kind, Zacharias; I can see that you wish to help. But I hope I have more pride than to marry anyone who offered for pity!"

"You mistake me," said Zacharias. He fixed an unseeing gaze on the teacups on the table, his pulse beating high in his throat. "I said that I fulfilled all the conditions you specified. If—if profound attachment is what you require in a suitor, you should have no cause to complain of me."

Prunella turned and fixed Zacharias with an intent gaze.

"Zacharias," she said, "do you mean to say you offered because you are in love with me?"

Zacharias nodded. "I have always believed marriage without affection to be indefensible—the cause of much misery and sin, that might easily have been avoided."

Prunella came closer, walking light-footed and cautious, as if she were approaching a wild animal. She surveyed his countenance closely. Her own was grave, as free as a child's of cruelty or design.

"Then you would not approve of *my* marrying for money," she said.

"That is a matter for you to settle with your own conscience," said Zacharias. "If you were inclined to accept my offer on those grounds, I would be content that the principles under which you operate permitted me to attain happiness in accordance with mine. I would not presume to sit in judgment upon your decision."

"Quite right. It is not for you to judge me, indeed," said Prunella, with asperity. "You do love me?"

"Yes, Prunella."

"Then," said Prunella, scowling with inconceivable ferocity, "you may as well know that in accepting your offer, my reasons accord with yours—that they could not be faulted, judged according to your principles."

Greatly daring, Zacharias touched her cheek with the tips of his fingers. Prunella went pink, but her brow remained furrowed.

"Lady Wythe will be pleased," she said. "She always said it was a shocking thing to marry for money."

"So it is."

"She told me I ought to marry for love, but contrive to fall in love with a man of substance," said Prunella. Her frown deepened. "It will gratify her that I have followed her advice."

"I beg you will forgive my impertinence," said Zacharias, "but would you object very much to a kiss?"

Prunella looked crosser and pinker than ever. "I should have thought I had spoken in terms suited to the meanest understanding. If you need to ask I cannot think you have understood me at all."

"I thought it civil to ask," said Zacharias.

Prunella stuck out her chin in a manner Zacharias recognised to be more comical than becoming. He found it inexpressibly charming nonetheless.

"Well," she said, as one daring another to do something very dangerous, "why do not you try it, and see what happens?"

Zacharias did, which served to divert them both sufficiently that conversation was suspended for a time. Youko came over to investigate, but grew bored when her mistress paid her no regard, and wandered out of the cottage in search of amusement. Tjandra, more discreet, put his head under his wing and went to sleep.

"You will come back to town?" said Prunella, after a period of deep interest to both had passed. "Lady Wythe misses you, and so do Damerell and Rollo."

"I will come," said Zacharias. The caterpillars could be dealt with somehow, he reflected.

"You will be a great help with the papers," said Prunella, brightening. The sunshine, streaming in through the window, haloed her in golden light, turning her hair to a rich burnished brown. Zacharias curled a silken lock around his finger, marvelling at its hue and texture, until the next thing Prunella said made him drop it. "I have been feeding my letters to Tjandra and Youko, but I cannot do that forever. I fear too much will interfere with their digestion."

"Prunella—!"

"Oh, I almost forgot!" she exclaimed. "When it was the whole reason I came to see you! Mrs. Daubeney would not countenance the teaching of magic at her school, but I wrote to Henrietta Stapleton—we could never break her of levitating in her sleep, you know—and sure enough, she was delighted, and she has got together a group of old girls as contrary as she, who wish to teach. Lady Wythe has found us a suitable building, and the renovations will be complete within a few months, but I have not been at liberty to give them the assistance they need. It is persuading the parents that requires the most work—they will have enough students to open the school with, if that can only be achieved. They will be delighted to have you to help them. I must say it has all fallen out admirably."

"What are you talking about?"

"Why, the school," cried Prunella. "The school for *magiciennes*. Not that it will be restricted to girls—we intend to open it to the labouring classes, and foreigners, and half-castes, and irregular persons of all sorts. That is all a great secret, of course; if the parents were to have wind of it, we should never bring it off. Lady Wythe is prodigiously fired up about it, and goes about all the great houses in town, demanding that they contribute either funds or daughters. Though we have enough money to start out with, for the Society has given us all we need for the nonce."

"The Society is funding it?" said Zacharias. This was the greatest shock he had received all morning. "How did you contrive that?"

"You of all people ought to know, Zacharias," said Prunella, surprised. "You said it yourself. I am very, *very* good at being Sorceress Royal."

ACKNOWLEDGMENTS

I am grateful to my agent, Caitlin Blasdell, for her infinite pains with this book, as well as to Hannah Bowman for her comments on the manuscript.

Thank you to Diana Gill and Bella Pagan, and the fantastic teams at Berkley/Ace/Roc and Pan Macmillan.

I am amazingly fortunate in my loving, creative, plain-speaking and hilarious family. Thanks for everything, Mom, Dad, Ko and Rin.

This book could not have been written without the unfailing love and support of my husband, Peter. No writer could have a better companion. I didn't write this book *for* you, but I hope you accept it anyway.

I have started a lot of stories in my life, but I might not have completed any of them if not for the belief, enthusiasm and eyeballs of my imaginary friends who live in the Internet. Thank you. You know who you are.